"Know what I want more than my next breath?"

Heather shook her head as Caleb leaned in, close enough for his breath to stir her hair. "To kiss you."

Her mouth parted softly. Her pulse leapt at the base of her throat, and her pupils flared in a show of nerves and excitement. "Are—" She swallowed hard, then licked her bottom lip. "Are you asking permission?"

He shook his head. "A kiss loses the lure of spontaneity if one has to ask."

"Are you trying to lure me, Caleb Edge?"

"Not lure. Seduce."

Skimming his fingers along the curve of her jaw he watched her eyes darken to aged whiskey with anticipation. She dragged in a ragged breath.

Helpless to prevent it, good intentions be damned, Caleb's vision blurred as his mouth touched hers. Not giving her time to think.

Soft and unthreatening, he brushed his mouth back and forth until her lips parted on a sigh. His blood pooled in his groin as the slick heat of her tongue came to greet him. She tasted amazing, and her response sent a jolt of pure possessiveness through him.

Mine, he thought. *Mine*.

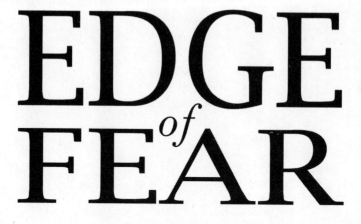

EDGE
of
FEAR

A Novel

CHERRY
ADAIR

BALLANTINE BOOKS • NEW YORK

A Ballantine Books Mass Market Original

Copyright © 2006 by Cherry Adair
Excerpt for *Edge of Darkness* © 2006 by Cherry Adair

Published in the United States by Ballantine Books, an imprint of The Random House Publishing Group, a division of Random House, Inc., New York.

BALLANTINE and colophon are trademarks of Random House, Inc.

This book contains an excerpt from the forthcoming book *Edge of Darkness*. This excerpt has been set for this edition only and may not reflect the final content of the forthcoming edition.

ISBN 978-0-7394-7128-9

Printed in the United States of America

To Rhonda Pollero
For curses, Curses, and laughter.
With the magic of hindsight,
I agree.
I *do* owe you
all the muffins
and bagels in the land.

A special thanks to
Heather Wieker from Sea-Tac Airport.
See? I was quite serious.

And for David, with love

Duty o'er love was the choice you did make
My love you did spurn, my heart you did break

Your penance to pay, no pride you shall gain
Three sons on three sons find nothing but pain

I gift you my powers in memory of me
The joy of love no son shall ever see

When a Lifemate is chosen by the heart of a son
No protection can be given, again I have won

His pain will be deep, her death will be swift,
Inside his heart a terrible rift

Only freely given will this curse be done
To break the spell, three must work as one

CHAPTER ONE

"What does it matter what she looks like?" Caleb Edge said into the phone, hoping like hell the dark, primal lust drumming through his veins didn't bleed into his voice. He frowned absently at his control's odd question as he shifted the compact sat phone between chin and shoulder, and the binocs left an inch for a better view.

A San Francisco street and a shitload of swirling fog separated the two apartment windows. The lights over there were on. The lights here weren't.

Desire tightened his body and clogged his throat. His heart, which was normally as steady as a rock, still pounded uncomfortably sixty seconds after he'd lifted the binoculars to his eyes and taken his first look at her.

Bam! Caleb felt as though someone had punched him in the solar plexus, grabbed his heart, and squeezed. *Hard.*

That's what Heather Shaw looked like.

Not that he'd share his physical reaction with his control, Lark Orela. She was like a frigging dog with a bone if she thought her people weren't focused. Unfortunately he was plenty focused.

"Earth to Edge?"

"She looks . . . I don't know." Classy. Beautiful. "Deluxe, expensive," he told Lark smoothly. His heart was racing, he assured himself, because his goddamned knee hurt like hell. He leaned a little more of his weight on the shoulder he had propped against the wall.

Heather had pushed the sleeves of the soft-looking purple sweater up her creamy forearms while she worked on something at the table. The fabric draped over her tall slender body as if it had been custom-made. Probably had. Heather Shaw had more money than many third-world countries.

"Interesting location for her to hide out," Caleb dragged his gaze from the gentle swell of Miss Shaw's breasts back to the top of her head. *Look up again, honey, let's see those gorgeous eyes again.* "How long's she been there?" Were her eyes green? Brown? Hard to tell from this distance.

"About six months," Lark told him. "Why?"

Reluctantly Caleb shifted the binocs. "Place's pretty stark. Chair. Bed. Table. Nothing personal that I can see."

"She's been moving around."

"Yeah." And not easy to track down, according to Lark. Finding Heather's father *first* would've expedited this op, and made it a lot more interesting, Caleb thought. Unfortunately, Brian Shaw had been missing for the better part of a year. Not surprisingly, he'd completely obliterated his trail, so he was a little freaking hard to find at the moment.

Which left his delectable daughter to the wolves.

Caleb figured he'd been in physical rehab for too damn long if just *looking* at the tango's daughter gave him a hard-on.

Long, elegant bones. Pale slender fingers. Silky-looking hair that would feel like sunlight on his skin.

He'd begged Lark to send him on a mission. Anywhere. Any damn thing to escape the hospital. This had been the best Lark claimed she could come up with at short notice.

Bullshit. Fact was: She didn't think he was ready to go back into the field.

This wasn't an op. A simple question needed answering. Hell, someone could call it in.

But here he was. Because anything was better than being stuck in a rehab center for months on end. Boredom seemed to be a family trait this week. His older brother, Gabriel, had visited him a couple of days ago on his way to Arizona to get intel from some scientist there. He'd been uncharacteristically cranky and out of sorts. Clearly needing a little action himself.

His younger brother, Duncan, was secretly lobbying to become head of the wizard council and was off somewhere, totally focused on his goal. And when Duncan focused he was pretty frigging single-minded.

So Caleb didn't even have his brothers to spar with at the moment. Too bad, he wouldn't mind a kick-ass, sweaty workout with Gabriel and his claymores, or Duncan and his knives—or both—right now.

Instead he was in San Francisco watching the daughter of the banker to some of the world's most lethal tangos.

Surprisingly, Caleb's reaction to the woman he'd been sent to find had been visceral and immediate. He liked women just fine. No, he *loved* women. But he'd never had such an instantaneous, energizing, chemical . . . jolt *looking* at a woman before.

Adrenaline junkie that he was, his physical reaction on seeing her—blood pressure up, libido up, temperature up—intrigued him. Pheromones were one thing, but he wasn't even in sniffing distance of her.

His reaction was so immediate, so *primitive* it shocked the hell out of him.

Why her? Why here? Why now?

"Okay, then let me ask you an easy question," Lark said in his ear. Caleb braced himself. Lark was an empath, and he didn't want her picking up any screwy signals. "How's the leg?" she asked, throwing him.

Yeah. Concentrate on something that made sense. The new knee still hurt. Which annoyed the hell out of him. One of his unique powers was the ability to heal, but the only person's injuries he couldn't fix were his own. Pissed him off no end. Caleb considered his body another tool in his arsenal against tangos. He needed to be in tip-top condition to do his job well, and he worked to keep himself in the peak of physical performance at all times. He was rarely ill, and this knee injury was the first time in his career that he'd been stuck in the hospital for so long.

"One hundred percent A-okay," he assured Lark.

He'd been pathetically grateful when he'd gotten the call an hour ago during his hopefully final physical therapy session in San Jose. Hell yeah, he was only an hour from San Francisco, he'd talk to Shaw's daughter. *Anything* to cut short the boring sessions. He'd been going stir-crazy.

He'd commandeered an apartment across the street, one whose windows looked directly into hers. A typical winter's day in San Francisco. Damp, misty fog eddied in gossamer ribbons between the tall, narrow buildings in an ever-changing screen that made it difficult to maintain a clear view into Heather's apartment, even with her lights on. Caleb had seen enough.

"Liar," Lark told him. "Dr. Long just told me you're still favoring that knee."

"Then why did you ask?" He'd had his knee replaced, but there'd been some nerve and muscle damage. It would heal. Eventually. These things usually did. He had plenty of scars to prove it.

Watching Heather Shaw was more interesting than discussing his knee. Which in turn made him bad tempered. Which in turn made him even more antsy to get back to work so he could forget about it.

Based on photographs, Shaw's daughter had changed some during the last year.

"To see if you'd lie," Lark informed him.

Lying was the least he'd do to get back to work. "I have a medical release from the doctor and the therapist. So, quit torturing me, honey. Find me something. *Anything*. I beg you. This lack of activity has made me a basket case."

"You're a workaholic, Middle Edge."

"You say that like it's a bad thing. Come on, Lark, help me out here. Send me to some exotic hellhole to kick some terrorist butt."

"Can you run?"

"Better than most." No. But he didn't want his control to know that his doctors were right. He wasn't fully back up to speed yet. But he'd get back into shape on the job. "And since when does an Edge need to run? We show up and take names."

"That may be, but you should still take some downtime until you're fully recovered. Think of it as a vacation."

"I don't want a vacation. I don't *need* a vacation."

Lark had a pretty laugh, even if it was mocking. "You sound like a truculent five-year-old. But I agree. You can do your job just fine limping. Your trigger finger's just fine. Your brain wasn't damaged—*much*—by that beating you took."

"Heartless, Lark. I'm sharp as a tack." Was she going to send him back in? Caleb imagined the young woman who was his control. Lark Orela looked like a cross between a biker chick and a Goth rocker. With spiked black-and-fuchsia hair, and half a dozen silver rings in each eyebrow, and one in her nose for God's sake. But behind that pale face and scary black eye makeup lived the brain of a brilliant tactician.

"Tell me what you see." She'd circled back to Heather Shaw.

This was a "look see." He wanted to get back to real work. "Are you sending me back into the fiel—"

"Observations, Edge?"

Lark was like a particularly friendly pit bull. Caleb shifted to do a quick scan of Shaw's one-room apartment. "How the mighty have fallen. Like I said, it's almost empty. The walls are bare. No pictures. No knickknacks. Nothing whatsoever to personalize her living space." The covers on the narrow single bed behind her were thrown about haphazardly. Restless night or lover?

His insides clenched at the thought of a lover, and his reaction surprised him. Good thing he would be with Kris-Alice in Germany within the hour. That was one of the benefits of being who he was. What he was. He could teleport with ease.

Caleb worked for T-FLAC/psi. T-FLAC was a privately funded counterterrorist organization. Psi was the psychic phenomena offshoot.

This wasn't a psi op. He'd been in Silicone Valley undergoing forced physical therapy on his knee—it had been just a *small* bullet hole—when Shaw's prints had been ID'd. Since he was closest, he'd been requested to get intel from the woman. Intel they sorely needed if they had a hope in hell of tracking down her father, Brian Shaw.

"She live alone?"

"Looks like."

Caleb found downtime redundant. Unlike his laid-back younger brother, Duncan, Caleb liked to be on the go all the time. But they'd insisted. Getting shot in the knee was a pain in his ass. Technically, he was supposed to be off duty for another three weeks. He'd never been real big on technicalities. All he needed was to be sent on an op now, and he'd prove to the team and control that he was in top form. And *this* wasn't an op. It was a frigging *conversation*. And a short one at that.

No action to prove he could still outrun, outjump, outshoot the best of them.

Right now even watching a woman through binocs beat lying around on a sun-drenched beach somewhere doing nothing. Give him action and he was a happy man. An op relaxed him. Hell, a fast-paced op made him sleep at night like a baby.

Watching Heather should have been a step in that direction. But instead his body grew even more coiled and tight. He needed to get a grip. And not—he thought with a mental thump on the head—on that perfect body of hers. Still, the mere thought of running his fingers through her honey-colored hair, of allowing his palms to slide over the gentle curve of her hip, was interfering with his assignment.

Time to focus.

Yeah. That.

He finished checking out Heather's living quarters. The kitchen occupied one corner, an open door led to the bathroom, another door led, he presumed, to the stairwell. The bed and folding table where she now sat were the sum total of her furnishings. The small, sterile accommodations, after living the high life, must really cramp the socialite's style.

She was seated at the table, some sort of small tool in her hand. Prying a stone out of a piece of jewelry, or putting one in. She made and sold her own jewelry to local jewelers. That's how she'd been found. Her finger-prints had been lifted from a jewelry store after a robbery there yesterday. The local cops had run them with all the other prints they'd found at the scene. Her prints hadn't been in their database. They were in T-FLAC's. Not under the name Hannah Smith, but Heather Shaw. The jewelry store had a current address for her.

She'd filled out some. In the last photograph they'd had of her—some high-society thing in Hong Kong a year ago—she looked almost skeletal. Now she had more meat on her bones.

Not that Caleb could see much of her, dressed as she was in jeans and a purple sweater. But her face looked softer, more appealing now. His heart, which had started a peculiar erratic beat when he'd first set eyes on her, picked up more speed as he took in the creamy curve of her cheek, the silky sweep of her hair, the stubborn jut of her chin.

His reaction to her was . . . weird.

The accelerated pounding was the staccato beat of fear. Or was it excitement? Or some sort of premonition? Damn, he didn't know what. Nor did he want to find out. Lark was the one with precognitive powers, not him. But every instinct in him flashed a big neon warning to keep the hell away from Heather Shaw. And in his line of work, Caleb trusted his instincts. They hadn't failed him yet.

"Earth to Middle Edge? Humor me," Lark said smoothly in his ear, snapping him out of his reverie. "*Expensive* doesn't exactly tell me what she looks like."

Touchable. Dangerous. Trouble. "She's not a blonde anymore." In all the pictures, Shaw's daughter was a golden, California blonde with about fifteen pounds of curls. Now the woman's thick, stick-straight, honey-brown hair hung to her shoulders in a shiny curtain. A nice improvement.

"Pretty?"

"Not particularly." No, not pretty, Caleb thought,

stunning. Appealing as sin. Her even features, and lack of makeup, made her appear younger, more . . . vulnerable, than her publicity shots had done. He didn't believe in tarring the offspring with their parents' brush, but the delectable Miss Shaw had run in her father's very fast, very public social circles. Stood to reason that there'd be nothing innocent or vulnerable about her.

"Who cares," he muttered, distracted by the way the lamp over the table brought out caramel highlights in Heather's hair. She was making some sort of necklace, he decided. Something with swirls of silver and purple stones. Pretty and delicate. As pretty and delicate as the slender hands holding it up to the light.

Her hair spilled over her shoulder as she tilted her head to inspect her work. "We have her. Send someone in for the interrogation. My work here is done." He was annoyed that he couldn't seem to take his eyes off Shaw's no-longer-missing only child. Surveilling her was one thing, *ogling,* for God's sake, quite another. Yet, for some mysterious reason he was drawn to this woman in ways he hadn't experienced in years. Years? *Ever.*

"Not so fast, Hopalong. This is now your op."

He frowned again. While he'd love an op right now—save him from more hydro-treatments, ultrasound tissue massages, and all the other crap—this wasn't it. Too low key. Too mundane. "Questioning Shaw's daughter doesn't necessitate a psi operative. I found her, now I'm ready to hand her off. Who are they sending? I'll hang around until he/she gets here."

They being T-FLAC proper. His particular talents weren't needed. He'd just happened to be in San Francisco when Heather's fingerprints had popped on the T-FLAC fingerprint database.

Gotcha.

"I'm assigning Shaw's daughter to you. Use your rakish charm to get that intel ASAP." For an extremely

Goth-looking young woman, Lark Orela's no-nonsense tone always came as a surprise. This afternoon it brooked no argument.

Made no sense, but Caleb figured he was there, might as well save someone the trip. Fifteen minutes and he'd be done. He'd report in, results in hand, then pursue Lark in person for a mission. A *real* one.

"Yeah. Sure," he told her easily. "I'll give you a shout when I get the father's location."

"Good luck." Lark sounded . . . odd?

Caleb's frown deepened at the strange inflection in her usually well-modulated voice. "What am I missing?"

"Life, love, and the pursuit of happiness?" On that cryptic note the phone went dead.

Caleb stared at it as he snapped it closed. Trust Lark to be enigmatic. She was a cross between a wizard, a mother figure, and a pain in the collective asses of her operatives. But as a control she had no match. Lark could juggle from one to twenty-one operatives simultaneously. Caleb would've staked his life on the fact that Lark *could* see the future. She never spoke of it. Ever. But the ability had saved many an operative's rear end, no doubt. Her advice and direction were always sound and spot-on. No one argued.

When Lark Orela said jump, intelligent people asked how high.

Caleb didn't bother glancing around the commandeered apartment to make certain he hadn't left anything behind. He hadn't. He'd shimmered in. He'd leave the same way. Sight unseen.

CHAPTER TWO

SAN FRANCISCO
MONDAY, JANUARY 16
3:22 P.M.

Hunched over her worktable, Heather barely regis-
tered the unfamiliar sound of the doorbell pealing
downstairs. The fog had gradually thickened during the
last few hours and now the opaque whiteness pressed at
the window, obligingly obliterating a boring view, and
muffling the sounds of traffic in the street below. She
sighed with satisfaction, enjoying the moment. Soft jazz
crooned from the bedside clock/radio, and the mug of
steaming chamomile tea beside her was almost steeped
enough and ready to drink.

Ignoring the vague, atavistic sensation stirring the
hairs on the back of her neck, she held the intricately
twisted white gold necklace up to the soft light filtering
through the lone window in the apartment. Taking a
moment, she admired the craftwomanship of the delicate piece she'd just made with her own two hands.
"Pretty, damn pretty."

The stones, suspended on delicate wires, danced and
prismed, giving off satisfying sparks resembling moonlight glittering off water and the rich purple of fine wine.
"Very poeti—" Narrow-eyed, she turned to stare at the
fog pressing against the window.

No one was watching her. Still, she rubbed the tingle, a primitive warning, on the back of her neck with her free hand. Her heart beat a little faster.

This piece was off to Klein's Jewelers the next day, a special order, but for a few hours, it was hers. Well, in some small way, it would always be hers. All her designs were made from gems—precious and semiprecious—pried straight out of her own jewelry.

In this case, the six round checkerboard-cut amethysts, held by three prongs, were from a necklace her father had given her on her thirteenth birthday. Those she was a little sorry to lose for their sentimental value. But she would be able to get two pairs of earrings out of the other stones still left in the original.

The .34 carats of pavé diamonds had been part of a bracelet her mother had picked up on one of her regular trips to her favorite flea market in Paris.

Heather's heart ached when she thought about her parents. God—If only . . . There wasn't a day in the past year that she hadn't thought about them. She missed her mother desperately. Her death had rocked Heather's world. The loss of her mother, and her father's actions, coupled with subsequent events, had flipped her world on its axis, irrevocably changing her life, and her, forever.

She'd never know for certain if her mother's death had been the accident her father had claimed it to be, or murder. She still loved her father and desperately wanted to believe what he'd told her. Her brain told her one thing, her heart another.

She missed her father as well. She had no idea where he was. Worse, she didn't know whether he was alive or dead. He'd promised to place an ad in a London newspaper to let her know when she could come out of hiding. But although she religiously checked the paper every Sunday, so far there hadn't been the hoped-for notice.

Her father was a brilliant man, and he had unlimited resources. She had to believe that he was alive and well and keeping a very low profile until this situation was resolved.

Situation.

She shivered, rubbing her upper arms, cold despite the cashmere sweater she wore. She had too few facts to work with to make any real sense of what had really happened that day a year ago. She didn't know what had precipitated her parents' violent argument. And she'd only heard snippets of their conversation. None of it enough to arrive at any definitive conclusion.

All she knew for sure was what her father had told her. One of his banking clients believed that he'd embezzled money—a *large* amount of money. The client was angry and unpredictable. Capable of killing, he finally admitted when she suggested they stick together to work it out. *That's* when she'd learned who her father's clients really were. Heather shuddered.

Terrorists. That's who had paid for her college degree, for her horse, for her clothes, for the roof over her head.

Terrorists. My God. She pressed a hand to the nerves jumping in her stomach. "How did I not *see* that?" The dots had joined up like a speeding bullet.

The thought of who she and her mother had been associating with for all those years, oblivious to the trail of blood and death those people had left in their wake, still managed to make her feel sick to her stomach.

Her father had made no excuses for his business associates. After assuring her that the current situation was nothing more than a misunderstanding, a bookkeeping error, he'd insisted she disappear until the matter was resolved.

Easy for him to say. The difference was that he had a

veritable army of security people. The two men he'd sent away with her were dead, and she was now alone.

Her father also knew what was going on, while she was in the dark.

Despite everything, she loved her father, but Heather had absolutely no illusions about him. He'd cover his own ass, and ensure his own safety and well-being before he remembered that he even *had* a daughter.

No matter how self-absorbed he was, though, she didn't doubt her father's love for her. Eventually he *would* remember, and he *would* place the notice in the London *Times*. Until then, she couldn't allow her life to be on pause.

"I have things to do and jewelry to make. And you, if I may say so myself, which I do," she said with determined cheerfulness as she briskly buffed the stones with a soft cloth, "are a thing of beauty." And would bring in at least two thousand lovely dollars.

"Not that I *care* so much about the bucks. It's just pretty damn astounding that I'm capable of *producing* something that someone wants to buy." She grinned. "And I'm talking to myself again."

Oblivious to the second peal of the doorbell, she wrapped the necklace carefully in tissue paper and laid the piece in a small silver foil box. It was only when her visitor held a finger to the buzzer that her head lifted at the intrusive noise.

"Damn. The cops are back."

One of her customers' jewelry stores had been robbed the day before. The police had come over last night, scaring the hell out of her when they'd buzzed. God. She put a hand over her manic heart and tried to take a deep, steadying breath. She'd managed to retain her composure as they'd questioned her. But inside she'd been a mess of tension and raw nerves.

Her fake ID was good enough to fool even the police,

but they hadn't asked for proof of her identity. They'd just questioned her because she'd been in the jewelry store the day before.

"Didn't you get enough information yesterday?" she muttered, striding over to the window overlooking the street. In the months she'd lived in the apartment she'd made a point of familiarizing herself with the cars that belonged in the neighborhood. Standing to the side she scanned the parked cars on either side of the foggy street below.

No unfamiliar vehicles. No police car. Parking was at a premium in this district of San Francisco. Yesterday the police car had double-parked. So, no car. That she could see. Someone on foot then? That perked her up. "Girl Scout cookies?"

She'd made no friends, no casual acquaintances, no personal attachments in the last eleven months. She'd purposely not developed relationships with her neighbors beyond saying hi when she went to and fro. But she'd bought cookies from the little girls in their green uniforms at the grocery store yesterday, and knew there were three little Scouts living several houses away.

She'd been so damned stressed after the police had left last night that she'd eaten the entire box of cookies before she'd even started dinner.

More chocolate would be good right now. She'd been bent over her worktable for hours. Cookies with her tea sounded terrific on this chilly afternoon.

She liked the Bay Area. It, and her new life, were vastly different from her jet-setting life before. Now everything was changed. For one thing, she'd never stayed in one place for longer than a few weeks. Even when she'd been a child she'd had a tutor because the family traveled so extensively.

It had been a nomadic kind of existence, and she'd

only realized just how odd it was once she was no longer doing it.

The doorbell buzzed again

"I hear you." Heather smiled at the persistence of the little salesperson as she grabbed her wallet and lightly ran down the stairs from her apartment to the front door. Because of the steep hill on which the apartment building had been built, her one-room apartment was on the second floor, while her front door and her minuscule entry hall were at street level.

Five other apartments were fitted around each other like the pieces of a jigsaw puzzle, over, beneath, and next door to her. A single, male schoolteacher, two young female flight attendants, a male bank teller, a female physical trainer, and a waitress and her young daughter. Each with their own street entrance. That was about all she knew of her neighbors. All she dared to know.

She had to constantly remind herself that the isolation was imperative. Her father had warned her what might happen if she were ever found. She got it. Boy, did she get it. But God—she missed human contact, the interaction between two people, the give and take of trust. Her guard had to be up constantly. She couldn't afford to let anyone scale the walls. Nobody had touched her in almost a full year. Forget sexually. She'd had no physical contact other than an impersonal handshake in what felt like forever.

She felt . . . invisible.

God only knew, she was thankful, and lucky, to be alive. But the constant fear, the constant looking over her shoulder, the constant knowledge that she could never let down her guard, was starting to wear thin.

And she was lonely. Acutely, deep down, desperately lonely, for the first time in her life. The loneliness had become almost a physical weight inside her. For a naturally outgoing, gregarious person, this was as close to purgatory as she could get. Like being thrown into solitary confinement indefinitely.

Eleven months of isolation. She wasn't the kind of person to dwell on the negatives in her life. But then she'd never had to. Her life had been filled with beautiful clothes, parties, and shopping trips. No one had ever told her "no." She'd led a life of privilege and pleasure and never given a thought to her future or how she would feel if it all ceased to exist.

That life had changed in the blink of an eye last March.

It had always taken her forever to make decisions, a mildly amusing trait when that decision was which designer to favor. Not so damned amusing when every decision could mean life or death. When the *right* choice might have to be made in a split second. Just the thought of going through that process again made her break out in a nervous sweat.

This past year had been a sharp learning curve for her. But she'd learned to depend on herself. Learned to make faster life choices. Learned . . . herself.

Since she'd moved to San Francisco, she'd taught herself to balance a checkbook, was teaching herself to cook, and was shocked and a little embarrassed to discover she could do her own laundry. Things other women took for granted were achievement milestones for her. She was damn proud of what she was becoming.

Too bad there wasn't anyone around to witness her little triumphs, she thought wryly. "Ha! Maybe that's the point of *being* a grown-up. Making good choices *without* any applause."

It had been almost a year, and they hadn't found her. She chose not to add the "yet." She was building a nice little business for herself. She was living in a beautiful city, and she was alive. For now that was enough.

One day soon her father would place the "all clear"

ad in a Sunday London *Times* and she'd know that it was over. Until then she'd learn and grow and become a fully functioning member of society.

Oh, Maman, Heather thought with an aching heart. *Look at me, independent. Who knew?*

She smiled. Fortunately, to keep herself amused she relied on her active imagination. Which came into play when she felt a tingle—something—an unexpected rush of excitement, as she approached the front door. In all this alone time, she'd developed a pretty acute sense of fantasy, based largely on the romantic old movies she often watched to break the tedium of her solitude in the wee hours of the morning.

She imagined that she'd open the door to find a nice-looking, nonthreatening man on her doorstep. Some normal guy who had a normal nine-to-five job. A nice guy who would have pleasant friends, a loving family, and—of course—would love her to distraction. A man who would look her straight in the eye when he talked to her.

A man with integrity, honesty, and honor. Someone rock solid and dependable.

Or, and she grinned, he'd be drop-dead gorgeous, shallow, and hot in bed. Been there, done that, but it had been a while. A hell of a *long* while, she realized. Hmm. He'd look into her eyes and without a word, sweep her into his strong arms and carry her off. Not happily ever after, just for a hot, fast, passionate encounter.

Those were fantasies. Reality was she'd open the door, find one of the little Scouts, make her purchase, and settle for cookies. At this point in her life a Thin Mint was safer than a brief encounter with a good-looking guy.

Bzzzz-bzzz-bzzz.

"I'm coming. I'm coming. Hold onto your merit badges, cutie. I'm just as eager as you are for this sale."

Heather smiled as she ran lightly down the stairs. "You're preaching to the choir. I *want* your cookies. Hang on a sec," she yelled through the door as she deactivated several locks. Both cylinder and electronic.

The day she'd moved in she'd replaced the front door with a metal, high-security model. No peephole. The door was too thick. But she'd had five locks installed, as well as a reinforced plate on either side to mount the strongest security chain she'd been able to find.

"Victory," she muttered as the last lock disengaged and she opened the door the six inches the sturdy chain allowed.

Because she was expecting a little girl, it took her a second to compute the large male standing in the gently eddying white fog of her tiny front porch. Her heartbeat kicked into high gear, and her mouth went cotton dry.

Stupid.

Stupid to open the door like this.

Maybe fatal.

Schooling her features to be nothing more than politely blank, Heather met his gaze in the narrow space between the door and the jamb. His eyes were ink dark, intense.

As authoritative as he looked, she recognized immediately that this guy was not a police officer. He was intimidatingly tall and broad. Despite the chilly January weather, he wore nothing more than jeans and a black T-shirt. He was unsmiling, his eyes a cross between dark blue and teal. His nose was straight, his lips clamped, his jawline slightly darkened by a five o'clock shadow. At three in the afternoon.

He looked . . . mean.

That was all it took. Her heart started to pound, and an icy cold shower of fear washed over her.

Run.

Too obvious.

She drew in a deep breath of cold foggy air touched with a faint hint of male. The hairs on the back of her neck stood up. "Can I help you?" she asked politely, wishing she'd grabbed her gun before coming downstairs.

Running scared, buying the gun, had been her last-ditch, back-to-the-wall, no-other-choice defense. She'd bought it in San Cristóbal where she'd gotten her fake IDs, after someone had tried to run her car off the road.

The gun was guaranteed not to set off airport security, and it never had. It was smaller than her palm. For months she'd been practicing, over and over again, to fit the tiny component parts together. She could do so in the pitch dark, in mere seconds, and under every adverse condition she could think of. But that damn practice couldn't pay off if she was here and *it* was in her closet.

"Heather Shaw?"

Her heart dive-bombed, and a spill of sick dread suffused her body. Oh, God! It had taken time, but they'd finally managed to find her.

How? She'd been careful. She'd—*Don't panic,* she told herself firmly as a familiar surge of fear made her heart manic, and her palms sweat.

Taking a deep breath, she met his eyes with effort, and said politely, "Sorry. No." When she tried to close the door, she realized the guy had his enormous foot blocking the way. Her breath came out in a strangled whoosh. "Hey! Move that foot. *Now.*" Fear made her voice shake. She put her weight against the solid surface of the door. But it wasn't going to shut.

"My name is Caleb Edge, Miss Shaw. I want to talk to you about your father."

There was a word that put the fear of God into her. "My father died years ago. I'm not the person you're looking for. Get lost or I'll call the police." Yeah, right.

Like she'd be dumb enough to do *that*. All she needed was one person to suspect she wasn't who she said she was, and she'd be on the run. Again.

And here he was. The devil incarnate's errand boy.

"You're not in any danger from me, Miss Shaw. Just tell me where your father is, and I'll leave you alone."

"This is Hannah Smith at 3249 Front Street," she said firmly, out of his visual range behind the solid bulk of the door. "I have a male intruder. Could you please send someone immediately? I'm afraid for my life."

"You don't have a cell phone."

Yes. She did. Unfortunately it was upstairs. "Wanna bet? I also have a gun." Also upstairs, damn it. "I'm a lousy shot, but I bet it would hurt a great deal if I fired at you at this close range." She couldn't imagine actually *shooting* someone, but if it came down to her life or his, she'd do it.

"You don't have to invite me in," his tone was smooth. Even. Unemotional. Everything she wasn't. "How about if we just talk through the door?"

Invite him in? Was he insane? "What are you? A moron? You're scaring the crap out of me! If you want to talk, move your foot, and stop trying to intimidate me."

"Okay. It's moved—No, don't—Damn it, woman!"

The second his foot was withdrawn, Heather slammed the door, then engaged all five bolts. Shaking, drenched in nervous sweat, she spun around, racing up the stairs as if the devil himself was after her.

Bzzbzzbzz.

Found, outed, and probably mere seconds from being killed.

She ran faster. "Shit. Shit. Shit!"

She wasn't safe in San Francisco anymore.

With every crazy beat of her heart she anticipated hearing the stranger's footsteps on the uncarpeted stairs behind her. Out of breath, more from fear than from racing up the stairs, she burst into her apartment, then slammed the door behind her and shot home those bolts too.

Leave. Now. No alternative.

Snatching the gun off the top shelf of the empty closet, Heather clicked off the safety. If the guy made it through the front door somehow, and God only knew he'd looked capable of that feat, she'd shoot to kill.

She'd have to. Because the man they'd sent this time didn't look like he could be conned or outrun. This time they'd succeed. This guy *would* kill her.

Ears tuned to the stairwell, she dragged her already packed suitcase out of the big, empty closet one-handed, and threw it on the bed. It took a matter of minutes to toss in the few belongings she allowed herself to keep out. And with every beat of her heart she anticipated the killer kicking down the door standing between them.

CHAPTER THREE

SAN FRANCISCO
SUNDAY, JANUARY 15
12:32:51

He'd handled their first meeting like a bull in a frigging china shop, Caleb thought, limping as he followed Heather into the grocery store the day *before* that aborted meeting at her apartment.

He'd struck out the *second* time as well, he thought with annoyance, which was why he was "redoing" this trip to the grocery store with her.

His special and unique ability to manipulate, or rewind, time frequently came in handy—in life-and-death situations. This incident hardly qualified on either front, and he wasn't thrilled to be wasting one of his lifetime allotments by using it on the delectable Miss Shaw.

While the aftereffects of a time jump weren't life-threatening, they *were* annoying. For several hours afterward he'd experience vertigo and nausea, and his ability to teleport was impaired. He'd jumped back twenty-four hours, and then back again another ten minutes. So here he was, limping on his bum knee, feeling like a drunk after a three-day bender as he followed Heather into the grocery store for the second time this miserably rainy Sunday morning.

Be careful what you wish for, he thought with annoyance. He'd wanted to be put back on active duty. And here he was. Tailing a woman in a frigging *grocery* store. He felt like an ass carrying the little red plastic basket.

How damn hard would it be to have Shaw's daughter answer one simple question?

Question: Where is your dirtbag father?

Answer: Argentina. Or Iraq. Or Bumfuck, Indiana.

Simple. No muss, no fuss.

Technically, his first attempt to meet her—the one where she'd summarily slammed the door in his face—wouldn't happen until tomorrow. He'd reversed time—did a TiVo, as his brother Duncan liked to say, to give it another shot.

Idiot. Of course she'd been scared. He'd heard it in her voice, and seen it clearly written on her face as she'd tried to close the door. Considering the people looking for her father, she should be freaking terrified. Heather had gone underground for a reason, and yet he'd tried to barge into her life as if he had the right to be there.

His lips twitched toward a smile. He guessed he was every inch the moron she'd called him.

Now that he understood her fear, Caleb had decided to shimmer back in time twenty-four hours. Hoping he'd have more luck if he approached her on neutral territory. The grocery store was a good place.

But unfortunately, after chatting her up for less than a minute, he'd realized that Heather was nobody's fool. She'd wanted nothing to do with him. She'd coolly blown him off and left the store without her basket of groceries.

If at first, he thought grimly as he watched her, you don't succeed—go back in time ten minutes and try again. Third time lucky.

It had to be; he was running out of options.

Except all those jumps so close together had drained him. All she had to do to get rid of him this time was blow hard. The thought of her anywhere near him with her lips puckered almost made him pass out right there.

He shook his head. She was too rich for his blood. Her sticker price was *way* out of his league. She'd dated princes and dukes and captains of industry. She'd dined, and probably a whole lot more, with presidents and kings.

Of course, he mused, watching the gentle sway of her hips as she walked, who gave a damn who she'd had dinner with, when she was naked in bed under *him*.

He almost groaned. *Not going to happen. Down boy.*

If he wasn't here to extract the intel on her father's whereabouts from her, Caleb would have turned around and walked away. Fast. There were dozens of excellent reasons to avoid this woman.

Besides her high-society social circle.

Besides her father's association with some of the most powerful and dangerous tangos in the world.

Besides her stratospheric D&B rating.

Beside all of *those* pesky little impediments there was an even bigger deterrent. He was Cursed. And he had no intention of starting something he knew he'd never finish.

No one had ever bucked the five-hundred-year-old family Curse, and he had no intention of trying.

Still, she had an astonishing effect on his libido. His attraction to her was intense, and more powerful than anything he'd felt before. He'd walked away from women who'd held less of a temptation than Heather Shaw.

But this was business. There was no walking away. Not until he had what he needed.

He hoped like hell he got the intel *fast*.

She picked up a container of hothouse strawberries. She'd turn the plastic box over—like that—to check the bottom for bad ones, then she'd bring it to her nose and inhale—like that. Then she'd put it in her basket. Just like that.

Been here, done this.

Caleb reversed direction as she proceeded through the produce section—the selection process would take her just over seven minutes—and walked slowly down a parallel aisle.

This time, he'd let *her* make the first move.

Chapter Four

Heather walked around the end of the tower of soup cans on special, heading for the bread aisle. To hell with the inflated price of the hothouse strawberries, she was in the mood to celebrate tonight. The ripe red berries sat beside an enormous baking potato in the bottom of her basket.

She'd added another boutique to her list of customers for her jewelry, and they'd given her a nice-sized order on Friday.

When she'd run she'd taken all of her own and her mother's jewelry with her.

The jewelry was far too recognizable to sell. The bracelets, necklaces, and rings were worth a large fortune, and had all been custom-made for her mother and herself. She and her French-born mother had been living trophies for her father to parade around to show his success and wealth to his "banking" clients.

Each distinctive piece that Heather melted down and remade gave her a double thrill. She was at last using her skills as an artisan to make the simple, stylish jewelry she preferred, and supporting herself at the same time.

It was a miserably cold and rainy day and there weren't that many shoppers in the grocery store on a Sunday afternoon.

A couple of Girl Scouts and their mothers were huddled at a table outside the doors to the grocery store, and Heather decided to stop on her way out of the store and buy several boxes of Thin Mints to take home to aid her in her solitary celebration.

A good book, a hot cup of tea, and a box of cookies sounded perfect. And for dinner, a nice thick steak instead of one of the fancy recipes that required all her concentration. Maybe a glass or two of champagne—

"Want to arm wrestle for it?"

The deep voice, coming unexpectedly from directly behind her, made her jump. Slapping a hand over her racing heart, she spun around.

The man was broad shouldered and a good six or seven inches taller than she, and she was five seven. *Big,* she thought breathlessly. Lord, he smells good, was the next fleeting thought. Despite the chilly weather he wore nothing more than a black T-shirt, jeans, and running shoes. Droplets of rain sparkled in his short dark hair.

Incongruously, he held an empty red basket in one large hand. The smile that had been forming on his lips faded away as their eyes met. A surge of warmth went through her, and she had to swallow hard. She had the strangest sensation of connection, and a strong sense of *déjà vu.* She didn't know him, but there was something vaguely familiar about his face. The angle of his nose, that little scar bisecting his left brow seemed familiar.

His eyes were an attractive dark blue with a hint of teal, his lean face a little pale beneath his tan. There was absolutely nothing threatening about his stance or his expression. Thank God.

But he did look dangerous in a different way. Dangerous to women in general, she suspected. There was that pirate, bad-boy, heartbreaker aura about him that had her heart beating double-time in a purely female-to-sexy-male response. She dropped her maidenly hand from her chest, and took a step back anyway, feeling a ridiculous urge to reach out and finger-comb his wet hair and lick the drops of moisture from his skin.

She curled her needy fingers around the handle of her basket instead, and tilted her head to look at his face. "I'm sorry. What did you say?"

"The last loaf of honey wheat-berry bread?"

Puzzled, she glanced away from his smiling blue eyes to the shelf. One loaf of her favorite bread left.

"You were staring at it for a while," he said gravely when she didn't immediately respond. "Please. You take it." He picked it up like a football and handed it to her. "I'd hate to think that those twelve children of yours would have to do without their breakfast tomorrow morning just because I wanted it for my solitary dinner tonight."

"Seven." When he looked blank, she clarified with a smile. "Seven children. Not twelve. Thanks." She took the loaf and set it on top of the strawberries in her basket.

"Your husband's a lucky man."

"I tell him that every night when he helps the septuplets with their trigonometry homework."

He choked back a laugh. "Brave woman."

No matter how strong the temptation to stay and play, Heather knew she had to nip the conversation in the bud. There wasn't any room in her life for a man right now. Especially not one as tempting as this one.

A short lifetime ago, she would have enjoyed the zing of interest in the pit of her stomach, the way her breath caught and her heart stumbled. Meeting a guy with a bone-melting smile in a grocery store had never been one of her fantasies, but she could certainly run with it. An ache, purely sexual and totally unexpected, spread through her as her mind flashed a slideshow of possibilities. In mere seconds, she envisioned him in her bed, their bodies tangled in the sheets as he did magical and thrilling things to her. With her. And she reciprocated.

Her fingers tightened around the handle of the basket. *Wow*. This was a first. Normally her thoughts on meeting a new guy ran toward a nice dinner, maybe taking in a show. She was the first to admit that it took her a long time to warm up to a guy, and even longer before she decided to sleep with him. But not with this man. No, her imagination had skipped the appetizer and main course, and gone straight to dessert.

Forget wheat-berry bread, she wanted sex. With him. Now.

But that was about as real a possibility as her faux husband and faux children. He thought she was brave? She nearly laughed aloud.

"You have no idea," she told him honestly, and forced herself to raise a hand in farewell before turning away. Feeling the heat of his intense teal gaze on her back, Heather crossed the aisle for a jar of apricot jam.

She knew that he was behind her, that he was following her toward the jam he probably didn't need. As tempting as it had been to linger and spend a few more minutes flirting with him, it was better not to. Loneliness wouldn't kill her. And it wouldn't be long before she was back to a life with a full social calendar and dozens of sexy guys vying to flirt, and more, with her.

The sensation of being watched was so strong, she slanted a glance behind her. He was standing in the middle of the wide aisle. Still there. He smiled, "Got ya," and Heather couldn't help smiling back. Just a smile.

She probably should have been nervous, but he wasn't threatening. In fact, his presence felt warm and almost familiar at her back. Lord, it had been fun to flirt again. Even if it had only been for a couple of seconds. She used to be good at it. It was one more thing she missed. And couldn't have.

The feeling would have to last her, she told herself firmly. She wasn't out of danger. Not yet.

She found her jam and continued down the grocery aisle without turning around, even though she sensed that the man had taken the hint and gone about his business. The knowledge depressed her and made her lonelier than ever.

Reining herself in, being something that she wasn't, was wearing on her more than she'd realized. Although she hadn't been that crazy about her life before either.

Perhaps one day she could find something between a useless Barbie doll, jet-setting around the world from party to party, and a jewelry designer holed up in a one-room apartment with no social life at all.

There must be some sort of middle ground.

For twenty-six of her twenty-seven years she'd taken the path of least resistance. She'd played dress-up from the time she could balance a plastic tiara on her head and had never looked back. All she had to do to make people happy was smile, look attractive, and listen attentively.

She was the only child of wealthy, doting parents, who had never expected anything of her. She and her mother were—had been—close. But Heather was a little embarrassed by how badly she always wanted to please her father. She'd adored him, and knew he loved her. But he also judged her. And at her age it shouldn't be so important to try to be what he wanted her to be.

Because what she'd ended up being was . . . shallow, and as useless as cotton candy.

Yet in the blink of an eye that had changed last March when she'd seen him standing over her mother's lifeless body. The scene in their Paris salon that fateful Saturday afternoon had played through her mind like a stop-action movie for months.

It had been the accident her father had insisted it had

been. Of course it had. Her parents were very fond of each other, and they'd never had a harsh word between them in thirty years of marriage.

She'd been devastated by her mother's death. And terrified that the French police wouldn't believe her father when he told them his wife had fallen during an argument. The circumstances and the situation had looked suspicious. Even to Heather, who'd come downstairs minutes after the accident.

Scared, out of her depth, Heather had done as he asked. She'd run.

Get over it, she told herself firmly. *I'm Hannah Smith now. I'm alive. I'll have my life back. One day.*

God, she was getting maudlin. She needed chocolate!

She still needed a couple of other things—a big, fat juicy steak for one, and a small bottle of champagne. Then the Girl Scout cookies and home.

She'd even grab a few society rags at the checkout stand so she could keep abreast of old friends. The more time she put between then and now, the more comfortable she felt in Hannah Smith's skin. But knowing what was going on outside her insular world still had the attraction of keeping her connected to her old life as Heather Shaw. Sometimes she missed her old life.

Mostly she didn't.

It was only after she'd run that she realized how unsatisfactory it had been. She'd never realized what a knife-edge of danger she'd been living with because of the people her father associated with. The people she and her mother considered friends. The families and friends of her banker father's clients.

How could she have been so blind? So incredibly gullible? So damned *stupid*? She considered herself reasonably intelligent; why hadn't she ever wondered how her father's banking clients amassed the fortunes they entrusted him to manage?

Strong hands grabbed her arms as she went barreling around a display of canned baked beans, and almost mowed him down.

"Whoa," he said with a smile. "Where's the fire?"

It was the same guy who'd given her the bread. "I'm sorry. Did I ste—" She stepped off his foot. Heat stole up her throat. "Sorry about that. I wasn't looking where I was going." Trying to outrun demons rarely worked.

His blue eyes held humor as he dropped his hands. "No harm done. Nice seeing you again." Without waiting for a response, thank God, he moved off down the frozen food aisle and opened a door to one of the freezers.

Feeling idiotic, Heather turned around and made a beeline for the meat cases in the back of the store. Making a lightning-fast steak choice, she hurried over to the dairy section for sour cream. Oh, no—

He glanced up, a brick of sharp cheddar in his hand, and a mock scowl on his handsome face. "Are you stalking me?"

Heather's eyes widened. "No. Of course no—No!" she choked back a laugh.

With a theatrical sigh he tossed the cheese into the basket he was carrying. "Damn. A man can live in hope."

There was an innate sexuality about him as his muscles shifted effortlessly beneath the black T-shirt clinging damply to his hard upper body. *Whew, it was hot in here.* "What about my husband and the children?"

"Do you *have* a husband?"

"No." And if she *did* he would be nothing like this guy. He was definitely a fantasy man, she thought, as her heart raced and her palms grew damp, *not* the father of her future children.

"Single mother?"

She smiled. "No."

"Will you have mine?" His eyes gleamed mischievously.

Her pulses leapt. "Your what?" she asked mischievously, enjoying the game. "Your mother?"

His smile widened. "My children."

"Hmm." She pretended to consider it. "Would I have to have seven?"

Eyes an unfathomable deep-sea blue regarded her with sultry appraisal. "How about three?"

"Three's good." Her heart fluttered beneath her rib cage at that hot gaze. She licked her dry lips. *Wow, he was potent.*

He stared at her for a moment, his eyes on her mouth, watching the small movement of her tongue. Short dark lashes flickered as his attention leveled out to meet hers. Heat blazed teal fire, setting off a heated response in her.

Two women, shopping together with a couple of toddlers, wanted to get by. He gave them a charming smile that made Heather weak at the knees. The two young mothers thought so too. One blushed, and the other fiddled with her hair. They started giggling as they neared the other end of the aisle.

His attention was on her when she turned back to him. "They'll be boys, of course."

Had he moved closer? Gripping her grocery basket in tight fists, she felt his warm breath fanning her cheek. "Why 'of course'?" Instead of moving back, she tilted her face a little more to better see his. Despite beads of icy rain still clinging to her coat, she was suddenly extremely—*extremely* warm. "What if I'd prefer six or seven daughters?"

"As much as I'd love to have *ten* beautiful daughters with eyes the color of sunlit whiskey, and hair the color of honey, all of whom look *just* like their gorgeous mother, I'm afraid if you insist on girls we'll have to adopt. There hasn't been a female born in my family for five hundred years."

Sunlit whiskey and honey? Heather bit back a smile. "Really?"

"Really." His lips curved, and for a moment it sent all rational thought from her head. "Does this mean you'll marry me?"

"Hmm." Silly, this was just an innocent flirtation in public, but her pulses leapt crazily at the desire in his eyes. "Isn't this a little quick?" she asked, a little breathlessly, feeling her body respond to him in a way that she immediately recognized, but had never felt this fast, this hot, before.

When his gaze moved gently over her face like that Heather swore she could feel the brush of his interest against her skin. A pleasant shiver of acute awareness traveled down her spine.

"Don't you believe in love at first sight?" he asked softly.

"Is that what this is?" The banter was charged with eroticism, and she could barely speak for the thickness in her throat. "I thought it was just hunger."

He gave her an enigmatic smile. "Of a kind."

"Yes. Of a kind." Something about this conversation had a serious undertone and she took a cautious step back.

"Now that we're engaged, will you let me buy you a cup of coffee at the Starbucks next door?"

"I—"

"Say I will."

Ignoring the warm liquid flutter inside, like being bathed in warm honey, Heather searched his eyes and saw nothing more dangerous than a casual flirtation lurking in the teal depths. Why not? How long had it been since she'd felt feminine? It wasn't as though they were going to get naked and roll around making love on the floor of a coffee shop. It wasn't going any further than a cup of coffee and a mild flirtation.

Unfortunately.

She bit back a moan, because of course, now the image of him *naked,* of touching his bare skin, was all she could think about. She cleared her throat and dredged up a smile. "How about if I say 'yes to coffee,' for now?"

"That'll work." His lips twitched and his eyes went hot. "For now."

CHAPTER FIVE

Carrying Heather's bag of groceries, Caleb walked, *limped,* damn it, her to the coffee shop next door. Unfortunately, the short trip was under cover; a quick detour in the pouring rain might have substituted for a cold shower.

Mine.

The thought slammed into his brain out of nowhere. *Whoa, pal!* He yanked on his mental brakes. Where in the hell had *that* come from? He was too damned pragmatic to be possessive. Especially about a woman.

Because of Nairne's Curse, it had always been a foregone conclusion that he'd never be in a relationship long enough to make it complicated.

Sex? Oh, yeah. Involved? Possessive? Hell no.

Unfortunately, no sex here. Too bad. He was hot for her, but Shaw's daughter was an assignment. And a short assignment at that. Anything was better than being bored out of his gourd.

An interesting, *sexy* assignment. But that was all.

Think cold shower.

Couple of hours, and he'd teleport to Berlin and Kris-Alice. Somehow the thought of the beautiful German woman became less appealing each time he saw Heather. *Hannah.* Once he was in Germany he'd start nagging Lark again. He was itching to get back in the field after three months of inactivity.

All he had to do now was get a location for Papa Shaw. He'd buy her a cup of coffee, flirt a little, subtly ask the question, and be done.

There were half a dozen people scattered about the small coffee shop when they walked in, some sitting, some standing at the counter, but Caleb spotted a small table in back and headed for it, Heather beside him. The shop smelled richly of coffee and rain-damp customers.

"This good?" he asked her, indicating the small table in the corner. He placed her bag of groceries on the third chair. She'd feel safe with the wall at her back. Clear view of the door. He stayed out of her personal space, lulling her into a false sense of security. The enemy had already breached her walls.

Then why the hell didn't he *feel* like her enemy? His body felt very . . . friendly toward hers.

"Great."

"What will it be?" he asked easily.

"Anything hot and with chocolate in it. Large. Thanks."

He brushed a damp strand of hair off her face with his finger, letting his knuckle linger on the softness of her cheek. "Think of our children's names." He dropped his hand before she could move out of reach. "Be right back."

He returned a few minutes later with two large coffees in tall covered paper cups. "One *venti* mocha for the lady with the pretty eyes." He placed the twenty-ounce cup in front of her.

Heather dragged her attention from the bank of windows overlooking the wet street as he approached. Her lips curved as she looked at him. "Thanks. Aren't you freezing without a coat?"

"Warm-blooded." *Hot-blooded looking at you.* Everything about Heather Shaw appealed to him. From her height, to her silky golden-brown hair, to her large, hazel eyes with their fringe of thick lashes. Her makeup was subtle and understated, but showed an experienced hand. Rain droplets beaded on the shoulders of her black raincoat and sparkled in her hair like jeweled netting refracting light. Her cheeks were still pink from the cold.

He didn't know a lot about clothes, but he guessed that what she was wearing now was off the rack—and an inexpensive rack at that—rather than the designer stuff she used to wear. *Where's Daddy's money, sweetheart? Hell. Where's Daddy?*

Had she and Shaw had a falling out? Was it her father she was constantly looking for outside, or some old boyfriend she'd changed her name to avoid?

"You should probably know the name of the father of your children," he said easily. Putting down his cup, he held out his hand across the table. "Caleb Edge."

She slid hers into it automatically. Hers was slender, her handshake firm, palm slightly damp. If that didn't tell him she was nervous, the fact that she was sitting perched on the edge of her seat did. She was a bird ready to fly.

"Hannah Smith." She withdrew her hand almost immediately and reached for her cup. She took a tentative sip through the hole in the plastic lid. Apparently her drink was too hot. She put it down and wrapped her hands around the base.

Caleb kicked out the chair not quite opposite, sat, then slouched back, intentionally relaxed and nonthreatening. He dragged his attention away from the rapid pulse at the base of her slender throat to gaze into her eyes. Hazel. More brown than green. Pretty. Despite the rich, dark fragrance of coffee surrounding them, he could smell her. Something light and floral and evocative of summer.

"So Hannah Smith, tell me all about you." He purposely broke eye contact, wanting to appear interested, not predatory, and pried the lid off his coffee cup. It was one thing to pretend an attraction to get what he wanted. It was quite another to feel this avalanche of sensations at her very nearness. His own heart rate was up, and he was preternaturally aware of everything about her. There was no pretending about it.

He needed to get this over with as quickly as possible. Everything in him was on a razor edge of arousal. Which was as bizarre as it was disconcerting. Lust at first sight was something new. He didn't care for it. Especially here and especially now.

He never mixed business and pleasure. And while he'd been tempted to break that rule a time or two, he never had. As a T-FLAC operative he had little downtime, and when he did he intentionally kept relationships casual. He wasn't stupid enough to try to buck the family Curse.

Caleb had no intention—ever—of testing the part of the Curse that stated: *"When a Lifemate is chosen by the heart of a son, No protection can be given, again I have won. His pain will be deep, her death will be swift, Inside his heart a terrible rift."*

Five hundred years of Edges had proven that the witch's Curse couldn't be broken. Over the centuries, all the women the Edge men had loved had *died*. He and his brothers weren't going to let Nairne's Curse continue.

The freaking Curse would die with them.

He'd been close to trying to buck it, damn close, *twice*. And in each instance he'd forced himself to walk away before more than a glimmer of emotion could blink into life. He'd never regretted doing so. Christiana was now happily married to a decent guy, had a cute daughter, and was living happily ever after in Maine. Donna had produced four girls and lived with her senator husband in DC.

Both women were happy. Both women were alive.

It was somewhat ironic that Christiana and Donna had both produced daughters. Edge men could only make sons. *"Three sons on three sons find nothing but pain."*

Yeah. Whatever. He'd never know.

Other than the fact that he'd been out of the ball game for almost three interminable months during his surgery and rehab, Caleb was happy as a pig in shit about his life.

So, as much as his body was yelling, yes, yes, yes right now, the answer to his rampant libido was an emphatic *no.* But *damn*—her skin was as soft as it looked. She was naturally fair, and her skin appeared smooth and flawless. Caleb had the insane urge to lean across the table and stroke her cheek with his lips.

He wanted to kiss her. Touch her. Everywhere. With lips and teeth and tongue. He wanted to rip off that bulky raincoat and the dark red sweatshirt beneath it. He wanted to drag the jeans free of her legs and bury his face against her stomach. Hell, he wanted to bury himself deep inside her.

But what he wanted was immaterial.

What he needed was a crack across the back of the head with a two-by-four. Then Shaw's address. Not necessarily in that order.

She wrapped both hands around her paper cup tightly enough to cause the plastic top to pop off. "Not that much to tell." She concentrated on picking up the lid and moving it a few inches to the side. Then she placed it on the lid he'd discarded earlier. She was neat. No, Caleb thought, watching her movements. She felt a need to control her environment. She also wanted something to do with her hands. Interesting. He could suggest any number of things this woman could do with her hands. All of which involved his body.

"I'm twenty-seven, and I design and sell jewelry for a living." She had the prettiest eyes, Caleb thought. Not just the color, which was a clear, almost transparent brown/green, but large, intelligent, and interested. "How about you?"

"Thirty-three, single." Under the table he stretched out his legs, *accidentally* brushing her leg with his foot. Only her eyes flinched. He kept his ankle against hers. She didn't move away. "Had all my shots and I'm in sales." He lifted his butt off the seat a few inches, yanked out his wallet from the back pocket of his jeans, dug a business card out, and handed it to her.

Caleb Edge, VP Sales and Marketing, Preda Enterprises. A Portland, Oregon, address. Preda could be anything the operative needed it to be. It worked well as a cover. The address was real. T-FLAC maintained similar offices all over the world.

She glanced briefly at the card. "What do you sell?"

"Tractor parts. Not that interesting, but lucrative enough. Been with them going on eight years."

"Do you live in the Bay Area, or in Oregon?" she asked, sticking his business card into her coat pocket. Her eyes flickered to the door, then back to his face. Who was she waiting for? Caleb wondered.

"I'm here often enough, but no. The bank and I own a house in Portland." Not true. He kept a condo in New York. One he rarely visited. "I always stay at the Indigo Hotel 'round the corner when I'm in town." The cover would work for her. He was solid enough to own his own house, close enough—almost—to be a local, and therefore not much of a threat. The shadow of fear in her eyes receded a little more.

Still, she wasn't completely comfortable, he noticed. She started to pick at the side seam of her paper cup. Nerves. Tension. The same sexual awareness that he was feeling? Interesting how her tone conveyed confidence while her body language showed that she was anything but.

Caleb wasn't a hand holder, but he took a chance and casually took her hand off the cup, lacing his fingers with hers on the tabletop. Her fingers looked ridiculously small engulfed by his. Her skin was soft, indicating to an extent her past privileged lifestyle, but her nails were short and unpainted, and she wore no jewelry, not even a watch.

"It's only coffee." He meant the event.

But it wasn't "only coffee." It was a razor-sharp mutual attraction that seared through him and made him want to grab her up and carry her off to his cave.

She gave a little start of surprise to find her hand in his, but didn't pull away this time. "Right. Just coffee. The Indigo's nice."

Roadblock. "Yeah, I guess." He traced the back of her fingers with his thumb and felt his own body echo the slight tremor transmitted from her hand to his. He found his attention focused on her mouth, which looked soft and silky and eminently kissable. He wanted to lean forward to taste her. Would tasting her be enough? He was afraid the answer to that was a resounding no.

"Hotel food gets old after a while," he said, trying to keep his mind on track with difficulty.

"Well, don't look at me." She really had the prettiest eyes, despite the wariness he saw in them. The color changed from hazel to a rich amber-brown when she smiled. It wasn't a fully fledged smile, but it did ease some of the tension around her lush mouth. "I'm not a very good cook."

He ran a thumb over the smooth skin on the back of her hand again, saw the nerves jump in her eyes. She was still a little wary, but she wasn't afraid. He tried to ignore his own physical reaction to touching her. The elevated heartbeat, the sudden sensation of euphoria were just his body's response to the closeness of a beautiful woman. "We'll have to hire someone then," he said easily, shifting closer into her personal space. Getting her ready to accept him.

"Absolutely," she told him seriously, eyes bright with amusement. "We both like to eat. And the children will need to be fed."

"No problem." He wanted to turn her hand over and press his mouth to her palm. He wanted to feel the rapid pulse that beat just beneath her skin. He wanted her soft pale hands on his body. "My folks will be delighted when Michael, Matt, and Mark arrive. How about your folks? Are you close?"

"Sorry. The kids will only have one set of grandparents. Mine died a long time ago."

She was a social liar. Good enough if one wasn't watching her eyes. She made just the right amount of eye contact. She didn't fidget. And if he hadn't been watching her so closely he would have missed the small tell of her pupils dilating.

"I'm sorry. Were you close?"

"I don't like to talk about them, do you mind?"

Hmm. Not even an attempt to bullshit about them. Interesting. Intriguing. "Okay," he said easily, taking another drink of his still-hot coffee and moving in another few inches so that their knees touched under the table. "We won't."

Well, damn. What had he expected? That she'd give up her father's address to a stranger an hour after meeting? Caleb wished he had his brother Gabriel's ability to read minds. It would be handy as hell right now. He was tempted to TiVo time back to when she and her father had split.

Unfortunately he didn't have an exact date or precise location, and without those he'd be screwing around trying to pinpoint the timing. A waste of valuable time and energy.

He could smell her soap or shampoo. Fresh. Clean. Female. Not expensive perfume, just soap and the natural fragrance of her skin. Being this close to her was like an aphrodisiac. Good in a torturous kinda way.

He'd never been this turned on by a woman seated three feet away. And damned sure not when in a public place. He wanted to lean over and kiss her. Ludicrous that he was even *thinking* it, let alone this freaking tempted to throw caution to the winds, give in to the craving, and do it. If she'd been any other woman in the world, he wouldn't have hesitated or given it another thought.

But she was Heather Shaw. Caleb was willing to go as far as necessary to extract the information he needed. But he doubted, unfortunately, that he'd have to make love to her to get what he needed.

He forced himself not to imagine teleporting her directly to the bed in his hotel up the street. Forced himself not to imagine burying his face against her creamy skin. Forced himself not to imagine the overwhelming release of burying himself deep inside her.

Caleb figured he was suffering for the good of T-FLAC and his country and took another drink of his coffee before asking, "How about brothers and sisters?"

The slight tension in her shoulders eased. "No. You?"

"Couple of brothers. One older. One younger."

"Are you close?"

Caleb held up twined fingers. "Like this."

"Lucky you."

"Yeah. Never more so than when I saw a beautiful woman ogling a loaf of bread an hour ago."

"We're strangers." Who was she reminding? Herself?

"Do you really feel that way?"

She bit the corner of her lower lip as their eyes locked. "No."

"Me neither. Fish or meat?"

She smiled at the non sequitur, but got it. And relaxed a little more. "Both. You?"

"I'm a meat and potatoes kinda guy. Dogs or cats?"

"Cats."

"You don't like *dogs*?!"

She shook her head. "Once bitten, twice shy."

"Where were you bitten?"

"In the kitchen."

"Funny. Not funny. Show me."

"Oh. I don't think so."

"I'll kiss it better."

"It happened when I was eight. It's quite better now. But thank you for the offer."

"Okay, the kids can have a cat."

"Thank you." She took a sip of her coffee, looking at him over the rim. "Raw or cooked?"

"The *cat*?" He gave her an exaggerated horrified look. She choked back a laugh.

"Food!"

"Ah. Definitely cooked."

God, she was sweet. Sexy and funny and damn cute as well. There was a vulnerability in her that he hadn't expected.

He didn't have a type, he enjoyed most women. But if he did have a type, Heather Shaw wasn't it, Caleb thought, playing with her slender fingers as he shifted closer still. Too bad his body wasn't getting the message.

"Yeah. Me too. Flying or driving?"

"Getting there the faster the better." Which was why this slow acquaintance dance, no matter how necessary, was making him crazy with impatience. Caleb let nothing of his thoughts show in his face, however. "Beatles or Elvis?"

"Beatles."

"Elvis." He needed to speed things up. Needed to get the answers he wanted so he could get back to—What? A frigging vacation? Jesus, he needed to get out there and kick some tango butt. Mano a mano would suit him fine right now. Preferably something violent that would relieve some of this excess adrenaline he felt just looking at this woman.

"Vacations?"

"Often," she answered.

He focused on her words, on probing for clues, and tried to ignore his body's reaction to her. Instead of fading somewhat with proximity, the lust factor was rising exponentially with every second he was with her. "Beach or mountains?"

Her brow knit pensively. "Mountains. I've gotten the beach thing out of my system."

He smiled. "Suffered the obligatory family vacations to the shore, did you?"

She shrugged. "We traveled a lot when I was growing up."

Brian Shaw was the banker *du jour* of some of the largest terrorist groups in the world. Taking his wife and pretty daughter with him when he went to see his clients was his MO. The family traveled extensively and often. "Favorite place?"

"They all look the same after a while."

"Humor me. I spent almost every summer vacation in Scotland. I would have liked variety." *Almost as much as I'd like to see you naked.*

"I love Paris," she mused. "Great shopping and great restaurants." Her mother had been French, and they'd had a home just outside Paris. As far as they knew, Shaw hadn't returned to France since the death of his wife a year ago.

According to their intel, Babette Shaw had been killed

in an armed home invasion. Both Shaw and Heather had been out of the country at the time, Shaw in South America, Heather at a close friend's in London.

"But no beach," Caleb teased. She wasn't telling him anything they didn't already know. "Where else?"

"Honduras—great diving there."

"Love diving. We'll teach the boys."

Honduras—hell, all of South America—was being checked as they spoke. His comment coaxed a small smile to her pretty lips. Caleb was distracted again as he imagined nibbling her lower lip.

"Yes, we'll want the children to be good swimmers."

It didn't task his imagination much to think of her in a tiny swimsuit. She'd look great in a skimpy thong, her skin oiled and—he shook his head to banish his off-track thoughts.

"The water's also nice in the Caribbean," she said. "Bermuda has beautiful pink sandy beaches. Then there's the Mediterranean, lots of private islands to rent."

Shaw wasn't in his usual haunts anywhere in the Caribbean, or Bermuda, or frigging around his known hangouts along the Mediterranean. They'd checked. Double-checked, and would continue to watch. But the man hadn't amassed the kind of wealth he had by being stupid.

T-FLAC wasn't the only group after the son of a bitch.

"Do you have a favorite?"

Shaw's daughter—*yeah, remind yourself who this woman is, smartass*—shrugged. "I used to, but that was a long time ago."

Time to change the subject. Preferably to an activity where he could imagine her fully dressed. He *had* to tamp down this attraction—bloody hell. *Attraction* would be like calling a forest fire a weenie roast. He had to beat down the sparks before he burned up. "Opera?"

Heather laughed at his expression as he'd wanted her

to do. Unfortunately her laughter shot to his groin like a heat-seeking missile, making his pants too tight and sitting damned uncomfortable.

Jesus. SOS. He was in big trouble here.

"You look like a kid told to eat spinach when you pull that face." She sipped her drink, automatically licking whipped cream off the corner of her mouth. "I love the opera," she told him cheerfully. "How about ballet?"

He turned her hand over and stroked her palm with his finger. She had a long lifeline, and newly formed little calluses on her fingers. Must be from the tools she used when she made her jewelry. "Love it as much as I do opera." The smell of her constricted his chest.

"Girls' night out, then."

"No problem. I'll stay home with the kids. We'll eat junk food and stay up la—" His fingers tightened over hers on the table. "Know what I want more than my next breath?"

Her gaze went from his mouth back to his eyes. She shook her head. He leaned in, close enough for his breath to stir her hair. "To kiss you."

Her mouth parted softly. Her pulse leapt at the base of her throat, and her pupils flared in a show of nerves and excitement. "Are—" She swallowed hard, then licked her bottom lip. A quick heated swipe. "Are you asking permission?"

He shook his head. "A kiss loses the lure of spontaneity if one has to ask."

Her pupils dilated. "Are you trying to lure me, Caleb Edge?"

Bringing her hand up to his mouth, he pressed closed lips to her slightly damp palm. *Scared, Little Red Riding Hood?* "Not lure. Seduce." *Trust me.*

Her fingers curled around his. Once again she didn't pull away. Their eyes met and held, hers heavy lidded. She had a nervous habit of biting the corner of her lower lip that drove him insane with hunger, and she did that now. Caleb almost groaned out loud.

He dipped his head, then paused, his mouth a breath away from hers. Skimming his fingers along the curve of her jaw he watched her eyes darken to aged whiskey with anticipation. She dragged in a ragged breath. Not fear. Excitement.

He wanted to kiss her so badly he shook with it.

Hoisted by his own petard.

As his pal Jake liked to say: "It's good to want things."

CHAPTER SIX

Helpless to prevent it, good intentions be damned, Caleb's vision blurred as he closed the gap. He shut his eyes as his mouth touched hers. Not giving her time to think. Not allowing himself a moment to shore up his resistance. He didn't *want* to resist her, damn it.

This would work, he assured himself. All part of developing that trust. Yeah. Right.

Soft and unthreatening, he brushed his mouth back and forth until her lips parted on a sigh. He'd meant it to be brief, a show of interest, nothing more. Instead he found himself plunged into unexpected depths as she responded.

His blood pooled in his groin as the slick heat of her tongue came to greet him. She tasted amazing, and her response sent a jolt of pure possessiveness through him.

He felt her hand on his shoulder, her fingers curling into the fabric. He did a slow exploration of the heated cavern of her mouth and felt a blinding, overpowering, *insane,* sense of homecoming.

Mine, he thought. *Mine.*

Cupping the back of her head in his palm he drew her closer, letting her long hair glide over the back of his hand. Slowly he deepened the kiss, exploring with long, lazy strokes of his tongue. She wasn't shy tasting back as her tongue met his, slick and agile. The flavor and texture of her was intoxicating. She smelled of soap, and tasted like chocolate-flavored coffee. Delicious. Intoxicating.

God, he thought, sinking into her sweetness, listening to her ragged breath, feeling the subtle tightening of her fingers on his shoulder. She tasted of promises fulfilled. Hope realized. Joy delivered.

His brain went blank as her essence filled him to the brim. God—*focus,* he told himself, *don't blow this. Don't scare her off.* But it wasn't *Heather* who was scared.

How had this suddenly become more than a casual seduction to get intel? More powerful. More intense, more—everything.

The very smell of her skin went to his brain like an aphrodisiac. Hunger simmered through his blood. Hot. Insistent.

He kept his touch gentle but his pulse hammered frantically. He wanted to taste her skin, wanted to rip off her clothes, wanted to take her, in *public* for Christ's sake! Right here, right now. Right on the small round table holding their coffee cups. He wanted to skim his mouth from her head to her toes. And then do it again.

He slid his hands down. Exerting gentle pressure on the small of her back, he brought her upper body even closer. His other hand, not quite steady, combed through her rain-damp hair, releasing the fragrances of sun-warmed flowers. The strands felt silken and cool as he buried his fingers deep enough to feel the warmth of her scalp. Lust, sharp and white-hot, raced through his bloodstream.

He wanted her in a thousand ways. Preferably naked, prone, and in private.

He wanted to feel the length of her body pressed to his. He wanted to wrap his arms about her naked body. He wanted to carry her off to his cave and ravish her.

He *wanted.*

Wanted all of her.

Christ.

Oblivious to the other customers, Caleb hauled her to her feet, wrapping his arms tightly around her. God, yes. She fit him perfectly. A sensual fire licked through his veins as her soft curves molded against him and her arms snaked around his neck. Pulling her more firmly against his body he felt a blinding, searing surge of connection that stunned him in its intensity.

Forgetting that he was pretending, he dipped his head and went back for more. He couldn't think clearly as everything about her consumed him. The need to bury himself deep inside her made his hands shake and his blood hot.

The kiss tore the breath from Heather's lungs, and she found herself on her feet without knowing quite how she'd gotten there. His tongue, wet and sensual and very sure of itself, slid between her teeth to taste and explore. Heat exploded through her body.

Her knees immediately went weak, and she leaned into him for support. His arms closed around her, molding her against the hard length of his body. Fisting one hand in the back of her raincoat he drew her more tightly against him. His fingers tangled in her hair as he crushed her mouth beneath his as if he were starving and she was a feast.

A long delicious shudder passed through her as he possessed her mouth with obvious relish. He used his teeth and his tongue and the hard press of his body to churn up sleeping desires deep inside her. Passion unfurled. Not like a lamb. But like a lion. With a deep roar, and a hunger that should've shocked her. Instead she moaned low in her throat, turning liquid inside as she arched against him, returning his passion with heat of her own.

His warm velvet tongue stroked, teased, played with

hers in an erotic dance that dissolved her resolve a little more with each stroke.

Pulse pounding loudly in her ears, she grew dizzy with pleasure as his need set fire to her own and the kiss became impossibly more intense in response to her participation.

Tasting his desire fueled her own.

The coffee shop, and everyone in it, disappeared. Standing on tiptoe she pressed even closer to his wonderful mouth.

A feverish rush of pleasure engulfed her as his tongue moved in slow, relentless strokes and his hands drew her more tightly into his embrace. The hardness of his thighs pressed intimately against her softness, and the solid muscles of his chest made her breasts ache to be touched by his hands, his mouth. His hair felt like damp silk between her fingers.

She'd been kissed before, she thought, dizzy with longing. This was somehow . . . more.

More intense. More erotic. More compelling.

Being held like this, by him, loosened something that had been tight inside her forever. Her tummy danced and her heart fluttered with the sheer pleasure of his touch. The constriction inside unfurled like a rose opening its petals to the sun. If she had a brain in her head she'd push him away and run. This wasn't for her. Not here. Not now. But, God. The danger of trusting him didn't compare to the strength of the temptation in his kiss.

Had she ever felt this way before?

Buoyant. Jubilant. Euphoric.

No. Never.

She'd never realized that a simple melding of lips could be so blatantly erotic. Caleb turned kissing into an art form. As if the kiss, and the kiss alone, was the prize at the end of the journey. She found complete and utter pleasure in the hunger of his mouth on hers, in the safety and strength of his arms circling her body.

His body felt deliciously big and solid pressed against hers. He kissed her hot. He kissed her hungrily. He kissed her impatiently. As if he couldn't wait one more second to taste her. God. He kissed her as if they'd kissed a thousand times before. He seemed to know what she wanted, what she needed. Delivering a million promises with his mouth.

Not that she was going anywhere. She whimpered into his mouth. This was pure Heaven and she realized with a shock that the last few years she'd been a desert, parched for water, and suddenly here was a flash flood. Her skin soaked up his touch. She gave in to the sensation of his warm mouth, to the strength of his embrace as he both claimed and protected her.

The kiss went on and on, deep and insatiable. Her core temperature rose until she burned, the heat fueled by nothing more than his lips and tongue and the press of his fully clothed body against hers.

The hard length of his erection pressed against her stomach, and Heather felt frenzied enough to climb his body so that he fit where she ached most. No, she had never felt like this before.

Someone in the coffee shop started to applaud. Others joined in. A male voice shouted out, "Get a room, dude!"

She almost moaned aloud when Caleb broke contact. How had he managed to come to his senses when she was still shaken and giddy with need and churned up inside? Her lips pursed and she tightened her arms about his neck, not wanting to separate from his heat. One more taste. One more kiss. Didn't he crave it, too?

"Jesus." His voice was thick as he lifted his head. The color of his eyes had deepened to almost black, and he looked as poleaxed as she felt. The skin across his angular cheekbones was stretched taut, and his eyes blazed as though he had a high fever. "Any more of this, and they'll call the Vice cops out. I want—Hell—*need* to be alone with you. Now."

She was used to good-looking, eligible men hitting on her. But she'd never met anyone like Caleb. In her social set, a lot of the men *tried* to look dangerously sexy. Caleb just . . . was.

This wanton public display was so unlike her, her cheeks grew hot with embarrassment as she realized everyone in the place had been watching them. But, God. She was so tired of being alone. She hadn't realized how badly she'd craved human contact until he'd touched her. She craved *this*. She craved *him*.

Dare she?

He slid the flat of his palms up her arms, then captured her hands, and gently extricated her hold from around his neck. So he had more sense than she did, she thought, relieved that he'd taken the initiative and stopped kissing her. She wasn't sure that she would have had the good sense and restraint to pull away. Not when her entire body throbbed with longing and her heart still raced crazily.

Caleb brought her hands to his mouth, his gaze holding hers as he brushed his lips over her knuckles.

"Let's get the hell out of here," he said raggedly. "Forget Vice. They'll have to call the fire department when we do that again. Your place or mine?"

Lips swollen and cheeks hot, Heather blinked, dazed and disoriented. She didn't blame him for being so sure of himself. She'd given him no reason to believe she wasn't on fire for him. "Your hotel's closer." She heard the suggestion spill out of her mouth and was only mildly shocked.

"How fast can you move?" He leaned over to grab

her purse off the table, then shoved it into her hand, already pulling her toward the door.

Stuffing the small purse in the pocket of her raincoat, she smiled up at him. Giddy, and ridiculously happy, she went with him, more than willing as they wound their way between tables of amused patrons. "Let's see," she told Caleb thickly, barely aware of the comments following their progress.

Groceries forgotten, they practically ran out into the steady downpour hand in hand. The rain beat down harder now, blurring the streets and building in a surreal moving sheet of grays and blacks. Beside her Caleb appeared painted in Technicolor. His blue eyes seared hot every time their eyes met. And that was often. How they didn't crash into people in the street Heather had no idea.

She laughed, tilting up her face to the rain as he urgently pulled her along. They dodged people and their umbrellas, newspaper racks, and sidewalk grates bellowing steam. The street shone, slick with water. The air smelled of damp wool and the sweet fragrance from the flowers in the kiosk on the corner. Tubs of bright yellow daffodils made brilliant circles of sunshine against the backdrop of dreary gray as they passed.

This was crazy. Insane. And as necessary as her next breath. She went with him. Oblivious to her surroundings now. Focused on nothing more than getting somewhere private with this man. It was as if he'd put a spell on her, and she truly couldn't care less about the consequences.

She didn't quite remember getting to Caleb's hotel or how they managed to reach the corridor outside his room without ripping off each other's clothing as they ran.

Her arm was around his waist, his around her shoulders. The heat from the hard length of his body burned down her side as they came to what was hopefully the door to his room. Behind that door was a bed. She wanted in. Now. She wanted him inside *her*. Now. Caleb curved his arm tighter, bringing her in front of him so he could kiss her.

"Open the door. *Fast*," she murmured against his mouth, taking a little nip out of his lower lip before she slid her tongue between his teeth to play with his. His arm tightened, bringing her flush against his chest and kissed her with unchecked violence. They were touching, their bodies flush, from lips to groin.

His erection pressed against her, hard and insistent. Heather slid her hand between their bodies to cup him through his jeans, and he groaned "Jesus," in a guttural voice.

"Hurry!" she told him urgently. The need to feel his bare skin against hers clawed at her. Ripping her mouth from his, she grabbed a fistful of his T-shirt and started tugging the fabric up and out of his jeans, not caring that they were standing in a public hallway mere steps from the elevator.

Hurryhurryhurrry. Baring his tanned torso, she hungrily ran her hands across the satin-smooth skin over the hard muscles of his six-pack, then up, to comb through the crisp dark hairs on his chest.

The smell of his skin went to her head. She pressed her face against his breastbone, inhaling deeply, then touched her tongue to taste his hot salty skin. "You taste like sin," she murmured, trailing her lips across his chest. "Better than chocolate. Better than—" There was *nothing* to compare it with. Nothing she wanted more.

Caleb swiped the keycard, his fingers gripping her shoulder hard enough to leave marks. She didn't care. When the light blinked green he muttered, "Thank you, Jesus!"

The second the lock disengaged he wrenched the door

open, pulled her inside, then shoved her against the door. It slammed shut at her back as he crushed her mouth beneath his.

Rain pounded at the windows, giving the room a liquid, underwater feel as Caleb unerringly found the closure on her raincoat with one hand, and started ripping at the buttons. Impatiently she tried to help.

"Coat. Off!" he said roughly as they both tussled to unfasten her buttons at the same time. She got the giggles as their fingers bumped and got in each other's way. Their breath sounded loud and ragged.

"You think this is *funny*, woman?" Before she could answer, he pushed her hand aside, then swooped down to take her mouth again as he finished unbuttoning her raincoat by himself. He captured her laughing breath on his tongue and devoured her as though they'd been apart for months instead of seconds.

The moment he freed the buttons, she managed to get her arms out of the sleeves, but no more than that since Caleb had her glued against the door with his body. She loved the feel of him. The weight of him. The sheer size of him as he pressed against her. The hard ridge of his penis pressed against her sent Heather's own need rocketing.

Caleb slid his hands underneath her sweatshirt and his clever mouth trailed a greedy path to her throat while his cool fingers learned the shape of her rib cage, one tantalizing rib at a time. "Your laugh tastes like summer."

It felt like summer inside, too, she thought. Hot and wonderful. Joyous. But she didn't want to distract him by chatting. Instead she squeezed her eyes shut and tilted her head against the door as he kissed her throat. The sensation went straight to her womb, making her moan.

Somehow she managed to pull his T-shirt off. He tugged her sweatshirt up, then took a moment to trail hot kisses along the edge of her bra while her head was covered and she could do nothing but feel the slick warmth of his tongue gliding across the hills and valley of her breasts. She could hear her own breath hitching as she tried to draw air into her lungs.

Her heart trip-hammered, beating so fast she thought the pleasure of his touch, the anticipation alone, might kill her. Blind, and desperate, she dipped her fingers into the waistband of his jeans and felt him waiting inside, hot and hard and pulsing with life.

He pulled back just long enough to finish yanking her sweatshirt over her head, then made quick work of the front closure of her bra. "Beautiful," he murmured reverently as her breasts were freed.

"Jeans!" she prompted urgently. It had been a long time since she'd done this, Heather thought frantically. Even while she hoped she could remember what to do, she knew that it didn't matter. She couldn't wait. Her body was burning up.

They struggled to get clothing off over hands that were fighting to strip the other bare. His hands were big, lean, strong, with clean, short clipped nails. Competent hands. Gentle hands. Hands she wanted to touch every part of her body. *Now*!

"The bed—"

Unsnapping his jeans with shaking hands, she managed to toe off her tennis shoes at the same time. "Here. Now." His forearms were lightly dusted with dark hair and strongly muscled. His abs were rock hard, his chest rock solid. She wanted to touch him everywhere. "Hurry!"

"Lift this foot. Here. Now thi—Excellent. Now." Caleb used both hands to pull her jeans and panties down her legs. She kicked them aside, then jumped up, wrapping her arms about his neck, and her legs tightly around his bare waist.

He was hard, and fully erect against her entrance. "I want you inside me—*now*," she urged, feeling him pulse against where she needed him most. Without further ado she impaled herself on his ridged length. His answering groan was raw. *Good*. She arched, tightening her ankles in the small of his back at the first deep thrust. All the breath left her body at the piercingly sweet sensation of him filling her. Her mind blurred with the wonder of it. His body seemed to envelop her. She'd never felt so safe, she'd never felt so secure. That alone was seductive. She sank into the magic of it. Tightening her arms about his neck and her legs around his waist, Heather covered his face with kisses.

"Don't," he said through clenched teeth, his arms like steel bands around her, holding her still. "Move."

How could she not? She tightened her legs, then rose slightly, sliding up his length. Then down again.

"I tol—Jesus. You're killing me!" He cupped her behind, his palms warm and hard as he moved her. Up and down. Up. Down. Their bare torsos rubbed together as they moved. Faster and faster. Up. Down. Updownup-downupdown.

She sank her teeth into his shoulder to muffle her cries as their bodies pulsed together and incinerated.

It was fast, powerful, and amazing, and when they'd drained each other they slid down the door to sprawl on the floor in a tangled heap.

Boneless, she collapsed on Caleb's chest. His arms came around her, holding her. Protecting her. There wasn't an ounce of energy left in her, but her chest felt constricted, and her eyes burned. She felt the most ridiculous urge to cry. She touched his face, her smile soft. "That was amazing."

Amazing? It had felt like a rebirth. Like she'd been loved for the very first time. Heather felt—as Madonna had sung—like a virgin, touched for the very first time.

"Oh, yeah. Jesus Christ. I died and went straight to Heaven." He stared at the ceiling, breathing hard. "Marry me. Bear my children. How soon can you find a white dress and a preacher?"

Heather's laugh was breathless. "Is the morning soon enough?" The game was so wonderfully real, she allowed herself to believe it for a little while longer. Just a little longer feeling safe and happy couldn't hurt, could it?

The hand he'd used to cup her behind slid up her back in a slow comforting caress. "We'll have to find something to do to fill in the time between now and then."

"Lapse into a coma?" She draped a limp arm over his waist. "Call a paramedic? Get up off the floor?"

He stroked a large hand over the back of her head, sifting his fingers through her hair, letting the strands fall against her bare shoulders. "Did I wear you out, sweetheart?"

The endearment fell easily from his lips. The sensation of his hand petting her felt strangely familiar. As if he'd done the same loving stroke a hundred times before. "It was that last two-minute mile." Eyes closed, Heather smiled against his chest.

Murmuring an unintelligible sound, she snuggled against him, listening to the uneven cadence of his heartbeat under her ear. Why hadn't this man walked into her life a year ago? Two years ago? she asked herself silently. Would she have appreciated him then? Would she have felt this same yearning to feel safe? Would she have jumped into bed with him within minutes of meeting him?

Yes.

The feeling she had, just being with him, transcended anything she'd ever experienced before. The physical aspect was strong enough, but there was something she couldn't explain. Something that drew her to *this* man as she'd never been drawn by any other. A feeling that he was the other half of herself.

The yang to her yin.

But the reality was, if *Heather* had met him a year ago, she would still have had to run. And *Hannah* couldn't take the risk of something happening to him if the people looking for her father eventually found *her* again. The world wasn't that big anymore. And her father's associates were highly motivated.

Suddenly Caleb drew in a sharp breath between his teeth, and he stiffened beneath her. His hand, which had moved down her back to stroke the curve of her butt, stilled.

Heather's heart thudded. "What's the—"

"Christ," he said at the same time. "I didn't use anything. I'm sorry. God—I've never gone off like that in my life. Not even my first time."

She lifted her face to meet his eyes. "It's okay." Of course it wasn't. She didn't *know* this man. "Okay, it's not okay. But I'm healthy, and I'm hoping you are too . . ."

There'd been a few years in her late teens when she'd been promiscuous as a form of rebellion. When she'd realized that the only person she was hurting was herself, she'd stopped having casual sex cold turkey. She hadn't had a lover in more than seven years.

He rested his forehead on hers. "I just got a clean bill of health, but still—if anything happens, swear that you'll tell me."

That sounded as though he expected to be in her life. If only. The clamp around her chest tightened another notch and she buried her face against his chest. "Nothing will happen."

"Swear it anyway."

"I swear. But nothing will."

"From your lips . . ." His fingers traced the faint

raised mark on her behind. "Are these the scars from the dog bite?"

"Wow. You have sensitive fingertips."

"I'm a sensitive guy." He rose in one fluid movement with her cradled in his arms. "I wanna see."

His physical strength was impressive. She was no longer as thin as she'd once been, and was in fact, fifteen pounds over her ideal weight. But she felt ideal just the way she was now. Thank God. She was happy that she had curves to give Caleb instead of countable bones.

Resting her head on his chest, she wrapped her arms around his neck as he carried her to the bed. "My butt?"

"I have to kiss it better." He laid her on the mattress and followed her down.

"I'd be incredibly grateful," she said, straight-faced. "Even after eighteen years the scar still hurts when it rains."

"It *does*?"

Her laugh was low and intimate. "No. But I want that kiss you promised me." Turning over onto her tummy, she cradled her cheek on her arm and closed her eyes.

"I'm a man of my word," he murmured, lightly skimming his fingers down her back.

CHAPTER SEVEN

Yeah. He *was* a man of his word. And his word belonged to T-FLAC, Caleb thought, ignoring his instincts to put a stop to this seduction *now*. This soft, sweet woman was merely a means to an end. He needed to remember that.

A tremor rippled across her skin as he stroked her butt, and a faint sheen of perspiration turned her skin to pink pearl. *God. Listen to me,* Caleb thought as he stroked her, loving the flex and play of her muscles as her body reacted to his gentle touch. *I sound like a poet. A bad poet at that.*

"Your skin feels like silk," he whispered thickly. "I love the feel of you under my hand. Soft, but firm with these beautiful long, elegant muscles, and lovely hollows. Made to fit my hand perfectly."

"I used to be skinny." Her voice, muffled by her arm, was drowsy.

Yeah. He knew. He'd seen pictures. "Well, whatever you did has made you absolutely perfect."

He glanced up to find her pretty hazel eyes watching him over her bent arm. "Really?"

How could she doubt her appeal? Any man taking one look at Hannah Smith would fall head over heels, insanely in love. Not himself, of course. Means to an end. Got it. But he wasn't blind. "Oh, yeah. Really."

How had he imagined that there was no time to build

her trust? How could they *not* be here, Caleb thought, doing *exactly* this? Suddenly it was no longer a quick Q and A. When had screwing Shaw's daughter become making love to Hannah Smith? Touching her like this, when the sexual heat within him burned and sizzled without abating, was foolish and highly dangerous. Caleb wanted to pull her over him, he wanted to absorb her. He wanted—What *he* wanted was immaterial.

The only reason he was here was to get a location on her father.

Unfortunately, the longer he was with her the stronger the pull, the more intense his response to her appeal. The more attractive she was to him. Damn it to hell. She was a dangerous woman.

What pissed him off the most was that for reasons he couldn't explain, he felt a twinge of guilt using her like this. He wasn't a man who usually felt guilty about *anything* he had to do. Why her? Why now?

When this was all over, he'd make sure to reunite father and daughter, even if it was only enough time for them to kiss and make up before Shaw was incarcerated for life. That would make up for him using her to get to her father.

Still, she was going to hate him for using her. Caleb gave a mental shrug. Couldn't be helped. He'd done worse in the past than screw a woman to get what he wanted.

He wished to God that what happened between them *had* felt like screwing. Unfortunately it had felt very much like making love.

Jesus. He was getting in too deep.

Get the information. Send her on her way.

Out of sight, out of mind.

The sooner the better.

So much for his carefully constructed plan to coax the

information out of her. He'd had no intention of making love to her. None.

Oh, yeah? He asked himself as he leaned over the side of the bed to pick up his discarded jeans. Pulling out three small packets, he shoved two under the pillow, and ripped at the third with his teeth. No, he'd had no intention of making love to her. That's why he had a wallet full of condoms.

He rolled one onto his still rock-hard cock while she dozed beside him. Better late than never, he supposed.

His knee hurt like hell, which also pissed him off. With the titanium implant he should be able to leap tall buildings et cetera. The fact that his knee ached just because he'd lifted a hundred and thirty pounds of woman bothered him more than he'd let on to the doctors. If he ever went back for a checkup. Which he wouldn't. His leg would be fine. Just fine.

A T-FLAC operative—even one in the psi branch— needed full mobility. It would heal, he assured himself as he tried to block the pain, eventually.

He cupped the pale globe of Hannah's ass, stroking his thumb over the scars marring her smooth skin. Scars that he could make disappear in a second if he wanted to.

Not only couldn't he remove her scars, which would necessitate an explanation he had no intention of giving, but he couldn't exactly bundle her into her clothes and kick her out of his hotel room—hell, out of his life either.

Wham, bam, thank you, ma'am.

Not just yet anyway.

He stroked a finger along the widest scar. "You must've been terrified." The punctures had been deep, and widely spaced. And *not* a dog bite.

"It wasn't pleasant." An understatement, Caleb knew. He'd seen people who'd been hit by shrapnel. This was bad. But it could've been a whole hell of a lot worse. He leaned over and brushed his lips across the slightly raised marks on her left butt cheek, feeling more than hearing her hmm of pleasure as his mouth skimmed her skin. "Where did you encounter this beast?"

"My bedroom."

What was the real story? Why in God's name did a socialite have shrapnel cuts? "How did a vicious dog get into a kid's bedroom?" *Where were your bodyguards? Who did this? And why?*

Not only couldn't he ask the questions, they were none of his damn business, he reminded himself.

Still, he also wondered *why* she was estranged from her father and living thousands of miles away from her friends. And having seen where she lived, she was clearly doing it without Daddy's money. Good for her.

What had happened between her and her father to drive her halfway around the world?

"He was a guard dog." Hannah wiggled as he kissed the small of her back, then trailed his lips up the bumps of her spine.

"Who the hell was it supposed to guard?"

"Me." Her voice was thick with sleep.

Caleb lifted his head. "You? From what?" He had a pretty good idea. Kidnappers. Assassins. The choices were numerous. God only knew the kind of enemies a man like Brian Shaw had collected over the years. Not only because of his incredible wealth, but because of the people he did business with. People it was Caleb's business to find and eliminate.

"I come from a life of privilege," she said matter-of-factly of her billionaire father. "That kind of wealth brings out the crazies. I had several bodyguards as well as two dogs that stayed in my room at night. I—I wanted to sneak out to see the fireworks. Fang had different ideas."

"They put the dog down, I presume?"

"Of course not. He was doing his job."

By biting his protectee in the ass? No matter what the true circumstances were, Caleb felt a surge of anger at Hannah's father. A father should protect his children, not shove them directly in harm's way.

His own father had been absentee, living in Scotland for most of his life. Caleb and his brothers had loved Magnus. But they rarely saw him, and when they did, their father was obsessed, consumed by protecting their mother. In his own way his father hadn't been able to protect his three sons either.

Gabriel had tried his best to be the man of the family, although he was only a year older than Caleb, and two years older than Duncan. MacBain, their factotum, had been a father figure. But he wasn't their father. None of the Edge boys had understood the blind, insane passion that drove their parents to the exclusion of all else.

His older brother had accepted the fact that his father lived away from them in Scotland, but Caleb had always thought it was bullshit. Magnus had married their mother, and then, instead of sticking it out, trying to find a way around Nairne's Curse, he'd run like a damned coward with his tail between his legs.

Magnus should never have married in the first place. Yeah, Caleb and his brothers wouldn't exist right now, but the Curse would have stopped with their father.

Caleb, Gabriel, and Duncan had made each other a promise when they were in their early teens. None of *them* would marry. They'd avoid love like the plague it was. And Nairne's Curse would unequivocally end with them.

That had been an easy promise to keep up until 1500 hours this morning.

Caleb felt as though he was being slowly and cleverly wrapped in the sticky silken web of a beautiful spider as he lay beside this woman who made his pulse pound and his brain forget minor details like the Curse. A T-FLAC operative's survival depended on mental as well as physical toughness. He had a bum knee, and he'd met Heather—*Hannah*.

"What were you doing in a grocery store when you're staying in a hotel?" Hannah asked without opening her eyes. He thought she'd fallen asleep.

"Maybe I followed you in."

Her eyes opened and her body stiffened slightly. "Did you?"

"No, of course not," Caleb lied easily. "You were stalking me, remember?"

Her eyes closed and she smiled. "You think you're hot stuff, don't you?"

"Hot enough to light your fire—Hey. Where're you going?" he demanded as she rolled from under his hand. Cheeks pink, eyes sparkling devilishly, she said, "Please, sir, I want some more."

Caleb laughed. "Oh, you do, do you?" He rolled onto his back, taking her with him. "Then you're going to have to do all the work. My knee hurts."

Hannah straddled his hips, bracing her hands on his chest. "Aw. Poor baby. Want me to kiss it better?" She lifted one knee from the bed as if she were going to unseat herself.

He pulled her mouth down to meet his. "Later." He tasted her smile as she met his mouth with eager heat. He stroked her breast, fitting it to his palm, learning the shape and texture in a slow exploration that had her breathless and him hot all over again.

She wrapped her fingers around the hard length of him, moving her hand up and down. When she brushed her thumb over the head of his penis, he shuddered convulsively. "You're killing me."

"Hmm." She guided him to her, then impaled herself

on his hard length with a groan. Her sheath closed around him like a benediction. Hands resting on his belly, she froze as her internal muscles clenched around him.

Caleb knew exactly what she was feeling. The sensation was so sharp, so intensely exquisite, he couldn't move either. Their gazes locked in the watery half light from the uncurtained window. He didn't dare move. He'd come in a heartbeat. He could tell from the tension in her face that she too was on the razor's edge and needed a moment. Carefully, he slid his hands over her hips, holding her still. Her breath heaved on a shuddering breath and her insides tightened.

The clawing need built and built while their eyes remained locked. His jaw ached from clenching his teeth to maintain a scintilla of control. The sharp bite of her short nails digging into his belly told him that she was literally hanging on, too.

"I can't—I c-can't—"

He couldn't hold it any longer either.

With a convulsive shudder he surged up, plunging inside her. With a cry, her back arched, sending him impossibly deeper. His eyes blurred as her entire body clenched around him. The pleasure was sharp and blinding. His hearing went muted. All he was was a penis in search of the next exquisite level of pleasure. Yes. Yes. Yes.

Teeth gritted, he thrust up, his hips arching off the bed, carrying her weight easily as he thrust hard and deep inside her, feeling her orgasm gathering. Caleb rode her through it, driving her orgasm to higher peaks as he controlled his own release to wait for her. Sweat poured off his body and his muscles shook with it. Reaching between their bodies, he found her engorged clit with the tip of his finger and pushed her over the edge.

His hips jerked as they came together. Hard. In shuddering, paroxysmal spasms of blinding pleasure.

She collapsed against his chest, her limp body hot as a furnace and damp with perspiration. "Oh. My. God."

"Yeah," he managed, too spent to move, barely capable of breathing. "That."

They dozed, still joined, their bodies glued together with sweat, his penis softening inside her.

More than spent lust had his heart beating like a sledgehammer. He'd never come like that before. So lost to his surroundings, so out of control. So totally unaware of the world around him. That kind of inattention could get a man killed. That kind of inattention made him sharply aware of just how dangerous this woman was to him.

The state of relaxation lasted all of ten minutes before Caleb felt himself grow hard again. Jesus. He wasn't a kid anymore. Normally it took him longer than ten minutes to be ready to go again.

"Hmm?" she murmured, pressing a kiss to his chest as he started moving.

"There's a lot to be said for taking it slow."

She sat up slowly. "I was having a lovely dream."

"Let's see if we can make that a reality." Holding her hips, he set the rhythm, then let go and ran both hands over her breasts, enjoying the curves and valleys of her body as she moved.

"This-is-hard-work-you-know."

And she was clearly enjoying every stroke of it as much as he was. "Uh-uh. Lean down a bit. More. There. Hmm." He closed his teeth gently around her nipple. Her back arched, which sent him in deeper. He gave the hard tip a small bite. In retaliation she started to move faster and faster. Caleb had to settle his hands back on her hips to keep her on target before she achieved lift-off without him.

A tremor shivered over his skin, and his heart did calisthenics as her sheath tightened around him, milking him dry. Sweat oiled his skin and blurred his vision as she moved.

This time was no less intense than the last. While her body was still clenching around him, he brought her down to the mattress beside him, then stroked a hand along her thigh, pulling her knee over his.

She lifted her face. "Kiss me," she demanded. Caleb complied, crushing her mouth beneath his. She made a soft, desperate sound low in her throat, and wrapped her arms around his neck. Despite hours of lovemaking, Heather still felt an electric thrill sparking across her nerves as he took possession of her mouth. Who needed air, she though fuzzily. She never wanted him to stop.

They broke apart, both panting, bodies damp, hearts racing. "Wow!" she managed, eyes closed.

Caleb groaned theatrically as he rolled onto his back. Heather laughed, not moving. "Water," she begged.

After the few minutes he needed to get his breath back, he got up to dispose of the condom, bringing back a glass of water and a warm damp cloth from the bathroom.

Climbing back into bed, he waited for her to drink, then took the glass and set it aside. "Lie back." His voice was husky.

Complying, Heather smiled, brushing his hair off his forehead when he leaned over her. "And think of England?"

He stroked the warm cloth down her tummy, following its path with his mouth. "Let's see if I can give you something more interesting to think about."

What followed drove every scrap of rational thought from her mind.

"I'm a noodle," she laughed breathlessly when he eventually lifted his head.

He tightened his arms around her. "Take a little snooze then." He dropped a kiss on top of her head. "Build up your strength."

He fell asleep instantly. Heather's lips twitched with amusement even as her gaze followed the contour of his face. No softening there. Not even in repose. A hard man. But tender with her. God. She wasn't sorry. She'd needed this. The sexual release—releases—had been phenomenal. Fantastic. But more, she'd needed the intimate interaction. Needed someone to *see* her. *Want* her. Give a damn whether she was alive or dead. If only for a few hours.

Caleb Edge had made Hannah Smith . . . *real.*

She looked at her pale hand splayed on his tanned, hair-roughened chest. That hand was becoming familiar to her now. The short, unpolished nails. The ringless fingers. All her jewelry had either been melted down or soon would be. Unadorned, her hands were a symbol of her new life. She liked them this way just fine. She loved them touching Caleb.

But the fantasy was over now.

Moving carefully, she slid out of his hold, pausing as he made a disgruntled sound as her body left the shelter of his. She stayed dead still, watching his face for signs that he was about to wake up.

Fortunately, he slept on.

Watching him the entire time, she picked up her scattered clothes, pulling on jeans and sweatshirt over bare skin. Tucking her panties, bra, and socks into her purse.

She paused with her hand on the door handle. Tempted, oh so tempted to go back to the big rumpled bed and the big rumpled man in it. Not just her body ached to return to him, her heart ached with the separation.

Appreciate it and move on, she told herself firmly,

opening the door quietly. She snuck out of his room carrying her shoes and purse like a thief in the night.

The moment the door snicked closed behind her, Caleb opened his eyes and sat up. He ran both hands through his hair in disgust. "Asshole."

He'd used her, plain and simple. And while that wasn't unheard-of in his line of work, he hated to exploit a woman who wasn't directly involved—

What in God's name was he thinking? Heather Shaw *was* directly involved. She was her father's daughter. Thank God she was worldly enough, sophisticated enough to understand a one-night stand. And while their lovemaking had been incendiary, that was all it was. A one-night stand to extract intel.

She'd given him zilch. Zilch intel, that is. She'd given him her body in ways that made his mouth water even now, and had made his body respond as he'd never responded before. There was some level to their lovemaking that he'd never before imagined. Having experienced it with Heather Shaw scared the living shit out of him.

Not just because she was the daughter of the man he sought, but because that kind of emotional entanglement wasn't for an Edge. Ever.

Sex was only sex.

Thank God, he thought wryly, getting out of bed to head to a cold shower. One more time and they'd have burned to ashes on the sheets. He absently rubbed a fist against the ache in his chest as he cranked on the shower, wondering at the strange unfamiliar feeling. Heavy and hollow. Heartsick?

Bullshit. Heart*burn*. By the time he walked out of the bathroom a few minutes later he knew that he could never see her again. They'd just have to find another way to track down her father.

Out of sight, out of mind, Caleb thought, strapping

on his watch after he'd dressed. His phone rang seconds before he was about to teleport to Germany. And if he hadn't delayed because he suddenly wasn't sure if seeing Kris-Alice was the answer to what ailed him, he'd have missed Lark's call.

"It was a nonstarter. She doesn't know where he is, or she's not telling. Either way, we do this without her," he said by way of greeting.

"So much for your legendary persuasive techniques," Lark told him, sounding annoyingly cheerful. "Not enough time? Not enough charm? What?"

Time enough to make love with Shaw's daughter. Time enough to—Damn it to hell. "I can't squeeze blood from a stone," he told her, his voice tight. He pressed a fist to his chest.

She made a noncommittal sound. "You have before."

"Move on."

She waited three beats before saying, "We found him."

God damn it. "Why didn't you say so in the first place?"

"Just wanted to see how it went with Heather."

"Her name"—Caleb's jaw hurt—"is *Hannah.*"

"Is it now?"

She knew it was. Damn woman was just jerking his chain. His gut already felt like a freaking pretzel. "Give me a break, Lark."

"My, don't you sound cranky."

"Just tell me where the fuck he is," Caleb snarled. "I'll bring him in and get this over with."

CHAPTER EIGHT

Shaw had chosen brilliantly.

The sonuvabitch was holed up at a UNESCO heritage site in the *sassi* district of Matera in the southern region of Basilicata, Italy.

The area had been a slum up until a few years before. Shaw had covered his tracks well by choosing to hide out in a site that was in the process of renovation, over one of his normal jet-setting, well-documented vacation spots. Damn smart, Caleb admitted again as he peered through the night. Not that anyone would deny that Brian Shaw, international banker to some of the biggest tango groups in the world, had a highly functional brain.

Originally, the billion-dollar question was why, just over a year ago, he'd suddenly put a giant target on his forehead by going underground. Then T-FLAC had uncovered some interesting intel. Billions of American dollars' worth of tangos' funds were missing. Shaw had absconded with his clients' money. Bad idea. Bad, *bad* idea.

Now the question was: why? Why risk certain death by stealing from groups that lived and breathed murder? Considering Shaw's clientele, it was a stupid move.

Damn stupid. Especially for a guy as savvy as Shaw. Caleb narrowed his eyes, ignoring the itch in the center of his back in favor of focusing on his hidden prey.

Everyone was looking for Shaw and the money. The good guys. The bad guys. Even the ugly ones. Why? Why had he thrown his carefully constructed, cushy life away? Criminal minds rarely acted on impulse, because when they did, they frequently made mistakes.

Like the one that had gotten T-FLAC here, first on the scene. But Caleb knew the various terrorist groups were highly motivated by both revenge and the need to get their cash back. Shaw had given them billions of excellent reasons to want to hunt him. And when they did, they'd keep the sonuvabitch alive just long enough to find out where their money was. Then they'd kill him. Slowly and painfully.

And while that was certainly no loss, and would certainly save the American taxpayers a chunk of change for his day in court, T-FLAC couldn't allow that money to get back in the tangos' hands. And soon the place would be crawling with bad guys. Everyone determined to catch the prize.

The good guys *had* to win.

The *sassi* was a fantastic version of a human anthill, an entire city of cave-houses dug out of soft tufa stone, rising out of an ancient river channel. The area was steeped in history, and the most outstanding, intact example of a troglodyte settlement in the Mediterranean region. Perfectly adapted to its terrain and ecosystem. The first inhabited zone dated from the Paleolithic period. The half-abandoned *sassi* was a popular stomping ground for filmmakers searching for a biblical landscape. Not that Caleb and his men gave a flying fuck about the area's history, or the fact that Mel Gibson had made a movie here.

What that all boiled down to was that it was a brilliant hiding place for Shaw.

Come out, come out wherever you are. There was no moon, and the star-filled sky was covered with thick banks of slowly drifting clouds. An excellent night to nab themselves an embezzling terrorist banker.

Caleb, Rook, Farris, and Dekker maintained their invisibility, keeping conversation to a minimum as they stood five hundred feet from the house. So far there hadn't been a sign of either Shaw or his men, but T-FLAC's intel placed the enemy within those walls. A dog ran down the cobbled path in their direction. Stopped on a dime, sniffed the air, and with a yip bolted back the way he'd come.

Dekker snorted. "Smart mutt."

Caleb allowed himself a small smile. It was common knowledge that animals could scent a wizard, invisible or not, and they usually stayed clear.

Three men and a woman passed within feet of the four wizards, talking in German about the dinner they'd just eaten at the nearby restaurant. Caleb could have reached out to touch them, yet they continued on their way, oblivious.

He wondered if that made the animals smarter.

The city of Matera had been built on a rocky plateau, which had then been sliced in two by the *Gravina* ravine. Shaw's house was in the middle of the steepest part of it. Surrounded by similar houses, fronting the original caves carved out of the cream-colored tufa stone.

Bastard was like a rat in a particularly impenetrable hole. Shaw also had a bird's-eye view of the canyon below. Nobody could approach his oddly shaped fortress undetected.

Nobody but an invisible wizard, that was.

Matera had been dirt-poor for centuries, but now the

educated sons and daughters of the people were returning, opening restaurants and shops for tourists and
locals alike. Gentrification had come to the *sassi*. Professionals. Families. Businesses.

Shaw had craftily padded his lair with innocents.
Above him, below, and on either side, lived and worked
hundreds of people unaware of whom they sheltered in
their midst.

T-FLAC considered all aspects when they went on a
job, including collateral damage. Caleb's stomach tightened, knowing that they had to get their mark and
get out before people got hurt. Tango assholes were a
different story. They wouldn't give a shit about the twin
five-year-olds in the house next door. Or the blind octo-
genarian one street over. Caleb remained motionless as
they waited and watched.

Surveillance gave a man a lot of time to think. On the
plus side, anyone new arriving would have to walk in,
right past four pairs of watchful eyes. While there were
vehicles on the plateau above in Matera, here in the *sassi*
it was foot traffic only. Good thing the four of them had
other forms of transportation, Caleb thought as they
waited for the last handful of the restaurant's patrons to
go home. Tourists mostly, headed back to the Sassi
Hotel on the opposite side of the ravine.

The warm, still air retained the savory smells of hundreds of dinners. Caleb rubbed an absent hand over the
ache in his chest. He'd felt an unexplainable hunger in
his gut for months. Not for food. He needed . . .

Action. Shooting. Running around. *Hannah*. Shit
happening. Yeah. All that.

He needed it soon.

He'd been pathetically grateful to get that call from
Lark in San Francisco after Hannah had left him. Man,
he'd been glad to get back to work. Get back into the
thick of things after three months of inactivity . . . Why

the hell did she have to sneak out like that? The least she could have done was say thanks for a great fu—, er, afternoon.

Rubbing his chest wasn't making the ache go away. It never did. Caleb dropped his hand. *Come on, people. Go home already.*

"Rook," he said softly. "Go check the restaurant." It was 02-frigging-hundred, didn't these people have to get up and go to work in a few hours? The sounds of restless animals and the susurrus of voices could be heard up and down the canyon as people settled in for the night, but the lights in the nearby restaurant were still on, and the sound of people laughing—God damn it—a *woman* laughing, grated on Caleb's last nerve.

Hannah's laugh was lighter, and why did he still remember that? They were adults. A one-night stand was no big deal in this day and age—but damn it, she hadn't even leaned over to kiss him good-bye. Just f-ing walked out with her shoes and coat in hand like a damned thief in the night. Clearly she hadn't felt the intense visceral response to him that he had to her.

Good thing, as it happened.

Yeah. A *damn* good thing.

A one-night stand was supposed to be just that. One night. Or, more accurately, one intense, incredible, transcendental damned afternoon.

Whatever.

He was grateful that she'd had the opportunity to leave first. The alternative was far worse. The knot in his chest tightened as he imagined the scenario in reverse. What if he'd been the one to slink away from the bed? Leave her? After all, he wouldn't want to leave her feeling an aching hollowness that nothing could fill. He didn't want to break the woman's heart.

No. Their parting had gone down fine. Great. Excellent.

He'd lost his quarry and the girl.

By the time he and his men had arrived in San Cristóbal three months ago, Shaw was gone. Of course he was. Lark had pulled Caleb off Shaw detail, claiming she was sick of looking at his pale face and listening to him bitch. He was in *pain* and damned-well better take that R&R, or she'd fire his ass. She'd sent a tracking team to follow the banker's almost invisible trail, chasing any lead they could find, and told Caleb to get lost for at least two weeks.

So he'd taken that damned vacation after all. He hadn't gone to Germany and Kris-Alice. She deserved better than Caleb Edge in a "mood," as Lark called it. Instead, he'd gone to Paradise Island, a T-FLAC training camp in the middle of the French Polynesian Marquesas Islands.

Sun. Beach. Rookies to beat the crap out of. A good vacation.

Besides, he hadn't been in a goddamned "mood." He'd been agitated and pissed off that Shaw was so elusive. How was she going to feel when he killed her father? How do you *think* she's going to feel? *Jesus. Don't even go there.*

After a week of Paradise he'd begged Lark to send him in—*somewhere*. Anyfuckingwhere. She'd obligingly sent him with a small team going to the Saudi desert. There was sun and there was sun. It had taken the T-FLAC/psi team three weeks to track their targets to their hideout, but they had found the tangos and dealt with them.

There'd been plenty of shooting, running, and dodging bullets. They'd been outnumbered seven to one. It had been fun.

Oh, hell, Caleb suddenly thought. What if Hannah and her father had reconciled and she was inside those tufa stone walls with him right now? His heart trip-

hammered and his mouth went dry. What if? Jesuscrap-
damn.

It had been eighty-nine days since he'd laid eyes on the
woman. Was she inside with her father? Anything was
possible . . . But if Hannah was this close, wouldn't he
feel her? Wouldn't he *know*?

A couple passed. *Get a room, people,* Caleb thought,
annoyed, as they stopped two feet away from him to
French kiss.

He pressed a fist to his chest and closed his eyes.

"Told you to stay away from the lamb chops," Farris
whispered.

He wished the damned ache could be relieved with an
antacid. Ignoring his partner, Caleb went back to his
memories of Hannah, a favorite yet torturous pastime.
He'd loved the fragrance of her. Lush and ripe. She'd
smelled of hope, and promises he knew he would never
hear. She'd smelled of Hannah. His Hannah.

No. Not his. Never his. Not ever.

And not *Hannah*.

Heather. Heather Shaw.

There were a dozen good reasons Hannah could
never be his. Forget about the last eight. Number two
was that her father was as dirty as they came, and deeply
enmeshed in the finances of his clients—a dozen tango
groups; drug lords, weapons dealers, child porn traffick-
ers. Hannah wasn't going to be Caleb's number-one fan
after he killed her father. And if he could, by some
strange miracle, bypass reason number two, number *one*
would cinch the deal.

There was that little matter of Nairne's Curse.

Duty o'er love was the choice you did make

Which showed what a dick their great-great-great-
however-many-great-grandfather *was*. The original Mag-

nus, then Edridge, had fallen for a village girl named Nairne. But he'd chosen duty over love when he had married the laird's homely daughter, Janet, as his family had wanted.

My love you did spurn, my heart you did break

Only—the beautiful village girl was actually a witch, and if Hell hath no fury like a woman scorned, ten times that is the anger of a scorned witch. Who knew?

Your penance to pay, no pride you shall gain
Three sons on three sons find nothing but pain

Five hundred years of three sons, not a daughter in the bunch. So Edges could *procreate* just fine. It was hanging on to their brides that was the problem.

I gift you my powers in memory of me

He and his brothers had often wondered: If the Curse was lifted, would they still be wizards, or would their powers disappear? Since five hundred years' worth of Edges had tried, and failed, to break Nairne's Curse, they figured the answer was rhetorical.

The joy of love no son shall ever see

Yeah. Whatever. None of them was willing to risk an emotional entanglement. Not when they'd been weaned on the consequences.

When a Lifemate is chosen by the heart of a son
No protection can be given, again I have won

Not even with a Lifemate, if there *was* such a thing. He and his brothers pretty much played the field. Some parts of that field were plowed a little deeper than others, but in the end there'd been no emotional ties. Safer that way. An image of Hannah, well kissed and sated, made him suck in a breath.

His pain will be deep, her death will be swift,
Inside his heart a terrible rift

Fortunately, with no entanglements that wasn't going to happen. Caleb pressed a fist to his chest; the couple kissed as though they'd die if parted. He shut his eyes again to block them out. Unfortunately he could still *hear* them.

Only freely given will this curse be done
To break the spell, three must work as one

He and his brothers had no problem with working as one. But they had no idea what the hell had to be given freely. Love? In that case he, Gabriel, and Duncan were screwed. Wasn't going to happen.

The woman sighed, her silk shirt rustling as the man drew her closer in his arms. Hannah had made just such a sweet sound when he'd—Get over her. Abandon hope all who enter here . . .

Caleb scrubbed both hands over his face.

Maybe he could get Hannah out of his head with brainwashing?

A frontal lobotomy?

Some sort of mind-altering drug?

He'd look into it when this was over.

Finally, *finally,* the lovers pulled apart and walked on, thank you Jesus. They were wrapped around each other, making one shadow as they disappeared down the bumpy path, their shoes clattering on the hard stone. Their soft, intimate laughter ratcheted Caleb's irritation level up another notch. The narrow, cobbled labyrinth of paths wound between the houses in uneven steps, making sound bounce deceptively.

Lights winked out, one by one, across the face of the ravine like fireflies. Hannah would think it was—Damn it. Caleb dragged in a sharp breath. Why couldn't he forget her? Why had he retained such a clear, sharp image of her in his mind after all these months? He was afraid he knew why.

" 'K?" Tony Rook asked softly out of the darkness.

"Never fucking better."

"Crap," Rook whispered. "Bad time of the month, Edge?"

Caleb ignored him. What if he just went to check on her? Not talk. Just check in. Make sure she was okay. She would never even know he was there.

"Keep out of the walls." Dekker showed up, interrupting Caleb's mental monologue.

"What happened?" Caleb heard something in the other man's voice.

"Got stuck. Be careful."

Yeah. Back on task. Better.

"Plan on the floor being rigged." Keir Farris could whisper more quietly than anyone Caleb had ever known. His voice was almost as quiet as a thought. Came in handy during that mission a while back in Gofuckistan when the terrorists' safehouse came complete with sound detection.

The good news was that they'd sensed no fellow wizards in Shaw's stronghold here in the *sassi* to detect their presence. The bad news was that Shaw's bolt-hole was a series of small, linked cave rooms, and each was filled with muscled goons loaded for bear.

Not that Shaw's firepower bothered them; in fact, they'd welcome some action right about now. But a shootout wasn't what was called for here. They needed

Shaw. Alive. He was the only one who knew where the money was stashed.

To do that they had to teleport to his exact location and shimmer him out with no one being the wiser. Not exactly rocket science. It was a simple retrieval now that they had the man's basic location. But while Caleb could backspace time should they be seen, he didn't want to waste his TiVo ability. He could only backspace in the same time and place three times. Each time had to count.

The problem was navigating those small, crowded rooms to *find* Shaw. He was in there. But exactly where? They needed to have a *visual* to teleport the man.

"I take it you didn't find him?" Caleb asked Dekker.

"No."

"Seen?"

"Unfortunately."

"I'll backspace five minutes. We're cool. No one will remember you were ever there." And none of his team would recall the do-over either. No one but himself was ever aware that time had been manipulated.

Chapter Nine

"I take it you didn't find him?" Caleb asked Dekker when he shimmered beside him for the second time.

"No. Fucked up. Minor miscalculation. Almost ended up embedded in mountainside forever. You?"

"Negative." Caleb sensed Rook's shimmering return seconds before the man spoke quietly from a couple of feet away.

"Restaurant's closing up. Owner and his wife. Another ten minutes I'd guess."

"Good enough," Caleb told him. "Let's do it."

Earlier they'd slipped into houses on either side of their quarry to see how far back into the mountainside they went. But that wasn't necessarily an indication of the depth of *Shaw*'s place. There'd been massive excavation over the past five years. Not surprisingly. With clients as dangerous as his, Shaw would know that one day he'd need a secure place to hide. None of the locals knew for sure how deep a new cave could be carved into the soft tufa stone. He was in here. Somewhere. Caleb was confident *one* of them would find him.

Thinking of Hannah, he hoped that one of his team would get to the bastard first.

He teleported to his guesstimated entry point some eight hundred yards in, almost landing on top of a man built like a defensive tackle. His hairless head was the smallest part on his body and he had no shoulders. A three-hundred-pound brick shithouse.

In these tight quarters, with twenty other men in the room, it was a wonder the guy could scratch his ass. Unless Shaw used him as sheer body mass, Caleb couldn't think of one useful purpose for the dude.

Ignoring Gigantean Man, Caleb quickly did a visual scan of the thirty-by-fifteen space. Beds lined the rough-hewn walls of cream-colored stone. No creature comforts here. Stone walls, stone floor. Bare bulbs, with exposed wiring, were strung precariously from a crumbling plaster ceiling. Beds. Foot lockers. Weapons rack.

The room might be light on accessories, but the gun rack more than made up for the lack of décor.

An opening on each end of the room indicated that the place had been set up like a shotgun house, with a passageway connecting each cave to the next. This was clearly a dorm, and it smelled like one. The stench of stale sweat, dirty socks, and leftover meals permeated the air, already too raunchy with that many unwashed bodies in a confined space.

The men were getting ready to sack down, with all the accompanying bodily noises and verbal bullshit. Ignoring them, Caleb went over to the weapons racked across the room. The usual shit; AK-47s, XM8s, G3A4s—the retractable butt version of the G3. A bunch of semiautomatic handguns, and a shitload of ammo.

There was plenty of noise to cover the sound as he disabled what he found by jamming the safeties or removing the firing pins. That done, he moved off into the next room. Another dorm. Bigger. This one held seventy-five sleeping men. Again he disabled the weapons in the rack, accelerating his movements to save time and escape detection. He might be invisible, but the weapons he was handling weren't. If anyone happened to catch a glimpse of movement it would be so brief they'd think they'd imagined it.

Man, he *loved* this part of the job.

The only thing better than being a T-FLAC operative was being T-FLAC/psi and walking among his enemies unseen. Too bad he didn't have the time to dick with their heads. He grinned as he moved unnoticed to the next room. A large galley-style kitchen. Clean and empty. They'd had fresh bread with their dinner, and the hot, yeasty smell made his stomach rumble. Shaw wasn't starving in here, Caleb thought dryly, looking around for some nuts. He'd had an insatiable craving for Brazil nuts in the last few months, but right now any kinda nut would do.

Shaw had one of London's top chefs working for him. Feeding his men well was a smart move. A full belly and good pay, very good pay, would ensure that the men stayed put. For how long? Caleb wondered, opening another pantry door.

Jesus. Forget the goddamn nuts! Shaking his head, he shut the door. Chairs and tables for a hundred. Instead of the salty nuts he craved, Caleb helped himself to a damn fine oatmeal-raisin cookie from an enormous container on one of the counters. Commercial refrigerators, commercial dishwashers, commercial, fully stocked pantry. Yeah. Shaw was feeding his men well. He'd have to in order to keep two hundred and fifty men incarcerated with him in these caves. This place certainly wasn't for the claustrophobic.

The man was well prepared. But then T-FLAC knew that about Brian Shaw. Knew that the man was fastidious, organized, some said anally so, and Mensa brilliant.

Had the death of Babette Shaw last year been the catalyst for Brian's out-of-the-ordinary behavior?

How had Heather felt when she'd learned her mother had been murdered?

Hannah. He—*T-FLAC*—knew where Heather Shaw was located. Still in San Francisco. And if she had any access to the billions her father had embezzled it sure as hell hadn't shown in her lifestyle.

And according to reliable sources, he thought, yanking his mind off Shaw's daughter and back to Shaw, *someone* had been digging away at this mountain for almost five years.

Which meant that the embezzling hadn't been spur-of-the-moment. Caleb grabbed another couple of cookies.

Maybe not spur-of-the-moment, but still f-ing stupid. He chugged some cold milk, then put the jug back in the fridge. First, according to T-FLAC sources, Shaw had been excellent at his job. He'd protected his clients' money, invested it, and laundered it. His commissions earned him billions of dollars a year. Most of it tax-free. It wasn't like he could report earnings from participating in a criminal conspiracy.

So why steal his clients' money? He'd already lived a life of affluence and privilege. He'd had everything a man could buy, and plenty of things that a man couldn't.

So why steal?

From tangos?! Stupid wasn't even the word.

There was nowhere on the planet that he could spend that money. Nowhere he'd ever be safe.

Shit. The man's behavior was illogical.

Caleb helped himself to a couple of fat olives, wiping his hands on a nearby folded towel as he chewed and walked. Why would any sane man rob the golden goose?

It was a given that when Shaw's ex-clients caught up with him, they'd extract the information as to the location of their funds in any way necessary.

Caleb came to a rec room. Everything any man re-

quired. Except a woman, of course. He wondered fleet-
ingly how Shaw handled *that* need for two hundred and
fifty men.

Men had killed for less than lack o'nookie.

Recliners, giant-screen TV. Hundreds of first-run movies.

Where the hell are you, Shaw? And please, God, don't
let Heather be with you.

Caleb had been so certain that Shaw was here, but
now he wondered if the intel was wrong, and they'd
made a mistake. He'd already traveled more than seventeen hundred yards in from his entry point—he was now
more than a mile and a half inside—and there was still
no sign of the man.

And still no indication that this maze-like pile of rocks
Shaw called home was ever going to end.

Satellite imaging indicated that there weren't any cave
openings on the other side of the mountain. And if there
were, Caleb had another team positioned there just itching to get the glory.

Shaw had been observed entering. There was no other
way out. He was still here.

Somewhere.

Next up, the latrine. Making sure no one was around,
Caleb took a leak. The thought that someone could
come in and see a sourceless stream of urine midair
made him grin.

Moving right along.

Ah. Now this *looked promising.* The next opening
was a hallway of sorts, intersecting three narrow tunnels. Unlike the areas he'd been through, there were no
lights in the tunnels.

Without hesitation Caleb went left. The natural inclination would have been to go right. There was enough
light from behind him to show the way for a couple of

hundred feet. After that it was blacker than a witch's heart.

He didn't bother with the NVGs. He saw pretty well in the dark, and after a few moments his eyes adjusted adequately to see the bends and turns in the pale walls.

He sensed, rather than felt, a presence, seconds before he heard the low-throated growl. Caleb paused, the hair on his arms standing straight up.

Make that growls. Plural.

The pack of black dogs, eyes gleaming, white teeth snapping, came at him from out of the darkness.

CHAPTER TEN

San Francisco
Friday, April 14
10:15 a.m.

She was pregnant.

Of course she was, Heather thought, pacing her far-too-small apartment. God had a perverse sense of humor. That day with Caleb had been magical, so of course there had to be penance.

She'd always been crazy about kids, and had no doubt that one day she'd marry and have a family. But not *now*. Not while her own life was on hold.

Not while one of her father's business associates was hunting her down like a bloodhound after fresh kill.

Arms wrapped around her body, Heather rubbed her upper arms as she speed-walked in a tight circle. "Ring, damn it," she snarled at the silent phone as she passed it for the nine hundred and ninety-ninth time in the last two hours.

After confirming her pregnancy, it had taken her a week to muster the courage to call the number on Caleb's business card. But now that the decision to tell him had been made, and she'd called and left a message, she wanted to talk to him this instant.

Perversely, just because she'd known he couldn't possibly contact her, Heather had spent the last eighty-some days pissed off that he hadn't. "And how could he?" she asked the room at large.

"He doesn't know where I live. He doesn't know my phone number. He doesn't know *me*." Worse, unlike herself, he'd probably forgotten that day altogether.

What was she hoping Caleb would do? Talk her out of the most difficult decision she'd made in her life? "Don't expect him to be thrilled," she told herself.

Not once in the hours that she and Caleb had spent together had he asked for her phone number or address. Not that she'd have told him, but damn him, he hadn't even *asked*. Which meant that he'd had no intention of seeing her again. No matter what he'd intimated.

"He is not going to be a happy camper when I tell him." What man would? She was as responsible as he was. She was a grown-up. She could have said no at any time. How responsible had she been not to put a stop to what they were doing when she realized they weren't using any protection? Oh, yeah. By the time her brain had caught up with her body it was a little late to put that horse back in the barn.

And as much as she hated to have to tell him, he had a right to know that they'd created a child together.

If he ever gave her the opportunity. He could very well ignore her message. Or it could've gotten lost. Or—

He'd call. She was pretty sure he would call.

"So I'll tell him. Without e-emotion." The break in her voice didn't bode well, and she cleared her throat as if he'd suddenly materialize before her right then. "And without an editorial." Then she'd tell him that this was her body and most importantly, she wanted nothing from him. "My choice."

Tears filled her eyes and she brushed them away. Hormones. And feeling sorry for herself. She desperately wanted her *mother*, which made the tears fall faster. Biting her lower lip, she wiped them away with both hands, wished she could be cool and sophisticated about this pregnancy and not feel so damn sad, and lonely and scared.

For that matter she'd been plenty lonely and scared *before* she'd found out she was pregnant. She forcibly pushed aside the mental image of a pink-cheeked, wide-eyed baby from her mind. The same sweet face that now gave her even more cause for nightmares and sleepless nights.

Everywhere she looked she saw pregnant women and babies. She awakened this morning sure she'd heard her baby crying. And then realized that it was her own sobs that had roused her. She didn't have any moral or religious reason to dismiss an abortion. But, oh, God. She had empty arms, and a heart yearning to give the love she had bottled up to the tiny life growing inside her.

She couldn't think of a logical, safe way to go through with this pregnancy and keep the baby. Or even go through the next six months and then give the child up for adoption. She couldn't risk another life, she just couldn't.

So the decision had been made. And she'd stick to it.

"By two tomorrow it'll be over." They'd told her to bring someone to drive her home afterward.

There was no one.

Substituting efficiency for emotion, Heather had arranged for a limo service to pick her up at the clinic. Despite her tight budget she hadn't had a choice. A cab wasn't dependable. She'd gone grocery shopping yesterday, stocking up on multiple comfort foods, there were fresh sheets on the bed, and new magazines on the bedside table. She was ready. It wasn't as though she'd be incapacitated for days or weeks. It was a simple procedure . . .

God. Her throat ached with unshed tears and her chest felt unbearably constricted and tight.

She was incapacitated already. *"Ring, damn it!"*

Human contact, a voice, even an *angry* voice right now would at least cut through some of her self-pity and the dreadful silence that seemed to throb with the sound of two heartbeats.

"Caleb Edge, where *are* you?"

CHAPTER ELEVEN

THE *SASSI*, MATERA
FRIDAY, APRIL 14
1900

Caleb avoided being mauled by a hair, two seconds, and his ability to teleport the hell out of Dodge. He shimmered outside PDQ. But not before one of the killer dogs attempted to take a chunk out of his leg.

Still feeling the hot fetid canine breath on his exposed skin, he thumped against the stucco wall at his back, waiting for his heart to go back down his throat. Holy crap. That was *close.*

Dogs.

Shaw had a pack of f-ing dogs in there.

Rotties? German Shepards? Damn Dobermans? Caleb hadn't bothered to find out. They'd come at him fast and furious, their barks serious as they charged to attack in a cacophony of sound loud enough to wake the sleeping men, and alert the ones who weren't.

Pandemonium reigned.

Men couldn't see him, but dogs sure as shit *sensed* something was there. Something dangerous. Something threatening.

He didn't TiVo that little encounter. Not that it really mattered. No one had seen him, and dogs frequently went off, barking at nothing. The thought of getting everyone up and running, only to find zip, amused him. Which made him feel marginally better about freaking when the dogs had come at him.

"Yo," he greeted Dekker, his internal "wizard radar" detecting the other man as he shimmered to Caleb's location outside.

"That you?" Dek was referring to the reason the dogs were still barking deep inside the cave. Faint, but unmistakable.

"Yeah."

"Get bit?"

"Suit's ripped." Practically unheard-of. The LockOut suit, invented by T-FLAC's science guy, Jake Dolan, was a modern miracle of fabrication and engineering. It was practically indestructible. He hadn't realized he'd been bitten, but then again the dog's teeth had been damn sharp. *Better the suit than me,* he thought, just as he felt warm blood dripping down his thigh. Damn. In a second, when the adrenaline rush passed, it was going to smart like hell.

"Medic?"

"Nah. Just a scratch." He'd had worse. Much worse. Limped out of that firestorm in Madrid six months ago with a shattered kneecap. Yeah. He'd had worse. A bullet to the knee trumped a dog nibble hands down.

"Don't suppose you got Shaw before you played with the nice doggies?"

"Negative."

"Damn," Dekker muttered harshly, disgust evident in his voice. "Where *is* this fucker? Could he have slipped past us?"

"No way. Unless he has some secret escape route." His stomach tightened. What kind of super brain only had one exit from a wormhole? But they hadn't located anything. "Okay, it's possible, but unlikely—Anything?" he asked as Rook shimmered to them.

"Nada."

A dog yipped in the distance, probably in response to the ruckus inside. A noise no human would hear through the soundproof walls. A radio's tinny voice softly played a love song. Caleb's mood, crappy for months, shifted up a notch to foul.

"Shit."

Caleb easily recognized Farris's quiet curse. The gang was all here. Since they all maintained invisibility, he could only sense where each man stood. "Regroup," he told them. As in how in the hell were they going to extract Shaw? Huff and puff and blow his house down? The four of them immediately teleported to a house they'd commandeered across town.

"Fuck it," Dekker muttered as they materialized in the living room of their safe house. "Let's just burn the son of a bitch out."

Hannah might be in there. "Can't," Caleb reminded him, grabbing the large can of Brazil nuts he'd left on the table before they left. He flipped off the lid. "Too densely populated." He poured several nuts directly into his mouth and crunched down. Better.

When he glanced up because it was suddenly quiet, he saw the others staring at him. "What?"

"What the flock is your obsession with those things?" Farris asked, pointing at the can Caleb had in his hand. "You must've eaten ten pounds of that shit in the last couple of weeks."

Caleb popped another fat nut into his mouth. "What're you? My mother? You don't like nuts?"

"I like nuts just fine. But I'd puke eating *that* many."

"Yeah, well I picked up some stomach thing last month, and these things make me *not* puke. Be happy." He glanced at the others as he poured a few more into his palm then closed the container. "Anyone else like to lodge a complaint about my f-ing eating habits?"

He got a lot of head-shaking in response.

Caleb peeled off the headgear of his LockOut suit and ran his hands through his flattened hair. His head itched, his chest ached, his leg stung like fire, and he was so pissed off and frustrated he wanted to chew glass. At least the Brazil nuts had eased the slight queasiness he'd been experiencing lately.

He ignored the fact that his annoyance and frustration were disproportionate to the job at hand because he was normally a patient guy, and waiting around to get things done was part and parcel of the job.

It wasn't the job. It was . . . Hell. He didn't know.

It was as if his life had somehow gone slightly out of focus. As though there was something missing. Something out of kilter. And he had no clue *what to do about it.*

Had he imagined those bites were shrapnel because that's where his head was because of the tangos he dealt with every day? Or had she been telling the truth? *Had* she been bitten when she was a kid? Had Brian Shaw had those goddamned dogs when Hannah was eight? He understood the need for guard dogs. But those were not the kind of dogs one allowed anywhere *near* a child. Caleb glanced down at the sluggish blood oozing from his thigh, and thought of the scars on Hannah's shapely butt.

Not dog bites. Worse.

He blinked the image away.

He grabbed the first-aid kit. Forcibly, he pushed the thoughts of Hannah, her ass, and her pale creamy skin out of his mind so he could concentrate. Absently he rubbed his palm over his chest. Unwilling to admit his true fears to the others, he simply said, "We're going to have to come up with a better way to do this. Too many civilians around."

He hadn't sensed her inside the house, hadn't seen her,

but he wasn't going to take that risk. Not even for T-FLAC.

Duty o'er love—

Yeah. That, he thought sourly.

"He's got to leave sometime," Keir Farris pointed out, doing the LockOut suit gyration to peel the tight black fabric down his body. It looked as though he was peeling away his shadow.

"Why?" Caleb put the box he was carrying on the table, and wrenched the cap off a bottle of water with more force than necessary. *Be careful what you wish for,* he thought, feeling feral. Damn, he should be used to it by now. He'd felt like this for goddamn months. He wasn't a touchy-feely kinda guy. He'd never been one to analyze his emotions. Jesus. He was doing nothing *but.* Emotions! He was losing it. *Get a grip. Just get a grip.*

He'd wanted to get back into the thick of things. *Well, sucker, here you are. In the thick of things. How's that working out for you?!* Shit.

"Think Shaw does his own grocery shopping?" he asked rhetorically, downing the water, before getting down to the business of checking out the damage to his leg. He was tempted to slap a Band-Aid over the punctures and call it good, but he didn't want to end up foaming at the mouth, or getting delirious and crying out some woman's name.

"Those two old women make the trek up the path with handcarts lugging food and supplies every morning. No one's come out in the two days we've been there."

"No shit, Rook, we know. We all saw them together, remember? Back to the drawing board." Farris stood there, bareass naked, his suit a black puddle around his feet. He was a big man, with a head of curly dark hair, a poet's eyes, and a crooked nose. Man was a brawler. He had one of the vilest tempers Caleb had ever witnessed. And the most control. He was one scary dude.

Caleb considered Keir a good friend. But he didn't need to see him naked.

Farris stepped out of his suit, hooked it with his foot, flung it in the air, caught it, and started toward one of the bedrooms. Hopefully to get dressed.

"The only way into his stronghold is through the front door. Right?" His voice, quiet as it was, carried across the room just to the other's ears. Remarkable.

"Been there, done that." Caleb pointed out, seating himself at the kitchen table—now their command center—and opening the first-aid box. He'd have to strip as well. It was useless trying to cut into the suit, no matter how sharp the scissors. The dog's teeth had slit it, though; he'd have to tell Jake to do an upgrade.

If he wanted to treat the leg out here he'd also have to get out of his suit. When had his life turned to shit? Maybe around the time Hannah had left—he rose, deciding he'd be more comfortable in shorts. The leg throbbed and pulsed. Had to be his bum leg of course. "Be right back." He strode into the other bedroom to change.

He came back a few seconds later wearing shorts, sat down, and expertly tended the bite. Since he couldn't heal his own wounds, he had to do it the old-fashioned way. The gash was four inches long, the skin around it already bruising. No big. He cleaned it and stuck a couple of butterfly bandages on it, preferring those to his own not-so-neat stitches. He put the items away and focused on work.

"Gather around, children." His sat phone vibrated on the table.

"Lark," he told the others, picking it up. "Hey beautiful. Whatcha got? Yeah, knew about them—Okay. Hang on, I'll put you on speaker." He punched the button and laid the phone in the middle of the table. "Want to go on screen?" he asked, reaching for the hookup to the computer.

"No thanks, I'm in the tub." Without waiting to see how that comment had been received, she continued. "Listen up, boys and girls," Lark sounded as if she were standing right with them in the room. Which was a little disconcerting for her operatives. "Research has just handed me what they swear on their mother's lives is Shaw's full banking client list.

"For those of you who whined because this op was too tame," she said dryly, "here's the good news. We already knew about Six March, Algeti National Army, and the Blue Wolves. Shaw has the Who's Who of Terrorists on his client list. But we've had a couple of surprises. You guys are gonna love this. *Worse* than the Sharks and the Jets," she told them almost with relish.

The Sharks and the Jets from *Westside Story* were Lark's barometer on the tango scale. Right up there near the top. The sound of water splashing came over the speaker and Rook wiggled his eyebrows.

"Whoever's doing that," Lark snapped, "stop it!"

"You have ears like a bat, Larkie."

"That's *Miss* Larkie to you, Anthony." Her tone went back to business. "Listen up. Because I love you guys the best, I'm giving you a special treat. We've just added a few more bad guys to Shaw's client list. Fazuk Al-Adel. Also Saif and Muhsin El-Hoorie. How do *those* three nasty boys float your boats?"

The way he was feeling, they floated Caleb's boat just fine. All three had had their moral compasses ripped off years ago. The El-Hoorie brothers had made their money with everything from drugs to white slavery. If it was profitable and illegal, they had their hands in it. They liked to blow things up. And they were damn good at it.

"Might be worth letting Al-Adel have Shaw for a couple of minutes," Farris said with a feral smile. Al-Adel's sideline was prolonged torture. He took his hobby *very* seriously.

"Watch your backs, boys," Lark told them before cutting off.

"That makes the party interesting," Caleb observed. Tossing the phone aside, he started shuffling through maps, photographs, thermal-imaging, ground-penetrating radar grids, and various papers to find the sat com pictures of the area.

The guys passed through the kitchen to grab drinks and snacks to chow down on while they pored over what they'd already pored over, studied, dissected, and reassembled. And they'd do it as many times as it took to get the job done.

"Ideas?" Caleb absently rubbed his knee as his men surrounded the table. Christ. He was thirty-four years old and already falling apart.

"Get him to come outside," Dekker offered, chugging a lemon soda.

"How? By dangling a magic carrot?" Farris asked, brushing a hand over a topographical map of the area and using his skills to convert the one-dimensional paper into a 3-D contoured landscape. He pointed. "Check out how deep he can go into the mountain." He glanced over at Caleb. "You went in—how far? Mile and a half? More? Can we even teleport that deep into sheer rock?"

"That's the point, isn't it?" Caleb asked flatly. "We're fucked if we materialize into solid rock. We have to figure out exactly how deep is just deep enough, get in, take him—*alive*—and get out. All at precisely the right second."

"Er—Didn't we just *try* that?" Rook asked, ripping open a bag of potato chips with his teeth. The chips went flying. "Sorry 'bout that." He started picking them up, eating them as he went, leaving dots of grease all over their paperwork.

Dekker handed Rook a paper towel before waving the grease marks off their paperwork. "Didn't your mama teach you any manners?"

"Orphan." Rook's country-boy, open face took on a hangdog expression. That face had gotten the twenty-two-year-old more women than Caleb had seen in a lifetime. Go figure that women liked Tony's blond, surfer-boy good looks, and that dimple that looked like someone had stuck the point of a pencil in his chiseled cheek. One side only. The girls seemed to like that.

Caleb liked that the kid was smart and quick, and thought on his feet. "Bullshit. I had dinner with you and your folks not two months ago." Rook's parents had been married for thirty-some years. To each other. And they still acted crazy in love.

Rook grinned. "Perfect, weren't they?"

"Yeah." Maybe that's when this annoying ache in his chest had started. Seeing a couple so happy, so content? *They* didn't have some f-ing medieval Curse to deal with. Tony Rook's plump, pretty mother wasn't going to die from some mysterious ailment or some improbable accident because she loved her husband.

"Know *why*?"

"No, Anthony," Caleb asked patiently. "Why?"

"Central Casting. Hired them to impress you." He grinned that choir-boy smile of his.

Interesting concept, but untrue of course. "Idiot." Caleb smacked him on the back of his head. "Let's compare notes, gentlemen. Where there's T-FLAC/psi, there's a way."

He started sketching the chambers each had seen, and what was in them, on his computerized illustration tablet. "Here." He X-ed groups of Shaw's men by numbers, location, and function. "Here and here. Dekker?"

Dekker put his feet on the chair beside him. Using the spatula he'd brought in from the kitchen to scratch his back, he pointed out the area he'd covered. "Latrine, dorm, dorm, gym."

Usually Anton Dekker wore brown contacts to disguise his eyes, which were an almost unreal shade of pale, Caribbean blue, and very distinctive against his dark, swarthy completion. He hadn't bothered on this op yet.

Caleb preferred him with brown eyes. He looked like a gypsy, he should have brown eyes. When Dekker looked at a guy with that pale, searing gaze it was as if he could read your freaking mind. Very disconcerting. Caleb didn't want his mind read. Especially by a man he wasn't sure he trusted.

What would Dekker think if he caught a load of all the erotic images in his head of Hannah?

Hannah's eyes were hazel. The color of a freshwater stream as it swirled around rocks and mossy pools— Good Christ. He'd lost what little he had left of his mind. Mossy pools, for God's sake?! Caleb chugged the rest of his water, then held the bottle against his shoulder as he addressed the others.

Oh, he trusted Dek's skills, and his dedication to T-FLAC and counterterrorism. But in four years, Dekker had never fully revealed all of his skills. He'd denied that mind reading was one of them. Why lie? No, the jury was still out on Anton Dekker.

"Two hundred and fifty men, plus a herd of wizard-hungry dogs," he added dryly, rubbing the cool damp bottle on his skin. Hannah's mouth had—*Shut up!* he told himself. *Just shut the fuck up.* Forget Hannah. He was never going to see her again.

Was it going to be like this until he was old and bent over and sitting out on the front porch of the T-FLAC retirement home? Crap. Was *this* what he had to look forward to?

He shook his head. Maybe he could have hypnosis? Or a brain suck, or . . . Get his shit together. Yeah. That. "All in *very* tight quarters," he told the others. "Stir crazy and ready to rumble." He glanced at each of them. "One TiVo op left, ladies."

"Teleport in." Dekker dropped his feet, pointing with the handle of his spatula. "All four of us, here where it branches. Two hold off the marauding hordes, the other two go find Shaw and teleport him out."

Caleb tossed the bottle he'd been holding into the trash. He gave Dek a hard look. "Kill two hundred and fifty witnesses we have no beef with? Those guys in there aren't tangos. They're soldiers. Bodyguards. Cooks and ass wipers."

"You have a point," Dekker said flatly, scratching his back, making Caleb want to scratch his too. The Lock-Out suit did a helluva job protecting them, but it was tight, and after it was removed your skin itched for an hour. "Okay, then the best solution is to draw Shaw outside."

Rook considered it. "Or find another way in."

"Pizza delivery?" Farris suggested tongue in cheek. "Two hundred and fifty hookers? What?"

Making the toughest decision in his entire career, Caleb stood. "I know a way I can stroll right through that front door and shake the son of a bitch's hand."

"Well, hell!" Dekker looked up. "Why didn't you say so!"

Chapter Twelve

The trick, Caleb thought, switching the flowers from his left to right hand, was to convince Hannah—*Heather,* he reminded himself. *Heather Shaw.* Brian Shaw's daughter.

Got it.

The trick was to convince Heather that he was in love with her.

Harder would be convincing himself that he *wasn't.*

There was no room for emotion. He needed her. She was his entrée into Shaw's bolt-hole. Time was ticking away. The longer T-FLAC couldn't get to Shaw, the more time his clients had to locate him. The more time Shaw had to escape.

Whoever found Shaw first would have control of billions and billions of dollars. Money was power. Especially in the terrorist world. If *one* group suddenly had access to that vast dollar amount it would be unstoppable. The thought of *that* much power in a tango's hands was bone-chilling.

T-FLAC *had* to find that money first. Had to.

Caleb left the others in Matera, keeping an eagle eye out for any signs of newcomers. The newcomers being any of the dozen tango clients Shaw had embezzled from. Logic dictated that none of them would be stupid enough to go inside, guns blazing. Without Shaw they wouldn't know where he'd hidden the money.

No one was going to get in there. Not without blowing the place to smithereens. No. The only way in was with a golden ticket for a front-row seat.

Caleb had that ticket. Hannah. He had to start thinking of her as Hannah so that he didn't screw up and blow his cover. But by calling her "Heather" he was effectively keeping her as job status.

What a Goddamned cluster.

He didn't want to see her again. She was too much of a distraction. He felt the familiar pain in what should have been his heart. A heart that had long ago acknowledged that any meaningful relationship was futile and doomed to failure.

He was A-okay, absolutely f-ing A-okay, with never having a permanent woman in his life.

The *un*permanent ones worked out just fine. Better than fine. Perfect in fact. Women like Kris-Alice who knew the score, and welcomed him into her bed with no strings attached.

Oh, yeah? Then why haven't I taken full advantage of her generosity lately?

Good question.

To which Caleb had no goddamned answer.

He'd received Hannah's message twenty minutes ago.

He hadn't called her back. He'd needed that time to gather his equilibrium, to marshal his thoughts, and to get himself under control to face her with equanimity. He couldn't afford to be vulnerable, even minutely, in this. He could not allow any trace of real emotion to cloud his reality.

Fucking up now was not an option.

He stood there like some pimple-faced teenager waiting for his first date to open the door. *First and foremost you are a T-FLAC/psi operative, try to remember that little factoid.*

His distraction when it came to Shaw's daughter could not be allowed to play a part in what he had to do. He was Cursed to choose duty over love. Unfortunately, right now the two were so intertwined he wasn't sure where one ended and the other began.

Hannah's call had been relayed through several switchboards. Lark had contacted him in Italy, minutes before he was about to teleport to San Francisco to see Hannah on his own. He had a hollow feeling in his gut about the reason for her call.

What a freaking mess. He was damned if he did, and damned if he didn't. To get close to Shaw he needed the man's long-lost, estranged daughter. But Caleb knew that seeing her again, being near her again, he'd feel that same inescapable pull.

That fatal attraction.

He'd put a lot of effort into not thinking about her in the last three months. Fat lot of good that had done him. Everything about her was indelibly imprinted on his synapses. He gave her front door a hard rap. Praying that his attraction to her had faded in three months. Praying that she wasn't as pretty, as sexy, or funny as he remembered. Hoping that . . .

The door opened six inches. "Caleb!"

He took her in like an addict snorted coke. Fast. The sight of her went straight to his brain, then shot directly through his bloodstream right to his groin.

The joy in her face, and the undisguised pleasure in her voice made his breath snag. Her honey-brown hair was half down, half up in a ponytail, and looked as though she'd just gotten out of bed. Her eye, the one he could see over the chain, sparkled, and her lips—Jesus God. Her soft pink lips, slightly parted, curved in a delighted smile.

"Hi." She didn't move.

Neither did he.

Caleb could just see half her face, a jean-clad hip, and her lightly tanned shoulder.

His mind went blank. She was *more* than he remembered. More everything. He knew he could go to the end of his life without seeing a more beautiful sight.

Half a Hannah was a feast.

Oh, man.

He swallowed fear.

Her beauty made the ache in his chest feel as though his heart had been hacked out with a pocketknife. For the first time in his life he had the overwhelming urge to run. Run like hell.

"Hey, beautiful." It was hard to push the words out through his dry lips. *I am so screwed,* he thought, like a drowning man going down for the third time.

"Hang on. Let me—" The chain rattled as she struggled to unlatch it. "Just a sec—Oh, damn it."

"Close the door first," he suggested, smiling. Really smiling. For the first time in months. When had he last met anyone so open and emotionally honest? Her sweetness sparkled in her hazel eyes, and curved her delectable mouth.

Heather closed the door. *Oh, God. He came. He's here. This is it. Show time.* He was wearing black slacks and T-shirt, and a cream-colored jacket, and looked even bigger than she remembered. Taller, broader, more solid.

She'd rehearsed this meeting all week, but now that he was here, she was all nerves and giddy joy.

Euphoric and terrified.

The recalcitrant chain wasn't cooperating. It didn't help that her fingers had a fine tremor, her palms were damp, and her heart was galloping in her chest.

This is going to be fine. She repeated her mantra.

She'd tell him. He'd tell *her* he was glad she'd told him, but that he was in agreement with what she had to do, and then . . . Then she had no idea. Her imagination hadn't allowed her to go any further than that.

By the time she managed to open the door fully, she had her emotions, the knee-jerk joy at seeing him again, a little more under control. The nervous anticipation of the conversation ahead was a little harder to manage. "Hi."

She put a self-conscious hand to her hair, shoved into a messy ponytail to keep it out of her way as she worked. Wearing jeans washed almost white, and a pink muscle shirt with no bra, she had a fleeting wish that she'd been dressed in something sexy. But then maybe it was a good thing she wasn't. Her core temperature shot up just looking at him. And the look he was giving her back was hot enough to melt glass.

All her juices started to simmer and bubble inside her until it was hard to breathe. Her eyes hungrily drank in every detail. He needed a haircut, and he definitely needed a shave.

His hot gaze slid from her face to her breasts, then slowly returned to her now-warm face. When had she last blushed? Only with Caleb. She'd felt the look as if he'd physically touched her. There was no hiding the sharp points of her nipples through the thin T-shirt material of her top, and she didn't bother trying.

She hungrily looked him over, curling her fingers into her palms so she didn't reach out and touch him. Touch him? She wanted to grab him. She wanted to bury her face against his throat and feel his heat. She wanted that magical afternoon back.

"Are you going to invite me in?" he asked, no longer smiling.

"Oh. Sorry." She stepped back. "Come in." Other than the police, briefly, several months ago, she hadn't had any visitors since she'd lived there. The tiny vestibule was immediately filled to capacity as Caleb stepped inside. The smell of him, fresh air mixed with coffee and the unmistakable scent of his skin, made her internal organs come to attention, and her heart started to flub-dub triple time.

"If you'd—" She indicated the stairs directly behind her, trying to get him out of the way so that she could close and lock the door. Her chest brushed his as they passed and her breath snagged in her throat.

He grabbed her by the upper arm with his free hand, spinning her around to face him, then crowded her against the wall, crushing his mouth down on hers. Heart knocking wildly, she grabbed his upper arms for balance. But she needn't have bothered. Caleb had her sandwiched between the wall and his hard body. She wasn't going anywhere. Every single thought went straight out of her brain as he sucked her tongue inside the rich dark cavern of his mouth.

She kissed him, holding nothing back as he cupped her face in his large hands. His raw moan tore through her, answering her own aching need. God, she'd missed him, she thought, running her hands up his arms to his broad shoulders. Missed *this*; she circled his neck with her arms, standing on her toes to press closer. Missed his heady taste. Her nipples felt unbearably sensitive, tight and hard against the plane of his chest. She'd missed his unique smell. Clean. Male. She'd missed the texture of his skin against hers. Missed the overwhelming sense of rightness she felt in his arms. Which was ridiculous because she'd known him all of one insane, erotic afternoon.

Caleb lifted his head, his pupils dilated, his mouth damp from hers. "Marry me."

Heather blinked, trying to clear the sensual fog from her brain. She half laughed. Not the ha ha kind, but a

"What the hell?!" kind. "What?" Her heart leapt. "No. You can't—We can't. It's impos—We've known each other for five minut—" She moaned, a soft, helpless sound of pleasure as he shut her up by kissing her again.

When she finally opened her eyes, it was to find herself on her back in the middle of her bed, with no idea how she'd gotten there, Caleb half on top of her.

"Oh, God," she murmured dizzily when he finally stopped kissing her and lifted his head. Her eyes were blurred, and her lips were parted and damp. Ready for more.

His eyes blazed teal. His mobile mouth twitched, the heated expression in his gaze turned to an amused gleam. "That didn't feel like a no to me."

She put a hand to his shoulder, but couldn't quite bring herself to push him away. Her hand slid around his neck instead. "No fair," she said weakly, loving the texture of his hair as she combed her fingers through the short dark strands at his nape.

He nuzzled her throat. She arched her neck to grant him better access. Her fingers tightened on the back of his head in an involuntary spasm as his open mouth found the frantic pulse at the base beneath her jaw.

"Why not?"

Hmm? "Because . . . Because I can't think when you kiss me like this." She forced herself to release her fingers. One. At. A. Time. With no help from her his lips found that magical place right below her ear. She shuddered as the sensation shot through her body like lightning. "Hmm . . ."

His chuckle vibrated against her neck, setting her nerve endings jumping and dancing with pleasure. She'd stop him in a minute . . . Maybe five. His teeth closed gently on the sensitive skin running down the side of her neck. The velvety swipe of his tongue tasting her resonated deep inside her. The sensation flashed straight to her womb.

"Caleb . . . Oh, God . . ." She moved her chin to give him access to yet another magical spot. "That feels so—"

"Oh, yeah." His voice was thick, his breath warm, his tongue cruising in a slow, unrelenting exploration as he murmured, "Amazing, isn't it?"

Amazing didn't even come close. She was melting. Imploding. Dissolving into a puddle of lust and want. Her fingers bunched the shoulder of his beautifully tailored jacket. Pushing him away . . . No, damn it. Holding him close.

If he'd slipped inside her right then she would have come in less than a second. She was that close.

"I've missed this." He lifted his head. "I've missed *you*—" he drew in a ragged breath. "Christ. Do you get it? I just can't get you out of my head. I feel you on my skin, and in my blood. I taste you on my tongue. I have the summery smell of you embedded in my brain until all I can think about is being with you. Holding you. Loving you." He cupped her cheek, his large hand gentle on her face. His thumb brushed across her hot skin. "Marry me."

The *L* word made her heart tremble, then start to beat double time. Oh, Lord. Temptation in a six-foot-three-inch package wrapped with sex appeal. His declaration ripped away the layers of protection she'd padded around her lonely heart. Her mind warned caution, but her heart softened toward him as though she were melting wax and he the flame.

She'd fallen in love with him in the coffee shop three months ago. He'd taken her hand. Looked at her. Seen *her*. And she'd plunged headfirst into love.

Over the ensuing months she'd tried convincing herself that it wasn't so. That what she'd felt was lust. Pure and simple. But even when she'd tried saying it aloud, and heard her own voice, the utter lack of conviction in it had depressed her.

Then she'd burst into tears. Because of course, love was impossible for her now. No matter how badly she wanted it. No matter how deeply she felt—her feelings were immaterial. She swallowed the aching lump of disappointment stuck in her throat. Not sure if she would ever have the luxury of knowing love again.

He'd called her *Hannah*.

Oh, God.

Hannah.

She rubbed her temples, feeling a headache coming on. Of course he had. That's who she was now. Hannah Smith. For a few blissful minutes, she'd been able to forget Heather Shaw. She couldn't think straight when he was kissing her neck, and tried to push him away. The fairy tale had to get back to cold, hard reality. Someone out there was determined to kill her. They hadn't found her yet. But they would. She could *trip* over one of them and wouldn't know it. They'd find her and they'd kill her and anyone near her.

That included Caleb. And the baby.

She was doing the right thing.

"Please let me go," she said quietly when he didn't release her immediately.

He sat back, holding up his hands as she rolled off him, off the bed, and walked away. Wrapping her arms about her waist, Heather went to her worktable, then turned around to look at him.

Band-Aid quick, she told herself. Just say it and get it over with. "W-would you like something to drink?"

He frowned. "You catapulted off the bed to offer me a *drink*?" He raked a hand through his hair, clearly puzzled by her odd behavior. "Got any nuts?"

She gave him a blank look. "Nuts?"

"Brazil. Cashews. Whatever."

How had she lost control of the conversation? How in God's name had they gone from a marriage proposal to nuts? She met his eyes, and on a single rush of breath said quietly, "I'm pregnant, Caleb. Or at least I will be until two tomorrow afternoon. I'm terminating the pregnancy."

CHAPTER THIRTEEN

Caleb shot off the side of the bed, his eyes now holding a different kind of glittering heat. The brackets around his mouth showed white against his tanned skin. He ran both hands through his hair, his throat working. "You were considering an *abortion*?"

"Not *were*. And not *considering*. I have an appointment tomorrow."

His lips tightened, and he sucked in an angry breath. "Bull," he said grimly. "Don't *I* get a vote in this?"

Heather's heart lodged halfway up her throat, but she gave him a steady look. "The voting is closed."

His jaw was so tight a muscle jumped in his cheek. "Then I suggest you reopen it," he said in a low, soft voice, all the more unnerving for its control.

Although he seemed to be staying where he was, she took a step backward—not so much retreating as putting a little more space between them. Okay. Retreating. He was big and he was mad. He'd gone from considerate lover to adversary in the blink of an eye. For a split second she had a moment of *déjà vu*. Caleb's taut features, and the way he was watching her with the eyes of a predator, were oddly *familiar*.

But in their short acquaintance, *very* short acquaintance she'd never seen this expression. Lord knew, it was a look she'd never forget. Caleb, the man she'd been so desperate for, looked like a wolf checking out a vulnerable place to bite. Her butt bumped into the worktable behind her.

Curling her palms over the edge of the table, her own eyes narrowed warningly. "I'm not doing it as a form of after-the-fact birth control, if that's what you're thinking."

"Don't try to second-guess me. *I* don't know what I'm thinking *myself* right now."

At least he was being honest. Her stomach clenched as his fists curled and he started walking—*stalking*—toward her. Her heartbeat sped up. She stood up a little straighter. "Hit me and you'll lose a hand, buddy," she warned, feeling behind her on the table for something to use in self-defense.

As if he'd slammed into a brick wall he stopped dead in his tracks. He stared at her for a few seconds, and time seemed to stand still. "Jesus. *Hit* you?" A flush rode his cheekbones as obvious effort controlled his emotions. An effort she appreciated a great deal. "I've never hit a woman in my life, and I sure as hell wouldn't start with you." Audibly grinding his back molars, he scrubbed a hand across his three o'clock shadow jaw. "Christ. I frightened you!"

Clearly on edge, he started pacing the room. She could have told him what a waste of time that was. "I'm sorry. I'm not mad at *you*. I'm mad at myself."

"I'll take your word for it. But don't look at yourself in the mirror," Heather told him flatly. "You'd scare yourself to death." She did a quick mental checklist of where she'd zigged instead of zagged. Obviously, the first thing was in assuming that he wouldn't want the baby. At the time, she'd figured that he write her off as a one-night stand. *Her* assumption had been that he was a man who wanted no ties. He had a job, a life that didn't revolve around her. She had done her best to ignore every pang of wishful thinking she had had in the last three months.

Inhaling deeply, she held the breath, then let it out slowly. "Are you in a position to be a father right now? Do you even want to be a parent?" She met his eyes unflinchingly. No matter how he felt, the anger and sense of unfairness that he was absolutely entitled to, she believed that he wouldn't hurt her.

She wasn't sure what he was reacting to. Her being pregnant? The fact that she'd chosen abortion? Or the fact that she'd made a decision without consulting *him*?

She didn't know. She'd gone through so many emotions in the past few months herself that she could hardly judge someone else's. Tears prickled behind her eyes and she watched him through a watery film, a clog in her throat. She'd never believed in love at first sight, never thought she could trust a man enough to give him her heart without reservation.

Until Caleb.

He'd walked in and demanded that she marry him. *Before* she'd breathed a word about the pregnancy. For the first time in her life, she was one hundred percent certain that a man wanted her, the woman. Not her, the only child of power broker Brian Shaw. Caleb knew nothing about her past. Nothing about her father.

And that, she thought achingly, was how it was going to have to stay. Be careful what you wish for, you might get it.

She almost hoped that he'd stay angry. Anything to break the accusatory silence hanging heavily between them. Maybe by defending her decision to him, she could make him understand that this was her only real choice. How could she protect a baby when she could barely keep herself alive?

"Bullshit question." Caleb rubbed a hand around the back of his neck. "I have no idea if I'm ready to be a father," he said with naked honesty. He tilted his head as he studied her. "You've had time to think about this. I haven't. The fact is you're pregnant with my child. Maybe the better question is how good of a father I'll be. I get a woman's right to choose, but . . . you left me that night. I didn't leave you. I thought that we had a special connection . . ."

His one-shouldered shrug pierced her guilt-heavy heart. She thought that she'd been protecting him, and herself, by leaving before becoming entangled in an emotional knot. Fate sure was a laugh a minute.

She tightened her fingers on the table's edge. "The decision has already been made. I'm not going to change my mind. Trust me, it's for the best. You have no idea how complicated my life is right now. *Too* complicated."

His left brow arched as he crossed his arms over his chest.

Had he heard the catch in her voice? Damn it, he'd see a sign of weakness and pounce on it. Her stomach tingled as she recalled the way he'd said "special connection." Was it possible that he really felt the same way? Had he given her a thought in the three months since they'd last seen each other? If she hadn't called him, would he be here now?

Had she made the biggest mistake of her life walking out on him?

She exhaled slowly, watching him pace restlessly around her small apartment. He was a man of action, a man of controlled power, and this place was too confining for him to unleash his energy. She knew, because she'd been trying to do the same thing for the past week herself. One couldn't pick up the necessary speed required to outrun the demons.

Walking to the bay window, he stood to one side, lifting the sheer curtain to look down on the street below.

Searching for an easy answer? Heather wanted to tell him there were none. He turned, jamming one hand into his front slacks pocket, his eyes unreadable. "Don't you want to be a mother?"

Yes! "No." Her hand unconsciously cupped the slightest bump of her tummy. She blinked back weak tears before he saw them. The decision was made. She'd thought, maybe, that by telling him about the baby he'd be supportive and heck, even offer to drive her to the appointment, hold her hand. Not make her go through the painful decision process all over again.

The ache in her heart would eventually fade, she told herself for the umpteenth time.

She was doing the right thing.

She knew she was.

"Liar."

She blinked. "What?" Distributing her weight slightly from one foot to the other, Heather bit her lip hard enough to shift the pain from her chest to a more manageable place. She had to control this situation before she ended up in a powerless puddle.

"I said, you're a liar." Caleb's eyes clashed with hers and kept her pinned there. "I think you *adore* kids. Tell me—when you had your first fantasy about getting married, how many baby names did you try on for size? What was the name of the not-yet-a-man you'd chosen as your future husband from the pubescent crop in high school? Billy? Bobby? Ralph?"

"Reed Newmark."

He huffed a silent laugh. "Bet you wrote his name over and over. And circled it with little pink hearts. Wrote Hannah Newmark on every page of your English Lit book."

Heather Newmark. "It was Social Science."

"Ah." He picked up a small shell she'd found on the beach from the bowl on her bedside table, and twisted it between his long, elegant fingers before looking back at her. "And how many babies did you picture that you and this paragon of virtue and manliness, Reed, would have?"

She glared at him. "Fine. I *do* adore children. Are you happy now? I've always wanted a big family—" She'd dreamed the same dream most women dreamed, until she saw how the dream could end. A loving husband turned murderer, a family torn apart . . .

"You're healthy?"

"Of course!"

"Married?"

"You know I'm not." She sent him a glare.

He had the nerve to grin. "Great. That's settled."

"What's settled?" Nerves danced up her spine.

"We can be married this afternoon down at City Hall."

The man was a human bulldozer. "I'm not marrying you."

He stepped toward her, and she moved quickly to put the table between them.

"I'm a good catch," he assured her with utmost seriousness.

"No!" No matter *how* tempting the offer. She had to remember that she was fighting for her life, something she couldn't do with a family. Her tummy jumped as she thought the word.

Eyes glittering, he tugged at his earlobe. She glared at him. The tension in the air was thick enough to cut with a diamond-tipped blade. And while Caleb's shoulders looked a little less tense, it was obvious by the way he stood that he was still—*what*? She wasn't quite sure. Pissed off? Stunned stupid? Feeling trapped? His face was closed, his expression unreadable.

Sphinx Man, for God's sake. She couldn't read him at all.

Of course she wasn't sure what kind of signals Caleb

was giving off. She didn't know the man. She was in love with him, pregnant with his child, but she didn't know him at all.

About ten feet separated them. A chasm.

She suspected that if she gave Caleb even a hint of how terrified and uncertain she was, he'd jump right in and take over. And while it was tempting to defer the impossible decision to him, it was still her body. Her life. He didn't know the consequences.

"Why not?" he asked, sounding annoyingly reasonable.

His voice was closer and she looked up, detailing his James Bond-ish style. A beautifully cut, rough-weave cream jacket stretched over his broad shoulders, his body hard and fit in the microfiber black T-shirt and casual but expensive black slacks.

He appeared so in control, while she felt like Wile E. Coyote headed for a cliff. "Because." She gathered the loose hair at her nape, tucking it back into the lopsided ponytail she'd put up some time earlier. Who was she kidding? Her life had been unraveling before she met him. Adding a baby and a mock marriage wouldn't change her life for the better, it would be worse. She'd be putting her new family in danger.

"Because?"

Because God only knew *who* was out there, waiting for her to make one slipup so he/they could grab her. She was tired of being scared all the time. And scared that there would be no end to this waiting for the other shoe to drop.

She'd spent the last three months weaving a lovely fantasy about Caleb to keep her fear and loneliness at bay, but the reality was just that—reality.

And it completely sucked.

"We'll make it work," he said softly, not waiting for her answer. He stretched out his hand.

"No way." She kept the inflection out of her voice with effort. If she looked at him right now she'd be lost. Metaphorically speaking, she was hanging onto her emotions with both hands, teeth gritted. She'd known when she'd decided to terminate the pregnancy that the decision would haunt her for life. She hadn't realized that it might be the same for Caleb.

She tried again, ignoring his hand to march toward the window. "We had a one-night stand. Hardly a solid basis for marriage."

"Are you telling me you feel nothing for me?"

Her pride was soothed by the disbelief in his tone. At least he didn't think she went around sleeping with whatever hot guy flirted with her in the produce section. "I didn't say that," she hedged.

Damn it. She never should have called him. So why had she? Had she subconsciously wanted to give him the opportunity to offer her options? What kind of person did that make her? She turned to face him.

"I shouldn't have told you."

"I'm glad you did," he said in his rough voice.

God! Why couldn't he act the way she'd thought he would? If anything, she'd imagined that he'd be *relieved* that she'd made the decision she had.

She pulled back the curtain as he'd done moments before. He was directly behind her, making him difficult to ignore. Somehow he'd moved from a safe distance across the room to right beside her without her noticing it. Damn, the man was stealthy. It was harder to be resolute when she could smell the faint tang of his soap, and the achingly familiar musky scent of his skin. Her mind flashed images of his naked body. Of the crisp feel of his chest hair under her hands. Of the weight and texture of his sex in her hand.

He took her shoulders, turned her around, and stared

down at her with a look so intense her knees trembled. "We made a baby together. Jesus. That's amazing."

"It was a *mistake*."

"That's something our son will never know," he told her harshly. He tilted her chin up with his finger, his eyes more teal than blue as he searched her face. "Our son." He shook his head slightly in wonderment. "Are you all right? Have you seen a doctor?"

"I'm okay." She wanted desperately to lay her head on his chest and rest there, just for a minute. Just a minute or two to catch her breath, and draw some of his seductive strength inside herself. "I went to the clinic last week. Everything is fine." *My life was turned upside down.*

But her body didn't care. Their baby was healthy and thriving inside her.

A muscle jerked in his jaw as he tucked her hair behind her ear with gentle fingers. "No morning sickness?"

"I don't think so. If so, it was pretty mild. Nothing really. I had the flu for a while and I—and then I finally went to the doctor last week and—and I'm pregnant—and God, Caleb!" Tears leaked over her lower lashes before she could stop them. She put her fingers on her cheeks as if she could stop them.

She'd cried more in the last couple of months than she'd probably cried in her lifetime. *I want this all to stop! I want my mother. And my father. Damn it, I want my life back.* "I can't have a baby now." Thank God her internal monologue didn't show in her voice. "I just *can't*."

CHAPTER FOURTEEN

Heather dragged in a liquid breath.

"Come here, sweetheart." He pulled her into the shelter of his arms. "There you go."

Lord, he felt *wonderful*. Solid. Big. Indestructible. He smoothed a palm down her back. "You've only known for a week? You didn't exactly give yourself a lot of time to think things through."

From this close she could see the individual hairs on his stubborn chin, and the spiky sweep of his short dark lashes on his cheeks as he looked down at her.

She used both hands to remove his arms from around her waist and stepped back. The hug hadn't been nearly long enough. But she considered herself lucky to get one at all.

"Not fair." Pulling the band from around her ponytail, she snapped it onto her wrist, then ran both hands through her hair. Caleb hesitated a beat before dragging his gaze off her breasts and back to her face. "I had to make a decision. Believe me, it was not a snap judgment. I'm the queen of ponderous decision-making. I took everything into account. Things are complicated. I'm making the right choice. For all of us."

"I handle complicated brilliantly. Give me a chance."

Shaking her head, she wrapped her arms around her middle to prevent them from going around Caleb's neck.

He looked larger than life. More vital. More virile. More *male* than her memories had painted him.

He stepped forward. "Can you feel him in here?" He nudged her folded arms out of the way and placed a gentle hand on her belly. He slid the hem of her top out of the way with his thumb, then spread his fingers wide over her tummy. The heat of his palm radiated through her, warming her soul.

He stared down at his hand over her as if he had X-ray vision. "How big is he?" His voice was hushed.

He was relentless. And charming, and sexy and—*Steel yourself. Get a grip,* she warned herself. *It's not all about me. I'm the only one here with all the facts. I have to think for all three of us.*

Caleb stroked her tummy as if he were communicating with the little life under his fingertips. The back of her throat went dry, and her eyes misted again. Damn these hormones. "I went to the library—about three inches." She shouldn't have read about the growth of their child. It had made the baby real. Made what she had to do overwhelmingly awful. Her throat hurt as she swallowed. "He can move around. He has little e-ears. I saw the ultrasound—He looks like a little bean—

"Oh, God, Caleb—" She shouldn't have said he. Or she. It *had* to be an it.

He pulled her tightly into his arms, and she let him hold her there. Was it so wrong to claim a moment of solace before her life really went to hell?

"Shh. Don't cry, sweetheart, don't cry." He rocked her gently. "Everything's going to be fine."

No. It wasn't. "We don't even *know* each other."

"We'll learn everything there is to know on our honeymoon, how's that?"

Not everything, she thought with a resurgence of fear.

"Enough to give Bean two parents who will love him."

Heather choked back a weepy laugh, slipping her arms beneath his jacket to circle his waist. She fisted the soft fabric of his T-shirt in both hands at the small of his back and pressed her face to the hard plane of his chest. The tears came in a flood, no matter how hard she tried to stem the flow. Who knew that Caleb would say all of the right things? And could she blame him if there was a little bit of strain to his words?

"I'm s-sorry—I'm—" *Sorry for being pregnant. Sorry for crying. Sorry for not being able to stop. Sorry my life is so totally screwed up and out of control. Sorry that I think I'm in love with you and in a minute I'm going to have to make you leave.*

Caleb lifted her face, forcing her to meet his intense gaze. "There's not a damn thing to be sorry about." He wiped her cheek with his thumb. "You didn't do this alone. We made this baby together. A miracle, in the grand scheme of things." He bent his head and traced her wet cheek with his mouth. "We're going to have a baby. *Incredible.*"

Damn it. Biting down on the corner of her bottom lip to stop her mouth from trembling, she asked, "You're p-pleased?"

He brought both hands up to frame her face, using both thumbs to brush the tears from her cheeks. "Yeah. Damn. I am." He paused and said it again slowly. "I. Am."

She watched as the same "oh shit!" look she'd been wearing lately crossed his features. "I know." A laugh escaped between her tears. "It's crazy. Lord, it still hits me like that sometimes, out of the blue, what it would be like." Her laughter faded as she remembered why she couldn't live her dream. She stepped back, but not out of the circle of his arms.

She glanced around the small apartment. "I don't have two chairs, but you can sit there, and I'll—"

Rolling her lower lip between her teeth, she asked softly, "What do *you* want, Caleb? Not what you think *I* want, but what do you genuinely see happening with us?"

"I want to get married, and do the right thing by our son. We care enough about each other and Baby Bean in here"—he was back to stroking her belly—"to make this work." He kissed the side of her neck, and she bent her head to give him better access. "*That's* what I see."

Oh, God—when he kissed that spot on her neck her insides did the happy dance and her brain went muzzy. "I can't think when you do that."

"That's the object of the exercise. Say yes."

Say no. Be resolute, she warned herself—but that little voice became fainter and fainter as he kissed the curve between shoulder and neck. *Just. Say. N*—Her lips formed the word, but she couldn't force herself to say it again.

She huffed out a breath. She wanted this. Wanted *him*. Wanted with every fiber of her being for this thing between them to work. She drew in a ragged breath. Held it. Then let it out.

"Before I answer, there are some things I have to tell you." *Shut up! Oh, Lord,* she thought, horrified that her body and brain weren't in sync, *just shut up.*

Don't drag Caleb into this. Don't let *your* needs, wants, hopes—*desire* for this man cloud the reality.

"The only thing you have to tell me is 'yes.' "

What she had to do, damn it, was *think*. Think for all three of them, she reminded herself firmly. Not just herself. But Caleb. And the baby. And she couldn't do that when Caleb was touching her.

She pushed out of his arms. "Don't touch me for a minute, okay? I don't even know where to start."

To his credit Caleb let her go immediately. She could tell he didn't like it, but he stuffed his hands into his pants pockets and stood there, his expression guarded. "Anywhere."

She bit her lower lip. Her father used to stand looking at her in loving exasperation, just as Caleb was doing now. He'd stick his hands—very elegantly of course—into his pockets, and jiggle his change, which used to drive her nuts. Now she'd do just about anything to hear that annoying sound again.

Where are you, Daddy? she wondered achingly. *When will this be over?*

How much was just enough? She didn't want to give Caleb information that, if it fell into the wrong hands, could get him as well as her father *killed*. And he sure as heck didn't need to know that it was her own father who'd embroiled her in this mess in the first place. No matter what he'd done, he was still her father, and as much as she hated him, Heather also loved him. She couldn't believe that she'd lived her entire life in ignorance about his line of work, and she hated him for lying to her and her mother for most of her life. She hated him for knowingly bringing vicious criminals into their home.

And she hated him for killing her mother. Accident or murder, her mother was just as dead. At his hands.

But that hatred was mixed with an entire lifetime of *loving* him. The two emotions were tightly intertwined inside her. Her feelings for her father were hard to define into clear-cut black or white. But love him or hate him, he was still her father.

The two of them had come up with a story. And she'd stick to it. As far as anyone knew, they'd had a falling out last year and had been estranged ever since. They'd gone their separate ways.

The truth was, Heather genuinely *didn't* know where he was. And she was scared to death that they might have found and killed him without her even knowing it.

God, Daddy, Heather thought. *How could you have been so damned stupid? And how could I have been so freaking oblivious?* There was more she didn't know about what her father had done, and to whom. But even if she knew all the facts, she wasn't going to give even *Caleb* full disclosure. They weren't her secrets to reveal. And she'd given her father her word. Complete secrecy was the only way they could hope to stay alive long enough for her father to figure this out. Until then, it was safer to keep up the pretense of a rift in the family.

Not such a difficult pretense really. She wasn't sure she was ready to see her father yet. Not when she was still so furious with him.

But for a chance at happiness, could she risk at least some of the truth? Caleb's strength let her think he could handle it.

She braced her hands on the window, looking out at the street. She was aware of Caleb's wavy image in the pane of glass as he stood behind her. "Someone's trying to kidnap me. Possibly kill me."

To his credit, he didn't laugh or tell her she was crazy. He simply waited for her to continue. "I've been on the run for almost a year."

"Who? Why?"

Heather turned and met his unfathomable gaze without flinching. "I don't know."

"All right. Wow. You've dropped a couple of bombs on me, sweetheart, you know that? Come and sit down, tell me what's going on." He sat on the side of the bed and held out his hand.

She shook her head, pulling up the single chair from the table, choosing to put some distance between them instead.

"You're a little pale. Want to lie down?"

If he had given her a little warning she would have had time to put on a little blush. Gee, maybe brush her hair before her life took another left turn. "I'm okay." About a solar system away from okay, but that wasn't his problem. That couldn't be his problem. Having nothing to do with her hands, she sat on them.

"Tell me about these attempts. How can you *not* know who's terrorizing you? Or why?"

"First of all, let me explain that my father is a wealthy man. An *extremely* wealthy man. Kidnapping me has *always* been a possibility. I'm his only child, and our family is high profile. More so in Europe than here, but if anyone put Hannah Smith in context with Brian Shaw they'd recognize me immediately. My name is Heather Shaw, not Hannah Smith."

"I don't give a damn if your name is Mata Hari. And I don't give a damn, other than how it relates to *you*, who or what your father is. Changing your name if you're keeping a low profile makes sense—Brian Shaw? The international banker?"

"Yes." International *terrorist* banker, Heather thought bitterly. A small detail about her father's business dealings that he had managed to kept secret from her for most of her life, and from her mother for almost all of their marriage. It was her mother's discovery that had precipitated all of this.

Heather couldn't figure out which emotion she felt more strongly at any given time. Betrayal. Anger. Fear. Or all three. And frequently in the last year, a powerful hatred too.

All churned up with the love she had for a man whom she'd always believed was her hero.

She'd learned pretty damned fast that there was no such thing. Her fault, she supposed, for believing in a man with feet of clay. He'd taken the two people she'd loved most in the world away from her. Her mother. And himself. The hole his actions had left in her heart was too vast to describe. She brought her bloodless hands into her lap, clasping them tightly. Briefly she squeezed her eyes shut. Remembering—*seeing*—

"Heather?"

"Sorry. I'm okay. It's been well publicized, on purpose of course, that no ransom demands will be met, not for my father's key employees, and not for his family. But the kidnappers might not have gotten that memo," she said, forcing a lightness to her voice that she didn't feel.

"My father warned me years ago that if I was ever kidnapped he, or his estate, wouldn't give in to extortion. He'd refuse to pay the ransom. I believe him. Besides the fact that he's so cheap he squeaks, we've never gotten along. And frankly, I don't think he'd notice or give a damn if someone *did* kidnap me. Or worse."

It was such an enormous lie she almost expected her nose to grow. Her father would go to the ends of the earth and beyond to protect her. Or would he?

The entire foundation of her life had been built on quicksand. She didn't know who to trust. Who to believe. *What* to believe anymore.

"So an attempt was made to abduct you. When? Where? And where the fuck were your bodyguards?"

"Mike was killed in Barcelona a month after we left Paris last March. He'd gone to get the car while Seth and I waited—remote-controlled car bomb." Amazing that she could utter the horrific words so calmly. She couldn't control the shudder, and rubbed her bare arms briskly as she remembered the force of the percussion and the unbelievable heat of the explosion as she was thrown back by the blast.

"Four men grabbed me. Tried to hustle me into a van. Seth managed to kill three of them and wounded the fourth. He was killed three weeks later in San Cristóbal."

"*Not* dog bites on your ass. Shrapnel from the explosion."

She nodded, sucking in air.

"Damn it, you're starting to hyperventilate." Without warning he swung her up in his arms and carried her over to the bed. "I want to hear this, but let me hold you, okay?" He lowered her to the head of the bed. "Nobody is ever going to hurt you again. I swear it."

Heather scooted back to lean against the wall. She pointed firmly to the foot of the bed. Caleb shot her an amused look and retreated. He promptly placed her bare feet in his lap.

"Let me finish this before you make crazy promises." How could she explain the situation to Caleb when she didn't fully understand all the ramifications herself? "It could be anyone, I suppose. My, uh, father was mixed up with some shady people."

"As in drugs?" He cupped one heel and started drawing his thumb up and down her sole. "Gambling? Why would a business associate of your father want to kill *you*?"

"I don't know," she said, adding a little bite to her voice. Now what? He was not going to buy that she hadn't a clue. Not at all. She could tell by his patient expression.

"You must have some inkling—an *idea*, of who his enemies might be. People don't put out a hit on someone, especially a woman, for no reason."

Lord. He said that so . . . calmly. *Put a hit out.* Was her heart beating at all? She put a hand up to her throat to check. Beating so fast it was impossible to count the beats. A *hit*. That's what her father had done to her. Since they couldn't find *him*, they were searching for *her*. She wanted—*somehow*—to believe that all they wanted was information. She'd never believed that. Not for a second.

She dragged in a ragged breath. "The next time someone takes a potshot at me, I'll run up and *ask* him. Think that will work?"

Using both hands on her foot, he massaged her toes with his strong fingers. She wanted to purr. "Someone tried to shoot you? When was this?"

"Right after I left Paris. In Hong Kong." She hadn't realized how dire the situation was *then*. "One of the safest cities in the world. And before you ask if it was an accident, I can assure you, it wasn't. I had Seth and Mike with me and was shopping. I stopped to have lunch at Pacific Place in the Admiralty area. The mall was crowded. We'd just sat down in one of the restaurants when someone, using a sniper rifle apparently, shot at me from across the mall."

His eyes crinkled at the corners when he narrowed them. Not laugh lines. He was serious now. His fingers stilled on her foot. "Were you hit?"

She shook her head. "Just scared to death, and covered in window glass." Scared hadn't covered how she'd felt. Terrified spitless came fairly close.

"He could have been aiming at anyone."

"He wasn't. That shot was meant for me." She'd been interviewed for hours by the local police while Seth did his own investigation. The bullet had missed her by mere inches. *They'd* had no doubt that the shooter was aiming for her either. But she'd assured the local police that there was no one trying to kill her. No reason anyone would want her dead. She'd been believable at the time, because at the time, that *was* what she believed.

When she ran again, it was with a low, make that *invisible,* profile. She'd been an idiot for going to Sonja's party the night before the shooting. Both of her bodyguards had strongly suggested that she not go. But in her own defense she had never imagined that her father's enemy, or enemies, would send someone after her, at least not with automatic weapons. Her father certainly hadn't appeared to give a damn when she'd left Paris. He'd been aloof and colder than ever.

But she had certainly not given a thought to her own safety. Sonja Chin's party had been a bigger event than Heather had anticipated, and the press had come out in full force. Her picture, always worth a ridiculous amount of money since she was the daughter of a very wealthy man, had been plastered on the front page of society rags around the world. In under twenty-four hours someone had attempted to kill her.

"Then, less than an hour later, I heard screams coming from outside my hotel." Heart pounding, sweating with fear, she'd been frantically throwing clothes into her suitcase like a madwoman when she'd heard the screams and shouts through her open window. She recalled pulling back the curtains just enough to see down below without being seen and getting another nasty surprise. She rubbed her bare arms, feeling the same dread she'd felt then.

"A crowd was forming around a blonde in a blue raincoat similar to the one I'd worn to go out shopping earlier. The woman was lying on the curb in a pool of blood. Dead. Shot as she got out of a cab outside the hotel I was staying in. If not for me, that poor woman would be alive today. Her death haunts me.

"That time the guys convinced me. I didn't wait for the police. We left by a side door, then took five separate cabs to the airport. We went to Barcelona, where Mike had friends who would help us figure out how to make me disappear. He was killed before we got to them. From there Seth took me to San Cristóbal. Way on the other side of the world! Yet *someone* messed with the brakes in my rental car. Probably while it was parked outside my hotel. I almost went over an embankment the next day."

"San Cristóbal? Sweetheart, those street kids would do anything to get their hands on a well-maintained rental car. You were lucky you still had tires. I believe that you believe what you're telling me. And if this *is* the case, then we'll do something about it. I promise. But consider this for a moment. If someone had wanted you dead—Let me restate that. If a *professional* had wanted you dead, he wouldn't have messed with your brakes. The car, with you in it, would have been a fireball."

Heather gave him a cool look, when inside she felt hot and agitated. He didn't believe her. "I guess you're just going to have to take my word for it that it was an intentional attempt on my life. Again."

She shuddered. The only reason she hadn't gone straight off the edge of that embankment was because Seth had been sneezing with allergies and had been driving slowly. One more curve, another two miles, and the grade would have changed from fairly flat to a steep downhill stretch over a suspension bridge spanning a ravine. Then it wouldn't have mattered, no matter how slowly they'd been driving.

"I believe that you believe it. And that's good enough for me. What were you doing in San Cris?"

"Getting new papers." New passports—plural, as well as the appropriate driver's licenses for the USA, Europe, and Japan. She hadn't had much in the way of clothing. Her suitcase had been filled with the cash she'd taken from her father's safe in Paris. And all of her mother's and her own jewelry.

"Ah. A good place to do so. Smart move. Then you came here to San Francisco?"

She had a fleeting thought: How did a tractor parts salesman from Oregon know about the underbelly of San Cristóbal? "Ah—From there I went to Utah. Then Arizona. Las Vegas, then Portland. Florida, then New Jersey, then Arizona again. *Then* California. First Los Angeles, then Santa Barbara, then Sacramento, then here."

"Excellent evasive technique. Did they try again?"

"I lost them."

"Not if they were professionals."

That's why she knew that eventually, they *would* catch up with her. It was just a matter of time. "Thanks. That doesn't scare the shit out of me or anything."

"Sweetheart, is it possible that you're being a little paranoid? The car bomb was on a rental car. Could have been rigged for someone else. A car accident in a place like San Cristóbal? Two shooting instances that close together? I don't blame you for thinking it was all meant for you."

"I'm not paranoid if someone really is after me."

CHAPTER FIFTEEN

"The police in Hong Kong believed the shooter was a hit man," Heather said tightly. "So do I."

Caleb saw that she truly believed what she was telling him. The difference was, she believed that someone was trying to kill her. And while he didn't doubt that the shots were meant for her, he suspected that someone was trying to scare the crap out of her.

Probably as an incentive, after they grabbed her, for her to reveal her father's whereabouts. It was what he'd do if he were a terrorist trying to track down Brian Shaw for stealing all his money. Damn. It *was* what he'd done. Tracked her down so he could find Shaw.

God damn it. He wasn't letting her out of his sight until this was over.

Ironically, if she and her father hadn't had a falling-out, she'd be safe as a bug in a rug with the bastard in his hideaway in Matera right now. Anyway he looked at it, he'd rather Heather were with *him*. Caleb stood and went over to her.

Startled, her eyes went huge. "What are yo—"

He reached down and scooped her off the bed. "I need to hold you." It was true. He did need to hold her. He wanted the words to be part of the seduction, but it was God's own truth. His arms had felt empty for months. Years.

The weight of her, the familiar softness of her body

cradled in his arms, made him feel . . . better. No—good. Hell. *Great.* Being with Heather felt like the missing jigsaw puzzle piece of his emotions had been slotted neatly back into place.

And he was a fool if he started believing his own propaganda. He needed her as bait, he reminded himself. That was it. What he felt for her was lust.

Not love. *Lust.*

Convince her I love her, he reminded himself grimly as he lowered his mouth to hers. *Convince myself that I don't.*

"This isn't going to resolve anything," she murmured, pulling her mouth away a scant quarter inch. "Put me down. Please."

He slid her down his body, keeping hold of her hand as he sat down on the chair she'd been in earlier, setting her on her feet between his spread knees. One hand on her butt, he eased the zipper of her jeans down. "I want to see you."

"There's not much to see. It's not like there's a window into Bean's room—or should I say womb?—down there." She sounded amused as she threaded her fingers through his hair and he traced the silky V of skin he'd exposed.

"He's not ready for his big reveal yet," Caleb told her, trying to picture a child curled beneath his hand.

His child. Their child. Jesus.

He could smell the womanly scent of her. Rich and musky, as he used both hands to peel her jeans over her hips to bare a triangle of blue lace and the smooth, silky skin of her stomach. Using his thumbs, he traced the juncture of her thighs, then the slight convex curve of her belly, refamiliarizing himself with the shape and texture of her body.

He leaned forward, and put his mouth to her cool skin, then had to remain still as the heady fragrance of her arousal enveloped his senses and made him hard enough to hurt.

"I missed you." Her voice was husky and her fingers tightened in his hair. "Missed *this*."

Oh, yeah. So had he.

Sliding off the bed to kneel at her feet, he trailed a path of kisses from her navel to the edge of sky-blue lace riding low across her hips. Using both hands, he stripped her jeans down her long beautiful legs as he pressed his open mouth to her veiled mound.

Heather put her hands on his shoulders for balance as she kicked off her jeans. "Caleb—" Her voice trailed away as he nuzzled his mouth against her intimate folds.

He got rid of the tiny barrier between his mouth and what he wanted by thinking the scrap of lace gone. Gripping her hips, he plunged his tongue deep, touching and teasing her intimately. Her taste was richer, more exotic than before, which in turn made him hornier than he ever remembered being.

He wanted to devour her. Sucking her clit between his teeth, he felt the bite of her short nails digging into his shoulders. She gave a sharp cry of pleasure, and her body vibrated beneath his onslaught, telling him her climax was inching closer.

Using his fingers to spread her open, Caleb stroked his tongue more deeply, alternating the rhythm of his penetration until she cried out, coming apart beneath his mouth.

While her body quaked in his arms, Caleb shimmered them to the bed. Stretching out full-length, he tucked her against his side, listening to her erratic breathing, and watching the pulse throb at the base of her throat. He stroked her hair as her breathing evened out some. He wanted to sink into her body and ride her hard. He was desperate to make love to her fast. And slow. And every speed in between.

But this wasn't *about* him.

Long, dark lashes fluttered, drowsy hazel eyes appeared more mossy green than brown as Heather looked at him. "I have to—"

Caleb pressed two fingers to her mouth. "In a minute. Close your eyes and enjoy the moment."

Her eyes closed, and she snuggled her cheek on his chest. Stroking his fingers down her back he felt her body gradually relax against his. Dropping a kiss to the top of her head, he inhaled the floral scent of her hair and the arousing fragrance of her orgasm.

He needed a minute to tamp down his own arousal. And just in case he wasn't insane enough as it was, he silently made the skimpy little pink top she wore disappear so her bare breasts pressed against his side. He loved her breasts. He'd always preferred his women well stacked, but Heather's small plump breasts were perfect. He almost—*almost* wished away his shirt so that he could feel her gentle curves against his skin.

He got a grip. It was bad enough feeling her warm skin through a layer of T-shirt. Skin to skin would send him off like a rocket.

Christ. He was a freaking glutton for punishment. He closed his eyes, then opened them again. Told himself he was doing this for a good cause.

Focus.

Damn hard to do with a naked Heather in his arms. He was in a constant state of arousal when he was anywhere near her. And often, he thought ruefully, when he wasn't. All he needed to do was inadvertently think about her, and *pow.* Hard-on. He was getting used to the problem.

He considered it a learning curve.

The pregnancy put a completely different spin on things. He'd never imagined having children. Ever. It had always been a no-brainer. Nairne's Curse was supposed to end with himself, Gabriel, and Duncan. They'd all agreed.

Duty o'er love was the choice you did make—

His *duty* was this mission, to find Shaw. And now, to ensure his unborn son's safety. Christ. As if this thing with Heather wasn't complicated enough, he was going to have to walk a damn shaky tightrope until her father was apprehended.

He pushed his long-ago promise to the side in favor of an image of his son. Would he look like an Edge? Or would his hair be lighter, like Heather's?

She stirred, draping a bare leg over his, and her arm over his waist. It was like being enveloped by a cashmere blanket. He loved the feel of her in his arms. Loved the way her body relaxed against his. Loved . . . His son. A swell of emotion tightened Caleb's throat. He rested his hand on Heather's stomach.

A son.

Now, far from being determined to marry her and then get a divorce and walk away, he was going to have to stay married to her. But never see her again.

He hadn't lied when he'd told her that people had made marriages just like theirs work. His parents had given it a shot. Not happily. Not successfully. And continents apart. An ocean and a Curse between them.

Knowing how this was going to play out, *had* to play out, he was still bent on seducing her into marrying him. It was the only way he was going to be able to gain entry into Shaw's Matera stronghold. The only way a man of honor could behave toward the mother of his child.

Duty o'er love. Yeah, he got it, he thought bitterly. Man, did he get it. But it was fucking exhausting trying to fight his desire for her. There hadn't been a day since they'd been apart that he hadn't thought about her. Wanted her. Craved her. She was sustenance and he was freaking *starving*.

Not wanting her was like trying not to breathe, a tide of urgency so strong he was helpless to resist it.

At least he didn't have to fake this part of their relationship.

This was the real deal. A thousandfold.

Lucky him. "Okay?" he asked against her flower-scented hair.

She looked up, some of the strain gone from around her pretty eyes. "Considerably."

He brushed her mouth with his, craving more, but knowing she needed to finish what she felt compelled to tell him. It wasn't like he could admit to knowing more about her father than she did.

He smoothed his hand over her tummy, his mouth suddenly dry as the reality slammed into him again. Jesus God. There was a child there. His child. If for no other reason than duty, he *had* to marry Heather. *Had* to become a father. A role he'd never allowed himself to envision, since every Edge knew there wasn't any such thing as a happy f-ing ending.

No picket fence, no Sunday dinners, just heartbreak. A difficult pile of crap for a man to swallow. Sheer brute strength couldn't beat the Curse, Einstein's brain couldn't break it. No one knew exactly how to end the damned words that stopped the Edges from being normal men, able to give their love freely, without killing the recipient of their affection.

The silken threads binding him to Heather tightened inexorably. *Duty o'er love was the choice you did make. And it seemed that yet another generation of Edges would be doomed to do the same.*

"So your dad was a glorified banker. To whom?" he prodded, wondering if she would tell, surprised that she'd said as much as she already had. "The Mafia? That goes with the hit man theory."

Heather hesitated, then gave a little shrug. "Maybe."

Caleb sensed her innocence, that she really didn't know what or who her father served.

Mafia? Not that T-FLAC was aware of. Shaw's clients were considerably bigger, and even more dangerous than the mob. But Caleb was pretty damn sure that none of *them* had a reason to be after Heather. Not unless she knew more about her father's business than T-FLAC suspected. The analytical team didn't think so, and frankly, neither did he.

Heather would never make a great poker player, since she broadcasted her emotions on her pretty face. It was why he'd been able to play the marriage card. Once he'd gotten beyond his egotistical male "no" response to her abortion announcement, he'd been able to see beneath the surface. Heather was scared, choosing what she saw as the safest way to "protect" her unborn child. By not carrying it to term. In that instant, Caleb renewed his vow to hunt down Shaw and kill the bastard for terrorizing his own daughter.

He hadn't needed ESP to realize that she already loved this baby and she'd be cut to the soul if she went through with the procedure. It hadn't taken much persuading, and yet here she was, next to him on her bed, spilling her guts. Guilt squirmed and he squashed it.

Shaw was a dangerous man. Unlike Heather, he'd make a mean poker player, one who held his cards close to his chest. It was highly unlikely that either his wife or daughter had ever been fully aware of what he did and the people he did it with.

A surge of protectiveness had Caleb pulling Heather even closer to him. "Well, now the bastards are going to have to go through me to get to you," he assured her.

Instead of relaxing, she went stiff as a board in his arms, pulling her head back so that she met his gaze straight on. Her brown eyes were wild with panic. "God no! This has nothing to do with you! I shouldn't have, damn it, I don't need a hero. See? This is why I can't have this baby, your baby. I can't have anyone in my life! I'm on the run, Caleb."

She bit her quivering lower lip as her eyes pooled with tears. "I have to tell you something . . . My, my father isn't dead." She sucked in a quavering breath and continued without looking up, "He and I—we had a huge fight and I haven't seen or heard from him in over a year. I think he pissed off someone enough that they want to hurt me in retaliation." She finally raised her eyes. "I don't want you to get hurt because of me, Caleb. I'd never forgive myself."

The look on her face was so honest and sincere that he almost, almost, told her the truth. About his job, his paranormal talents, and the Curse. He caught himself before majorly f-ing things up.

His heart constricted but his voice was smooth and assuring as he whispered into her hair, "Nobody's going to get hurt, sweetheart. Trust me." *The only thing I plan to break is your heart.*

CHAPTER SIXTEEN

Two hours later they were married and heading to Italy for their honeymoon. "It's a long flight," Caleb told her softly, although there were no other passengers in first class to hear him. "Try to get some sleep. You're going to need all your strength when we get there, Mrs. Edge."

Mrs. Edge. Hard to believe. It had all happened so fast. Caleb tucked a blanket she didn't need over her lap. As if she'd freeze in a pressurized cabin. Still, it was sweet.

For someone who debated a minor decision for days, if not months, Heather had gotten dizzy as she was swept along by Caleb's take-charge actions today. Lord, the man made split-second decisions, then lightning-fast follow-ups. He'd given her mere minutes to pack a bag and lock up her apartment before hauling her into a cab and taking her to city hall. Their wedding had taken four minutes. And two of those had been spent signing forms.

She hoped to God that she wasn't making a mistake by leaving the relative safety and anonymity of San Francisco for Europe. Wouldn't these people *expect* her to eventually go home? Europe wasn't that big. It was common knowledge that the family had a pied-à-terre in Paris, and her parents' estate was sixty miles outside of that city. Many of her father's banking clients had been to functions at both. Worry gnawed at her. What if they bumped into someone she knew while they were in Europe? What if the paparazzi spotted her at the airport? What if . . . What if . . .

"Relax," he told her with a smile. "We're going to Italy, not the salt mines of Siberia."

"I am relaxed." Sort of, she thought ruefully. She felt as though she'd been sucked into a vortex. She tried to smooth the anxiety from her face and forced herself to breathe slowly and deeply.

"Perhaps one day you and your father can patch things up," he offered, leaning over her to stuff a small pillow between her and the window. "It would be nice for our son to know his grandfather. Is there a chance of a reconciliation? Now that we have a baby to introduce?" Caleb's tone was light, but she sensed an underlying tension in his voice.

"He's not exactly the warm and fuzzy type, believe me," she said dryly. She couldn't imagine her elegant father around a small child, but it would certainly be interesting to watch.

Loving Caleb this much, this fast, was a little overwhelming. "Has anyone ever called you a human bulldozer?" she asked, intrigued by the way his eyes crinkled when he smiled.

"Only my brother Gabriel. And only when I'm eating MacPain's cooking."

"Mac who?"

"His name is Mac*Bain*. He's my brother Gabriel's— Hmm. I'm not sure what MacPain is called nowadays. Butler? Factotum? Pain in the ass? He runs Gabriel's household."

"Good grief. Your brother has a household large enough to warrant a *butler*?" So he came from money. Which explained the first-class seats purchased at the last moment at a premium, and the exquisite diamond band on her wedding finger. Things he probably wouldn't have been able to purchase on the salary of a tractor parts salesman. Not that she had a clue how much or little a tractor parts salesman made.

"Actually Gabriel's house is a castle."

"Literally?"

"Yeah. It was originally our family seat in Scotland. He brought it over to the U.S. and had it reconstructed, stone by stone, in Montana."

"That must've given the local cattle something to moo about." Heather smiled. "Does he have a horde of kids?"

"Nope. He's single."

One didn't have anything to do with the other, but she let it pass. "And eccentric apparently, living in a Montana castle with a butler."

"They're just friends," Caleb said, straight-faced.

"I'm married to a comedian," she teased. The diamonds on her finger sparkled, shooting off little shards of fire in the stream of light from the small overhead reading lamp. She'd felt the prickle of tears behind her eyes when he'd produced the ring for her during the ceremony. It had all happened so fast, yet he'd still made the time to buy her a wedding ring.

Before he'd come to see her.

Before he'd known that she was pregnant.

Had he called his family? Told his brothers he was marrying? Or at the very least, that he was going to be a father? Lord, there was a lot she had to learn about the Edge family. "Tell me about this Montana castle."

"Long, long ago—rest your head—yes, there you go. Close your eyes, sweetheart."

She yawned, slipping her arm around his waist as she listened to his deep voice vibrate through the wall of his chest and resonate inside her. "Long, long ago in a land far away," she mumbled, suddenly so sleepy she could barely keep her eyes open.

His chuckle reverberated in his chest. "Far away back then, but with jets, Scotland is a quickie these days. Anyway, five hundred or so years ago, Magnus Edridge, our great-great-something-grandfather, fell in love with a beautiful village girl named Nairne." Caleb stroked Heather's hair off her face, talking softly.

"At first he ignored his family's demands that he marry the Laird's homely daughter so that he could refill the family's depleted coffers. Those holy wars were hell on the old bank account. Instead, he lavished expensive gifts on the beautiful Nairne—the woman he truly loved—flaunting her in front of his father and the people of the village."

"Uh-oh."

"Oh, yeah. Worse, he gave his beloved the Edridge family betrothal jewelry."

"Shocking. The bastard."

"But his father kept working on him. He was too old to be plowing the local girls as if there was no tomorrow. It was time he married. Magnus, who was probably a teenager, said fine with me, Pop. I'm engaged to this gorgeous babe down in the village. We'll tie the knot and be done with it."

Caleb's quiet voice and the steady beat of his heart beneath her ear coupled with the monotonous drone of the plane's engines were relaxing her more than the overpriced massages she used to rely on. *"Plowing?"*

"In the vernacular. Finally Magnus got the message that if he continued seeing Nairne he'd be banished without a sow—"

Heather grinned. "I think that was a *sou.*"

"—and he had to marry Janet of the big castle and the even bigger fortune."

"Poor Nairne."

"Yeah, well that's where the Edridge family luck took a southerly turn," Caleb said dryly, playing with a strand of her hair as he talked. "Magnus trotted down to the village to tell Nairne that he had to marry Janet. He demanded that she return the Edridge betrothal jewelry."

"Clearly, and surprisingly, he lived to tell the tale."

"Nairne cursed him. Did I mention that she was a witch?"

"A Scottish witch. Cool. Did she shrivel his balls and turn them black?"

Caleb shuddered. "Bloodthirsty. No. She left those jewels intact, but cursed the ones she threw back at him."

"He was lucky to get away alive."

"Anyway, he married Janet, changed the family name to Edge to avoid the curse, and had three sons."

"And lived happily ever after?"

"From the look of old Janet in her family portrait, I'd say not."

"What was the curse?" Heather sat up to look at him.

"That was a bedtime story, Mrs. Edge. If you're not going to sleep I have another activity in mind."

"Dream on, big boy. Curse?"

He reached out and tucked a strand of loose hair behind her ear. His finger traced the outer edge, making her shiver as he quoted: " *'Duty o'er love was the choice you did make, My love you did spurn, my heart you did break.'* " His fingers gently brushed the soft pad of her earlobe.

Heather's breath got tangled in her lungs as his thumb stroked her jaw. "And?"

" *'Your penance to pay, no pride you shall gain. Three sons on three sons find nothing but pain.'* "

"Geez Louise," she whispered thickly, trying to concentrate on what he was saying, when all her attention was on what he was doing. "She—" Lord. What were they talking about? Oh, yes. "She cursed his kids as well? That was cold."

"Only five hundred years' worth," Caleb told her dryly, unsnapping his seat belt with his free hand.

"Ah. Now I get it. That's why you think we're having a boy. Because of the curse."

"Five hundred years of only boys . . . Your skin feels like satin," he murmured, distracted. "What were we— Oh, yeah. And only three to a family. We Edges take Nairne's Curse *very* seriously. *'Only freely given will this curse be done,'* " he finished. " *'To break the spell, three must work as one.'* "

She frowned, trying to tamp down a shudder of anticipation as his hand smoothed down her throat. "It doesn't quite rhyme."

Two fingers rested on the frantic pulse throbbing at the base of her throat. He smiled. "Hey. She was a witch, not a poet."

"What has to be freely given?"

Caleb shrugged. "Haven't a clue."

"Come on. In five centuries none of the three sons on three sons has figured out what will break the spell?"

"Nope."

"Maybe we can figure it out."

He sat up a little straighter in his seat, and lifted an eyebrow. "On our *honeymoon*?"

"Why not? What else—" His hand skimmed down the side of her rib cage, and she wiggled in her seat. "Don't do that—Caleb, I am *so* ticklish—Shh. People can *hear* us."

"*I* don't have the giggles," he whispered, hauling her into his lap, blanket and all.

Beneath her thighs she felt him. Hard and ready. Desire shot through her, molten and immediate. The bubble of laughter died on her lips as he kissed her softly. His lips were firm and smooth, his taste familiar as he rubbed his mouth across hers in a maddeningly erotic dance that promised paradise.

"You do know, husband mine," she whispered thickly as heat chased up her spine, "that you're making false promises here?"

God, she was lucky. Lucky to have met a man like Caleb in the middle of the mess her life had become.

"Relax, sweetheart." Her new husband rested his chin on top of her head and rubbed her bare arm in a caress that was anything but comforting. Her heart rate shot up, and she wished they weren't in public. No matter how secluded she felt, behind a curtain just feet away sat a planeload of other passengers.

Eyes closed, she felt him reach up with his free hand, and seconds later the overhead light winked out, leaving them in semidarkness. He slipped his hand beneath the blanket and spread his fingers over her tummy. "Hi, little guy, this is your dad. How're you doing in there? You take a nap now. Mommy and I have to have a private conversation."

"What private conversation?" Heather whispered.

Caleb gave her a stern look. "Shh. He's too young to learn about the birds and the bees just yet."

He was positive she was carrying his son because of some fairy tale that had been passed down through the generations. She didn't care if the baby was a boy or a girl. As long as he was healthy. She'd make sure their baby knew nothing but love and security his whole life. "He's fast asleep," she whispered, her hand over Caleb's for a shared moment.

The plane's engines hummed. Resting her head on his broad chest, she listened to the steady beat of Caleb's heart. Yes. She was lucky. Damn lucky. And she wasn't going to waste the first day of the rest of their new life together by bringing up her past.

The first-class seats were wide and comfortable. Caleb reclined his seat, holding her snugly against him. She felt the brush of his lips on her hair. God. She felt ridiculously, dizzily happy.

He skimmed his hand under the blanket.

Her heart literally skipped a beat. "Stop that," she said on a whispered laugh as she wrestled his busy fingers. "Someone will walk through here and see us. Tell me what it was like growing up with two brothers in a Scottish castle in Montana." She could barely concentrate because now he was stroking her thigh.

Her desire for this man saturated her. She wasn't making much of an effort to stop him, merely holding onto his wrist. Absolutely no deterrent to his marauding fingers at all.

His hand cruised beneath the hem of her dress and stroked along the inside of her thigh. She shook her head, reading the intent in his dark eyes before he moved his hand higher. "Are you a member of the Mile-High club?" she asked, her voice unsteady.

Angling his body into her, he gave her a slow, wicked smile. "Wanna join?" He slid his fingers a little higher, the brush of his fingers making her skin burn.

She bit the corner of her lower lip, eyes dancing. "Not with three hundred plus other passengers onboard, I don't."

But it was a lie. She'd take this man anywhere, anytime, anyhow. Damp heat started between her legs, and her heart skipped several beats as he lazily rubbed her mound through her sheer panties. Running her fingers through his hair, she drew his mouth down to hers. The kiss was slow and sweet and made her blood heat and pulse lazily in her veins.

"Should I stop then?"

"Of course," she told him primly, spreading her knees

a little to grant him better access to where she wanted, needed, to be touched.

He chuckled, sliding his palm up her midriff under both dress and blanket to feel the weight of her lace-covered breast, teasing the already hard nipple between his fingers. The erotic glide of his tongue against hers made her shift in her seat. His tongue tasted her, exploring her as his fingers drew down the lace covering her and skimmed beneath to bare flesh.

Heart fluttering, senses swimming, she murmured against his lips, "Somebody's going to come . . ."

Caleb's eyes absorbed light. "Yeah." His voice was raspy and filled with tenderness. His mouth covered hers again, hot and hard. And brief.

She tasted his wicked smile against the underside of her jaw as he cupped her left breast. "Your breasts are bigger," he whispered, skimming his lips across her cheekbone, as his thumb rubbed her nipple to an aching hardness. His mouth found the curve of her neck. She wanted his mouth where his hand was.

"Tender, too—No," she grabbed at his wrist as he immediately lifted his hand away. "Don't stop. I love your hands on me." Vaguely she glanced around the first-class cabin. But they were completely alone. Of course someone could push through that curtain at any second—

Breathless, aroused, she tried for reason. Okay. Not very hard. "You can't—"

Apparently he could.

Blindly her mouth found his again as he skimmed his hand over her rib cage, hesitated at her tummy, then dipped beneath the tiny triangle of fabric of her thong. Pleasure swamped her as he cupped her intimately, then slid a long finger deep inside her wet heat. Burying her face against his shoulder, she tried to muffle her moan.

"I love touching you. Can't get enough. Love the way your body moves when I touch you—Yes. Just like that.

I love the way your eyes lose focus, and that little frown of concentration as the fever builds." His clever fingers moved inside her, knowing just where to touch, where to stroke.

Desire, already razor sharp, clutched at her belly, and her hips lifted off the seat without her brain giving instructions. She had to clear her throat to get any words out. "The flight attendant . . ."

"Won't disturb us, I promise." He eased another finger inside her slick heat. She gasped at the exquisite sensation, arching her hips off his lap, her body bowed as arrows of pleasure shot through her nerve endings. Heather pushed against his hands, at the same time using her own over his to press them down harder, increasing the pressure. Biting down on his shoulder, she managed to muffle her cry as he drew a climax out of her that went on and on.

When at last her body was once again her own, Heather lay limply against him, her breath snagging, her heart going a mile a minute.

"Close your eyes, sweetheart."

Like bubbles in Cristal champagne, her joy fizzed and danced inside her. When she was with him time seemed to stop. He loved her, this man with the hot teal eyes and incredible mouth. And she loved him back.

There was just a small, annoying little voice in the back of her mind whispering that although her new husband had kissed her senseless, heated her beyond boiling, and made her come, *he* hadn't lost control for a second.

CHAPTER SEVENTEEN

Heather was cradled on his lap, her head tucked against his shoulder, her body lax, breathing slow and even. Caleb touched his lips to the top of her head, inhaling the fragrance of her hair.

Most of the passengers had their overhead lights off, casting the cabin into a relaxing dusk. She'd been too wired to sleep, so he'd put a light sleep spell on her. With the pregnancy she needed to rest. And the next few days were going to be hard on her.

Yeah. That was *one* of the reasons he wanted her *sleeping* right now. The other was that it was becoming harder and harder to remember that the crap he was telling her was . . . crap. He had to be one hundred percent convincing when he looked into her amber eyes and told her, with utmost sincerity, that he loved her.

He wasn't surprised to find that he was a damn fine actor. Didn't hurt in his line of work either.

He couldn't love her, of course. That wasn't in the cards for him. But it *was* an interesting, and extremely dangerous, game he was playing, seeing just how deep he could go into shark-infested waters before he had to pull back.

Was it good or bad that just *looking* at her made him want to devour her? That just *looking* at her made his body jerk and pulse and made him almost manic to bury his cock deep inside her? 24/7.

He watched her in repose. God, she was beautiful. Thick, dark lashes rested on her lightly flushed cheeks. Gently he brushed a heavy strand of honey-brown hair off her face; it clung to his hand. Instead of releasing it, he rubbed the silky filaments between the tips of his fingers. She smelled of warmth and light and color.

She stirred and muttered and hazily brushed his hand away from her face, but didn't waken. His heart turned over as he thought of her response to him earlier. Fresh need stirred.

He hadn't known it could be like this. Resting his head against the high-backed leather seat, Caleb watched the even rise and fall of her breasts as she breathed.

Four months ago he hadn't known she existed. Now he wondered how he was going to let her go.

He suddenly had a flash of memory of a long-ago summer. The picture was crystal clear. Crouching beside the small, man-made lake outside the solarium at Edridge Castle, his older brother Gabriel beside him. They'd been seven and eight. Brilliant orange and gold koi swam lazily beneath the shining transparent surface of the water. The sun beat down on their heads as if summer would never end.

"Do you think he'll stay longer this time?" Caleb had whispered, grubby fingers rippling the surface of the lake to tempt the hungry fish. Gabriel had caught one with his bare hands last week, and Caleb wanted to see what a fish felt like. *Slimy I bet,* he thought with relish.

Gabriel picked at a scab on his knee. "Leaving day after tomorrow." He sounded as if he didn't care if their father stayed longer or not.

Caleb wished *he* didn't care so much. "I'm not going to fix that cut again if you're going to keep picking at it." Disappointment made his voice sound angry.

"It's good practice for you."

He was pretty proud that he was in charge of "fixing"

all the injuries around the castle, but his brother was annoying him today. Next time he fell off his bike, Caleb decided, he'd let him bleed for a while. "Yeah. Whatever."

A yellow fish the size of a monster bumped his thumb and he froze, eyes glued to the koi's opening and closing mouth. "Ew, gross. The fish's *kissing* me. Yuck." He left his hand where it was. "Are you sure?"

"Been five days."

He and his brothers had seen their father twice. Once the night he'd arrived. And yesterday for breakfast. "I guess." Caleb cupped his palm under the fish's belly. "How do I do this again?"

"Close your hand carefully—*not too hard*—and pull her out quick. Hey! You did it." His brother slapped him on the back as Caleb brought the fish out in a sparkling spray of water. "Good job."

His chest swelled with pride. It wasn't easy; it wiggled and wriggled like crazy, but he cupped the golden fish in both hands, caged against his chest. "I'm going to keep her in my room." She didn't feel slithery and slimy at all. She was so pretty. And felt smooth and silky, like the cover on his mother's bed.

Mine, he thought.

Gabriel ruffled his hair, which annoyed him. "Put her back, Caleb. She's not a pet. You can't keep her."

Caleb pulled away. "Says who? I caught her. I get to keep her. I'm going to train her to do stuff."

"She'll die."

His chest hurt. "No, she won't."

"Yes," Gabriel said, sounding way older than eight. "She *will*. Throw her back in, dirtwad."

Weird damn thing to remember, Caleb thought, cupping Heather's cheek and feeling her warm moist breath on his palm. He hadn't thought of those koi in years. He'd have to check them out next time he went home.

"Is she asleep?" Lark asked, suddenly appearing without fanfare, butt perched on the arm of the seat across the aisle.

"Yeah, she is." So much for enjoying the moment, Caleb thought ruefully. "That's interesting." He motioned to the spiked black leather dog collar around Lark's throat, which she wore with a skintight LockOut suit. "Do you bite?"

She wiggled her eyebrows, both pierced with rows of little silver balls. "Often and well," she assured him in her lilting, husky voice, amused. "But not you, Middle Edge."

Caleb grinned, relieved. "What's up, beautiful?" She actually was quite lovely under the Goth makeup and assorted piercings. Not that he'd ever been interested. No spark.

She stood for a moment before crouching down beside his seat, giving him a quite spectacular view of a nice pair of—

"Up here." Lark pointed two fingers at her eyes. "Interview process starts next week for Master Wizard. Do you think Duncan will run?"

"Ask him."

"I did. He wouldn't tell me."

"There's your answer then." He pointed to the pile of small foil bags of cashews on the tray table across from him. "Pass me those, would you? Thanks." He tore a couple pouches open with his teeth.

Amusement sparkled in her eyes. "You know what *that's* about, don't you?"

"What what's about?"

"Your craving for nuts and the rest of it."

He frowned. What the hell was she talking about?

"You have couvade syndrome."

"I'm going to hate myself for asking," he said, tossing

a small handful of nuts into his mouth. "But what the hell is couvade syndrome?"

Her lips curved. "Comes from the French word *couvee,* which means 'to hatch.' In other words, Middle Edge, you're having a sympathetic pregnancy with your Heather."

"Bullshit."

"It's been researched and is quite real, believe me."

He wasn't *sure* if she was jerking his chain or telling the truth, for Christ's sake. "How do I get rid of it?" Losing the nausea would be nice.

"The only cure I've heard about is—birth."

"Jesus! Will I go into labor too?" The thought was too horrific to imagine.

"Nope. That she'll have to do alone."

Thank God. "Any more intel on Shaw's client list?" He ate a couple of nuts, which settled his stomach, which in turn made him damned nervous. Sympathetic pregnancy. Ah, man, that was too weird.

"The Blazing Path has been added to the list of those we know about. Which explains their low profile for the past year," she said dryly, resting her arm on his armrest to look at Heather.

"Hard to buy weapons when your banker splits with all your cash. We're backtracking to see who else has been quiet in the last year. Shaw had an excellent reputation. His clients trusted him to take care of their money, invest it, bulk it up. Pretty surprised after twenty, twenty-five years of trust to find out that he was greedy. It's not like they can file a complaint with the FDIC. They didn't know he'd placed their offshore accounts in his own offshore corporation. One messy lump sum. Another transfer to a Swiss account, and voilà. The man has a death wish, apparently. There are a lot of angry factions out there looking for blood. She's really pretty, isn't she?"

Caleb digested the specifics of the situation, then glanced down at his sleeping bride. Lark was dead on. Heather was beautiful. "I don't want her hurt, Lark. No matter what happens."

"As long as your protection spell works."

"Why wouldn't it?"

"No reason. You amped it up, right?"

BARI, ITALY
SATURDAY, APRIL 15
0850

From Rome's *Leonardo da Vinci/Fiumicino* they'd boarded a domestic flight to Bari, one of the largest cities in southern Italy. And just under a hundred miles from their final destination of Matera. Caleb's adrenaline kicked in. Ninety miles to Shaw.

Heather was sound asleep, her head on his shoulder. Picking her up in his arms before everyone started to deplane, Caleb teleported outside the small terminal, bypassing security and the crowds clogging the building, which was always congested since it was the hub for plane, rail, and bus travel in the area.

The air outside was blood temperature, and stank of diesel fuel, stale sweat, and strong cigarettes. The smell pushed nausea up his throat, and he had to swallow hard to control his queasy stomach. Great. Just f-ing great.

Tony Rook, and a black town car, waited outside to drive them to Matera.

Rook glanced from Heather to Caleb. "I see your legendary charm has failed you. You've put the poor woman to sleep with your scintillating conversation." He grinned as he checked her out, opening the back door so Caleb could put her inside the air-conditioned vehicle. "Man. She's even hotter than the intel pics."

Caleb settled her full-length on the backseat, bunching

up his jacket to slip under her head. Rook's observation had him taking another look. Hell, Heather wasn't just hot. She was gorgeous. He touched her hair. The silky strands fell fluidly through his fingertips. As a blonde, as a brunette . . . He jerked his hand away, curling his fingers around the top of the door instead.

"Sleep," he whispered.

"Hmm." She turned over without opening her eyes. Her fingers spread open on her slightly rounded stomach beneath the thin cotton of her dress. She mumbled, "Love y—," and was off again. Even fast asleep she was making sure their son was safe. Throat tight, Caleb resisted touching her again and closed the door carefully, shutting out the dozens of conversations being conducted at high volume all around them.

He and Rook got into the front seat of the car. Caleb checked that the window between the passenger and driver's sections was firmly closed before getting down to the real business of why he was there. "Any activity?" he demanded as they wended their way slowly through a clot of cars, taxis, and buses jamming the street outside the small airport terminal.

"Nada," Rook told him as they drove through the city proper to reach the road to Matera. The younger man expertly maneuvered the car through the narrow, congested streets, where the college kids double- and triple-parked their cars in total disregard of other drivers. "No ins, or outs."

"Any sign of the tangos?" While none of Shaw's clients had thus far tracked him down, every hour brought that possibility closer. And while he and his team would be more than happy to engage a few bad guys after they'd secured Shaw, Caleb didn't want to have yet another element of danger brought into the mix. Not until he made sure Heather was out of harm's way.

"Not yet."

"You bring my Brazils?" Caleb asked, turning the air up high and angling the vent for best chill distribution. Grabbing what he hoped was a clean napkin from the stack on the dash, he wiped his forehead, realizing that his entire body was dripping with a cold sweat. His stomach cramped. The nausea was back full force. Weird. Very weird. Teleporting had never affected him like this before. Could his powers be changing? Could Lark have it right? He didn't know which answer freaked him out more.

"Glove compartment." Rook's voice held a hint of disbelief, but Caleb hardly cared, snapping open the door and feeling an intense sense of relief at the sight of a brand-new can of Brazil nuts. He pulled the lid off and poured a handful directly into his salivating mouth. Once the food hit his bloodstream, the nausea subsided, thank God.

"Man, you're going to turn into a nut if you keep eating those things like that."

"You only brought *one* can?"

"There's a whole frigging *case* in your hotel room," Rook told him with a puzzled glance. He thumbed the backseat. "How'd you persuade her to come?"

"I married her," Caleb said dryly.

"No shit?"

"No shit." They lapsed into silence, driving through the city before Caleb spoke again. "Heather's pregnant," he told the other man baldly, picking two of the biggest nuts out of the can and eating them together with a satisfying crunch and grind.

Really. He felt better already.

Rook's eyes gleamed in the lights from an oncoming car. "So, what?" he motioned to the can of Brazil nuts Caleb had clutched in his hand like a life preserver. "You're sharing her cravings?"

"Say what?" Caleb stared across the car at Rook as if he was speaking Aramaic. The same Aramaic Lark had been sprouting, apparently. Damn it to hell.

"Cravings. You know. That weird phase pregnant women go through when you never know what they'll be hungry for? My sister Lisa craved black olives and marshmallow cream." He shuddered. "*Together.* Totally gross. I wanted to puke just watching her take each olive and dip it into a bowl of marshmallow cream." Rook used one hand to mime the action as he drove. "Do you know how nauseating *gray* marshmallow cream looks? Especially with little black chunks in it?"

Caleb swallowed hard, and slapped the lid back on the nuts.

"Did that for the first three, four months she was knocked up. I love my sis, but man, she was damn lucky she didn't give birth to an olive with white fluffy hair." Rook chuckled at his lame joke, then reached over to punch Caleb in the arm. "But, hey! Congratulations. When this party's over, let's get shitfaced and celebrate."

"I'm not telling you so we can smoke a cigar and have a bonding moment," Caleb said. Then wished he hadn't mentioned the word *cigar* as bile burned the back of his throat. Promising himself that this would be the very last one, he took another nut from the can and chewed furiously until the nausea subsided.

Morning sickness—all freaking day and night sickness, if the truth be told. A sympathetic pregnancy? Geez. What kind of f-ing cosmic joke was *that*?

He needed another nut.

He switched from "feelings" to business so that he wouldn't have to think about it. "I'll fill the others in as well—this is a heads-up that not only do we have an innocent civilian in a dangerously explosive situation, but that she's carrying a child. And before you ask, you inquisitive little shit, no, her getting knocked up wasn't intentional. Although it helped, you know, getting her to marry me so fast. She and Shaw had a serious falling-out.

"The only thing preventing me from feeling like a total asshole dirtbag is that I think it will make her happy to reconcile with her father." Even as he said the words, Caleb's gut told him they weren't true. She'd made no bones about how much she disliked her father. He'd spent the entire flight holding her in his arms while he convinced himself that what he was doing was just and right.

Shaw had to be stopped. Shaw's *clients* had to be stopped. The only way to extract Shaw was to use his daughter as bait to gain entrée to the man's stronghold. There was no other way.

He'd keep her safe, keep the baby safe. But it was a losing proposition. She'd probably hate him for forcing a reunion with her father. Probably, hell. Marriage or no marriage, there'd be no way back from this kind of deception. Which didn't matter since they couldn't have a traditional relationship anyway. If he stayed with her, according to the ancient family Curse, she'd die.

Sometimes life could really suck.

Caleb had put a protective spell on her in San Francisco. He'd strengthened it before they'd started the trip. But just because she had a protection spell in force didn't mean that someone wanting to do her harm couldn't attempt to do so.

No one could touch her physically because of the spell, but he didn't want her terrified. And he sure as shit didn't want anything upsetting little Bean.

"She'll be safe inside Shaw's place," he told Rook, told himself, knowing that was true. That last comment of Lark's about amping up the protection spell niggled at the back of his brain, but he wasn't quite sure why.

He knew the spell was solid. Trust Lark to jerk his chain.

Shaw's digs were a fortress, and she was his daughter. They didn't have a shred of intel to indicate that he'd ever harmed Heather in the past, so it was a reasonable assumption that he didn't pose a threat now.

Caleb had a quick flash of the scars on her shapely ass. Did her father suspect that his clients were after his daughter? Caleb suspected that more than one group was trying to nail her. To scare her? Or to prove to Shaw that they could get to him through his daughter? Another possibility was, he speculated, trying to kidnap her. To do what he'd done, flush out her father.

Whether Shaw knew that the bodyguards he'd sent away with his daughter were dead or not was immaterial. She'd been out in the cold, *on her own* for a year, while her father was safe and cozy and surrounded by more than two hundred armed men.

She was damn lucky Caleb had found her first. Yeah. Damn lucky.

They might have had a falling-out, but Caleb suspected that he'd witness a tearful reunion. It would be brief, but he could give her that much before he extracted Shaw and started grilling him like a cheese sandwich.

Before he left Heather with nothing but a prompt monthly child support check.

God damn it, he hated feeling like an asshole. Hell, not just feeling like one, *being* one. He'd left out *the* most important parts of Nairne's Curse when he'd told it to her during the flight.

I gift you my powers in memory of me. He was a wizard, hard to explain and unnecessary information to one's *temporary* wife. The mother of your child. To a woman who was going to inflict her own curses on him when she found out what he'd done.

The joy of love no son shall ever see. When a Lifemate

is chosen by the heart of a son, No protection can be given, again I have won. He was damned if he'd do anything that would remove that protection spell from her. Heather Shaw—Heather Edge—was safe from everyone but her husband.

He was *pretending* to be in love with her. *Pretending,* he reminded himself for the umpteenth time, as he absently ground up three large nuts at the same time—and doing a damn fine job of it too, he thought, rubbing the now-familiar aching void in his chest.

His pain will be deep, her death will be swift—
Not going to happen.

Inside his heart a terrible rift. Yeah. There was that little zinger.

None of it was going to happen. He was here to make sure it didn't.

Not. Going. To. Happen. He'd live with his guilt. He'd take being an asshole. As long as Heather stayed safe, and with her, his son. It was a fair trade.

"I cast a powerful protective spell on Heather and my son, but I still want all eyes vigilant and ready for trouble until this is over," Caleb told Rook. Barring his first mission, Caleb had never felt even a glimmer of fear before an op. He prided himself on his absolute focus when he was in the field. Or out of it, for that matter.

It had taken him half a plane trip—Jesus, *that* was a slow form of transportation—to recognize that for the past three months he'd felt edgy, out of sorts, and irritable as hell. Coupled with that shit were his strange, and sometimes bizarre, new eating habits. Not to mention this damned weird and annoying hollow sensation in his chest.

If he were a touchy-feely guy, which he sure as shit *wasn't,* he'd say he was having a goddamned meltdown.

Fear?

Before, during, or after an op? When he was a rookie, yeah. Since? No.

He loved his job. Thrived on it.

No. Obviously he'd picked up some freaking bug in the Saudi desert last month. That, coupled with some residual medical crap tied into spending so long in rehab for his leg, was why he felt like shit on a shingle half the time. And as if someone had whacked him in the chest with a two-by-four the other half of the time. Temporary.

Leg was fine. *He* was fine. Never better. Great. Excellent.

CHAPTER EIGHTEEN

"What're you gonna do?" Rook asked as the lights of Bari winked behind them. "Knock on the front door?"

"Yeah." Caleb looked over his shoulder. Heather hadn't moved in twenty minutes. She was still fast asleep. Moonlight streamed a cool white beam of light through the vehicle's window, illuminating her profile.

He'd considered and weighed the pros and cons of backspacing time to before they'd slept together. Erase the past three months. But one: He wasn't sure if he *could* TiVo Heather back before the baby was conceived. He had no idea how backspacing would affect either Heather or the baby. He'd never tried it with a pregnant woman, and he sure as shit didn't plan on starting with Heather and Bean.

And two, and three, and fricking *four*: He wasn't going to risk either mother or child or mission in an attempt to be chivalrous.

No. He was on a course. None of this had come about by accident, he reminded himself. He was doing his job. His duty.

Jesus. He was so screwed. "I want her to rest. Then we're going to walk in there bold as brass to let Shaw wish us well."

"And then?"

"Then I teleport them to our safe house. No fuss no muss."

Rook shot him a glance. "You told her you're a wizard?"

"Hell, I didn't even tell her I was T-FLAC."

"Man, I'd like to be a fly on the wall for *that* conversation." Rook was still young enough that the trauma, the disbelief, the horror of full disclosure were nothing more than a vague thought. Each wizard had to decide if and when and to whom they would reveal themselves.

"Pull over," he told the younger man absently. Caleb wasn't sure telling Heather anything about himself would mitigate the hate she'd have for him when she realized how he'd used her. Whether a wizard divulged who and what he was was a matter of debate among the wizard council as well. He, Gabriel, and Duncan had discussed the pros and cons—briefly.

The only time they deemed it necessary to tell someone that much info was if a long-term association was anticipated. Caleb could count the people who knew he was a wizard, other than T-FLAC/psi operatives and his immediate family, which included MacBain, on either hand.

It was on a need-to-know basis, and other than his fellow operatives, no one needed to know.

Rook pulled over onto the shoulder and turned off the car. "What are we doing?" The engine pinged and hummed for several minutes as it cooled down.

Caleb stared blindly at the moon-swathed road ahead. Jesus. Would *Bean* be a wizard?

Yes. Christ. Of course he would.

The knowledge hit him like a blunt force blow to the belly, and he shot out a hand to brace himself on the dash. He was going to *have* to tell Heather. About himself. And about their child. His son would be a wizard. Had he wanted to, he *couldn't* disengage himself from the child. Which meant that, like his own father, Caleb had to have contact with Bean's mother. There were things that only another wizard could teach him . . .

His brothers? Caleb thought a little desperately. Gabriel had practically raised himself *and* Caleb and Duncan . . . *He'd* make an excellent father . . . He would and could teach little Bean everything he'd need to know. Bean would certainly see a hell of a lot more of Gabriel, and perhaps Duncan, than all three of them combined had seen of their father.

His mother had taken them to Scotland to see Magnus, or he had come to Montana, *once* a year. Alternating between the States and Scotland for sixteen fucking years. Jesus.

Of course the boys hadn't spent a whole hell of a lot of quality time with their father, because their parents had spent most of that week upstairs in the master bedroom. His parents had been completely self-absorbed. *Obsessed*. Insane with love and lust. They couldn't bear that they had to remain apart. They spent their days whispering to each other on the phone. Living for that one week together.

His mother, who was always weak and melancholy, would get paler and paler, and more frail in that week they spent together. As if by being with her husband the very life was being sucked right out of her.

The three boys had grown up just fine without a mother tucking them in, or a father watching the Super Bowl with them.

It was amazing to Caleb that a man who was basically a stranger had been such an enormous presence in his children's lives. It was their father who'd taught them swordplay. Their father who brought his manservant MacBain to Montana to keep an eye on them. Their father who had encouraged all three of them to try out for T-FLAC.

The counterterrorist organization was HQ'd not far

from Edridge castle in Montana. Magnus had been aware of the T-FLAC/psi branch, and had offered up his sons when they'd been in their late teens.

It had been a perfect match.

Early discipline, rigorous training, and a love of their country had given Caleb and his brothers something to fight for. Something to believe in. Something, God damn it, to *love*.

Fortunately they'd learned early not to expect anything back.

Annihilating tangos was an often thankless, unnoticed, and extremely violent job. Caleb's smile was feral as he reached for another Brazil nut and crunched down. Man, he *loved* what he did.

And that was the point of this mental masturbation. He, Gabriel, and Duncan had turned out fine without the guidance of their father. Bean would do the same.

And what? Caleb could watch his son grow through a chink in the hedge? An emotional fuckaroo. God, he was going to be his father. Flitting in and out of his son's life like a blue-assed fly. He'd be leaving Bean's training and the honing of his skills to others. Because to keep her safe, he couldn't be anywhere near *Heather*. And she would no sooner give him custody of their son than fly to the moon.

He cursed under his breath.

Shooting Caleb a glance, his face demonic in the lights from the dash, Rook asked, "You okay?"

Not by a Curse and a million miles. His life was fucked and going to get a hell of a lot worse. He wondered if this deep, unrelenting ache in his chest would ever go away. "I'm going to teleport us in so Heather can get a decent night's sleep. She needs it."

He had, what? Twenty-four hours to keep her safe? Then he was going to break the small thread of trust they'd built, and destroy her.

THE *SASSI*, MATERA
SUNDAY, APRIL 16
1000

Heather lay in the curve of his body, her butt pressed against his erection. Caleb buried his nose in her hair, and tightened his arm around her. He spread his fingers over the gentle curve of her belly, and felt that weird, painful void open in the center of his chest.

This time tomorrow she and Bean would be on a flight back to San Francisco. He'd keep the protection spell on her. He'd contact Gabriel and ask him to— Crapshitdamn. He didn't *want* another man raising his son. Even if that man was his brother. Partial custody? She might go for that.

He'd at least have an excuse to see her. Once in a while. How often? Once a year? Once a month? He could move closer to San Francisco. Hell, he didn't care where he lived . . .

She didn't move, but Caleb felt the rhythm of her breathing subtly change. *"Buona mattina il mio cuore,"* he said softly.

She wriggled against his body, taking his hand and shifting it from her stomach to her breast. Her nipples were hard, her body soft as she rolled over into him.

Giving him a sleepy, seductive smile, she wrapped her arms about his neck. "Hmm. Loosely translated that means: It's a glorious day, we're on our honeymoon, wanna fool around?"

Shifting over her, he separated her legs with his. "My God, you speak fluent Italian."

"Hmm, I do actually. But aren't Scotsmen supposed to speak Gaelic?"

"When in Rome . . ."

*   *   *

"You look good enough to eat," Caleb told Heather, sending her a heated glance as she removed an orange sherbet-colored cotton jacket that matched the flowers on her sundress. She'd slipped it on before going into one of the many small churches dotting the *sassi* neighborhood across the ravine from their hotel. The midmorning sun beat down on the creamy, tufa stone buildings, sending the temps way up. They both wore sunglasses to shield their eyes from the glare, although Heather slid hers on top of her head as soon as they walked in the shade of a row of houses.

His breath snagged as she shot him a sultry look from under long lashes. She was a natural flirt. Sweet and seductive, and for a little longer—his. "A sweet ripe peach," he said thickly, running his palm down the curve of her shoulder.

Her skin was warm and silky smooth. The sundress bared her pale arms and the swell of her breasts, but covered her gorgeous legs and swirled around her shapely ankles. She wore sandals and carried a disposable camera she'd insisted on buying in the gift shop of their hotel.

"Yeah, well, honeymoon or no honeymoon, I want to sightsee, so keep contact to hand-holding for a few more hours, Romeo," Heather told him dryly, looking ahead to where the cobbled path leveled out for a couple of houses, before stair-stepping up the hill to where hundreds more houses were situated almost one on top of the other. Caleb cared about only one of them.

Around that next corner their lives would change irrevocably.

He knew his team was in place even though they were invisible. Now, more than ever, he was determined to keep Heather and his child safe. In an hour, maybe less, they'd have Shaw in custody. And pretty damn soon after that he was going to have some explaining to do to the man's daughter.

And then he'd have to tell her good-bye.

"Geez," Heather said on a laugh. "Don't look so grim. If you want me to, I can rip off your clothes right here and have my wicked way with you."

Not wanting to telegraph his dread of what was to come, Caleb eased his expression into a smile. "Five feet from a church, Mrs. Edge? I had no idea pregnant women got so hot."

"Really? How unobservant of you. I thought I had your full attention this morning." She grinned, tucking her arm into his as they walked. She lifted her face to the sky, inhaling deeply.

"This day is absolutely perfect. And you chose *the* perfect, most wonderful place for a honeymoon."

He stopped, Shaw's house directly across the street, and pulled her inside a doorway alcove. "*You're* perfect. I love you, sweetheart. Remember that." He brushed her lips with his. Her hands clutched the front of his shirt as she stood on tiptoe to welcome his kiss. He kept it dry and brief with determination.

This was the last time he'd allow himself to be this close to her. He'd tried to store up memories this morning, when they made lazy love. Yet he still craved her. Still wanted her.

Convince her I love her, he reminded himself. *Convince myself that I don't. Yeah. That.*

Got it.

"I'll never let anything hurt you," he promised, wanting, *wishing,* he could promise her more perfect days in their future. He lay his hand on the gentle curve of her belly. "Or Bean. Ever."

She reached up to stroke his face. "I know. I think this is the first time in memory when I've felt so completely and utterly at peace." She grinned. "And the sex ain't half bad either."

Jesus. The glow of love on her face, the unmitigated trust he read in her beautiful big hazel eyes, twisted his gut into knots. The best he was going to be able to do was assure her that she'd be well taken care of. That they'd live in different states, rarely see each other.

And that she and his son would want for nothing.

He'd spend the rest of his life wanting *her*.

Too f-ing bad.

It was what it was.

History repeating itself, he though grimly. His parents had given love a shot. They'd sucked at it. And the Curse had still been in effect. No matter how freaking hard they'd tried to stay apart, they just hadn't been able to do it, and his mother had eventually died.

He *had* to let Heather go. But first he had to finish the job he'd come to do. He dropped her hands and stepped away from her. Once this was over he'd never see her again. That would be best. Clean and quick. Out of sight, please God, out of mind.

"Stay right here for a second, okay? I have a surprise for you."

"Really? What kind of surprise? Can I kiss it out of you? Tickle it out of you?"

"Give me a couple of minutes. I'll come and get you when I'm ready."

"That sounds extremely mysterious. I'll come with you."

He smiled as he shook his head. "Stay put, I'll call you over when it's . . . ready."

"Hmm. Okay. Kiss me good-bye first."

He made himself laugh. "I'll only be a minute—"

She pulled his head down for a quick kiss. Her lips felt smooth against his. Closed. Chaste, if he hadn't known what her mouth promised. No tongue. Still, he couldn't help it as his lips clung for an extra beat.

"Hurry back," she said, her voice husky. "I miss you already."

Caleb briefly touched a honeyed strand of hair curved on her sunwarmed shoulder before turning to stroll across the cobblestone path. The fifteen feet seemed like a hundred miles.

"What's up, boss?" Farris said quietly from beside him. "You're walking so freaking slowly it's like a rat crawled up your ass. What gives?"

Caleb kept walking. He knew the men inside Shaw's place were watching as he crossed between the houses. They would see a guy alone. Nothing threatening about a tourist in a loud red-and-yellow Hawaiian shirt, jeans, and running shoes.

"Doesn't feel right," he said almost as softly as his invisible friend, lips barely moving as he took his time getting to Shaw's front door.

Once he started the final stage of this op in motion, there'd be no turning back.

"Dekker and Rook are with her," Keir pointed out.

Yeah. Caleb knew. And he trusted his men to be his eyes and ears when his own weren't trained on her, but he still had this persistent itch between his shoulder blades.

Keir's hand settled lightly on Caleb's shoulder. "It'll be quick and painless."

"Yeah. I know," Caleb said under his breath.

Heather admired Caleb's loose-limbed stride as he strolled across the "street," if the wide path that allowed no motorized vehicles could be called that. He should have looked incongruous wearing that bright, tropical shirt in a historical place like the *sassi*. It was almost sacrilegious. Instead he looked confident and deliciously sexy.

She felt someone's gaze on her back and spun around, but there was no one there. Of course there wasn't. This scenic, historical area was *so* not her father's or his sophisticated banking clients' cup of tea.

"Relax," she said out loud. Lord, it was hot. She gathered her hair off her neck, holding it up in a ponytail, hoping for a bit of a breeze. There wasn't one. Wishing she'd brought a hat, she let her hair drop back to her shoulders.

She rested her hand on her tummy. Even through the heat, she felt oddly energized and ridiculously happy. And why wouldn't she? She was on her honeymoon, for goodness' sake. If a woman couldn't be ridiculously happy on her honeymoon, when could she be?

And just look at the long, lean hard body striding away. She gave her tummy a little rub. "Your daddy is a hunk, do you know that, sweet baby? He assures me that you're a boy. And *I* think you're going to be just like him, aren't you? Sweet and kind and funny. I suppose we'll spend the next twenty-one years paying for your therapy, because I have a feeling you'll always be Bean to us." She smiled.

"I hope he hurries up over there. I wouldn't mind getting inside where it's cool and I can have something to drink." She gave her middle a little rub. "I love you, sweetheart. We're so lucky, you and I, to have your father." Shoving her slightly damp hair off her face, Heather admired Caleb's butt as he reached up to knock on someone's front door.

Whose? He hadn't mentioned that he knew anyone here. Perhaps it was a restaurant, or a jewelry store, or—She grinned, remembering the heights he'd taken her to earlier. "Who cares. Anywhere your daddy wants to take us is fine with me."

After a few minutes the door opened. Caleb's body blocked whomever had opened it. He talked for a few minutes, then gestured behind him—presumably at her. The door closed, leaving him outside in the brilliant white sunshine. Hmm. Intriguing. Her hand curled over her stomach and time seemed to still.

"Heather? Sweetheart? Come on over." He didn't leave the doorway, but held out his hand with a smile that melted her heart and chased away whatever had spooked her.

The sun beat down ferociously on top of her head as she crossed the street. She took his outstretched hand just as the door started to open again. "Close your eyes," he murmured, tugging her against him. "I don't want to spoil the surprise."

She smiled, shutting her eyes. How sweet and romantic. He drew her forward, inside, where the temperature dropped dramatically. Heather shivered, getting a quick premonition that something wasn't right.

"Cold?" he asked softly. "Want to put on your jacket?"

She shook her head. Caleb tucked her beneath his left arm, his hand warm on her waist as he guided her across a slightly uneven floor. It took a surprising amount of energy to keep her voice light. "Can I open my eyes now?"

"Yeah. Open."

Heather blinked the fuzz from her vision. The blood drained from her head. "Oh, God, Caleb," she whispered. "What have you done?"

CHAPTER NINETEEN

THE *SASSI*, MATERA
SUNDAY, APRIL 16
1209

"Hello, Daddy."

"For God's sake, Heather," her father said by way of greeting, clearly furious. He sounded shockingly American, and looked completely out of context in this medieval setting. "Have you lost your goddamned *mind* coming here? And in *broad daylight*?"

His harsh words, and the fury on his face, directed at *her*, his princess, shocked her into taking an involuntary step backward. She needn't have bothered. Making no move to approach her, her father remained where he was. Irritated. Distant. She could have called this one, Heather thought bitterly. He was either the attentive, doting father or oblivious to her very existence. It had always been that way.

Right now he was not a happy camper seeing her here.

She'd only seen him truly angry once before this. The day her mother died.

Seeing him now, without warning, made the unpleasant mixture of love and hate she felt for him churn uncomfortably in her stomach. She held his gaze. *Are you all right? I miss you. Will this ever be over?* Her throat ached. Did *you kill my mother?*

His contact lens–enhanced blue eyes were disapproving. Her father, the original metrosexual, wasn't impressed by what he saw. He made a *moue* as he inspected her from top to toe, but didn't comment. As he tightened his lips, she watched him mentally putting her husband and her clothing choices in the same garbage can. *Oh, Daddy, you are such a damned snob even under these extreme circumstances.*

"Are you well?" he asked her after a moment.

Always a gentleman, Heather thought dryly at the polite inquiry. The question, she knew, was pretty much rhetorical. She wasn't sure if she was imagining the concerned subtext underlying the question. "Fine, thank you," she said automatically. Did he have any idea that both her bodyguards had died within a month of her leaving Paris? Since their only communication was supposed to have been when he discovered who had stolen his clients' money, probably not.

He gave a slight nod. "Excellent."

She smiled, despite the throbbing tension in the air. It had taken her years to realize that he was considerably more demonstrative in public. Clearly he didn't consider Caleb and his staff "public." She really could have done with a hug, but since that wasn't going to happen she merely said, "You look wonderful as always, Daddy."

And he did. Heather had absolutely no illusions about her father. Incredibly vain, he enjoyed being compared to Sean Connery in his later Bond movies, and dressed accordingly. He looked exactly like what he was, an obscenely wealthy man who took very good care of himself. He was obsessive about his macrobiotic diet, and unrelentingly disciplined about his rigorous exercise and weight-training program. His twice-a-week facials kept his skin smooth and vibrant, and his personal tanning bed kept him lightly bronzed all year long.

At sixty-three he was fit, attractive, polished, and sophisticated. And *always* number one.

Memories of a doting and attentive father when she was a small child kept the love she felt for him alive, but she sometimes wondered if he was the same man who used to push her on the swings and carry her on his shoulders. It had been a long time since they'd had that connection.

She was vaguely aware that the chilly, rough stone foyer of what appeared to be a giant catacomb was filled to capacity with many of his key personnel, and a phalanx of bodyguards. Worker bees in a hive, expressionless machines, armed with the most high-tech weaponry that only too much money could buy.

Still, he had a right to be livid, since he'd gone to a lot of trouble and expense to stay hidden. But they hadn't seen each other for more than a year; it would have been nice for him to greet her as if he'd missed her just a little.

His bodyguards were watching Caleb as if they expected him to pull out a machine gun and mow them down.

Right now she wasn't so sure she wasn't expecting the same thing. She was bewildered as to how this meeting had come about, and as she turned around, she shot her new husband a puzzled glance. Sometime in the last few seconds he'd managed to disengage from her, leaving her to stand alone. Cold suspicion trickled down her spine.

How had Caleb known where to find her father? Even she hadn't known where he was. "Why did you bring me here?"

This meeting didn't make any kind of sense. Suddenly *Caleb* didn't make sense. She realized, perhaps too damn late, that she knew very little about the man she'd married. She loved him, but she didn't know him at all.

She seemed to be batting zero in the love department.

"To reconcile with your father, sweetheart."

"That doesn't explain how you knew where to find him." Her lips felt numb. Oh God, her entire body felt numb. Was *Caleb* the "client" whose money had disappeared? No. That couldn't be. Could it?

He shrugged. "Just enjoy the moment."

Heather frowned at the nonanswer. *Enjoy* wasn't exactly the word she would use, she thought bitterly. She turned away from him. The very air in the room seemed to crackle with animosity. Her father was clearly not happy to see her, and seeing *him* again made her realize that she was as furious, saddened, and bewildered today as she had been a year ago. "We'll go," she told her father flatly.

"You'll stay until the matter has been resolved," Brian Shaw told her just as flatly. He motioned one of his men to search Caleb. "Who *is* this man?" he demanded in his most autocratic voice. "And what in God's name were you thinking bringing him here?"

Heather took a calming breath before saying mildly, "This *man*"—she lifted her chin a notch, not sure if she was just as angry as he was, totally confused, or living a nightmare. Or all three—"is my husband. Caleb Edge. And we're here on our honeymoon." How could something so right turn into something so wrong? How *had* Caleb found her father? Why had he found her father? And what part had she inadvertently played in this meeting? The questions and doubts tumbled around in her brain like rocks in a dryer.

Her father raised a brow mockingly. "Coincidentally in *Matera*?"

Excellent point. "I—" To which she had no answer. She gave him a cool look. "You could congratulate us."

She wanted to believe that Caleb had somehow tracked down her father for her sake. That he'd believed her when she'd told him she and her father were estranged, and he'd wanted to help.

But that didn't explain how a tractor salesman from Portland had managed to do what no one else had. Nor did it really explain why he'd done so.

Caleb's hands were raised shoulder high as her father's man searched him, none too gently.

"Daddy, don't!" Heather said, clinging to the hope of Caleb's innocence for a few more seconds.

Caleb didn't look particularly concerned. If anything he looked mildly amused, and a little bored.

She really didn't know him at all. She'd placed her safety and that of her unborn child in the hands of a man who could very well be the death of both herself and her father. Even doing her damnedest, Heather found it impossible to believe that he was completely innocent in this. What was he thinking? Was he scared? And trying to bluff it out? Or had he expected to be searched?

He caught her eye and deliberately winked. "Is this how they say hello in Matera? Kind of strange, but I'll go with it." He ignored the man frisking him. "Talk with your dad, honey," Caleb said easily. "We can't stay long."

We can't stay long? Heather repeated mentally. *We can't stay long? What are we* doing *here?* Caleb now appeared as relaxed and at ease as if he were attending a cocktail party. Neither the fact that he was in the process of having his jean-clad legs patted down nor the fact that he had a dozen guns pointed at his chest seemed to faze him in the least.

Which by rights should have fazed him a great deal. The situation sure as hell freaked *her* out. What man was ready to handle being frisked on his new father-in-law's orders, while on his honeymoon? Her mind raced as she tried to assimilate the *tableau vivant* before her so that it made a *modicum* of sense.

She understood her father's reaction to seeing her. He'd been adamant about them having absolutely no contact until he discovered who had killed her mother, and what that person had done with the funds stolen from one of his client's bank accounts. Terrified for her safety, positive that her mother's death was business related, and fearing that the killer would come after his daughter or himself next, he'd sent her away.

What she *didn't* understand was Caleb's motivation in bringing her and her father together. And it *had* been intentional, she had absolutely no doubt. She didn't believe in coincidence, which had kept her alive against a nameless, faceless enemy. She sent her handsome husband another glance. He smiled, tugging his clothing back into place, and jerked his head toward her father. She put her hand over her belly, and couldn't even force a smile to her stiff mouth.

Had he stumbled across her in San Francisco, immediately recognized her as the daughter of the wealthy Brian Shaw and decided . . . what? To extort money from her father? Threaten him? Blackmail him, or blackmail *her*?

Or worse. Her blood froze in her veins, flushing her body with ice. Had he used her to somehow track down her father to *kill* him? She rubbed the goose bumps on her bare arms.

Who could she trust?

She was the focus of all eyes, standing partway between the two men. "Have you two met?"

"No." The answer came from her father and Caleb simultaneously.

One question answered from the dozens churning in her brain right now. If they didn't know each other, how *had* Caleb tracked him down? Oh God, more important—*why, why, why*? She shot another glance at her husband. His face was inscrutable.

"How did you two meet?" her father demanded, accepting a glass of spring water from his aide, but not offering anything to his guests.

"In San Francisco. I'd like a water, please." After a brief nod from her father, the man went off to get another glass of water for her. Her knees felt rubbery, and she would have loved to sit down. But there were no chairs in the room. And she was so cold now her teeth were practically chattering. Or was that nerves?

Both. Either.

"We bumped into each other in the grocery store . . ."

Caleb tuned out their conversation, observing the body language between father and daughter with a slight frown. Heather didn't know it, but he'd allotted five minutes to the reunion. He'd honor that time frame.

And then the proverbial turd of all time would hit the fan. He wasn't looking forward to it.

Unobserved, as Heather and her father spoke, key men in Shaw's employ were quietly disappearing one by one from behind him as Dekker effortlessly teleported them to a secure location across town. Not the safe house where they'd been staying, and where they'd take Shaw directly after he was teleported. And where Caleb was going to have to tell Heather a little more of the truth before handing her father off to another team for interrogation. If she'd listen to him.

Then he'd be gone. Off, hopefully, to a mission filled with violence, aggression, and shit blowing all to hell. The more fucking down and dirty, the worse the odds, the better, he thought with desperate relish. He needed to pound the living crap out of something. Soon.

Against his own better judgment, and the strong suggestion of his team, Caleb had wanted Heather to have her reunion with her father here. Where he lived. In his own setting, instead of across town. Not because it was a great location, but because *here* was not the cluster *there* was going to be.

He was almost ashamed at how cowardly that decision was, God help him. As far as the mission went, taking the Shaws directly to the secured area would be the most expedient course of action, he knew. Less fuss, less muss. Took extraneous elements out of the equation.

Bringing Heather here had done what he'd needed. Visual range of Shaw was necessary for teleportation. The problem was, once *Heather* was teleported there'd be shitloads of goddamned fuss and muss.

If she was confused *now*, wait ten minutes. Caleb wanted to put that confrontation off for as long as possible.

Giving her five minutes wasn't going to kill them. She was in no danger inside her father's stronghold. Hell, she was in no danger *period* because of the protective spell he'd put over her.

He knew Rook was back there, sealing Shaw's foot soldiers inside their quarters with a simple holding spell. The garbage team would be in later to sweep them up. He knew, thanks to the preplanning, that Farris would be behind Shaw. If Shaw or the men standing in a semicircle behind him made so much as a hair's movement toward Heather, the team had instructions to cut the reunion drastically short.

With coded sign language, so subtle no one but another T-FLAC operative would notice, he had Farris move his position between Heather and her father while he ambled over and held up a wall with his shoulder, watching father and daughter through hooded eyes. He mentally continued the five-minute countdown. Minute to go. Observing them together, he considered even that short a time together too long. Unless they were communicating telepathically, they had nothing to say to each other.

It was painful.

Time to shimmer. His lips twitched slightly as a man across the room behind Shaw suddenly noticed that the guy next to him had vanished into thin air in the middle of a whispered conversation. His eyes rolled, and he started falling to the stone floor in a dead faint. Then he vanished too as Dek snatched him into the teleport with his buddy. Show-off.

Brian made a grab for Heather's arm, startling her. Her eyes went wide. Caleb pushed away from the wall with a frown as Shaw pulled his daughter closer. "You can't keep it, Heather. You must know that would be a death sentence."

Caleb's radar tuned in.

"What?" Heather blew out an exasperated breath, tugging at her arm. "Good grief, Daddy. What on *earth* are you talking about?"

"God damn it! I should have known." He was even more pissed off. "I've had my people searching all over the world for her accomplice, and all this time it was you!"

Heather pulled out of his grip, rubbing her arm. "Are you out of your mind? Accomplice to what? And who is 'she'?"

CHAPTER TWENTY

Good questions, Caleb thought with a small amount of pride.

"You were the last person to see your mother alive," her father said. The thought seemed to please him, as if a puzzling piece of information had finally come to light. Caleb didn't like the man's tone. And apparently Heather was having none of the triumphant hug her dad wanted to bestow on her. She stepped several feet out of reach.

Brian took a step, too, his eyes bright. "She did give it to you, didn't she?"

"I wasn't the last person to see Mom alive, Daddy. *You* were. She and I spent that morning at the flea market, and then—" she shrugged a very Gallic shrug. "You know the rest."

Say what? Caleb, on the presumption that one or more of his men were there, motioned *hold*. He wanted to hear this. As far as they knew, both Heather and her father had been out of France when Babette Shaw had been murdered. Instead, they had both been at the house with her that day?

"Your memory is faulty, my dear. Now. Where is it?"

"It?" Heather repeated hollowly, her gaze flickering to the back of the room as the last of her father's men was removed by Dekker. She blinked, rubbing her temple with her fingertips. "What?" she asked, clearly confused.

"The *money!*"

"*What* money?" Her shoulders were so stiff Caleb thought she might shatter. This could wait until—

"My *client's* money," Shaw snapped. "The money that mysteriously disappeared out of my client's account last March. *That* bloody money, Heather. Forty-eight billion dollars and change that your mother stole.

"She gave it to you, so now what have you done with it? You have to tell me!"

Obviously stunned, Heather stared at her father as if she'd never seen him before. "Money? You think *she* stole money? My *mother?*"

"Of course your mother! Who do you think I mean? Queen Elizabeth? Why do you think I've been stuck in this godforsaken *anthill* for more than a year? What did you think I meant that day when I said the money was gone?"

"*One* client. A few million, for God's sake, Daddy!" She rubbed her forehead. "*Forty-eight billion dollars?* I had no idea. Why would *she* steal money from you?"

"Punishment. Retribution. Who knows."

"She was upset when she found out who you did business with, I'll grant you that. But she wouldn't steal—" She turned to look at Caleb, her expression haunted. "My mother would never steal anything. She wasn't like that."

"You told *him?*" Brian spun around and glared at Caleb.

"That you misappropriated forty-eight *billion* dollars of assets from your clients?" He whistled while shaking his head no. "Jesus," he said with false sympathy. "No wonder the Jets and the Sharks are pissed off and hunting you down like a dog. Gonna get ugly."

"No one was supposed to goddamned *find* me until I had the money back where it belongs." His attention stayed on Caleb, but he was still speaking to his daughter. He stepped closer to her, not noticing that he now had no security at his back.

"Your mother wanted it all, my darling," Shaw modulated the ugly tone for something more controlled. "Every cent. Babette cleaned out all my client accounts. Cleaned them out. *All* of them. That astronomical dollar amount is just my *client's* account; she didn't touch our personal finances at all. She wanted me dead, Heather. Do you understand what I'm saying? She knew what my clients would do to me when they discovered what she'd done. She wanted me to die slowly and without mercy. *That's* what this was about. A vindictive woman and revenge."

Heather was slowly shaking her head in disbelief.

"Help me, darling. Just tell me what you did with whatever she gave you before she died. Or what she said. She had to have said something."

"Daddy, Maman was dead when I came downstairs, remember?" she said gently, with a small, telling catch in her voice. She was scared, and confused, but she was also starting to get pissed off with her father's line of questioning if not his tone. "She didn't say *anything*."

Instinctively Caleb knew she was lying. And he'd bet his last paycheck that the woman *had* given her daughter something.

Shaw stroked his mustache pensively, "You must be mistaken! Think, Heather!"

Hell, Caleb thought furiously. *What* a clusterfuck this simple mission had turned out to be. All this for nothing. Not *nothing,* a small voice whispered in his head.

Without Shaw he wouldn't have met Heather. There'd be no Bean . . .

Yeah, asshole, he mocked himself. *But you don't have them either, do you?*

Crapshitdamn.

He'd take the man in, until this information was authenticated, but God damn it, the trail for the money had suddenly gone stone-cold. The *mission* had turned to shit. They'd wanted Shaw so that they could confiscate and cut off the funds to the terrorists who right now thought that *Shaw* still had their money. If Shaw didn't have the money, he was just a cold-eyed, shitty father in a good suit.

If the bad guys couldn't have Shaw, the next person they'd go after would be *Heather.*

Not *would be. Was.*

The kidnapping attempts, and attempts on her life—the tangos wanted what Shaw wanted. The money. They wouldn't believe that she didn't know. Nobody would believe that she didn't know if Shaw was suddenly taken out of the picture.

Caleb would be damned if he would let her out of his sight until he had someone to keep an eye on her—

He had an idea. A damn fine idea.

She wasn't going to be happy, but for the foreseeable future his lovely bride was going to make her home at Edridge Castle. Gabriel and MacBain could keep an eye on her and Bean.

Christ, that was brilliant, he congratulated himself.

"The only thing I took when *you* hustled me out of the house that afternoon was the jewelry," she said through clenched teeth. "And *you* gave me that."

Hustled Heather out of the country, Caleb knew, with a box of jewelry and only two men to guard her against some of the worst, most violent tangos on the planet. How she'd managed to survive this long on her own, he had no idea. Fury rose inside him at this man's casual disregard for his daughter.

It was clear that Heather loved the man; why, Caleb had no idea. Thank God it was also apparent, to him at least, that she wasn't willing to take her father's bullshit.

The son of a bitch waved a well-manicured hand, dismissing several million dollars' worth of jewels. "The transfer was made the night before—Damn it! Did she converse with anyone at the street fair that morning?"

"Not that I saw. We were together the entire time."

"Someone she could have given something to? Something small. Papers? A key? Bloody hell, Heather, a goddamned scrap of paper with a bank account number on it? *Anything*?!"

"She wasn't out of my sight all morning. Not for a second."

"Are you positive?"

"Yes." A fine tremor shook her body. She didn't take her eyes off her father as he approached. "Yes, I'm positive."

Shaw took his daughter's jaw in his cupped hand, looking into her eyes. "I don't believe you, my darl—"

Pop. The distinct sound of a silencer.

A bullet hole appeared between Shaw's brows. Heather jerked in response, opening her mouth to scream—

Jesus Christ. He'd been a hundred fucking ways wrong on this mission, Caleb thought, watching fear follow surprise and leach the color from her cheeks. She did scream as her father fell against her. Unable to brace his full weight, they crashed to the floor together. Eyes wild, she cradled her father's body in her lap.

"No. Neither do I," a new voice inserted coolly, from a partially open side door. The man stepped into the room. Caleb recognized him instantly. Oh, Christ. Lark was right. *Worse* than the Sharks and the Jets.

Fazuk Al-Adel.

"No." Al-Adel motioned Caleb to stay where he was as his men flooded the room. "Don't move. One of my men might accidentally hit the girl."

Caleb raised a brow. He didn't waste time wondering if his own men were in position. Why Dekker hadn't been on this guy before he got in. If Farris had returned, or if Rook had finished securing the grunts in back.

He, Heather, and her dead father were the only ones here. And *she* was Caleb's only concern. His eyes locked on Heather as he ignored the man's directive. Looking shell-shocked, she crouched on the floor, holding her father.

Even in quadruple time, faster than anyone's eyes could possibly see him, Caleb kept his body between Heather and Al-Adel and his men as he raced to her side.

Her eyes went wide, confused, as she frantically looked around for him. *"Caleb?!"*

She didn't have time to draw in the breath needed to scream. He yanked her onto her feet, and into his arms, and got her the hell out of Dodge.

CHAPTER TWENTY-ONE

Heather lay in the curve of his arms, her back pressed against his chest. He'd TiVoed time back to that morning. Caleb buried his nose in her hair, tightening his arms around her.

Been here. Done this.

His heart pounded as hard as it had the last time. But in *this* version of this morning the reaction was caused by residual fear, not anticipation. And *this* morning he didn't have a giant cockstand. And frankly, even if he had one, right now he felt too enervated to do anything about it. He frowned. He was accustomed to losing some physical strength when he TiVoed time. But lately the aftereffects had been excessive. He was weaker for longer. He didn't like it. More, it concerned him because it was something that had only been happening recently. Lark may have been right. Damn.

He'd just have to keep Heather in bed for the next couple of hours until he recovered, he thought with a small smile. Not a bad way to recuperate. In a few minutes she'd stir, stretch, then roll into him and lift her mouth to his for a kiss. And in the meantime, he'd have a few minutes to regain his equilibrium.

When she woke up she wouldn't remember what had just transpired. Thank God. He sometimes wished he didn't have to remember each version of each event, either.

Gliding his hand between Heather's breasts he paused, surprised to find her heartbeat manic instead of the steady beat from sleep as he remembered.

"Get your goddamned hands off me, you bastard."

One moment she'd been snuggled supple and sexy in his arms, the next she was scrabbling across the bed in a tangle of limbs and sheets. Palm to her forehead, she staggered to her feet, obviously light-headed from the teleportation, the backspacing of time, and the pregnancy.

White-faced, and not able to stand, she sank onto the foot of the bed, dazed and disoriented. Pressing her hands to her face, she moaned. Caleb tried to get up to help her, but God damn it, he was too weak to even sit up. Fear grabbed him by the throat. What the fuck was going on?

He couldn't take care of her like this . . . A sharp surge of panic washed through him. Jesus. This was bad. *Really* bad.

"What happened, sweetheart?" He managed to keep his fear out of his voice, while his mind raced. It scared the crap out of him that his voice was so weak. "Bad dream?"

He had to contact the team. Farris had to teleport her to Edridge Castle and Gabriel stat. "Sweetheart, talk to me."

Heather blinked several times to bring Caleb into focus. The son of a bitch had somehow found her father. How and why she had no idea. But as soon as she'd taken care of her father she was going to damn well find out.

The world spun crazily for a moment as a kaleidoscope of memories and sensations flooded her. She frowned. God, she was dizzy. And sick to her stomach. Had she been hurt and not realized it? She didn't see any obvious injuries. Oh God! The baby! Automatically, she touched her belly, comforted to feel the little bump of Bean.

Heart racing, she tried to open her eyes so she could find out what hospital was treating her father, but vertigo and nausea kept her pinned where she was. Squeezing her eyes closed, she sat very still, hoping the disorientation would soon pass. She must have fainted after he'd been shot. Although she'd never fainted in her life. But then she'd never been pregnant either.

Bean. Was fine, she knew instinctively as she lifted her hand away from her stomach.

Caleb was anything but. Unluckily for him, he was in the room with her. She had questions for him to answer. The son of a bitch.

It was her father who needed help. After he recovered, she'd shoot him herself. Damn him. She was so freaking furious at both of them.

How convenient for her father to forget that *he* was the one responsible for her mother's death. Accidental, or murder. He'd been the one to push her. Perhaps all of this business had driven him to some sort of breakdown? She bit her lip.

How badly had her father been hurt? God, there'd been a lot a blood . . . Where was he? Had that man taken him before he could get proper medical attention? Oh God . . .

"Daddy?" She blinked. Frowned. Blinked again, and slowly looked around the room. Their *hotel* room. A second ago she'd watched as a bullet slammed into her father's forehead.

Heart pumping as though she'd been running, she remembered the sensation of warm wetness as her father's blood soaked the front of her dress.

She looked down. She was naked.

That wasn't right. Her head shot up and she found Caleb watching her with concern. He too was naked. He looked like a *Playgirl* centerfold sprawled out on the bed, all bronzed and sexy on the white sheets; the morning sunshine streaming through the open window made his skin gleam.

No. That wasn't right either. He'd been wearing *jeans*. A Hawaiian shirt . . .

Wait! her brain screamed. She wasn't in her father's house. There were no armed men around and no blood. But it seemed so vivid. How could something that real be nothing more than a nightmare?

"That was no freaking nightmare," she insisted, talking out loud. Oh, God. She desperately wanted it to have been nothing more than her active imagination following her into sleep. But something warned her that somehow, how she had no idea, what she'd experienced had been real.

"It must've been pretty damn terrifying. You're white as a sheet." He held out his hand, looking as pale as he'd accused her of being. "Come back to bed, sweetheart. Let me hold you."

She held up a hand. "Give me a minute." When she thought she could stand without falling over, she got up and crossed to where her suitcase had been placed on a chair under the window.

Opening it, she took out the sundress she'd been wearing. No blood. Other than a few creases, it was spotless. "Did I wake up last night?" she demanded, frowning.

"No. I carried you in from the car. You slept from the airport until a few moments ago . . ."

"If I was asleep the entire time, how do I know that

the bathroom is down those steps?" Stepping into a skimpy peach-colored thong, she put on the matching bra, then pulled the dress over her head. "How do I know the tile in there is green?" She did up a loose button between her breasts. "How do I know the hallway to the bathroom leads out onto a patio overlooking the ravine? How could I *possibly* know all that if I was asleep and this is the first I've seen of this room?"

"Obviously you were awake enough to look around. And you did go into the bathroom during the night."

Okay, that was a possibility. The rational side of her weighed his perfectly reasonable explanation against the sensation churning in her gut. That feeling you get when you know something is wrong but can't quite pinpoint what.

She decided to go with her gut. Slipping on her sandals, she made a derisive noise in her throat and glared at the virtual stranger who was her husband. "The first time I wandered around this room was this morning after we made love. Why are you lying to me, Caleb?"

Odder still, why hadn't he at least got out of bed for this conversation? He wasn't the kind of man to lounge around—or maybe he *was*. She really didn't know.

"About what?"

"Everything, I suspect." Her chest was tight; she could barely catch her breath. She felt more than a flicker of apprehension as she watched him carefully, trying to read his closed expression. My God, she thought sickly, did I really believe that I could trust this man? Was I really that stupid, that desperate to think he loved me? Love at first sight? Lord, what a fool she'd been.

She swiped her tongue across her dry lips. "You brought me to Italy to see my father, didn't you?"

"What makes you say that?"

That wasn't a no. Was it her imagination or did his

eyes flicker a little? Was that his tell? The subtle action
that he couldn't control when he was lying, or was it
genuine surprise? Affronted annoyance?

"Up until half an hour before the wedding," he said
calmly—irritatingly calmly—"I thought both your parents were dead, remember?"

She regarded him for a heartbeat and a half. "That
was the first you knew about my father?"

Again with the flicker eyes. "Of course, honey." He
patted the mattress. "Come back to bed."

"I don't believe you." She held his gaze, as if that was
strong enough to hold him back. To keep him away
from her. "He lives in that house right there across the
ravine." She half turned to point, then spun around to
pin him with a glare, stunned as the answer came to her.

Oh God, now everything made sense. It had all been
one big setup. Love was supposed to be blind, not stupid. He'd played her, perfectly. "You were trying to find
my father," her voice flattening out on the last word.
"*That's* why you 'accidentally' bumped into me in San
Francisco, wasn't it? What did you do? Hypnotize me?
Drug me?" She took her purse out of her suitcase, then
slammed the lid closed and went to stand at the foot of
the bed.

"We showered together, we had breakfast in the din-
ing room. There's a picture of Mary and Jesus over the
buffet—"

"Almost every public building in Italy has a picture of
Mary and Jesus somewhere, sweetheart."

"Not one with the top left corner torn. We had fruit,
bread, and coffee. We shared a strawberry yogurt. Then
we walked around the *sassi*, went to the little church
right there. Then you told me to wait because you had a
surprise for me. The surprise was my father's execu-
tion." Her knuckles showed white as she tightened her

fingers around her purse. "That was no damn *dream*. Who the hell *are* you?"

"No way." Cold clammy sweat suffused Caleb's body as he managed to haul himself up on his elbows. His stomach protested big-time. He'd give his right nut for a Brazil nut right now. He swallowed the nausea and concentrated on Heather.

No way. There was no f-ing way she could possibly remember. Except that he'd *heard* her. She *did* know. How? He had no idea. But she had full recall.

"No way?" she repeated incredulously. "*No way* you're going to tell me who you really are?"

God damn it. When was this fatigue and nearly continual feeling that he was about to hurl going to wear off? He was about to have one of the most important conversations of his life. He sure as shit didn't want to have it while he was flat on his ass.

His eyes narrowed. "Are you telling me you *remember*?"

"Make it fast, and don't insult my intelligence by lying. And would you *please* get up and put some clothes on?"

"Amazing. I mean—Shit, you have no idea how fu-freaking amazing it is that you re—" He rubbed a hand across his jaw as his mouth flooded with saliva. "Look." He swallowed hard, hating to have to ask. "I'll tell you anything you want to know, if you'd hand me that can of nuts on the table behind you."

She stuck her hand on her hip. "You're going for the insanity defense. Is that it?"

"Please?" Christ, if he hurled now, he'd . . . Caleb caught the can in midair. "Thanks." He held up a hand. "Sec—" Pried off the lid and tossed a handful into his mouth, barely chewing, the salt on his tongue enough to calm the storm. *Ahh.*

"I'm pissed, waiting for an explanation, and you're

snacking?" Her lips clamped in anger. "Keep it up, bud, and that insanity defense might work."

"Know what this is?" Caleb held up the can.

"A can of Brazil nuts, being eaten by the biggest nut of all?"

At least she was still there. Unfortunately he could almost hear the tick-tick-tick of a metronome counting off the seconds until she walked out that door. He couldn't let her do that. He needed to buy some time. Even now the nutmeat was soothing the sickening gurgle in his stomach.

"I'm apparently having your cravings."

Suspicion gleamed from her eyes. "I don't have any."

"*Exactly.* I'm having them *for* you. The nausea? I'm having that for you too. Backaches? Check. If a pregnant woman gets leg cramps—I'm experiencing those as well."

She snorted, disbelief in the sound. "Are you going to have the baby for me too?"

Caleb closed his eyes, said a quick prayer for patience, then looked at her. "That would be one hell of a trick, don't you think?"

She tucked her purse under her arm. "I'm done. Had enough. I'll alert the AMA and Jerry Springer, 'cause I'm sure the world will be fascinated by the first man to ever have such severe sympathy pains. Where's your extra five pounds? Never mind, just tell me who the hell you are so I can get it right on *Oprah.*"

"You're a riot." Caleb found himself totally drawn to the fire in her glare. "Let me just figure out the best way to—No. There isn't—You're right. Get to the point. Yeah. Got it. I've never had to do this before. Never."

"Yeah, fine. Whatever. This better be good. Let me make it easy for you. Start with name, rank, and serial number. Are you after my father? Is he really dead? How did you get me back here? Who do you work for?"

"T-FLAC. It's an independent counterterrorist organization. We were onto your father long before the funds were misappropriated last March."

She frowned. "What does a counterterrorist group want with my father? He's not a terrorist. He's a *banker*."

"His clients are tangos. Terrorists."

"N—" She started to deny it, then bit her lower lip. "But *he* isn't a terrorist. He's a victim. He was shot, remember?"

"Yeah, I remember, but *you* aren't supposed to."

"Hypnosis? I've never been susceptible. I could have told you it wouldn't work."

"Not hypnosis—"

"No? What drug *did* you give me? Damn it, Caleb! Don't you know that anything I put in my system goes directly into the baby. You—"

"I didn't drug you and I would never hurt Bean. We'll get to that in a minute. It's easier if I explain things to you one topic at a time. Terrorists first. Specifically, your father."

He could tell the leap hadn't been that hard for her. "So what does he have to do with me? Why track me down—And how did you do that? Oh, shit. The robbery at Munzinger's jewelers. You found me by my fingerprints, didn't you?"

Damn, she was smart. "Yeah. My assignment was to get your father's location."

She scowled. "I didn't know it. I was an assignment?"

"I had no way of knowing that you and your father had parted ways."

"So you just opted to seduce me anyway?" Heather lifted one hand. "Don't bother answering that. It was rhetorical," she said bitterly. "Stupid me. It never occurred to me to wonder why a man on a business trip, a man staying in a hotel, was shopping for *groceries*. Or how you knew where I lived when I'd never given you my address or even my real name. And I was so freaking careful! How'd you get past my defenses?"

"Making love to you was never the plan. I was supposed to get the information about Brian Shaw and get out. It wasn't about seducing you." He kept his gaze locked with hers, trying to make her understand. "It's not supposed to get personal."

"Here's an update, Caleb. It doesn't get much more personal than screwing me senseless. Might not have been the 'plan,' but it happened anyway. Did you not use protection on purpose? Did you want to impregnate me?"

"Jesus, Heather!" Most of the vertigo from the time jump was dissipating, thank God. He managed to drag himself to a sitting position and lean against the headboard. "No. Of course not."

"There's no 'of course' about it. It happened. And you did it for power—No. Not power. You have that already. No. You did it to manipulate me into doing exactly as you wanted. And how did you imagine that I wouldn't remember what happened yesterday?"

This was the tricky part. Caleb knew he had to do this right. "It happened today."

She glanced at the bedside clock. "Yesterday. It's only eight A.M. You took me to him, like a possible lamb to slaughter, at about ten yesterday morning."

"Believe me." Why should she? He shook his head and forged on. "It was *this* morning. This is our second shot at today." He watched her face and saw that she was ready to call bullshit on him. "You're asking me to tell you something only a few people, people like me, know."

"Like you? What? Other lying, cheating, opportunists?"

"I have the ability to manipulate time." He braced for her reaction.

She looked ready to nail him in the head with her purse. "Manipulate *people,* you mean."

"That too. I'm a wizard."

Heather tossed her head back, an incredulous expression crossing her face. "Beep! Wrong answer."

CHAPTER TWENTY-TWO

"No one has ever been aware of it when I've manipulated time. No one who was present when we confronted your father will remember that we, my team, were there at all. For them, it'll be like it never happened."

"A wizard who can reverse time? Do I look like I have *stupid* tattooed on my forehead?"

"It's the truth."

She leveled her gaze on him. "That's the lamest load of garbage I've ever heard."

He merely looked at her.

"If it is, then prove it. If what happened this morning didn't happen, then my father wasn't shot."

"That would be partly correct. Some of what happened this morning won't happen on the second replay. You and Bean were my concern. The op was going to hell, I had to get you out of there."

She slowly lowered her arm. "Is my father alive?"

"No, I'm sorry." Her chin trembled and Caleb gulped past the surge of nausea. "Someone on my team teleported him when I took you. He was dead then. He's dead now."

"*Teleported?!*" Heather shook her head, and cut to the chase. "Pretty damn convenient for you." Caleb could see the wheels turning before she blurted, "But if he'd been left there, he'd be alive?"

"Yeah. But he wa—"

"Do it again. Do whatever you did." She waved a hand. Her ring, the wedding band he'd put on her finger, shot sparklers of refracted light against the walls in the sunlight, illuminating the tears welling in her eyes. "Undo whatever."

"It doesn't work that way." His gut clenched.

"Really." She knelt one knee on the bench at the foot of the bed, swiping away the moisture from her face. She didn't look like a woman settling in for a heart-to-heart. But she wasn't running for the door either. "How *does* it work then? Is my dead father on another astral plane? Will we have to get a Ouija board? A crystal ball? Some eye of newt?"

Caleb decided to treat it as a genuine question. He chewed on a nut and thanked God that his strength was gradually returning.

"If I'd had the time"—he didn't add *and the f-ing inclination*—"and had gotten to your father fast enough, then *possibly* I *might* have been able to perform the revivification spell."

"Reviv—" She took her knee off the bench and stood. "Ah-huh."

"Frankly, I'm not sure that I can perform that on anything other than animals. This isn't an exact science. The only success I've had was with animals when I was a kid. It didn't always work."

"Ah-huh."

"Like twenty percent. There's a finite window of time in which it has to be attempted, anyway." He had to buy more time. "If too much time passes after a death, it's too late." He glanced at his watch. "It's been more than half an hour since your father was shot. Too long. In my experiments, the most time that could lapse between death and revivification was just over a minute. And that was for a twenty-pound *dog*." Duncan's Dixie. Caleb's kid brother had been grateful for months.

"Tell you what," Heather told him. "Put it all in a memo and e-mail me, okay?"

Oh, crap. She was going to split. "Hang on. Didn't you have other questions?" Caleb asked desperately, tossing his can of nuts on the bed.

"Yes. I do. About a million. But apparently, you think what you've done to me is one big joke. So don't bother. I'm sure I won't believe your answers anyway!"

"I swear to God, I'll answer truthfully."

"Do wizards believe in God?"

He grit his teeth. "Yes."

"You contacted me in San Francisco to track down my father?"

"Right. But you didn't know where he was. We found him another way."

"Did you get that woman pregnant too?"

"No other woman. And I swear on Bean's life, getting you pregnant wasn't intentional."

"Don't bring Bean into this, damn you."

"Okay. Okay. I was a bastard to sleep with you, I admit it. But damn it, Heather. I'm not sorry. We had—"

"And if I hadn't been pregnant, would you have come back? Would you have married me?"

Shit. "It was the only way I could get at your father. I have to be in visual range to teleport someone else. But no matter the assignment, the minute I found out about the baby I would have convinced you to marry me."

"Let me see if I'm getting all this right. You married me for access to my father. Then you planned to teleport him somewhere else. After that he'd—what? Go to jail? Be put to death for treason or something? And it didn't cross your mind that that would hardly be conducive to a happy marriage? Or didn't you plan on this marriage lasting after you got to my father?"

The skin across her cheekbones grew taut, and her dry eyes glittered. "It wasn't love at first sight, was it?"

His stomach lurched. "No."

"Well, that at least is honest—assuming I buy the whole wizard thing. I guess I should thank you for setting me straight. Well, good luck with your hunt. I presume my lawyer can send the divorce papers to your office? Or was Preda as fake as you are?"

Caleb scooted toward the edge of the bed, wishing he was freaking dressed, but not having the juice to do so yet. "What did your mother give you, Heather?"

"Not a damn thing."

"Your father was scared. And he had just cause. If *he* didn't embezzle the money from his client, then someone else *did*. With your father dead, that person will come after you. It's the logical next step. They've already made a couple of half-assed attempts at grabbing you. Now they'll get serious."

She paused by the door, her hand on the knob. "Well, I can't help you."

"The funds were transferred out of your father's account at three A.M. the day your mother died. The transfer was done from a computer on the grounds of your family estate in Paris. Who had that kind of access?"

He saw that he'd hit an emotional bull's-eye as she bit the corner of her lower lip. "My father," she finally said. "My mother. Me."

"It wasn't you. And it wasn't, apparently, your father. So that leaves your mother."

"Who's *dead*."

Caleb stroked his chin as he worked the sequence through in his head. "Between three A.M. and the time the two of you returned from your outing and she was killed, she must have passed that information on to *someone* else. Who could it have been?"

Heather was obviously rattled, but prepared to bolt.

"I have no clue, but good luck finding them," she said, turning the handle.

Desperate, Caleb shouted, "You can't leave!"

The door slammed behind her.

Blinded by tears, Heather ran, stumbling down the uneven path outside their room. She slowed down a little because the cobblestones were treacherous underfoot, but she still moved fast. As if the hounds of Hell were after her.

"Bastard!" She stumbled. "Damn it!" Choking back sobs of rage, embarrassment, and disbelief, Heather caught herself before tripping. She had to keep going. The sun, golden warm, beat down on her head and bare shoulders. Rain should have been boiling out of a black sky to suit her mood. Didn't she deserve crappy weather after being taken advantage of by a madman?

Hearing women talking in rapid Italian behind her, she walked faster, not wanting anyone to hear her talking to herself—crying, raging, and berating were more accurate terms.

She didn't have her freaking sunglasses, so she crossed to the shade on the other side of the path. "Son of a bitch. *Wizard,* my butt."

Damn it. She needed her suitcase. Which was back in their room, probably with her shades. All she had in this purse were a few hundred American dollars, a brush, a lip gloss, and Hallelujah! She sniffed, gaining control of her careening emotions. Her *passport.* She wasn't without resources. Any number of friends would send her money if she made a phone call . . .

And involve them in this mess? After having disappeared for a year to avoid exactly this situation? No. She'd rely on her own common sense, she'd already proven she could. Until Caleb, she thought, fresh tears heating her eyes.

What a gullible, stupid fool she'd been. Love at first sight? In real life? In *her* real life?

She'd been desired by men countless times. For her wealth, for her looks, for her social connections, for a hundred reasons that men and women played the mating game. Because it was fun. Because it was what men and women did. She'd cared for some of the men in her life, and they had genuinely cared for her. Some had tried to use her. But she'd never been played for such a fool. She'd never been used like this.

And as for her father—Heather's stomach roiled. She pressed her fist to her middle as she walked. "Sorry Bean. *Hearing* the word *terrorist* from my father a year ago doesn't even come *close* to meeting them face-to-face." Probably because he'd intentionally only told her the tip of the iceberg about his business dealings. Just enough to make her scared enough to run, and stay hidden, while he tried to find the money.

She thought of her mother, and sorrow clutched at her throat. Knowing what she knew now, Heather believed her father *had* killed her in a fit of rage. Rage brought on by the very real fear of what his client would do to him when he discovered that his money was missing.

Her entire life had been built on quicksand.

Not had been—still was.

She'd never fallen so hard, so fast for a man.

She'd never before been quite that vulnerable, Heather thought bitterly, angrily swiping the moist streaks from her cheeks. Never been that open. That damn *needy*. The tears dried stiff on her cheeks as she continued down the winding path toward the foot of the steep ravine, propelled now by anger, muttering furiously to herself. "You used me, you bastard," She walked faster. Worse—"I *let* y—"

She screamed, scrambling backward, her back thump-

ing into a wall behind her as Caleb suddenly materialized out of thin air right in front of her.

He was gloriously, unabashedly, stark naked.

Hand over her leaping heart, she stared at him, open-
mouthed in shock. Her blood still ran hot, and her pulse
throbbed beneath her skin. She was surprised. Angry.
Confused as hell. Not even a teensy bit turned on to see
his bronzed skin gleam satin in the brilliant sunlight,
as she followed the dark line of hair pointing down to
his heavy sex. She dragged her attention up his chest
to his face. Her mouth was bone-dry. "How—"

"You can't be out here alone, Heather," he told her
grimly, stepping forward, seemingly unaware of his
nakedness, as comfortable as a warrior. "Al-Adel obviously knew your father's location. I don't want that sick
son of a bitch anywhere near you. Come back to the
hotel. Please." He held out his hand, palm up.

Two elderly, black-garbed women, shopping baskets
on their arms, passed behind Caleb. Their eyes went
wide as they saw him, and then they giggled, heads together like teenagers as they continued down the hill,
shooting backward glances as they walked.

Heather swallowed hard. "I'm going over there to see
if my father is really there, or . . ."

"He's not." His hands clamped on her upper arms,
and his nearness immediately spiked her internal temperature, throwing her off balance. "If you want to see
his body, I swear I'll take you to see him. But you have
to get inside. Now."

And then they were inside their room. Heather blinked
at the dimness, dizzy and disoriented. Caleb held her
steady for a moment, his eyes, his lying, deceitful eyes,
filled with concern.

"Okay?"

"Peachy." She wiggled. "Let go."

"You'll experience a little dizziness . . ." He released

her but didn't move away. "Teleportation," he said by way of explanation.

The vertigo subsided. Thank God. She struggled to make sense of the impossible.

"To quote Sir Arthur Conan Doyle, 'When you have eliminated the impossible,' " Caleb told her quietly as she plopped down on the side of the bed and just sat there staring at him. " 'Whatever remains, however improbable, must be the truth.' "

After a few minutes, she rose to her feet. Her knees were still a little watery. "Was Doyle talking about wizards?" It was all both impossible *and* improbable.

She walked over to her still-packed suitcase. In the lining were three more passports. Ten grand in loose diamonds that she'd strung together to make a cheap-looking necklace, and a handful of credit cards in various names. This same small suitcase had traveled around the world with her. Right now everything she owned, barring her tools and the jewelry she had stashed in a safety deposit box outside San Francisco, was right here. She could go anywhere in the world. And disappear. Again.

Caleb came up behind her as she slammed down the lid and locked the case. "Maybe." He rested his hands on her shoulders.

His breath shifted the hair brushing her shoulders. He was that close. She felt the heat of his skin, his bare skin, all the way down her back through the thin cotton of her dress. She closed her eyes against the desperate ache in her chest. Because by rights she should have been able to turn into his arms. To lift her face for his kiss—

That fantasy was gone. Burst like a toxic bubble in a shower of splintery black shards.

"You can't force me to stay here." She spun around, the suitcase clutched in both hands, and shot him a furious glance. "And for God's sake put on some clo—Oh, God."

He was fully dressed.

Black jeans, a dark blue T-shirt, and black running shoes. He smelled as though he'd just stepped out of the shower. Even his dark hair was wet. "You—" she watched a drop of water run down his temple and forgot what she'd been about to say.

His eyes were serious. He looked nothing like the man she'd thought she'd married. There was nothing sweet nor kind about this hard-faced stranger.

"What do you want to do?"

"Don't tempt me." She was shocked at how *violent* she felt. "I'm going over there." She indicated the view outside the open window. The brilliant white tufa stone house on the hillside opposite them. "If my father is there— or *was* there—his security team will tell me what happened. I can't think beyond that."

"I'd rather you didn't go back over there." Caleb's voice was annoying reasonable. "Al-Adel isn't aware that your father is no longer there. But," he glanced at his wristwatch, "in about an hour, he'll show up, guns blazing."

"If this load of crap is the truth, then you don't have to worry. If my father is really dead, then I'll be on the first flight back to San Francisco." *To pick up the jewelry, then I'm going to lose myself in Mexico. But first I'm going across the ravine to that house we went to . . .*

"I'd rather you went to stay with my brother Gabriel until this situation has been resolved. I can have you in Montana in a flash."

Not just no, Heather thought, shuddering. *Hell no.* "I don't think so. No to the brother, and no to the mode of transportation. I'll take a commercial flight."

"Will you at least let me have a couple of my guys go with you? Make sure that everything is safe?"

"Are they . . . wizards too?"

"Yeah."

"I want to go *now*." If this was all true, then her father's security team would—oh, my God. She'd seen her father's men disappear one by one without a sound. She rubbed her temples. "I'm not hanging around for some strange guys to show up."

"Heather," Caleb said dryly. She flinched, the blood draining from her head as two men appeared between her and the door. "Meet Anthony Rook and Keir Farris."

CHAPTER TWENTY-THREE

Rook teleported back to the safe house to fetch the car and bring it to the top of the ravine. Caleb, Rook, and Farris would escort Heather up the hill and into the vehicle. She wasn't budging on the Gabriel issue, so Caleb was grateful that she was at least willing to accept two of his men as bodyguards. Until the situation was resolved.

She'd gone to take a quick shower while they waited for Rook to return. Of course it had taken Rook less time to teleport to the car and teleport it back to where they needed it than it had taken Heather to walk down the stairs to the bathroom. But the least he could do was permit her to shower before she started the long trip back.

Caleb could hear the water running and tried to drag his mind from Heather, wet and naked in the shower back to his associate.

"The Six March group showed up at a small private airfield fifteen minutes ago," Farris told Caleb. T-FLAC had people monitoring all forms of transportation in and out of the area. Al-Adel and his group weren't the only terrorists with a vested interest in Shaw and/or the money. Once word got out—which it surely had—tangos would be on this place like flies on dead meat. Of course they didn't know yet that Shaw had been removed.

Not unexpected. The vultures were starting to circle. Whoever had access to the missing funds would control the whole terrorist financial pie. Forty-eight billion dollars would buy any damn thing they wanted for any type of nefarious, maximum-destruction plan.

"Where are they now?"

"Matera," Farris told him, helping himself to a Brazil nut as he leaned against a table next to the window. "Dekker's with them."

"Listen, I know it sucks that I'm sending you away from the action, but keeping Heather safe is important, too," Caleb reminded his teammate and friend. Caleb was in charge of this mission, and he could tell his men to do whatever he damn well pleased, knowing they'd instantly obey. He also knew that Keir and the other wizards, like himself, chafed when the missions were this tame. This white-collar. Usually there was a ticking clock, a literal bomb about to drop, keeping them motivated.

Yeah, tangos were everywhere, but it would be bad guys killing bad guys until the money turned up.

He rubbed his jaw, almost wishing he could undo Shaw's death. For Heather's sake, if nothing else. How would it feel finding out that your flesh and blood was one of the bad guys?

Caleb had no idea how or even why Babette Shaw had managed to steal the money from that account. But he'd bet his last dime that the consequences hadn't occurred to her.

By ransacking her husband's client's account, moving the money to an unspecified location, Shaw's wife had placed all that power up for grabs.

Now Caleb was asking two highly trained T-FLAC operatives to basically act as bodyguards. Worse, to take a trip that could've taken them minutes via teleportation. Now they'd have to endure it for fifteen hours.

His friend stole another nut and nodded, but kept his opinions to himself.

"I appreciate you going on my behalf. She won't— She's stubborn."

Laughing, Farris arched a brow in a gesture for Caleb to continue.

Caleb shoved a hand into his front pocket. Heather had summarily refused his original plan to teleport her back to San Francisco. She had some issues with teleportation's effect on Bean—not that there was one, but his protests had fallen on deaf, uninformed ears. "See if you can change her mind on the drive to the airport," he advised, half listening to the water still running in the bathroom. "If not, I want you and Rook to stick to her like white on rice until this is over. I don't want her threatened or frightened by *anyone*."

Remembering her fire as she confronted him earlier, he figured it would take a lot to scare her. "None of those assholes gets anywhere near her, *comprende*?"

"Got it. And where will *you* be in the meantime?"

"I'm positive her mother gave her something the day she died. If Heather knows what that was, she's not exactly inclined to share the intel with me. I gotta tell you, Farris, I could get it out of her, but after everything I've already put her through, I just don't have the chops to do it. She wasn't supposed to remember her father getting shot."

Caleb stalked to the window and looked out. "She might not even actually know what it is her mother gave her. Hell, it's quicker just to backspace to last March and that Parisian bazaar. See what the hell it was for myself. By the time you guys land, I'll be in San Francisco waiting. Hopefully with the information we need to get that money."

"She does appear to be a little, uh, upset, with you at

the moment," Farris said with a small smile, watching Caleb pace.

"She hates my guts. Which in the grand scheme of things is for the best." His stomach twisted.

"So, are you gonna dump her?"

"Heather?" Caleb asked, as if there were any other woman on his mind. "She was part of the op." He didn't have to lie anymore. "The assignment is almost over."

"And I guess it's a minor detail to the legendary Caleb Edge that the woman is not only his wife, but pregnant as well?"

"Heather and Bean will be well taken care of."

"Bean?"

"The baby. Damn! What the hell's taking her so long down there? She's not gonna have any skin left."

"Is there a window?" Farris asked, clearly enjoying himself.

"Yeah. There is. It's this size." Caleb indicated about two feet square. "She's not stupid, Keir. She knows there are bad guys out there, even if she doesn't fully believe everything I've told her. She's not going to do anything to put herself and Bean in danger. She might not like me giving her orders, but she'll do what needs to be done to protect the baby."

He hoped he was right.

THE *SASSI*, MATERA
SUNDAY, APRIL 16
10:20 A.M.

Heather flicked a glance at the car clock. According to what Caleb had told her, twenty minutes ago, she had walked into her father's house and seen him get shot. On this day, at about this time. It made absolutely no sense whatsoever.

She sat in the back of the car, Caleb's men in front, on the way to Bari airport. Like Caleb, they'd tried to convince her that it would be safer, not to mention more expedient, for them to teleport her back to San Francisco. She'd politely and adamantly refused. She couldn't dispute what she'd witnessed with her own eyes, but that didn't mean she was willing to put Bean through something she didn't know was one hundred percent safe. There wasn't anything on "Wizardry During Pregnancy" in any of the books she'd read about what to expect when you're expecting.

The first thing she was going to do when she got back was go and see her doctor. Just to make sure Bean was okay. She rubbed her tummy, *knowing* that he was curled up, safe and warm, totally unaffected by what had been going on in his mother's world—"Oh. My. God!"

The guy in the passenger seat—Keir?—whipped his head around. "What's the matter?"

"Ah—Nothing. I thought I forgot something." Heather told him, short of breath. He gave her a small frown, and turned around again.

Let's just say, she thought, her brain going a mile a minute, say Caleb really *is* what he claims to be. Does that mean that his son would be a wizard too? My God. She couldn't wrap her mind around *any* of this.

Could a nonwizard raise a wizard? She almost groaned at the ramifications of what Caleb had revealed. It wasn't as if she could turn around and go back to him. Pretend that his lies now meant nothing and she could forgive him for the sake of the baby. No, Heather was neither that naïve nor that stupid. The faster she got away from Caleb, the better off she'd be. She knew that with every fiber of her being. Well, almost every fiber. Her heart refused to cooperate. It still ached for him, wanted him— or the illusion of him. That's all it had been, an *illusion*. None of it was real. Well, except the baby.

After she'd checked in with her OB/GYN in the Bay Area, the second thing she had to do was access her safety deposit box and look at her mother's jewelry.

Heart heavy with sadness, Heather recalled how her mother had handed her the small bag after lunch. "An early birthday present. Open it later." Heather had stuck the gift in her tote, and in all the chaos of what had happened in the next few weeks, promptly forgotten about it. She'd been too busy trying to stay alive.

Had her mother somehow managed to use the antique pieces as a way to access the money she'd stolen from her husband's business accounts? Clever if she had. No one would think to look there. For? Heather frowned. Her father had mentioned account numbers. Painted or engraved discreetly on one of the pieces? Or perhaps there was a key to a safety deposit box among all the earrings, bracelets, and necklaces? She'd retrieve the pieces, and look for clues about the missing money.

She'd love to dump forty billion dollars—in cash—in Caleb's lap.

By the time they reached the airport, Heather was desperate for a bathroom. Bean had taken up a determined position directly against her bladder. The two men she was with were nothing if not patient as they escorted her to two restrooms; unfortunately both had little yellow cones blocking the entrance to indicate that they were closed for cleaning. She was almost desperate enough to ask the guys to teleport her to the closest available bathroom ASAP.

"This one looks promising," Keir Farris told her with a smile, putting her small suitcase down beside him.

"We'll wait out here," Tony Rook assured her, leaning a shoulder against the wall beside the door to a ladies' room thankfully open for business. "Better move it though." He jerked his chin down the concourse.

"Ah damn it." Heather saw a cleaning woman approaching with her cleaning cart. Taking up the now-familiar yellow cone, she waved Heather in front of her with a smile. Heather smiled back. Whew. Good timing. She didn't think she could make it to another restroom. "I'll hurry," she promised. With a smile.

The woman followed her in, cart and all, and was already spraying cleaner on a sink as Heather raced into a stall. Much relieved, she emerged a few minutes later. Crossing to one of the clean sinks, she glanced at herself in the mirror as she dried her hands. "Good grief! I look like the Wild Woman of Borneo!"

She shook her head as she popped open her purse. Caleb had been in such a damn rush to get her out of the hotel that she hadn't dried her hair. Taking out her brush, she left her purse open, knowing she'd need the lipstick too.

As she raised her hand to run the brush through her hair, she was bumped into from the side. She half turned to see the cleaning woman and a nun standing behind her. Heather smiled. *Mi scusi—*

She felt a pinch, like a particularly nasty bee sting, on her upper arm, then everything went black.

CHAPTER TWENTY-FOUR

LES PUCES DE SAINT-OUEN
PARIS
ONE YEAR EARLIER
1207

Because there were dozens of flea markets in and around Paris on any given weekend, Caleb saved time and started his tail of Heather and her mother from their home to this particular flea market on rue Jules Vallès.

It was fascinating for Caleb to see Heather the way she was before events had set her on a course melding her fate to his.

She was considerably thinner here, almost to the point of emaciation. Even seeing *this* Heather, he couldn't imagine his Heather wearing the skintight jeans, high-heeled boots, and short mink jacket that she wore now. Diamonds sparkled at her ears, throat, and wrists. Her nails were dangerously long and shellacked a deep burgundy. He preferred them the way she wore them now, short and unpainted. Her hair here was a creamy, expensive blond, cut in a mystifying style that was probably fashionable, but looked untouchable to Caleb. His fingers recalled a tactile memory of the texture of Heather's hair in the present. The way the silken honey-brown tendrils had felt as she'd let strands drift across his chest when they'd made love.

He'd have to store away the memories of their love-making and everything else they'd shared. For good. Time to move on.

Invisible, he'd followed the two women from stall to stall for the better part of the morning. He observed most of their morning at the flea market in double time, sometimes triple time. All he wanted to see was what, if anything, Babette Shaw gave her daughter.

It was a nice day to be outside, and the two women were enjoying the first sun break in several days. They weren't alone, of course, Caleb noted. A dozen men were with them. All packing. It was expected of the wife and daughter of such a wealthy man. The bodyguards were unobtrusive, dressed in jeans as were most of the other shoppers, but they never forgot what their job was. Their eyes were everywhere. Caleb was glad to be invisible, they were that good at their job.

Heather and her mother walked arm in arm. Every now and then Heather would comment on something in English, but for the most part the women spoke in French. Their driver, an older man, was in charge of their numerous packages, and he'd been back to the car a half dozen times already this morning to deposit their purchases.

Caleb had checked everything they bought as it had been selected and wrapped. Mostly they'd purchased small antiques: a writing desk, a bronze urn, a pen set, several vases, a length of old lace. They'd bought flowers, some produce. Nothing of any importance. Still nothing had been given from mother to daughter. And Caleb had watched closely.

They stopped for lunch, the bodyguards taking up their positions at the surrounding tables. The driver had trotted off to deposit more packages in the car and hadn't returned yet.

Two women Heather's age came up to their table, and were invited to join them for lunch.

Caleb leaned against a wall nearby, keeping his eyes on Heather and her mother. He listened to the four women discussing a party they'd all attended the past week, but his mind kept drifting back to the Heather of present day.

She, Rook, and Farris would be at the airport by now. Even with the powerful protective spell he had on her, Caleb was grateful the two men had accompanied her. He rubbed the back of his neck, feeling a niggle of . . . What the hell *was* it?

Concern? Yeah. But he knew he didn't have to worry about Heather and Bean's safety. Rook and Farris were with her, and would stay with her until he got to San Francisco.

He'd have felt better still if Heather had agreed to go to Gabriel's. But once this money situation was resolved, he'd try to persuade her that staying at Gabriel's was her best course of action. She and Bean would want for nothing.

And he'd be able to see them . . . once in a while. Absently, he rubbed the tightness in his chest.

And how long would she stand for that? he asked himself, gazing at the long line of her neck as she laughed at something one of her friends was saying. The same laugh. Of course it was. The same sparkle in her hazel eyes.

This, you idiot, is the life Heather will return to when this is all over. *This* life. He couldn't imagine she'd be happy living in a tiny one-room apartment in San Francisco, especially with a baby, for long. She came from enormous wealth. The kind of wealth most people couldn't even imagine.

So yeah. She'd want to come back to France when this was all over.

Back here. To Paris. To her old life.

Heather and Bean.

His son would learn to speak French before he spoke English. Christ. He'd probably eat—Caleb shuddered. *Snails.* Okay. Bad idea thinking about a plate of *escargots* swimming in garlic butter. He waited for his stomach to protest. Nada. Well, hell. Happy days.

The group rose from the table for their good-byes, then moved off, Caleb beside Heather. She turned her head, a small frown between her brows and looked right at him. Jesus! Could she *see* him? Not possible . . . She shook her head and turned back to talk to the driver, who'd returned and met them en route to the car. Caleb let out the breath he'd sucked in.

She hadn't seen him, he was pretty sure, but somehow she'd sensed that he was there. *How* he had no idea. The idea that Heather was so attuned to him that even a year before they would ever technically meet she'd be aware on some level of his presence freaked him out a little. Okay, more than a little. Especially since he knew she was the first and only one to remember a backspace.

The driver discreetly passed a small paper bag to Heather's mother. Not something that either woman had purchased earlier. "Here is the gift for you, my darling," Babette Shaw said in lilting English, handing the small sack to Heather as they walked.

Heather smiled. "Now what did you do? It isn't my birthday for two weeks, Mom."

"Put it away, my darling. Save it to open on your birthday. It is quite valuable, so have a care with it, yes? Put it somewhere very, very safe."

Bingo.

What woman wouldn't be curious, and insist on opening a mystery gift right that second?

Heather.

She pushed the small paper bag deep into the tote she

carried slung over her shoulder. "You're being very mysterious."

"It is something quite old that I had embellished especially for you. If it needs sizing or polishing, you must"—Babette warned, her hand on her daughter's arm—"you must take it personally to Switzerland to have it repaired. I put the address of the shop inside the bag. You understand, yes?"

Caleb certainly did. Heather clearly didn't.

"I will take very good care of my present," Heather said with a teasing smile, tucking her arm into her mother's as they strolled along. "I'm sure I'll love it whatever it is."

With the information he needed, Caleb viewed the rest of the shopping trip in fast-forward. While he wanted to be sure the package Heather received was what everyone was looking for, he felt an almost overwhelming need to go back to real time. Now.

Feeling the exigency, Caleb placed a tracking spell on whatever the hell was in the package, and shimmered back to real time. Still invisible, he transported himself to the flight that Heather and his men were on. She didn't need to see him, but he sure as shit needed to see her.

Drastically weakened by the backspacing of time, Caleb had to grab a seatback at the front of the cabin to prevent himself from crumbling in the aisle. Lately, each time he TiVoed back took more and more out of him. Locking his knees, he scanned the first-class section for her. He just needed to see her lovely face, assure himself that she was okay, then he'd be gone. One look.

Just one.

Surprisingly, the stairs hadn't been pulled away from the aircraft, and the door was open. Again, he scanned the first-class section. There were three empty seats in the back.

Nobody looked happy. He didn't give a flying fuck

about the annoyed passengers strapped in place, muttering and looking impatiently at their watches.

What the fuck was going on?

He did a quick walk-through of the rest of the aircraft. No Heather. No Rook. No Farris.

Mouth dry, heart thumping, Caleb went into the cockpit. " . . . ten more minutes," the captain told his crew. "If they haven't found the missing passengers by then we've been given permission to take off."

"Weird, isn't it?" The male flight attendant twisted his wedding band around his finger as he glanced from the pilot to the copilot. "How could a woman disappear out of the restroom in a crowded terminal and no one see her?"

"The police are curious as to why she and the two men she was traveling with don't—"

Enough. Caleb was gone.

He materialized inside the terminal beside a magazine stand and then went in search of his men. How the hell could this have happened? With such a powerful protection spell on her, nobody should have been able to get near her.

She'd run.

The little fool had run.

CHAPTER TWENTY-FIVE

"Strike her again," a man's voice said flatly.

Heather came to in a surge of sheer terror; heart manic, icy sweat bathing her body as she was hit across the face. She barely had time to register what had happened when she was hit again. This time she screamed. The back of her head slammed into something hard and she bit her tongue. Salty, metallic blood filled her mouth, and the cry of sheer terror lodged in her throat. What was going on? Her fuzzy brain tried to make sense of where, when, and who she was.

Her stomach tensed just before she was slapped again. She attempted to open her eyes, but they immediately filled with tears of pain, flooding her vision. Bam! She heard a loud crack, and realized it was her head breaking the back of the chair she was in. The violence had come out of nowhere.

"What the—?" Her tongue, swollen, refused to articulate the words. The blows came, methodically, without giving her a chance to think or protest. Dizzy and disoriented, she tried to figure out what was happening. *Nothing* made sense. Her entire world revolved around her pain.

Fire blazed across the entire right side of her face. Ears ringing, arms stretched behind her, legs numb. Heather catalogued the feelings, envisioning herself strapped to a straight-backed chair, arms tied, ankles tied. How long had they been hitting her? What was the human capacity for suffering? She'd never felt this much agony in her entire life.

She screamed again as an especially hard smack brought her around. Her brain started piecing together fragmented shards of memory. The airport, running from the bad guys and Caleb, the restroom, the nun and the cleaning lady—how had she ended up here?

"Hold," the flat voice instructed.

She carefully turned her head, frightened to the core. Who wouldn't obey a cold voice like that? Heather peered through slitted eyes in his direction. She was already terrified. Now her fear ratcheted up another notch as she recognized the man who'd shot her father. She blinked rapidly, attempting to clear her blurry vision. It was hard to hold onto a thought, hard to concentrate, yet she knew she had to. Touching the tip of her tongue to her split, swollen lip, she felt the ridges of a tender cut. Her head felt like it weighed fifty pounds when she tilted it to the side.

"Why?" she managed to choke out, images of her father lying dead in his own blood giving her a spurt of courage.

The man propped her head upright with his fist under her chin. "Where is your father, Miss Shaw?"

"He's . . ." Blinking rapidly, she played the scene of her father's murder in her head. He was dead. This man had killed him. Right? God, this was a nightmare.

His hand dropped away from her face, and her head flopped forward. Only to fly back as she was hit again. "Stop!" she yelled, choking on the blood in her mouth. Adrenaline and fear were starting to scare her "sober." With the continual barrage of blows, she was having a hard time bridging terror and truth. Sagging against her bonds, she dragged up reserves she didn't know she had to stay conscious.

It would be easier to give in to the darkness beyond

the pain, but she couldn't. She was her baby's only hope. "Who *are* you?"

"Fazuk Al-Adel. I am a client of your father's." He shot a sneaking glance at the bulky shadow of a man standing beside her chair. "If you would be kind enough to inform us where he is, Miss Shaw, we will be finished with you."

That didn't sound promising. "Finished" as in they would stop beating the shit out of her and send her on her merry way? Or "finished" as in they would just shoot her and be done with it? She could only see out of one eye, and when she turned her head to look at Al-Adel, she almost threw up. This was so unreal. "You— you s-shot him."

Al-Adel's expression hardened to stone. "Your father was shot? Are you telling me he is *dead*?"

The room was starting to come into focus, although Heather still felt as though she was seeing everything underwater. She continued blinking her good eye, trying to see the two men more clearly. Her abused tongue was a hindrance as she argued, "Of coursh he'sh dead. You killed him."

"It was not I," Al-Adel assured her with some heat.

She repeated the words in her mind. Rearranged them until they made some sort of sense. "Yesh, it was." She nodded, or tried to. "I saw you do it."

Heather closed her eyes, spent. She dimly remembered a sting in her arm at the airport, which meant that the cleaning lady must have drugged her. Swallowing, she thought of her baby. Poor Bean. Poor Caleb. He'd tried to send her and Bean away, to keep them safe, and they'd ended up right in the enemy's arms.

Al-Adel's eyes darkened to angry slits. "You make no sense!" he growled, then turned to one of the other men. "She is useless to me like this. I specifically said I wanted her awake and aware of what was happening. Bring her around."

Groaning, Heather really wished that Caleb would swoop in and do some of that wizard shit right about now. Something that would save her and Bean from this hell.

Time freezing, teleporting, anything to get her and their baby away from these terrifying men. God, what good was being in love with a wizard if he couldn't get her out of this kind of situation? Her heart ached at the realization that despite everything they'd gone through, she really did love him. There was something ironic about Caleb being a Master Manipulator of Time, and yet for his family, time was running out.

"Wake up," the cold, flat voice instructed.

Not wanting another blow to her throbbing face, Heather attempted to lift her chin from where it was resting on her chest. Slowly, she opened her eyes and gave him a deliberately vacant look. She glanced around, trying to take a quick inventory of her surroundings while maintaining a look of drugged stupefaction.

The room was vast, and the only light came from a giant fish tank against the far wall. She counted six or seven shadowy figures she assumed to be men, plus Al-Adel.

Her terror intensified. So did her resolve.

Returning her attention to the effortless movement of the brightly colored saltwater fish in the tank straight ahead, she prayed for a plan. Quick. If Al-Whatever thought she was drugged stupid, that could buy her some time. Hopefully.

Almost hypnotized by the back-and-forth, back-and-forth swimming fish, Heather let herself sway side to side, as if she'd had a few too many glasses of champagne. The way her stomach was knotted with nausea, it wasn't that much of a reach.

The man's cold voice held an angry edge. "How much phenobarbital did the women give her?"

"Sophia told me a double dose. Four hundred milligrams."

Phenobarbital? Her thoughts skipped and jumped again, coming back to the baby's safety. What would that do? She bit back a sob, wondering if it would even matter. If Caleb didn't come soon, she and Bean would both be dead. She tugged against her restraints. It didn't matter how desperately she wanted to leap out of the chair and run like hell, she couldn't break the tight ropes cutting into her wrists and ankles.

She received a whack on the back of the head for her efforts.

"She's coming out of it," Heather heard one man say.

"Not fast enough," Al-Adel snapped.

"Time was of the essence," the other man said defensively. "She had two bodyguards right outside the door. She had to be wheeled out in the cleaning cart. Any noise—"

"Yes. Yes," Al-Adel snapped. Heather cringed as he put his hand under her jaw and lifted her face.

Heather licked her cracked, bloodied lips. "My husband will come for me. You won't get away with this." *I love you, sweetheart. Remember that. Promise me if anything happens—Promise me.* If he was a wizard, maybe he could hear her thoughts. She began to scream in her head. "Something is happening! *Rewind me, or whatever it is you do!*"

"Where *is* this husband of yours?" When she didn't answer he flicked her cheek with something icily sharp. "Does he work for your father?"

"No, and stop poking at me, damn it!" Would it help her if he thought she was crazy? The truth might just get her there. "Caleb is magic. He has powers, but even he couldn't bring my father back to life."

Al-Adel cursed and stepped away. "She's too out of it to make any sense. No. No more drugs for now. Last chance, Miss Shaw, before I just end the game. Where is your father?"

She blinked, so scared she couldn't even cry. "Dead."

His lips were one straight angry line across his hard face. "And where is my money?"

"Your money? Oh, right." Suddenly everything in her *life* seemed to be about this damn money. It was why Caleb had used her. Why her mother was dead and why Al-Adel had killed her father. Heather made her tone especially flippant. To hell with the money, where was Caleb?

"Daddy didn't steal the money. From what I hear it was lots and lots of money. Not all yours, though. Is it?" She pictured forty-eight billion dollars in ten-dollar bills. That much money would fill a room. Fill a suitcase. Fill—her whole damn world.

"Who *has* it?" she asked, intentionally slurring her words. It was an excellent question. Too bad she didn't have the answer. She was loopy, trying to get sensible, and *pretending* to be loopy. Loopier?

She choked as he squeezed her throat between his fingers in a grip so painful she couldn't hear or see for several seconds. "—*you* know who moved the money?"

If she gave him something, maybe she could stay alive another day, giving Caleb a better chance to find her and Bean. "My birthday present. I *think,*" she said with the precision of a drunk. "I *think* that it's a clue. *I* think my *mother* stole the money. Can you *believe* it? My *mother*? Who would have thunk it? Would *you*? Did ever you *meet* my mother? Grace Kelly. That's who she was. Grace . . ." Heather listened to her slurred babble and tried to rein herself in.

God. Was she overdoing it? Scary, how easy it was to imagine that this was all happening to someone else. But she wasn't the rich, spoiled heiress anymore. She was Bean's mother, and with Caleb missing in action, she was her baby's only shot.

Focus. Concentrate on what you're saying, and focus, she warned herself sternly. Concentrate. This is really,

really bad. And not likely to get better. She shivered, digging deep for the strength to do what she had to do.

Al-Adel flicked open a knife, the blade glinting dangerously close to her face.

Heather nearly fainted as she pictured the blade slicing smoothly across her throat. Gritting her teeth, she lifted her chin a notch, silently daring him to make her death quick. Steeling herself, she waited for him to make his next move.

Al-Adel cut the restraints from her arms and legs, then grabbed the front of her dress in a hard fist. The fabric ripped as he yanked her to her feet. "Hey!" she muttered, staggering.

An ice-cold hand gripped her upper arm, jerking her upright as her knees buckled and her head flopped. "Can you walk?"

She didn't bother trying. The pins and needles racing through her arms and legs as the circulation returned was nothing compared to the sharp cramp in her stomach. Hang on, baby, hang on.

One hand had her arm, and with the fingers of the other hand he grabbed her hair to hold her head up.

Think drunk, think happier times, think . . . "I've been doing it for year—"

"How old are you, Miss Shaw?" He started walking, holding her so tightly her shoulder was hunched up to her ear, and her neck strained against the yank of her hair. "Thirty?"

He'd never know how bad it hurt her to talk, to push the smart-ass words past torn and bleeding lips. "It's not polite to ask a woman her age. Even for a terrorisht."

"When is your birthday?"

She frowned, trying to figure out what he really wanted. "March twenty-ninth . . ."

The room they were in was some sort of medical office, with certificates on the wall nearby, and models of human organs and a vertebra mounted on black bases and lined up along a credenza. Even without bright lighting she could tell that the office was plush, with gray fabric-covered walls, and thick charcoal carpet underfoot. Tasteful paintings and plaques were illuminated by the surreal ebb and flow of the fish tank's lights rippling across the walls.

"And what did your mother give you for your last birthday, Heather? Tell me what she gave you."

Her knees buckled again, this time partially because her legs really felt like Jell-O, and partially because she wanted this man to believe she was still out of it. He'd taken the bait—would it be enough to keep her alive? He would need her to show him where the bracelets were, to get into her safety deposit box. It could give her an opportunity to escape. She needed every advantage she could get.

Her teeth snapped together as he jerked her upright again.

"I feel sick," she blurted. Her eyes filled with tears, and she managed to curl one hand over her belly. "Don't hurt me. Please."

"Then tell me what your mother gave you. Tell me how to retrieve the money you say she stole."

"I can't. I don't remember, I—"

Growling, he half carried, half dragged her toward the fish tank. Terror kept her silent. Had she gone too far? Heather struggled like a worm on a hook, thinking fast. Keir and Tony would be searching for her right now, she knew that without a doubt. They would certainly have contacted Caleb the second they realized she was no longer in the restroom at the airport. Caleb would *definitely* come looking for her.

So why wasn't he here? she thought achingly as Al-Adel threw her against the side of the enormous fish tank. Her face took the brunt of it as she hit the solid glass wall. She literally saw stars as her nose connected with a thud, followed by a sickening crunch that ricocheted into her brain and vibrated through her body. Her legs refused to hold her and she crumpled to the floor.

Heather blocked out everything but Caleb. Caleb *would* come.

Not just for *her*.

For Bean.

Caleb would come for his son.

Wouldn't he?

And if he did, would it be in time to save them both?

"If you want to live, Miss Shaw, answer these two simple questions." Al-Adel wrenched her to her feet. Barely conscious, Heather couldn't stand. His words blended and merged, pulsing in time with her manic heartbeat, which pounded deafeningly in her ears, and throbbed excruciatingly around her broken nose.

Calebcalebcaleb.

He shook her violently. Her head flopped backward and forward like a rag doll. Half blinded by the swelling of her face, Heather gagged on the blood filling her mouth. *Calebcalebcaleb.*

"What did your mother give to you?" he shouted. Shake. Shake. Punch. Oh, God. Agony. Heather left her face open to the blows so she could protect her stomach. "And where is it?"

She felt herself being lifted off the floor, strangely light, yet there was this dreadful heaviness inside.

Metal scraped against glass. The top of the tank? Something heavy fell to the floor with a loud metallic crash. With Al-Adel's unshakable grip on the back of her torn dress and a handful of hair on her crown, she was pulled up and over a hard edge. Blurry light hurt her eyes. What . . . ?

Water. Close. So close. Didn't make any sense. Something hard cut across her middle as she was bent over. *Bean . . .*

Cold water rushed over her face, shocking her into semiawareness. Her eyes flew open. Blood and her long hair floated in front of her face. Struggling to break free, she flailed her legs weakly. Her lungs burned as if she'd sucked in fire.

He held her head underwater with an inextricable grip in her hair.

A teal-and-yellow fish swam right in front of her nose. *Ohgodohgodohgod.* She tried to lever herself off the side of the tank, but he was pressed against her legs, holding her body against the side of the fish tank with his own, and she was weak. Dangerously, lethally weak. Water went up her nose and filled her mouth as she fought to hold her breath as all sound—save the thudding, erratic beat of her own heart in her ears—disappeared.

Red blood mingled with swirled black to obscure her vision as she started losing consciousness. *Bean. Nooooo.* The harder she struggled, the weaker she became.

Al-Adel jerked her head up. Out of the water. "Answer the questions."

She hung limp, choking, coughing, desperately trying to drag air into her burning lungs. Sucking in deep, desperate gulps of air, Heather tried again to get free. But with no purchase she was pinned there, caught between Scylla and Charybdis.

"Brac—" *lets.*

His words were lost as his fingers tightened painfully in her hair. He forced her head under the water again. Her lungs burned as she held onto her last, rushed gasp of air.

CHAPTER TWENTY-SIX

BARI AIRPORT
SUNDAY, APRIL 16
1415

"Hey, Middle Edge. Your presence is req—"

"Unless this call is about Heather, I'm not interested." Caleb cut Lark off, his voice flat. Grim. Oh, fuck— *terrified*. He was in the women's bathroom where Heather had last been seen. *Last seen*. Jesus. It felt like he hadn't drawn a breath in the past half hour. "She's missing."

His gut twisted in a knot of fear for the safety of both Heather and Bean, Caleb was almost out of his mind with worry. She *couldn't* be goddamned missing, he thought savagely for perhaps the thousandth time in the past thirty minutes.

Impossible. He'd put a protective spell on her. A powerful spell. A reinforced spell. Unless she'd chosen to walk out of this bathroom on her own two feet, nobody, but nobody, should have been able to get near her to do her any harm.

Yet Caleb knew, with every fiber of his being, that not only had Heather been abducted from beneath the noses of two highly trained T-FLAC operatives, she was in danger. Grave danger. His fucking protective spell hadn't protected her at all.

How was that *possible*?

He raked his fingers through his hair, feeling the knot of frustration tighten in his chest. Another wizard? he wondered. He shook his head, dismissing the thought. He'd sensed no other wizard at any time during this op. No other wizard. But then why had his spell not worked, God damn it?!

Maybe his powers were screwed up. Testing the possibility, Caleb turned to the mirror, gave a small flick of his finger, and splintered the glass into a million little shards. Then just as easily, froze the shards and reversed their momentum. The mirror was back in place, complete with water spots and fingerprint smudges. Jesusshitcrapdamn.

How? Why? What the fuck was happening to his magic that a relatively simple protection spell had failed? And for Christ's sake, he was ridiculously weakened by his recent backspace and wouldn't be capable of doing it again for *hours*. Heather might not *have* hours. God damn it. He had to find her in real time.

Real time.

Real fast.

Thank God his morning sickness seemed to be over. He didn't have time to be anything but at the top of his game.

Dismissing his own physical discomfort—it would pass—he started searching the far right-hand stall. Again. Searching for anything. Any clue.

He'd half forgotten he was still on the phone with Lark. "What do you mean missing?" his control said in his ear as he closed himself inside the stall and ran a hand down the door panel. What he thought he'd find there, he had no idea. Something. Anything. *Where are you, sweetheart? Where the hell are you?*

Unfortunately, mental telepathy wasn't one of his powers. "Where's Stone? How fast can you get him here?" Alex Stone was telepathic—he'd find—

"Terrorist Summit," Lark informed him. "Prague. And

before you ask again, he's on his way to Gabriel and *his* problem in Montana. Getting a shiny gold star for doing what his control asks of him."

Caleb stepped out of that stall and went into the next, starting the search all over again. Same result. Nada. "Jesus, Lark—"

"Gabriel has called a meeting. His place. Today. 2030. Emergency. Psi/spec ops. Levels one and two only."

What was going on? His brother was a big boy, and the choice between attending the meeting of powerful wizards or finding a powerless female wasn't even a choice.

"Can't make it." He closed the phone and shoved it in his back pocket. Then he immediately started checking out the next stall, Lark and the emergency meeting already forgotten. He, Farris, and Rook were still at the airport. It didn't take a rocket scientist to figure out that they'd moved her out in the cleaning cart. Farris had found the cart quickly enough outside in a parking area. But there was no sign of Heather or the cleaning woman.

Or the woman who'd posed as a nun.

And no clue as to who they were, or who they worked for.

Why? Caleb closed his eyes, imagining what had taken place. Rook, blaming himself, was watching surveillance footage supplied by the airport security people while Farris was interviewing anyone who might have seen the women. Caleb had sent Dekker and another team to watch and wait at Shaw's house. The invisible cats waiting at the entrance to a rat's hole. His chest burned with impotent fury.

Caleb continued to hunt high and low for anything that might lead him to Heather. His nostrils filled with the sickeningly sweet scent of industrial-strength pine deodorizer.

"What do you mean you *can't make it*?" Lark demanded, materializing in front of Caleb in a swirl of leather and black lace just as he came out of a stall. He had to stop on a dime as she blocked his way.

She pointed a long fingernail at his chin. "That was an order. We have a rogue wizard out there assimilating powers—"

"Does this rogue wizard have my wife?"

"No," Lark assured him.

"Then screw orders. My wife is my immediate problem. I have to find Heather. Help me find her, Lark. Please."

"I'm not in the lost-and-found biz, sweetcheeks," she said with only a trace of sympathy. She stepped back, folding her arms over her chest, watching as he tipped over a trash can to inspect the contents. She pulled a face, high-heeled boots clicking on the terrazzo floor as she backed up.

"There's not a damn thing here to indicate a struggle," he muttered, frustrated. The second he'd seen Rook and Farris's faces he'd known that Heather hadn't just decided to go it alone.

"But damn it, I feel—She's in trouble. Jesus Christ. It's bad. Christ, Lark—You have to tell me where they took her." He quickly filled the empath in on what he'd learned from his men.

Lark raised a brow. "Are you telling me that Farris and Rook were standing *right outside* and had no idea she was being smuggled out right *in front* of them?"

It was no secret that Lark had a heart of gold. It was just buried under five or six feet of concrete. But if he could reach it, she'd be the best help a wizard could ask for.

"Heather came in. A cleaning woman and a cart followed, right on her heels. A woman dressed like a freaking nun came in, then went out a few minutes later, conning Rook and Farris with some bullshit about Heather needing something 'female' from the shop across the concourse. While the fake nun was talking to

Farris and Rook, the cleaning woman strolled out. We found the empty cart in the parking garage."

"Ah, the old 'woman's problem' ploy." Lark shook her head, the fuchsia stripes in her hair picking up the fluorescent lights above. "At least three women involved. Sounds like a riddle, doesn't it? The cleaner, the nun, and someone left behind to impersonate your lady love. Bad guys—bad *girls* in this case, had upward of nearly fifteen minutes' head start?"

"*Seventeen* fucking minutes. They could have her *anywhere*. We're at an *airport* for Christ's sake. They could have . . ."

"She's still here in Bari," Lark assured him, placing a hand on his arm, which had an immediate calming effect.

Which he shook off. "Where? Isn't this your special skill? Clairvoyance?"

"Don't believe everything you hear, Middle Edge. If I told you your future you'd freak. Besides, telling anyone what's supposed to happen might alter their behavior, thus changing what should happen. It's a total karma thing."

"Fuck karma. This is my own damn fault." He thumped his fist on the towel dispenser, effectively buckling it and making it inoperable. "God damn it! Nobody should have been able to get anywhere *near* her! The spell didn't fucking *work*," he said through gritted teeth.

She observed him, her gray eyes clear. "Why do you think that is?"

"Don't, Lark. Not now." Ah, shit—"I'm losing my powers, aren't I?" he said hoarsely. "Jesus." He pounded the towel dispenser again. It fell off the wall with a clatter.

She raised a multi-pierced eyebrow at his display of frustration. "Your temper, maybe. But you are *not* losing your powers, Middle Edge, that I can tell you for sure. I'd suggest that you clue in on why they don't work on *Heather*. Before it's too late."

Too late? The words hit like a punch.

Bathed in an icy sweat of foreboding, Caleb rubbed a fist across the familiar ache in his chest. She wasn't dead. He'd know it. *Where are you, Heather? Where in God's name are you?*

"Tell Gabriel he can give me the CliffsNotes on that meeting. Later. Right now all I give a damn about is Heather and Bean."

Thanks to Lark, Caleb and Rook had a location.

While the talented empath could give the men a sketchy description on the interior of the building, she couldn't pinpoint where in the fifty-thousand-square-foot medical center Heather was being held.

It was after hours, and the parking lot behind the two-story building held only a dozen or so vehicles. The second he materialized inside, Caleb smelled the familiar stench of death.

"Report?" he asked softly into his lip mic. Rook had teleported to the other side of the building, and the Big Plan was for the two men to check each room until they met in the middle. Or until they found Heather. His mind raced along with his pulse.

Picturing his wife, his *wife,* damn it, he sent out a desperate, but useless, thought. *Where are you?* He'd give anything to be telepathic right now. A simple mind-meld, and she'd be safe, with him.

He ignored the weakness that caused his muscles to feel like Jell-O. It would pass, but in the meantime, it was a stark reminder that there could be no magic for him until the end of this rescue attempt. Not *attempt,* damn it. *Rescue.*

He couldn't afford to expend energy rendering himself invisible. He had used up his store of power backspacing, followed immediately by this short teleportation. He was damn well out of juice. And frankly, he thought, feeling feral as he ran down a corridor, weapon drawn, he didn't give a shit if anyone saw him or not.

His stores were so depleted that unless it related directly to Heather, this takedown was going to have to be done without utilizing any of his wizardly skills. He had to replenish what he'd lost so that he could teleport Heather and himself out of here when it counted. And the only way to do that was wait.

"Woman dead in her car. Side parking lot," Rook said in his ear, sounding grim. "Throat slit. Oh, shit. There's a kid strapped in a car seat in back—Man, I fucking *hate* when kids get—Holy crap. It's *sleeping*! I'm porting the baby to Lark."

Bean. Jesus. Bean. Caleb's heart clenched. He'd never had this much to lose. When he'd gone into that bombed building in Beirut a couple of years ago to rescue some diplomat's daughter from a tango kidnapping, he hadn't given the girl more than a second's thought. She was nothing more than a job.

This was no different, he reminded himself. He *had* to put his emotions, along with the personal connection, aside. Had to, in order to function on all cylinders.

He glanced down the long, doorless corridor as he ran toward the front of the building. Weapon raised, he recognized the incessant ping as that of an elevator door opening and closing. He sped up, his long legs making short work of the hallway.

Caleb paused to take a quick glance around the corner. A chilling calm settled over him as he came across more of the tangos' handiwork. He spoke softly into the mic. "Couple of bodies by the elevator near the pharmacy."

Three mutilated bodies sprawled on the floor, half in and half out of the open elevator. The door dinged and opened. Then it tried to close but was obstructed by the bodies, and dinged open again.

Caleb did a lightning-fast visual, trying to maintain his professional detachment. "Three women. Jesus—"

"How bad?"

Professional detachment was impossible, because with this kind of evidence he knew with a sick certainty who, God help her, was holding Heather hostage.

"Fazuk Al-Adel bad," Caleb told Rook hoarsely, stepping over the tangle of arms and legs and other severed, indistinguishable parts. Avoiding the seeping pool of coagulated blood darkening the carpet, he kept going, his sole focus: Finding Heather. *Please God, don't let me be too late.*

"Al-Adel?" Rook said in his ear. "Oh, shit. This century's Dr. Mengele."

Tightening his grip on the gun, Caleb recalled that Al-Adel derived perverse pleasure out of performing his atrocities. He remembered some of the photos T-FLAC had posted and winced. The sick bastard had clearly indulged his sick proclivities for some time with the center's staff and patients.

"He had time to entertain himself with these kills." There were more ahead. The inside of the building was as cold as an f-ing meat locker. Air conditioning turned up high. A notorious Al-Adel idiosyncrasy.

"While he waited for Heather?"

Caleb's mouth went dry. His thought exactly. "Christ. Smells like a slaughterhouse."

At any other time he'd have at least paused to ascertain whether any of Al-Adel's victims were still alive. Today the thought barely crossed his mind as, on a razor's edge of urgency, he ran down the corridor.

They already knew from Lark that each floor of the two-story building consisted of two parallel corridors. Caleb had come through the back door. This corridor was clearly used for wheeling patients outside in wheelchairs or gurneys. He could see the lobby ahead. Off that was yet another hallway, this one leading to a row of exam rooms and various doctor's offices, according to Lark. Who was rarely wrong.

"Shimmer upstairs to the recovery room," Caleb instructed Rook. "I'll stay down here."

In real time Al-Adel had had close to two hours alone with Heather, doing—his throat constricted. Couldn't go there. Not now. *Focus.*

Caleb raced through the luxurious reception area, where phones rang unanswered, a couple of computer screens swirled with screen savers, and a fax machine spewed out papers onto the bodies of the two young women gutted and left on the floor behind their desks.

Two more women had been killed and left in the middle of the reception area, where a shattered fish tank spewed water, vegetation, and dead fish. Bullet holes riddled the floor and ceiling. The path of gore led from the front doors, through the waiting room, and down the corridor with all the exam rooms.

"Three nurses dead up here," Rook reported. "More than one bad guy did this shit. What a bunch of sick sonuvabitches, you should see—Sorry," he said quickly.

Listening to Rook lose his normal rigid control at what he was seeing up there, Caleb slammed open an exam room door. Empty. He prayed a quick fervent prayer that his powers would return to full strength quickly. *Instantly* would be even better. He opened every door as he raced down the corridor.

Jesus. Where the fuck are you, sweetheart?

He paused only long enough to glance inside each exam room, then ran to the next, and the next. Pretty much every room had the tango's brutal touch, as evidenced by dark crimson pools or blood-splattered walls. Gruesome reminders of the futile efforts of his victims attempting to escape. His stomach lurched. Not because of the gore before him, but simply knowing that his—

that Heather might very well be counted among the victims of the sadistic Fazuk Al-Adel.

Cold sweat broke out on his brow and he ran faster.

Heather? Tell me where the fuck you are. I swear to God, when this is all over I'll let you do whatever you want to do. I'll never see you again. I won't—

He didn't know what the hell she was going to want him to do.

Go jump off a bridge, most likely—especially after that confrontation in their honeymoon suite just this morning.

He couldn't even swallow past the rock in his throat. Whatever it was she wanted, he'd give it to her on a platter.

Just be alive. That's all I'm asking you. Please be alive.

Caleb couldn't imagine his world without Heather in it.

A woman moaned when he opened one of the doors. Barely conscious, and in bad shape, but alive. Caleb hesitated. Jesus. He hated this. His first inclination was to teleport the woman immediately. Lark was at their private medical facility in Switzerland, waiting. But he couldn't, he just *couldn't* teleport this woman and then find that he couldn't do the same for Heather when he needed the juice. "Room 121B. For teleportation."

"Now?"

"Now—"

Rook materialized to teleport the woman. He didn't have to accompany her, but he did have to have line of sight. "Go," he told Caleb as the woman disappeared, leaving the outline of her upper body on the sheets she'd been lying on.

Caleb went.

CHAPTER TWENTY-SEVEN

Caleb felt the guilt weigh on his shoulders, and despite the frigid air, a film of sweat bathed his entire body as he methodically searched behind every door.

Chaos, brutality, murder. More of the man's vile trademarks. No more living victims. He gulped and spoke into the mic. "I'm holding you to that promise, Tony."

The promise that no matter what happened to *him*, Rook would get Heather out. No matter what.

"Shit, you're a lazy dog. Get your lady out of here yourself. The sooner, the better, man."

Caleb intended getting her out of here himself. But he always had a contingency plan or three. So long as he thought of Heather as his responsibility, he could make it another step. Because if he thought of her the way Al-Adel had left these other victims, he'd be a worthless excuse for a wizard.

An arrowed sign pointed to the Chief of Staff's office, and the surgery center at the end of the corridor. Fifty-fifty. They were the last two places downstairs that he hadn't checked yet.

Caleb's blood froze because he knew which area Al-Adel would choose.

The surgery center. Where there was a plethora of lethally sharp instruments. Al-Adel had a history of doing his reprehensible deeds in an operating theater—

there was something about the sterile environment and the harsh, revealing lights that turned the sick son of a bitch on.

Caleb had never moved so fast without magic. He was highly motivated, and so damned scared he wasn't rational anymore. He practically flew the five hundred feet to the double doors at the end of what seemed like a million miles of charcoal carpet. The doors opened with a crash as he blasted inside. They swung out into the hallway, then closed again behind him with a soft swish.

A group of men was circled around an operating table in the center of the room. They turned as one at the noise of his entry. Even as he fired the first shot, Caleb subliminally took in a woman's pale naked legs, visible between the bodies of the men. She was spread-eagled on the table.

Every bit of moisture in his body turned to dust, and his heart stopped beating in his chest.

Was she . . .

"Not Heather." *Thank you, God.*

It helped that the guy at the end of the table, the one about to position himself, had his pants around his knees, and his dick waving in the breeze. The second guy was clearly surprised to be wearing a hole in the middle of his uni-brow.

"Need help?" Rook asked hopefully in his ear.

"Nah. Two down, only five to go. Dumb asses have their weapons tossed on a cart thirty feet away." Didn't mean that they weren't armed anyway. Caleb hoped they weren't. While he would have enjoyed a close encounter of the violent kind, he damn well didn't have the time. He popped off Number Three before Number Two hit the floor. And by the time Four, Five, Six, and Seven came at him at once, he had his knife in his other hand just to speed things up.

He hated to rush his work, especially since he itched

to take these guys on and build up a real sweat. But somewhere in this building, Heather needed him. He had to go.

Not only weren't they armed, but they sure as shit were predictable, Caleb thought, almost disappointed. They poured all their energy into rushing up at him. Way too fucking enthusiastic.

He shifted to the right, knowing someone was behind him.

He snapped back his elbow with hand support. The man shifted just before the blow landed, rendering Caleb's defense ineffectual. The guy grabbed him, binding his arms at his sides. Not for long, but long enough for Caleb's gun to fly out of his numb fingers.

Shit.

He dropped his head forward, then reared sharply, slamming the back of his head into the man's nose, at the same time spinning out of his way.

Guns were handy. But at this close range, mobility and balance were almost as good. And being quick, better still. And he was *quick*.

Bending his knees slightly to lower his center of gravity, Caleb asked conversationally, "Who wants to die first?"

Rook snorted in his ear.

Number Five came at him with blood in his eye, literally. Blood poured from his nose, and his eyes were already swelling closed. Jesus, where did they find these guys? Caleb waited until the guy was three feet away, then gave him a roundhouse kick to the temple that took him out. A kick above the waist wasn't always the smartest of moves; one snap kick in the balls from the bad guys could leave the good guy on the floor clutching his groin for a good five minutes.

But these guys didn't have the spin-and-kick mentality.

And not only was Caleb faster, he knew how and where to kick, plus he was motivated to kill them all—preferably slowly. He'd keep one alive, just to force the son of a bitch to take him to Heather, even if he had to drag the guy there by his scrotum.

Number Seven scrabbled to pick up Caleb's gun. Unless he happened to be employed by T-FLAC, the terrorist wasn't going to get off more than one shot. It was the way he held the gun that gave him away. Hand shaking as he babbled in Arabic, he fired, only managing to hit Five as he was falling to the floor.

"Now see that?" Caleb told Seven sternly. "I *did* that already. Number Five got killed twice. How do you expect world dominance if you have a shaky trigger finger?"

He circled, watching Seven and Four's eyes as they came at him. Six was creeping up behind him to his left. Caleb couldn't see him, but he knew exactly where he was.

"You guys watch too many American movies. Straighten up, for God's sake," he told them, looking at Four. Seven wasn't as dumb as he looked, and got it. Four straightened up immediately after. He heard Rook snicker, and had to agree. This was like taking freaking candy from a baby.

Four's nose connected with Caleb's fist. Since Caleb's fist was going, oh, sixty miles an hour right then, the guy's eyes rolled. He tripped over his own feet as he crumbled, bounced, and crashed into the wall before he lay down on the floor in a heap of bloody unconsciousness.

Six was still behind him and to the left. Caleb shot a glance at his watch. Forty-three seconds since he'd walked into the room. Too long. "Gotta go, gentlemen."

He spun around, grabbed the man coming up behind him by the wrist and collar with two fingers, his knife in his left hand, and jerked Number Six toward his body and off-balance. Then drove his right foot into the front of the guy's knee. *Hard.* Six yelped, of course. They always did when a bone snapped.

While he dealt with Six, Caleb slashed to the side, connecting with Number Seven's gun hand in a downward sweep that went through flesh and tendon to the bone. The man screamed, and his weapon dropped to the polished floor with a clatter. Caleb did a cool move his brother Duncan had taught him. He stepped up on Six's leg—his whole body weight, and practically walked up the man's body. Six ducked, trying to get away from the force of Caleb's foot on his broken leg.

When Caleb was high enough, he kneed Six in the face with a satisfying crunch to the nose.

You just never got this kind of satisfaction from just *shooting* a guy.

From his higher vantage point, Caleb twisted and jumped before Six collapsed against the wall. With his leg still extended, Caleb kicked Number Seven to the ground. Seven scrabbled across the floor, then turned on his back, blasting Caleb with Six's fallen weapon. A good move.

A little too good. Because Caleb had miscalculated and thought the weapon was Seven's and without ammo. The first shot missed, the second connected with his side.

"Shit!"

Lark had been right. Probably should have taken the time to suit up.

Annoyed, Caleb rushed forward to kick the weapon out of Seven's hand before he had a chance to squeeze off another shot. The man was like a frigging Weeble as he rocked up and tried to stagger to his feet. Caleb grabbed Seven's wrist as if to help pull him up, then forced his booted foot between the man's legs, and stomped down hard on his balls. The guy screamed like a girl.

"Dude, I seriously feel your pain. Didn't your mother ever teach you that if you shoot someone, you've got a good chance of taking one in the balls?" Of course Seven couldn't hear him down there in la-la land.

"Tell me you left some for me," Rook bitched in his ear as Caleb took a quick glance at his opponents scattered about.

" 'Fraid not. Hell, I barely broke a sweat." A bullet to the side didn't rate a mention. Been there. Done that. Right now, with adrenaline pouring through his system, he barely felt it anyway.

"Anyone capable of moving—eventually—won't be going anywhere for a good ten minutes," he said quietly into his mic. "Order the garbage detail since you appear to have time on your hands."

He bent to pick up his weapon, checked the clip, then spun around to leave. He paused at the door. With a quarter turn, and a small flick of his wrist, Caleb covered the dead woman's naked body with her clothing, which had been scattered all over the floor.

He glanced at his watch and cursed. Minute five.

The head honcho's private office was right next door to the OR. A feeling of intense dread weighed Caleb down as he opened the door silently. Thanks to his training, his eyes adjusted immediately to the dimness after the bright lighting in the outer hallway.

There was a double click in his ear, the signal indicating that Rook was right behind him, invisible yet lethal as he covered Caleb's back.

The room was washed with an undulating glow. Caleb glanced left to see the source of light. It came from an enormous fish tank situated across the room. The tank was supported on a black stone base that made it look as if the huge glowing body of water was floating three feet off the floor.

Heather and the tango were behind the tank, their shadowy forms undulating in the reflection of the water. Bile rose up Caleb's throat.

Jesus—

Al-Adel had Heather by the hair as he held her head under the water.

Caleb sucked in a breath. Held it. Jesus. How long could she stay under? How long had she been submerged? No sign of air bubbles. Not movement other than her hair, which floated around her face like seaweed.

"Al-Adel!"

Was she alive? Pushing emotion aside, Caleb's attention was pinpointed on his prey.

A flicker of movement from the left. Without removing his attention from the horrific spectacle, he got off a shot at the guy coming up out of the darkness. Rook blasted the dude too. They hit him at the same time, as evidenced by the gurgled scream and thump of a falling body. Caleb didn't give the asshole another thought.

"Release my wife nice and slow," Caleb said in clear Arabic as he approached, his gun out and steady. He didn't have a fucking one hundred percent clear shot. Heather's bent form was sandwiched between the backside of the tank and Al-Adel's body.

Caleb, who'd never hesitated over a shot in his career, hesitated now.

Jesus. Al-Adel was using her as a shield. Heather stood on something behind the tank—a stool or a chair. He was behind her, standing on the floor. The only part visible was the small section of the man's arm holding Heather's head under the water and the top quarter inch of his head.

"Your wife?" the terrorist said blandly in unaccented

English, not bothering to look up. He plunged her upper body deeper into the tank. "She is being *most* uncoopera- tive. And unattractively stubborn. I've been compelled to punish her. No. Stay where you are if you want her alive," Al-Adel warned when Caleb continued to ap- proach him in ground-eating strides.

He couldn't feel his heart beating, Caleb thought vaguely, his eyes fixed on Heather's limp and lifeless form. All his internal organs seemed to be paralyzed, and his eyes burned as he searched for the slightest sign of life. Terror reverberated in his ears.

"Stupid woman refuses to tell me what I wanted to know," Al-Adel said conversationally, foolishly believ- ing that if he assured Caleb of Heather's relative well- being, he could use her body as a shield. "Perhaps you can persuade her where I cann—"

Caleb didn't hesitate, squeezing off the shot.

The bullet sliced off the top of Fazuk Al-Adel's head as neatly as a knife through a hard-boiled egg. Brain mat- ter sprayed the wall, and bloody bits plopped into the tank, dissipating swirls of red through the water.

"Go, go, go." Rook yelled unnecessarily behind him. Caleb had already closed the distance between his posi- tion and Heather's. Oh, Christ . . .

Hips supported by the rim of the tank, she was bent over the edge, her entire upper body submerged. With- out Al-Adel's hand holding her under, her torso floated just below the surface. The underwater lights leached every vestige of color from her face.

Kicking the dead man out of his way, Caleb vaulted onto the base where she'd been standing. Her feet swung free as her body was more inside the enormous tank than out.

No time for being gentle or using finesse. He hauled her limp body out of the water, sending up a formless prayer. Water and blood immediately soaked into his clothing as he cradled her limp body against his chest.

Eyes half open and lifeless, her head flopped back, baring the pale, still line of her throat.

No pulse.

No fucking pulse.

Pain stole his breath, almost incapacitating him in its intensity. His brain knew what his heart refused to acknowledge.

Heather was dead.

He teleported her the hell out of there.

Shimmering into the safe house, he was grateful to see his men waiting for them. He took in at a glance the medical supplies neatly laid out beside the bed. Lark had warned his men, and they were ready for anything.

"Stopwatch." He had no idea how long she'd been dead. "Start at a minute ten," he instructed Farris calmly,

He was already sending energy through to Heather as he laid her on the bed. Her hair crackled and dried instantly, then surrounded her face with static electricity as he passed his hands inches above her face. Gently he closed her lids over her sightless eyes. His hands shook.

Jesus. Oh, Jesus. Her beautiful face . . . Nose and left cheekbone shattered. Throat, contusions. Left arm broken in four places, two ribs . . . *Bean*—Caleb blocked out everything but pouring healing energy into her ruined body.

"One twenty-two," Farris told him. "You're bleeding like a stuck pig yourself, you know?" In some dim recess of his brain, Caleb felt his shirt tear away from his side, then the prick of a needle as Farris did his thing, sewing him up without touching needle and thread.

Whatever.

The front of her delicate flowery sundress was torn. There was so much blood . . . *Bean,* he thought again, throat aching. He ripped the fabric down the front of her dress with both hands, exposing her blood-soaked bra and panties, and the cold, marble whiteness of her skin.

Dekker came over, felt the side of her throat for a pulse. His hand came away bloody. He shook his head at the other two men as he straightened. "She's dead," he said carefully, stating the freaking obvious.

Caleb held out both palms, inches above the swell of her breasts, directly over her heart and lungs, willing every particle of magic at his disposal to flood through her body. His own body vibrated, but Heather remained still. Her skin was as pale as the sheets on which she lay. Her lips were slightly parted and bloodless.

She'd been battered. Beaten. There was no purpose to Al-Adel's vicious treatment before he'd successfully drowned her. Caleb doubted if the son of a bitch had even bothered to question Heather about his missing goddamned money. She'd been sport. As had everyone else the tango and his men had tortured at the medical center.

Sport. Nothing more.

Sick to his stomach at the excruciating pain she'd endured, he braced a knee against the edge of the mattress and yanked his thoughts away from Al-Adel. Away from anything and anyone that would take even a fraction of his attention away from what he had to do.

Dek put a hand on Caleb's shoulder. "I'm sorry, Edge. You didn't get there in time. She didn't—"

"Jesus," Tony Rook said urgently. "TiVo time quick!"

"One-fifty-three," Farris inserted.

"Can't," Caleb said hoarsely. "Not until—Won't work if she's dead. Christ . . ." He almost took a second to magically make the blood covering her disappear because he couldn't stand seeing her covered in it, but he didn't want to take away even that much juice from healing.

Palms warming, he moved his hands slowly across her chest. God help him, he wasn't sure if he was doing it right. What if he wasn't?

Was he using the right power?

The correct intensity?

There was no one to ask.

He was it.

"Two-nineteen. You can bring her back, right?" Farris, who'd known him for twelve years, asked quietly.

I don't know. Christ. I don't know. "Yes," he said flatly. Yes was the only acceptable answer. *Yes. God damn it. Yes.*

He willed his hands steady, his mind clear. He had to give this everything he had. "Tony, get rid of this blood on her so I can see what they—"

He only noticed dimly that the red streaks were immediately gone, leaving behind the obscene bruising and contusions that mottled her skin.

Deep inside his core a fine vibration hummed like an approaching electrical storm. The pulsations traveled quickly from his shoulders through the muscles of his forearms down into his wrists, then sparked through his fingertips inches from Heather's skin. Every atom of his body was involved, all his focus. All his attention was on the broken woman beneath his hands.

His body was on fire now, an internal heat that pulsed and hummed through his veins, building hotter and brighter. A translucent sheet of metallic violet-colored energy pulsed from each fingertip, connecting to Heather's chest in a brilliant stream of magic. As much as he wanted to heal the obvious damage to her face, he concentrated on her core.

"Come back to me, sweetheart. Listen to my voice. Concentrate. Jesus—Heather—Please—"

The only experience Caleb had was "resurrecting" family pets. He and his brothers had been fascinated by his skill. He'd tried backspacing time to before Gabriel's gerbil had been attacked by a cat. It hadn't worked. He'd found that he couldn't manipulate time to prevent a death that had already occurred, not even the few seconds they'd need to get the animal up off the floor and out of harm's way.

"Two-thirty-eight."

"What can we do?" Rook asked, his voice thick. "Anything? What? Say the goddamned word—"

"There are so many fucking factors involved—I have a finite amount of time to bring her back."

"He has to bring her back to life before he can TiVo to before the shooting," Farris told the others quietly. "Three."

"Crap," Rook whispered. "And if he can't?"

"If I can't," Caleb said grimly, "Heather stays dead."

When his mother's cat had died after eating poison, twelve-year-old Caleb had brought it back within seconds, and then TiVoed to before the dumb cat had gone foraging. It had worked.

Trial and error had given him the period of time after death that he had to perform the revivification. He'd brought back Dixie, Duncan's dog. Under four minutes. For an *animal*.

Was it the same for a human? A *pregnant* human? This woman who he . . . This woman who didn't deserve to be in the wrong place at the right time. Because of him?

Would the fact that she was human possibly buy him more time?

Less time?

Did it even *work* on a human?

Farris leaned against the wall, his eyes on the stop-watch, not Heather. "You have more than a personal connection with her. That's a big part of it working, right?"

More personal than shooting a tango, then remembering that he'd forgotten to ask the guy something. In his line of work when someone was dead, Caleb wanted them to stay that way. But not Heather. Not her. "My fucking personal connection to her *killed* her." His hands burned. Hot as fire.

He clenched his teeth as his body vibrated hard, and the stream from his fingertips turned from violet to the color of watery wine.

"Holy crap. Never seen anything like it. Lookit, her cheek is starting to heal," Dekker said, clearly surprised.

Good to know, Caleb thought savagely, but it wasn't her face he was worried about. *Bring her back,* he bargained with God, *and I'll give you any damn thing you want. Just, please. Bring her back to me.* He refused to imagine his world without Heather in it. Somewhere.

Please, God . . .

He locked the knee supporting him as his body shook violently, and the light purplish stream emitting from his fingertips darkened. What did the color change *mean*? he wondered, refusing to give in to the panic, rage, and grief gnawing at his resolve.

"Three zero nine."

Caleb had either been too late to bring his mother back, or he wasn't capable of performing revivification on a human. But he'd tried, damn it. He'd tried.

And *failed.*

Maybe he'd been too young? Maybe *he* just couldn't make it work on a human—"Come back to me, sweetheart."

Ignoring the pain in his hands, arms, and shoulders, he noticed that the color of the current coming from his hands was changing to a deep blue. Were more of her contusions fading? Or was it his imagination?

And Jesus. God. His son? What about his *son*?

"Three thirty-three." Farris's voice barely carried. "Fuck. I feel useless. What can I do to help?"

"Pray," Caleb told his friend, voice grim.

His pain will be deep, her death will be swift. Inside his heart a terrible rift.

Christ. What the hell chance did he have against a Curse that powerful?

No, he told himself with brutal honesty, Heather's death had had nothing to do with Nairne's Curse. He'd known up front, when he'd dragged her willy-nilly into this, that the cost to her would be enormous. Known it. Weighed it. And decided that she was worth the sacrifice to put several powerful terrorist groups out of business.

Heather was dead now, not because of some ancient fucking curse. But because *he'd* put her in danger and sacrificed her life.

The cost had been astronomical.

"Three fifty-eight."

Static electricity moved over her skin and teased her hair as the shimmering, pulsing dark blue light vibrated and danced just above her body. The electricity-like current changed to green, then a mustard yellow, then a brilliant orange—

He didn't give a shit. He had no fucking idea *what* the color changes meant. Whatever the interpretation, nothing seemed to be making a damn bit of difference.

Very little scared him. He was pretty stoic about pain and death. He'd seen shitloads of both.

Oh, Christ. Did he have *seconds*? Minutes? Would his skill be strong enough to bring them back?

He was terrified he knew the answer.

No.

CHAPTER TWENTY-EIGHT

No-air-no-air-no-air.

N

   o

         a

           i

              r

Fight. Him.

Bean.

Caleb—

Oh God. Take another breath and hold it. Hold it. Hold it. Hold it—

Lungs on fire.

Panicked, filled with oppressive dread, Heather couldn't help herself and dragged in a deep shuddering breath, pathetically grateful that she had time to do so before she was submerged again.

"Good God!" A man said, sounding incredulous. "You *did* it. You brought her back."

Her lungs burned from holding her breath for so long the last time he'd held her under. Struggling to open leaded eyes, she knew she'd rather see what was going to happen next than anticipate it. The room swam into focus, soft blue and hazy. The sound of her thudding heart filled her ears.

Disoriented, she blinked away the fog, even as she struggled, fighting to get up. To get away—

"Shh. You're okay." A gentle hand touched her shoulder. *Caleb. Oh, God. Caleb. She would recognize his touch anywhere.* "Lie back, swee—Just lie back and take another deep breath. You're safe."

She didn't feel safe. She felt terrified. And freezing cold. All made worse when Caleb withdrew his hand. A cruel hallucination?

Heather frowned. She was lying on a bed? What new torture was this? A shudder traveled through her body as she forced her eyes to open and stay open.

No terrorist. No fish tank.

The room they were in was unfamiliar. But a quick glance through the window told her they were back in Matera. It was dusk, and the lights across the ravine were just starting to wink on. Warm, balmy air drifted through the open casement window and fluttered the short drapes. The breeze probably smelled of tomato sauce, a dinner staple, but Heather imagined the stench of fishy water, and a shudder rippled down her spine.

She shifted her head to see Caleb sitting on the mattress beside her, elbows propped on his knees. He looked like hell. Jaw shadowed by stubble, he was watching her from sunken eyes. When she shivered he stuck out an imperious hand. "Another blank—" A red blanket materialized in his outstretched hand. He added it to the others already covering her without breaking eye contact.

"How do you feel?" His voice sounded as though he hadn't used it for a while. Or like he'd been yelling. A lot.

She didn't feel . . . pain, she thought, forehead scrunched, and that made no sense at all. She instantly remembered everything, and her hand flew to her belly.

Heart pounding with a sick dread, she licked dry lips.

"Bean?" All her fear came out in that single whispered word.

He balled the hem of the blanket in his fist. "He's—" His throat worked, and his eyes darkened with intense emotion.

The breath left Heather's body and she went completely numb. "Nooo!" she wailed, slammed by unspeakable grief. Tears flooded her eyes. "Caleb, *no.*"

"She thinks he's dead," someone out of sight said quickly. "Tell h—"

"He's *fine.*" Caleb put up a hand, interrupting the other man. "Heather. Jesus. I'm sorry, I didn't mea— Damn it." He brushed her wet cheek, as if afraid to touch her, as sobs erupted from her raw throat. "Listen to me. Bean is okay. Swear to God, he's okay."

Overwhelming relief surged through her. She sat up, sobs ripping from her throat. Impatiently she swiped at her cheeks with both hands as she tried desperately to regulate her uneven breathing and calm down. Her breath hitched. Caleb was many things, and he'd probably told her lies that she'd never ever find out about, but she was certain he wouldn't lie to her about the well-being of their son. "You're s-*sure?*"

"One hundred percent positive."

Sheer, unadulterated fury followed closely on the heels of relief. "Damn it, you scared me to death."

"I'm sorry."

"Y-you're sorry?!" Heather's emotions went from empty to relieved to annoyed to *homicidal* in the space of three heartbeats. "*Sorry?!*" Everything *he'd* made happen in the last few months surged through her in a molten rage.

The "accidental" meeting in the grocery store. The clever seduction. Her pregnancy. His proposal. Bringing her to Italy to flush out her father. Al-Adel drowning her . . .

Every incident had Caleb's name scrawled all over it.

Worse. Much, much worse, she thought, clenching her fists hard enough that she couldn't feel her heart breaking, worst of all—he'd never loved her.

He'd *used* her.

Each separate ingredient churned up a slushy, unhappy stew of emotion deep inside her and erupted like Mt. Vesuvius.

It shocked the hell out of her when her temper totally snapped and she lunged at him with newfound energy. She hit him. Hard. Pummeling him with her fists. His arm. Whack. Chest. Whack. Head. Whack, whack. She wasn't aiming; she could barely see for the tears. She just wanted to hurt him as much as she'd been hurt. Impossible. His lies and deceit had shattered her heart.

"Want me to grab her?" one of his minions asked.

Caleb flinched as her wedding ring caught his temple, but he did nothing to stop her from venting her rage. "It's warranted," he said, meeting her eyes and recoiling slightly as she punched him in the belly. His rock-hard stomach felt like iron against her knuckles. She hit him again, knowing that he was letting her, which just pissed her off more.

"*Your* stitches just busted open, and you can't and won't hold her off—"

That was his friend Keir, Heather realized. Well, she could take him on, too. He's aided and abetted—the sons of bitches.

What was that saying? Hell hath no fury like a woman scorned? Ha! She punched any part of Caleb's lying, scheming body she could reach. His chest. His neck. His face. She pummeled him with every ounce of strength she had in her as she wept uncontrollably. God. She couldn't stop crying. It was as if now that the floodgates were open she was powerless to stop them. Terror, stress, hormones, all conspired against her.

"Get lost, Keir." Caleb's voice sounded old and tired, and she wasn't blind to the hand he put out to stop her from toppling off the bed when she missed his skull with her swinging fist.

She shook his hand off her arm, and slugged him again.

"Using *that* fucking degree and concentration of magic for as long as you did could've killed *you*, dickhead," Keir announced loudly. "I'm sticking around until I'm positive you won't die on me. Or die on her and the baby."

"Then go in the other—Ah, shit—room and close—Christ, sweetheart, that was a good one—the goddamned door, Farris. This is—ow!—private."

Harsh racking sobs ripped through Heather's body, blinding her, even as her mad, furious strength ebbed. She didn't need to see him to know he was right there. Caleb's very essence called to hers, no matter what plane of existence she was on. She couldn't forgive him for that either.

"I hate y-you," she choked. "I'll bloody well hate you *forever*. And s-so will Bean."

"I know," Caleb whispered, his voice raw with emotion. She felt his warm breath on her cheek.

"You p-put us in da-danger," her voice rose. "You put us in a p-position for that lunatic to *k-kill* us. On purpose! Oh, God. This is insane. C-crazy. I can't st-stop crying!" The last came out on a blubbering wail.

"I know, sweetheart. I know," he said softly, finally pulling her into his lap and tucking her head beneath his chin. Wrapping the blanket around her, he held her tightly against him. "Get it all out. I know you were frightened out of your mind, sweetheart. Anyone would've been. He was a horrific, sick bastard. But he's dead now, and we've rounded up most of his followers."

Head as heavy as a fifty-pound bowling ball, Heather

let her sore lids close as she sorted through what he was telling her. Exhaling, she rested her cheek against the solid rock of Caleb's chest, the fight draining out of her.

Caleb's arms tightened protectively around her and he continued whispering foreign words that made little sense, but touched every particle of her being with a sadness that was bigger than they could handle. He rocked her as the sobs tore from the depth of her soul, raw and uncontrollable. She slid her arms about his waist, grabbing the back of his shirt in her fists, burying her face against his throat.

Everything that had happened, everything that Caleb was, was too impossible to wrap her exhausted brain around. It all boiled down to her loving a man who couldn't, wouldn't, love her back.

Tired beyond words, drained, limp, Heather finally stopped crying.

Caleb kept rocking her, rubbing a hand up and down her back. "Christ, sweetheart," he said thickly. "I'm sorry. So goddamned sorry."

"You're sorry?" she repeated, her voice muffled against his chest. "Are you sorry that I was drugged by that madman? Or are you sorry that my introduction to Al-Adel was watching him slit the throat of some poor, whimpering twenty-year-old who'd gone there for her first mammogram?

"Maybe you regret the fact that a bunch of lunatics trained loaded g-guns on me while I was dragged to a chair and tied in p-place? Did you think you could undo it all and I wouldn't remember a damn thing?

"He beat the crap out of me, you bastard. Over and over until my face was on fire. He punched me in the face. B-broke my nose. It *hurt*. I—My lip split. I tasted my own blood. Nobody has ever hit me in my *life*. And you allowed it to happen."

"Honey, I—"

"Do *not* say a word," she warned, lifting her head to glare at him. She'd never felt as much impotent rage as she did right now. Ironically, as furious as she was with Caleb, she made no move to get off his lap or out of his arms. As livid as she was, there was still comfort staying right where she was.

"He punched me so hard, and so often, I knew I'd lose our baby." She squeezed her eyes shut. "I was helpless. I couldn't protect Bean any more than I could protect myself." She curved her arm around the swell of their son, safe inside her. By miracle and by magic, their son was alive, well, and safe. But she hadn't known that then.

Caleb's skin was drawn taut over his cheekbones, and his eyes glittered feverishly as he wordlessly listened to the nightmare spilling from her lips. He looked anguished. As well he should. She damn well wasn't going to spare him the details.

Hearing about it didn't even come close to experiencing it.

"Heather, I—"

She silenced him with a single pointed glance. "He dragged me to that—that freaking *fish tank* and forced my head under the water. The first time it happened so fast I didn't have time to hold my breath—My feet flailed around as I choked in water. My lungs were filling up and I knew I was about to pass out, and all I could think about was calling your name. Over and over and *over* before I lost consciousness."

His lips tightened into a straight line, but he didn't release her.

"At the last possible second—when my lungs screamed for one *sip* of air—he'd pull me out. He did it again and again and a-again. And the whole time I was thinking about *you*. I needed you, Caleb. Bean needed you. Instead, you and your wizard brigade were off doing God knows what. We were *dying*. Do you get that?"

Her jaw clenched as she ground her teeth together. "So, despite the fact that you . . . somehow fixed me, do you see how freaking *comical* that last statement was, given the circumstances? 'You're sorry'?" It was damn hard to be pithy with a runny nose and a tear-blotched face.

He made no excuses. Which in turn pacified her because he *was* damn well *wrong,* and also pissed her off because he should at least have *tried.* Tried to make it right. Some insane part of her psyche still insisted that Caleb Edge, Wizard with a Cause, would always hold her heart.

His lips brushed the top of her head. "I'm the biggest ass on the planet."

"Yes. Y-you are." Jumbled, racing thoughts spun in her head. She lifted her eyes. "How do you know for *certain* that Bean is okay? I'm assuming you, um, vaporized us to get here?"

"Teleported," he corrected softly, his fingers gently tucking her hair behind one ear. "Cut me some slack, sweetheart. You were dead. Instant teleportation was the only hope I had of successfully reviving you."

You were dead. Dead. That concept rattled around her brain for a few numbing moments. "You brought us back." Not a question; the answer was obvious. Somehow thanking him seemed inappropriate.

"I swore I'd protect both you and Bean," he said flatly, his voice thick. "The protection spell I wove didn't work. The reasons why are moot at this point. The spell didn't f—didn't work, and I'll have to live with that for the rest of my life. You were never supposed to be in any real danger.

"Do you hurt anywhere?" He lifted her chin on his finger, forcing her to look at him. Her throat closed painfully at the tenderness she imagined she saw in his eyes.

"Other than the obvious—swollen eyes, red nose, raw

throat from getting hysterical—I'm surprisingly okay." Alive. Bean safe. Heart broken. Yeah. She was fine and dandy.

"I'm sorry, Heather. Sorrier than I can ever tell you. I'm sorry you and Bean got caught in the middle of this. Men like Fazuk Al-Adel and his ilk are responsible for hundreds, if not thousands, of deaths a year, but you were never supposed to be anywhere near them. Swear to God.

"If I'd known that *you* were the key to the missing money, not your father, I would have done this very differently. But I can't change what happened to you now. And for that I'm honest to God sorry. And as apologetic as I am, I still need access to those funds.

"Having their money misdirected has been slowing the tangos down. Not stopped them. If T-FLAC gets control of their billions it will slow the bad guys down even longer. Give us more time to root them out and exterminate them."

She forced herself to break away from him. His voice was so matter-of-fact when he spoke about what "had to be done." Out of the safety net of his arms, she scooted across to the other side of the bed and slung her legs over the side. She sat there for a moment, gathering herself, putting her thoughts into words.

"You were doing your job," she said quietly, not turning to look at him.

"Yeah." Was it her imagination, or did his voice have a bitter edge to it? "That I was."

Grateful that the crying jag was finally over, she rubbed both hands over her hot face. Her eyes were swollen, and her nose was stuffed up. "I need a tiss— Oh." A box of tissue appeared in her hand.

Face hotter than ever, she was horrified to find Keir Farris leaning against the wall watching them. Not attractive. But then she wasn't trying. "How long have you been—forget it." She blew her nose. "I probably need to thank you for whatever part you played in saving me and the baby, but I'm still pissed off about the whole T-FLAC thing, so could you, uh, hit the road?"

His lips twitched, but his eyes were serious. "That part was all Caleb. And I was just sticking around to make sure you didn't kill him." He disappeared.

Would she ever get used to it? Knowing about magic? Would Bean . . . she stopped herself from going there.

"My favorite wizardly skill." She jerked her chin to where Caleb's friend had been propping up the wall. "Why don't you give it a try—" She glanced down to see a smear of still-sticky blood staining her fingers. Not hers.

Her eyes shot to his. "Are you *bleeding*?"

"Where do you want to go?" Caleb asked tightly as he rose. He looked like he'd been to hell and back. His jaw was dark with stubble, his eyes were sunken, and one side of his ripped T-shirt was covered with dried crusty blood. The other, where it was ripped, was dark red and shiny. Worse, it was clear that he was so weak he could barely stand.

She stood, too, pulling up the strap of her torn sundress as it slid down her shoulder. She wanted to be glad he was bleeding. He deserved to bleed, and worse. But somehow she couldn't quite work up the enthusiasm. She didn't know what to think, what to believe anymore.

Pressing a hand to her stomach as it heaved, she thought she'd seen enough violence during the past two days to last her a lifetime. Caleb didn't need her sympathy. If he was hurt, he'd fix himself.

She rubbed her forehead, where a monster headache bloomed. "What day is it? Is my father still dead?" She had no idea if she was in the past, the present, or the damned future.

"Still Sunday. Yes."

"Before I was kidnapped? Before all those poor women at the clinic were butchered?" Please God let all those women be alive.

He shook his head.

Her heart clenched. "Caleb! For God's sake. Why *not*?"

"You were my priority."

She didn't know what to say to that. "Beam me to San Francisco. And beam yourself straight to wherever you need to go—just keep the hell away from me and Bean." Her baby had to be her number-one priority.

"We have unfinished business—"

"Oh. I *so* don't think so."

"If you want the bad guys to stop trying to kill you, you have to give me that early birthday present your mother gave you that day at the flea market."

God. That bright sunny day seemed like forever ago. "How do you know she g—You went back, didn't you?" Instead of feeling like he'd invaded her past, Heather was struck by the familiar sensation of loss. What she wouldn't do to have one more day like that with her mom. To tell her about—everything. And Caleb could pop in and out of time as if he were riding an elevator.

"What was it she gave you?"

The point of prevarication was long past. She just wanted out. She wanted her apartment. Her life. Pick a life, any life, as long as it was . . . a *normal* life. "A few pieces of antique jewelry."

"Can we teleport to San Francisco and take a look?" he asked politely, "or would you prefer going the conventional route?"

"Swear it won't hurt Bean?"

"I've been assured that it won't."

Her eyes narrowed. "Who assured you? The Association of Wizard Midwives?"

His lips twitched with the struggle not to smile.

"Something like that. Believe me, I won't do anything to put you or the baby in jeopardy."

"That ship has sailed. But I want to get this over with as fast as possible. Zap away." She closed her eyes. "Hang on. I'd better use the bathro—Oh." She looked around. "We're here!"

Her apartment was just the same as it had been that fateful day he'd proposed. A lifetime ago.

Caleb shot out a hand to support Heather as she wobbled with reentry. Under the hectic flush on her cheeks from her bout of crying, her face was pale, her pretty eyes a little glassy. She'd had a hell of a day.

"Sit." He deposited her on the side of her very own bed, then pulled over the straight-backed chair from her table. He wasn't feeling so swift himself. He'd almost died bringing her back from death. It had taken every vestige of juice he'd had, and when that was depleted, he'd dug for more.

When the others had tried to tell him it was hopeless, he'd grit his teeth and channeled more energy into her lifeless body, and that of his son.

She looked around her apartment with red, swollen eyes, clearly exhausted. "Weird," she mused. "Everything looks exactly the same as when we left."

Her hair was tousled, she had a smear of dried blood, his, below her ear, and she looked so beautiful, Caleb's heart ached. She was everything he wanted. And everything he couldn't have.

"Is that jewelry here?" He wanted to get this over with. Once and for all.

"No." She ran her fingers through her hair, as if she'd caught his thoughts, and scooted back against the headboard. "I keep most of it in a safety deposit box at a bank in Concord."

"Will you let one of my people bring it here so I can take a look at it?"

"One of your pe—No. You get it." She lifted her chin in what he'd come to recognize as her "hell no" look.

"Unfortunately I have somewhere else I have to be," he told her coolly. Black particles obscured his vision. He clamped a hand tightly on the seat of the chair he was sitting in to remain upright. He had to get out of here before he passed out.

"Yeah. I bet you do. Then sure. Someone *else* can go and get it. I need some pieces myself." Swinging her legs off the bed, she paused to glance at him. "I'm going to get some tea."

Caleb ground his teeth and yanked his phone out of his back pocket as Heather went into the kitchen. Water ran into the sink, followed by the slamming of pots on the tile counter in a very female, nonverbal form of communication.

Still pissed.

And God help him, justifiably so. He closed his eyes and spoke into the phone. "I need you, plus two, here at Heather's apartment, stat."

Caleb flipped the phone closed. Even that took effort. He was physically tapped. Out of juice, and in danger of passing out any second. It had been a fucking miracle that he'd been able to maintain consciousness back in Matera for as long as he had. Adding this teleportation to his already dangerously depleted store of magical energy could very well kill him. There was still a chance Heather could have her wish.

Thank God the cavalry was on its way.

Lark materialized with a bottle of nail polish in her hand, and a dark look on her face. Under a long, swirling black skirt her pale feet were bare and sporting little yellow foam things between her toes. "You look like shit on a shingle," she told him unsympathetically. "This better be important. I was right in the middle of giving myself a pedicure, Middle Edge. What do you want?"

Before he could answer, Dekker arrived, followed by Rook. They both glanced around with interest. "Long time no see," Tony Rook said, grinning.

"The gang's all here," Lark told Caleb, one pierced eyebrow raised in haughty inquiry. Nobody summoned Lark. She was usually the one doing the "get your ass over here, *now*" commands.

Caleb didn't give a shit if he paid for it later. Right now he had, oh, a few minutes at best before he passed out.

"Heather's mother gave her several pieces of antique jewelry the day she was killed. She has it in a safety deposit box about an hour away. Rook—find out where, and go get it. Lark, I want you and Dekker to stick to Heather until—" *Hell freezes over, which is when she'll want to see me again.*

"*Until?*" Lark scowled. "I'm not a babysitter."

The kettle in the kitchen whistled. "Until this business of the money is resolved." Caleb rose, gripping the chair back in a white-knuckled fist. "Promise me—" He pushed the words out, capturing the empath's gray eyes. "Promise that if *anything* happens to me . . . You'll get Heather to Gabriel. He and Duncan will protect h—"

Black rolled over him in a wave.

CHAPTER TWENTY-NINE

Heather spent five minutes in the kitchen trying to get a grip on herself. Her hormones weren't cooperating and she sure as hell didn't want to cry anymore. Particularly when she said her final good-bye to Caleb.

Which she knew she'd be doing as soon as he had that damned jewelry.

Fine. She'd deal with it. Too bad she didn't have Caleb's ability to reverse time. This would be a lot easier if she hadn't married him. If she didn't love him. If she weren't *pregnant*? No. Now, more than ever, she wanted her son.

She'd washed her face in the kitchen, then held an ice-filled towel over her eyes while the kettle came to a boil. Too bad there wasn't any makeup in here. She looked like hell. It would have been nice to wave good-bye to him looking strong and beautiful, a little like Charlize Theron in one of her good movies instead of a lot like Charlize in *Monster*. People had commented on her resemblance to the actress before, but right now what Heather really needed was some of the woman's acting talent.

Strolling out of the kitchen with a mug of tea in her hand, as if she didn't have a worry in the world, took a ton of effort. Glancing up to casually offer Caleb a cup of tea, she did a double take. There was a strange woman with her foot propped up on the worktable, painting her toenails. The woman, a girl really, had red-and-black-striped hair, silver balls pierced into her eyebrows, and red lips. She wore a long flounced black taffeta skirt and a long-sleeved black baby T. Her feet were bare except for yellow toe separators.

Heather didn't need to look around to know that Caleb was gone. Her entire body felt his absence.

The stranger didn't bother with a greeting, but Heather would bet her favorite emerald pin that the woman knew to an inch exactly where she was standing.

Leaning against the doorjamb, Heather dunked the tea bag in her cup. *Where the hell is Caleb? And why couldn't he at least say good-bye?* Her eyes burned. Damn it. *And if I cry again I'll never forgive myself.* "Can I help you?" she asked mildly.

"Not unless you have some cuticle cream." The woman didn't even glance up as she continued painting her toenails poppy red. "I'm here to watch you."

"Watch me do what?" Heather took a sip of her tea, and observed her visitor over the rim of the mug. All recent events considered, seeing this strange young woman in her apartment was the least shocking.

Her visitor took her foot off the table and capped her nail polish before giving Heather a friendly smile. "Hey, I'm Lark Orela."

That didn't tell Heather anything. "Okay."

"Is that herbal?"

"Black currant. Would you li—Ah." Lark Orela had produced an identical steaming mug in her own hand. "I take it you're a wizardette?"

"That's funny," Lark said, amused, eyes twinkling. "I'm an empath, and in theory, I'm Caleb's boss." She wrinkled her nose. "As much as that's possible. Bed or chair?"

"By all means, take the chair." Heather settled cross-legged on her bed, feeling as though she'd fallen, once again, down a damned rabbit hole. Her guest sank gracefully onto the chair in a swirl of taffeta.

"I must say"—Lark blew on her tea, watching Heather over the rim with penetrating gray eyes—"you're more than I expected."

"More what?"

"More substance. More depth. Just . . . more."

"Wow. That's so nice to know," Heather said sarcastically.

"He's cursed, you know."

"*Bean?*" Heather asked, horrified, placing her hand over her tummy in an instinctively protective gesture.

"*Caleb.* He told you. Right?"

Pausing, she considered the story he had told her on the plane. "Frankly, I thought it was a cute fairy tale. I didn't believe it. Not at the time."

"And now you do?"

"Now I know that there are things in this world that nobody would believe. But since I've seen these things with my own two twenty-twenty eyes, I don't have a choice. It's either be flexible on what I thought I knew or be crazy."

"That's a start." Lark smiled. "He didn't tell you the entire Curse, you know. He left out the important bits."

"Which, apparently, you are dying to share with me." Heather leaned over to put her empty mug next to the bowl of seashells on her bedside table. She straightened, leaned back on her hands, and tilted her chin. "Have at it."

"You know his parents tried to have a marriage?" Lark asked, holding Heather's gaze. "Man, those two were *insanely,* crazy in love with each other." She sipped her tea. "But of course it didn't work. Nairne's Curse and all. They gave it their best shot, and it so didn't work. Hell on the three boys. Hell on *them.* End of story."

"Caleb didn't marry me for love," Heather said coolly. "He married me to get to my father. We'll be getting a divorce as soon as he gets back, I'm sure."

"You're sure?"

Heather shrugged. "He's given no indication that he'd want it any other way. I have no desire to be married to a man I can't trust." *And who doesn't love me back,* she added silently.

This was such a freaking weird conversation. How could this *girl* be Caleb's boss? She looked like a beautiful runway model who had zigged instead of zagged. Heather forced herself not to a put a hand to her hair, but she couldn't help wishing that she could have half an hour in her bedroom in Paris, with all her makeup and a huge wardrobe of designer clothes to choose from.

"And what *do* you want?"

"I don't—"

"Never mind," the woman interrupted. "What you want isn't important."

Ha! Maybe not to her. But it was damned important to Heather. "The Curse?" she asked, a feeling of dread in her heart.

" '*Duty o'er love was the choice you did make,*' " Lark quoted in a musical voice. " '*My love you did spurn, my heart you did break.*' That was Nairne talking to Magnus Edridge when he told her he was marrying the Laird's daughter. '*Your penance to pay, no pride you shall gain. Three sons on three sons find nothing but pain.*' Five hundred years of three sons to each wife," Lark explained. "Caleb told you all that. Here's the bit he left out.

" '*I gift you my powers in memory of me.*' She made them wizards. Nothing wrong with that part." The empath smiled. "Now this is the part that these boys take very seriously. So listen up. '*The joy of—*' "

"I've heard this. And frankly, I don't care." Heather

suddenly had to get away from Lark. She slid off the bed and avoided the woman's piercing gray eyes. Remembering that the damn apartment was too small to pace effectively, she leaned against the wall beside the bed and folded her arms.

" '*The joy of love no son shall ever see,*' " Lark continued, skirts swishing. " '*When a Lifemate is chosen by the heart of a son, No protection can be given, again I have won.*' "

She cast pale eyes in Heather's direction. "Do you get that? *No protection can be given. That's* why Caleb's protection spell, as powerful as it was, didn't *work* on you."

Heather straightened away from the wall. "I'm not his Lifemate."

" '*His pain will be deep, her death will be swift. Inside his heart a terrible rift.*' You *died.*"

"Oh, for—Because Al-Adel kidnapped and tortured me. It had nothing to do with the damn *curse!*" Shivering now, as if she were about to come face-to-face with another horrible truth, Heather bit her lower lip to keep from screaming.

" '*Only freely given will this curse be done. To break the spell, three must work as one.*' "

"What is it that must be freely given?" Heather asked tightly. "Because someone should do whatev—" Tony Rook materialized behind Lark's chair without warning and Heather jumped back. "Damn it, can't you people *knock* or ring a bell when you do that!" Honest to God. She should be used to people appearing and vanishing by now. Which just showed how off-kilter her life had become lately.

"Sorry." He glanced at Lark.

"How's the package?" she demanded. Black brows, shiny silver balls and all, came together in a scowl as she looked up at him. She sounded a lot older than she looked.

Tony shrugged one shoulder. "Beat to shit."

"Can it be fixed?"

"Twenty-four hours."

Heather wondered with rising annoyance if they thought she was stupid. Caleb was in trouble. He'd been bleeding when she came to. *Someone*—Tony? Keir? had commented on him opening his stitches while she'd been having her minibreakdown back in Matera. Why had he required stitches? *When* had he had stitches? Those were just a few of the pressing questions she had for him.

If she ever saw him again.

"Heather?" Tony said as if he'd called her name before. "Can you give me the bank's address so I can pick up that stuff? Caleb put a tracking spell on it, but the um—code—kinda slipped his mind."

Nothing slipped Caleb's mind, Heather thought with alarm. Not a damn thing. A small notepad and pen materialized in her hand. She wasn't even surprised. "Only if you promise to bring it to me first," she told him, writing down the name of the bank, the location, and her pin code. "I'll know which is which." She looked up just in time to observe Tony Rook glancing at Lark. The woman nodded.

Heather handed over the piece of paper, hoping against hope that she was doing the right thing. "Maybe I should go—"

Lark shook her head. "Rest. It'll be fine."

Tony knocked twice on the back of Lark's chair, then disappeared.

"Cute," Heather said, almost smiling before remembering what she'd heard. "What's wrong with Caleb?"

"He ran out of power." Lark pointed at Heather's mug on the table. "More tea?"

"In a minute—Okay. Thanks." Heather reached over and picked up the full mug, taking a sip through the steam. The heat was calming. "How and why 'out of power'?"

"His special power is manipulating time—But you already know that. When he shifts, he loses strength when he returns to real time. He went back to see your mother. He was gone for four hours. Normally it would take him under an hour to recuperate when he got back. It's always been that way. He compensates for it. But your pregnancy changed that. This time it took four hours for him to regain his full strength."

"My *pregnancy*? What has that got to do with Caleb's powers?"

"Couvade syndrome. From the moment you conceived he's experienced most of the physical discomfort of your pregnancy. The nausea. The fatigue. The cravings." Lark grinned. "The irritability."

"I still don't see—"

Lark's smile faded. "Each time shift uses more . . . juice . . . for want of a better word. If he needs to backspace, teleport, or use any of his other skills, each one depletes him more." She sipped her tea, then said matter-of-factly, "You were dead. He brought you back. Your face was pulp. He fixed it. Any one of our acquaintances would have said what he did was impossible. He's the only wizard known to have ever performed a revivification on a human. It took him five hours."

Lark got up, pacing the room as if searching for answers.

Been there, Heather thought, watching her. *Done that.*

"Why didn't he take a break? Doesn't he have some sort of apprentice or assistant?"

Sniffing, the woman said in her husky voice, "It doesn't work that way. Sure, we all have shared talents—teleporting, that kind of thing, but each wizard has a unique skill. Some, like Duncan, have lots of unique skills."

"Okay, so Caleb drained himself to save me and the baby." *Still didn't completely erase the fact that he'd put them in danger in the first place. But it helped.* "Did he run out of . . . juice before he could fix himself?"

"Can't fix himself. Ever. But it's more than that," Lark said. "Even if he hasn't admitted it, Caleb knows you're his Lifemate."

Heather rolled her eyes. "He's got a strange way of showing it."

"He returned from the four-hour backspace to Paris. Immediately teleported to find you without having time to regenerate. Got shot. Teleported you back to the safe house. Enough of his juice had already been depleted to flatten him like a pancake right there. *Then* he performed an incredible feat of revivification on you and your son. Two people. Five hours. Sounds like a lot of 'showing' to me."

Heather heard the controlled anger in Lark's voice, which only made what she'd just said more real. Her throat closed with a terrible fear. "Is he going to die?"

"I have no idea."

Heather's heart skipped several heavy beats. "That's pretty damn cold."

Lark shrugged her elegant shoulders. "He knew the risks. He took them. He had to keep your baby safe."

Heather curved an arm across her middle. Her mouth went cotton dry. *Please say it was because he loved them.* "Why?"

"Because your child is going to grow up to have unimaginable powers. Believe me, I know."

"Oh, God," she whispered weakly, the news overpowering her feelings of being used. Even if it was for a higher good.

"Not quite, but close." Picking up Heather's ringing phone, she said. "Hi, this is Heather."

Heather felt a chill run up her spine. Lark didn't just sound like her, she sounded *exactly* like her. "I will," Lark said, again in Heather's voice. "It will take me at least an hour to get there." She put the phone down and drew in a deep breath.

"How did you do that? No. Never mind. I want to see Caleb. *Now.*"

"You can't." Lark's vibrant face had drained of color. "The El-Hoorie brothers have him. They're holding him for ransom."

The blood drained from Heather's head, and her heart went manic. "That's impossible. He's . . ." *Invincible. A wizard. A T-FLAC operative.*

"Barely alive," Lark finished grimly.

"But Caleb barely alive is better than any *other* man on steroids, right?" When Lark didn't respond, Heather repeated, *"Right?"*

"Not this time."

Don't panic, Heather told herself as she felt a surge of sheer fear swarm through her. Her experience with Al-Adel had been so recent that she couldn't help immediately flashing back to what had been done to her. How scared she'd been. How much pain she'd had to endure.

And the final result of the terrorist torturing her.

Caleb had brought her back, at great loss to himself.

Who would bring him back if—

No one.

He'd told her that, to his knowledge, he was the only wizard who could revive a person, and Lark had just confirmed it.

"My number is unlisted. How did they—"

"Used Caleb's cell phone."

Heather forced herself to remain cool and calm. It wasn't easy. Her brain was darting about like a gerbil on a wheel. She opened the door to her almost-empty closet. "They don't know he's a . . . a wizard fighter/agent/super spy, though, right?" That gave him a huge advantage.

"They know he's T-FLAC. They got him at the hospital. And the fact that's he's a powerful wizard is moot right now. His magical powers are completely on the fritz."

"The ransom they want is the forty-eight billion dollars my mother stole or they'll kill Caleb?" Heather swallowed nausea, still reliving her brief, but interminable experience with the terrorists. She couldn't bear to think of Caleb in similar circumstances. She pulled out a pair of jeans, a T-shirt, and sneakers from her suitcase.

"They'll settle for the location and access to the money. They insist you deliver."

Heather went into the bathroom to change out of her ripped sundress, leaving the door ajar so she could hear Lark. "Of course they do." Just the thought of going anywhere *near* the people Caleb and Lark dealt with in their line of work made her sick to her stomach. The other part of her was fully focused on Caleb's plight. The images in her head of what they'd be doing to him this very second weren't pretty.

The beatings and drowning *she* hadn't survived were crystal clear and debilitatingly fresh in her memory.

"You're not going, of course," Lark told her. "I'm sending a female T-FLAC operat—"

"*I am* going." Heather stepped out of the bathroom dressed for combat in jeans and a black T-shirt. "My mother took that money. My father did business with these people." Her mouth settled into what she knew was a stubborn line. "It's a Shaw problem, and a Shaw will fix it." *Caleb is there.* In some wacky, insane way, she had to be the one to bring this full circle.

"You may be a Shaw," Lark informed her, her tone unbending. "But you're carrying an *Edge* child."

"Then an invisible someone, *several* invisible some-ones better be with me to ensure our safety." Heather sat on the chair to put on her shoes. "What condition is Caleb in?"

"If they were able to take him? Pretty damn bad."

Heather tightened the laces of her shoe, her heart speeding with surging adrenaline. "Does his power come back in a rush or is it incremental?"

"Incremental."

She finished tying that shoe, and went to work on the other. "Okay. So it's been building up in the last hour or so. Right?"

"What's the question?"

"I'm trying to figure out how strong he is, and if he's got any of his powers—" There was a hard double rap on the table next to her before Rook materialized. She stood, brushing her damp hands against her jeans. "Thank you, Tony. Caleb has been kidnapped by some brothers."

"Ah, shit." He glanced at his boss. "Saif and Muhsin El-Hoorie got to him? How? Is he suddenly jinxed or something?"

Lark's pretty face showed her concern. "He is not jinxed, he's being stubborn. And the answer to the first question is: at the hospital. He was in a coma."

Heather spun around to glare at her. "You didn't tell me he was in a coma!"

"If he wasn't, do you think anyone could have snatched him?"

Heather scowled. "But wasn't he in a . . . *T-FLAC* kind of hospital? How the *hell* could bad guys just waltz in and take him like this? What kind of flaky freaking se-curity people do you guys *have*?"

Like Heather, Tony Rook gave Lark an incredulous

look. "Couldn't've happened," he said flatly. "Not possible."

"Oh, I'll find out how, don't worry." Lark told them flatly. "Heads will roll. Literally. For now, let's concentrate on what we *do* know. Start with that stuff." She indicated the briefcase Tony held.

"Dump it on the table," Heather instructed, tucking her shirt into the waistband of her jeans. "Let's see what my mother gave me."

He emptied the contents of the sleek leather case on the table. "Where and when for the drop?" Rook's attention was turned to Lark as Heather started sorting through the various pouches. She pretty much knew what was in each of the silk or chamois bags on the table. About three mil in pretties. Diamonds, various semi-precious gemstones, and pearls. But she wasn't interested in any of those pieces.

She searched the colorful pile for the small gray silk drawstring bag her mother had given her at the flea market the day she'd been killed.

"Monterey Bay Aquarium."

Heather's head shot up as her brain immediately filled with the image of bursting lungs and sheer, unadulterated terror. "More *fish tanks*?! No way!"

"Way. Don't worry about it. You won't be going."

Heather found and opened the familiar small bag. Lark and Tony were nuts if they thought she'd sit idly by when the father of her child was in danger. "Here it is. Let's see what's worth almost fifty billion."

Lark and Tony came closer. "That's it?" he asked, openly disappointed.

So was Heather. A pair of earrings, a brooch, and half a dozen old-looking bracelets rattled onto the wood surface of the table. Each bracelet was between two and five inches wide. Heather suspected that her mother had bought all the similar-looking pieces together, probably tied with a ribbon, or in a pretty box. Her mother had loved the chase of finding treasures; their value was immaterial. As far as Heather knew, her mother had never worn any of these pieces. They were all discolored with tarnish, age, and years' worth of dirt. And then she noticed the slip of paper that had floated onto the table with an address on it in her mother's handwriting.

"Well?" Lark demanded.

Heather picked up her jeweler's loupe and the closest bracelet. "What am I looking for?"

"Microchip, maybe?" Rook suggested.

"Numbers," Lark said impatiently. "Probably a Swiss account, and this address is most likely the bank's location."

Whatever it was, Heather wanted to find it *fast*. The thought of Caleb held hostage and powerless made her insane. Was this how he'd felt when he found out *she'd* been taken? "This looks like a mixed alloy. Probably an imitation of something far more valuable." She twisted it slowly between her fingers, inspecting the outer surface. It was so black with grime it was hard to make out the stamped relief design. She turned it so she could see inside, her curiosity aroused. "It's filthy, and frankly, I have no idea what a microchip would look like if I saw one."

"It's not a microchip," Lark said impatiently. "It'll be numbers. Some offshore account. Trust me."

Heather, fighting her own flare of impatience, said, "I can't see anything with all this gunk on it. All this stuff needs to be cleaned. And that's going to take forev—"

The pieces transformed before her very eyes, and she laughed. In under a second, Lark had whisked away years of grime that would have taken Heather hours of tedious, painstaking work. The sooner she could get the information, the sooner they could save Caleb. Heather turned and smiled at them both. "It's good to know people with skills."

All the pieces were pristine save for one. "I wonder why that didn't work on this piece?" Picking up the blackened bracelet, she twisted it to the light. "My God—" She met Lark's eyes. "The numbers *are* here." A long string of them, circling the inside of the bracelet. If she hadn't been specifically looking for something, she never would have seen them. The piece was black and cruddy, the indentation of the numbers almost filled in with the dirt and tarnish of years, decades, hell—*centuries*.

"This is so weird. Weird and *impossible*. My mother must have had this engraved a year ago. In which case all this black crud would have been cleaned away with the engraving tool." She twisted the piece, trying to read the numbers. Almost impossible. If she hadn't been looking closely, she would have missed them completely. Dismissed the little she *could* see as some sort of pattern on the inside of the metal circle.

She picked up a sheet of pale pink tissue paper, used when she boxed her own designs, and placed it on the inside of the piece of jewelry, then ran a soft pencil gently over the numbers, hoping they'd be able to read them a little better.

"Is that working?" Lark asked, watching her intently from across the room.

"Amazingly, yes." Heather removed the thin sheet of paper from the circle and laid it on the table. All the numbers appeared to be there, revealed by the rubbing of the lead pencil. "We have what we need." She slipped the heavy metal bracelet onto her left wrist and stood. "Let's go."

"I'd prefer you didn't," Lark said in a neutral tone. "We have professional operatives who are trained to do retrieval."

"Excellent. Then send a bunch of them with me. Because I have to tell you, the thought of going anywhere near A, terrorists, and B, large tanks filled with fishy water scares the bejesus out of me."

Lark gave her a cool-eyed look. "And what do you think *you're* going to do when you get there?"

"I'm going to do exactly as they tell me to do." Heather returned Lark's stare. "Hand this damn bracelet over. Then I expect your 'professional operatives' to get Caleb and myself the hell to safety. How long do I have to wait, and how many are coming?"

"You're out of your mind. You know that?"

"In case you aren't as empathetic as you claim, I'm in love with the damn man. Which absolutely makes me out of my mind. Is *that* reason enough?"

"Not if your craziness gets you killed."

"Is *Caleb* the only person who can put a protective spell on me?"

"If you recall, that didn't work worth a damn."

"Because *he* did it." The fact that Caleb's spell didn't work gave her a warped sense of satisfaction. He might not like it, but if what Lark had told her about the Curse and a Lifemate was true, Caleb did love her. Despite his actions and attitude.

That remained to be seen. But first things first. "Can you protect me?"

"I can," Keir Farris said grimly, appearing over by the window in a shadowy flash.

"She likes us to knock," Rook told him.

Four raps sounded in quick succession. Two on the table in the middle of the room, one on the closet door, and one on the wall by the kitchen.

"Excellent," said Heather dryly. "Gratifying to know that wizards can be trained."

CHAPTER THIRTY

The El-Hoorie brothers looked more like their Greek mother than their Arabic father, Caleb though, his brain thick and fuzzy from the drugs they'd pumped into him. Apparently their parents had hit every branch of the ugly tree on the way down, then added insult to injury by breeding a pair worse-looking than themselves. Both brothers were large mounds of too-tanned flesh, curly black hair, and the flat features of a pair of identical gerbils. Kicking their asses could only be an improvement.

Hell, being capable of *moving* right now would be nice.

Unfortunately, he was weaker than a baby, and freaking drugged to the gills to boot. They'd propped him up on a bench and left him there half an hour ago, knowing he wasn't going anywhere. He'd just mastered *blinking* five minutes ago. The exercise had left him dizzy and exhausted.

Twin sets of mud-colored eyes had bored into his, daring him to fuck up their plans as they'd slapped Flexi-Cuffs on his wrists and ankles tightly enough to instantly cut off his circulation. Considering at the time that he was barely conscious, he guessed they weren't quite as stupid as they looked. He wasn't going to be out of it forever.

It only fucking *felt* that way right now.

He tried to snap open the cuffs magically. The effort

left him limp and sweating, and the cuffs secure. Damn it.

From his forced perusal of the three-story-high kelp forest tank, he caught sight of a watery El-Hoorie image as they directed the men to various positions in the semi-dark aquarium behind him. The aquarium was obviously closed, and the enormous building was empty save for himself, the El-Hoorie brothers, and their men. About twenty of them in all. Other than an occasional squeak of a rubber sole on the floor, and the susurrus of voices, it was eerily quiet.

The brothers weren't actually stupid at all. They hadn't gotten where they were in the world of terror—Number 4 on T-FLAC's terrorist watch list—by not thinking things through all the way. The fact that they'd also managed to think on their feet and grab him was an indication of the level of their intelligence.

And, Caleb thought groggily, trying to force his brain to come onboard, him being here, showed the level of *his* intelligence. Swamp scum was smarter than he was at the moment. Un-fucking-believable that he'd walked directly into their hands. It sucked that it was his own fault he had prime seating for this event.

He'd come to in the hospital—apparently it had been touch-and-go, and he'd fallen into a coma. Yeah—whatever. He'd woken up, back at the same San José facility where he'd spent those endless months after his knee replacement. Even before he'd opened his eyes, the first thought as he swam back to consciousness was *Heather.*

In his more dead-than-alive addled brain he'd had some crazy notion that he should talk to her. Make her not . . . hate him. In a mental fog, he'd even thought about the "L" word. Stupid. It was just that he couldn't shake the feeling that they had unfinished business.

He'd yanked out the IV and found his clothes. He wanted out of there. He wanted, God damn it, *Heather.*

It was a minor detail that he was only just ambulatory, and his brain was uncooperative. He'd been on auto-pilot.

Heatherpilot.

The first person to ream his ass, if he got out of here in one piece, would be his doctor. Barely able to stand, sure as shit not thinking straight, he'd slipped out AMA. Against doctor's orders, and feeling the warm drip down his side indicating that he'd messed up the man's handi-work before he reached the front door of the hospital.

The second would be Lark. The list went on from there.

Heather, with the way he'd left without saying good-bye, probably just thought he was out of her life. And she probably wanted him to stay there. She didn't need to know how close he'd come to biting it for good in her apartment.

He'd stuck close to a hedge in the dark and made it down the long, private driveway without being seen by security personnel, who were watching for people trying to get in, not break out. They were good, but even in the condition he'd been in, he was better.

By the time he slipped through the gates and walked three blocks in search of a cab, he was holding onto walls to keep upright. Drenched in sweat, barely conscious, he knew he'd done something unbelievably stupid.

Shit, he might as well start a list. A *long* list of all the stupid shit he'd been doing lately.

Maybe this whole couvade syndrome had somehow eaten up the majority of his brain cells. He had no idea. But he'd better freaking snap to it and find some smarts *fast*.

The El-Hoories must've lain in wait and followed him from the hospital. Later, he'd figure out how the hell they'd tracked him down. He hadn't been quite able to get his cell phone off his belt, and they'd snatched him up as he'd been searching his pockets for the change he needed for the pay phone.

That injection into his throat had come fast.

He'd woken up here. With the fishes.

Whatever drug they'd given him was still sluggishly floating around in his system. That, combined with his already drastically weakened state, made him an easy freaking mark.

Note to self: Revivification sucks the juice out of a man. Got it.

They'd used some sort of paralytic, which had been extremely effective. And here he was, tied to a bench. Damned uncomfortable, but not life-threatening. He tried to move. His eyelids were still all he could control. Hard to kill a guy with a fast-moving lid, he thought, too doped up to be as scared as he knew he should be.

He wasn't used to being or feeling helpless. He wasn't used to operating without his powers for this long either. *That* scared the crap out of him and got a good bit of adrenaline surging through his veins.

He'd depended on magic to get him through almost every type of situation, had depended on it *being* there, all of his life. He'd always taken his powers for granted. Yeah, he was a good shot, sure he could use hand-to-hand combat to take down his enemies. But it was his *powers* that always saved the day.

Yet here he was—powerless. For how frigging long? *That* was the billion-dollar question.

Caleb almost wept when he found that he could now manage to wiggle his thumbs. Yes! He concentrated on moving each finger in turn, relief washing through him as they each seemed to work. Sluggishly, but mobile.

It took every scrap of concentration, but he magically snapped open the cuffs on his ankles and wrists.

With the paralytic added on to everything else his body was trying to fight, he needed to flush out his system. Fast. Keeping an eye on the activity, Caleb conjured a matte-black jar containing a high-potency vitamin/energy drink.

He chugged it down, filled it with water, and kept drinking until he couldn't manage any more. While he'd managed, at great effort, to summon it, he was still incapable of enough movement to hold it in his hand, and he didn't have enough power to keep the glass suspended near his mouth for long. It fell to the floor with a soft clatter, then rolled beneath the bench. No one appeared to notice the sound.

The water seeped into his parched cells, reviving him while he waited for the vitamins to go to work.

He opened and closed his fingers. Made fists. Yeah. Getting there.

The brothers' main claim to fame was a proclivity for blowing things up, and they were chillingly good at it. Preferably locations where loss of human life could be counted in the hundreds, if not thousands. Like the London Underground station they'd blown up last spring. Or the Tokyo baseball stadium they'd made a big nasty hole in six months ago. Killed seven thousand people. It didn't take any wizardly skills to know this aquarium was their next target.

Since arriving, he'd watched their men positioning enough C4 to blow the lid off the place. For what purpose Caleb had no idea. Who the hell were these guys planning on killing? A handful of schoolkids on a field trip tomorrow? Didn't make sense.

There was an easel with a sign on it at the far end of the room, but he couldn't read what the poster was announcing. Whatever the event, the brothers planned on killing it in their usual spectacular way.

While Caleb exercised his fingers and tried to bring blood back into his hands, he watched for the brothers' return. Since he had already played the Who-has-it-where-is-our-money game for the better part of half an hour, with various new bruises to prove it, he knew they were waiting for his brain and mouth to connect before giving him another opportunity to answer their questions.

In the meantime they knew, and he knew, that he wasn't going anywhere, and wouldn't be chatting for a while.

The kelp forest in front of him would have been cool, if he hadn't felt like the proverbial axe was about to fall. He knew enough of the plan to realize they were waiting for someone tonight. Who?

Bad guys didn't have a toll-free number to T-FLAC, so he was curious to see just who they'd called. Who did they think could tell them where their money was?

Couldn't be Heather. They didn't know where she was, and even if they did, she had Lark and his team with her. No one was going to get near her now.

A leopard shark did a lazy one-eighty through the gently swaying kelp. The glass on the giant tank was a good seven, maybe eight, inches thick and the air filters and mechanics were merely a faint hum in the silence. The tank was open to the room, and pale moonlight filtered through the gently undulating amber-colored fronds, highlighting the silver scales of a school of sardines as they darted about.

Unobtrusively, he tested his ability to move to see just how much longer he was going to have to pretend a drugged fascination with the flora and fauna of Monterey Bay. And when he'd be able to make his move.

Soon.

Definitely before any bad shit went down.

His thoughts went straight to Heather. As soon as he got the hell out of here he was going to talk to both Gabriel and Duncan and start the ball rolling as far as her and Bean's safety went. Their future.

The last few days had been a grim reminder of what the future held for him. Years of unfulfilled longing and torturous concern as he constantly chose his work over the family he'd created. At least he knew he could depend on MacBain to send him pictures and daily updates.

The Gerbil brothers and their entourage were spread out behind him, but he could see them just fine in the reflection of the kelp tank. He watched as they became animated, muttering amongst themselves. The brothers grinned, creating an even uglier expression on their almost identical pug faces. He concentrated on reading their lips, but his Greek was marginal at best. And lip-reading a reflection damn well impossible.

The squeak of a tennis shoe on the polished cement floor alerted him to a new player. It was time.

When Heather's reflection swam across the surface of the glass, Caleb thought he was hallucinating. Hallucinating or not, his heart stopped.

"She is alone," one of the brothers' minions told them in Greek. He sounded as incredulous as Caleb felt.

"I have the numbers for a Swiss bank account, gentlemen." *Heather's* voice. Here. Not only was it totally un-fucking-acceptable, it was *insane*. What had Lark and the others been thinking? Sending her, a civilian, into the lion's den? Caleb's heart trip-hammered as the sound of her tennis shoes came closer. Rubber soles against cement. Fingernails down a chalkboard. Jesus.

Had she slipped out? How had she known where to go? Had he, in his bid to win her back, actually given her position away to the enemy? The base of his skull tightened with fear.

One of the Ugly Brothers held out his meaty hand. "Give it over."

"You let my husband go, and I'll give you the number."

"You give me number, and we don't kill." He gave her a grotesque smile. "Him. You. Where is the number?"

A fair enough question. And while they sorted that out Caleb finally felt confident that his body was back in working order. He did a mental inventory and decided he was strong enough to kick some butt. Physically at least. Not magically just yet.

Heather was thirty feet away. His primary concern was for her safety. He couldn't afford for her to get a freaking *hangnail* right now, because this time it would be impossible to revive her. He couldn't even heal her if she got hurt. Not for at least another six hours, if he'd calculated his skills right.

And he still didn't have the juice for any fancy shit.

A quiet double click sounded directly behind him. Someone was improvising. Nice to know he wasn't alone. He felt a welcome spike of adrenaline knowing that Heather wasn't defenseless.

This was where Keir was supposed to teleport her and Caleb back home and out of harm's way. She braced herself.

Nothing happened.

She bit the corner of her lower lip. Hard. *Come on, Keir. Do it.*

Nothing.

Beside her Keir hissed, *"Shit."*

Uh-oh. What did *that* mean? *Shit*? Oh God. *That* didn't sound good. "Problem?" she asked, not moving her lips. The brothers might not hear her speaking, but she bet if they listened they could hear the hard fast knock of her heart trying to escape.

She couldn't ask what was going on, but she couldn't just stand here mute either. They expected her to negotiate, and she'd damn well better do it.

She gave them each a cool look, as if she faced down

terrorists every damn day. "Kill him and *I* won't tell you. Come on. You're businessmen. Caleb and me versus how many of you? Fifteen? Twenty? We walk out of here and you get your account number. We both know you have forty-eight billion reasons to do this deal."

"Forty-eight?"

"Billion American dollars," she said confidently. What on earth was taking Keir so freaking long? Why had she even imagined she could play the role of hostage negotiator? She was frightened spitless. And despite her bravado with Lark and Caleb's men back at her apartment, half, hell, more than half of her courage had come from knowing that Caleb's men would keep her safe in this situation.

An almost-silent verbal question mark came from behind her. Tony or Dekker.

"Fuck if I know." Keir's almost-silent voice in response. "You try."

Try? Heather repeated in her head. *Try?* "Yes. That's all of it," she told the El-Hoorie uglies. "I'll give you everything from Fazuk Al-Adel's account." *Anytime now would be good, guys.*

A chill rippled up her spine as she remained exactly where she was. In the aquarium. Feet away from two terrorists who looked ready to rip her apart any second.

"And Six March," she added desperately, playing for time. "*And* the Algeti National Army *and* a dozen more of Brian Shaw's clients. You can have it all. In exchange for my husband. Where is he?" *CalebCalebCaleb!*

Even though she knew she wasn't alone, Heather sure *felt* alone. Her T-FLAC/psi protectors were invisible, and apparently having technical difficulties.

A pale, artificial glow of the larger-than-life saltwater tanks filled the entire space, surrounding her with brightly colored fish, seaweed, and really bad memories. Honest to God. If anyone could've come up with a more terrifying place for her to be right now, she couldn't imagine what it could be. Her stomach churned as she remembered vividly the salty, disgusting taste of tank water, and the mind-numbing sensation of not being able to breathe—Don't think about it now, she told herself firmly.

She was scared enough already without superimposing what she knew could happen with what *had* happened.

Then she saw and recognized the back of Caleb's head. He was slumped on a bench facing the thirty-foot-high kelp forest. He wasn't moving. Was he unconscious? *God . . . please don't let him be dead.*

Thoughts of what they might have done to him terrified her. She got a grip and focused on the men in front of her.

"I did as you asked," she told the two ugliest, biggest men she'd ever seen. Every fiber of her being was aware that the Aquarium was crawling with armed men. Other terrorists, men as horrible as Al-Adel, as these El Hoorie guys. They had to have about twenty men, while she had only six, apparently malfunctioning, wizards. The odds seemed pretty damned uneven to her, although Lark and the team hadn't seemed worried.

Heather was worried, and scared enough for the entire T-FLAC organization, *and* all their friends and families. Why were she and Caleb still *here*?

Instinct and emotion urged her to go to Caleb. But she wasn't going to do anything to piss either of these guys off.

Having the social skills to converse adequately, but charmingly, in four languages at a cocktail party hadn't exactly given her the experience for what she needed in this situation. Charm and BS could only go so far.

"I'm here, alone." She infused confidence and authority into her voice by sheer necessity. This wasn't a dress rehearsal. "Alone." It sure was starting to feel like it, which ratcheted up her nerves another few notches. "I just told you I can give you what you want. Bring Caleb to me. Let us walk out of here, and everyone leaves happy."

One of the brothers motioned to the two men flanking her. "Search her."

"Right here with you, honey," Keir Farris said softly. *So* softly that Heather thought it was in her head. Was that even possible? "Start backing up slowly. Straight back, that's a girl. Keep going." How was it that nobody else could hear him? The trouble was, there was still that "Oh, shit!" tone in his voice.

One brother was apparently fascinated by the sea life swimming through the thick strands of kelp. The other scowled at her as he observed her taking a step back. "Where do you think you're going?"

She stopped in her tracks and lifted her chin with false bravado. "I don't want your goons to put their hands all over me. You asked me to come. I'm here. You told me you'd let my husband walk out of here with me. So"— she held out her arms—"back off." She slid her feet backward, inch by slow inch.

"Look. No purse." She pulled her pockets inside out, the bracelet ridiculously heavy on her wrist. "No weapons, no microphones, nothing."

"And no account information," one of the brothers snarled. "Do you think we're fools?"

Heather figured that they didn't want her honest answer. She gave them her cocktail smile. "I think you're businessmen. The numbers are in my head; isn't that why you demanded that I be the one to deliver them? You knew that already," she said, flattering their intelligence. "I'm prepared to do the deal as agreed."

The situation was surreal, and her stomach was knotted with tension and nerves. At her apartment earlier, Lark had told her to just hand over the bracelet to the brothers. Just give them what they wanted and her invisible bodyguards would take care of the rest. Every instinct in Heather urged her to do just that. She wanted to get out of here so badly she could barely think of anything else. But a cautious little voice in her head reminded her that Caleb had thought he'd placed a protection spell on her, and it hadn't worked. Boy howdy hadn't it worked.

What was there to say that Keir's spell *would*? For God's sake—he was having problems teleporting her! "Oh, shit" was right.

The second she gave these guys the bracelet there was no reason for them to keep either herself or Caleb alive. If the protection spell didn't work, she and Caleb might both end up very, very dead.

In a very, very permanent way.

Her tension eased slightly as the El-Hoorie brothers' men started disappearing. One by one, they were being picked off and teleported out of the room. So Caleb's men could teleport the bad guys, but she was stuck here? That didn't make any sense at all. Still it was pretty funny watching people disappear into thin air. Thank God she'd seen this before or she'd think she was going stark, raving nuts.

"Keep going," Keir told Heather softly. "Don't stop until you get to the wall."

One of the brothers motioned his two men to stay where they were. "Our money is where?"

Heather's back hit the wall. "Sw—"

Caleb's people had been teleporting the brothers' men at a dizzying speed. Suddenly the brothers noticed that their number was dramatically decreased. They might not know why or how, but they could obviously count. Surprise, surprise.

One brother raced across to the bench where Caleb had been. Had been? She blinked. Where was he? Had Lark teleported him out already? She almost shouted out his name when the other brother leveled a big black gun at her. Oh, shit. Again.

There wasn't even time to brace, if such a thing were possible. It happened so fast she just stood there paralyzed. A split second later she heard a chink as something metallic—the *bullet*?—dropped to the floor a few feet in front if her as if it had hit a force field. Not waiting to confirm her suspicions, she ran like hell for the exit. Okay. Good to know.

The protective spell *did* work.

The plan had been for her to hand over the bracelet, and then quickly have Keir Farris teleport her back to her apartment. If for any reason that wasn't possible, she was to head for the exit, where either Tony Rook or Dekker would teleport her. Supposedly, in wizard theory, she shouldn't be in any physical danger.

Running all out, she prayed she wouldn't be slammed in the back by a bullet, or flattened by a ricocheting piece of cement. Behind her all hell was breaking loose as Caleb's men engaged the terrorists in a no-holds-barred fight to the death.

Gunfire strafed the Aquarium. The sound bounced and echoed off the cement walls and the thick glass of the tanks in a deafening cacophony. The noise set off the alarm systems, which not only added to the rising decibels, but turned on bright lights across the exhibits. Chunks of cement become projectiles, and as dangerous as the bullets.

Heather didn't look back. Raising one arm to protect her head, just in case, she used the other to protect her stomach and ran. Her heart was in her throat, and sweat poured down her temples as she raced toward the closest EXIT sign. Maybe she should have just handed over the bracelet. Where was Caleb? More importantly, was he safe? Or, heaven help them, bleeding and powerless? She wanted to scream. Scream for the gunfire to stop. Scream her husband's name. Hell, just scream until the panic stopped surging through her system.

She saw Dekker, a gun in each hand, running to intercept her at the designated exit. She paused, bracing herself to be teleported. Nothing happened.

He scowled, got off a shot at a man charging behind her, and kept coming. He stopped a few feet away and reached out to take her arm. "What the hell?"

"Oh, God, now what?" But she saw "what." He couldn't touch her. His hand was stopped—blocked—a foot from her body. That, apparently, was as close as he could get.

"Rook," the op shouted into his lip mic. "To Heather. *Now.*"

Rook materialized beside her with a cocky grin. "Hi, beautiful. Ready to go home?" He shot the man beside her a sneaking glance.

"He can't teleport me, either." She didn't even try to keep the panic and nerves out of her voice. "Where's Caleb? What's going on?"

"We're on it," Rook insisted. "Let's get you out of here. Ready?"

"Ye—" She didn't teleport when Tony tried again either. She was suddenly very afraid.

Farris glanced at Rook. "Take her outside. I'll get Caleb." He was gone in a poof and a blink.

She and Rook ran side by side. The first EXIT door was locked and Heather tasted the burn of panic. "This way." Rook pointed to the left with the barrel of his gun.

Okay. This wasn't supposed to happen. She was here to save Caleb. And she'd seen nothing but the back of his head. Heather's heartbeat faltered, and she slipped on something on the floor. She threw her hands out as her feet shot out from under her. Tony tried to grab her.

Three things happened simultaneously. One, Tony couldn't touch her, two, somehow she was upended and placed gently back on her feet, and three, Caleb arrived wearing a scowl. "What the hell are you thinking, Rook? Why is she still here?"

"Can't teleport her. Neither can Dek or Farris."

"Bullshit." Caleb's eyes narrowed when she didn't go anywhere. "Who the fuck protected her?"

"Farris. But I'm telling you, he can't teleport her either."

"Impossible. Probably," Caleb amended.

"What *probably*?" Heather shot back. She grabbed fistfuls of his shirt. "Do something. Conjure up some eye of newt or whatever it is you have to do but—"

"*Bean*," Caleb said with dawning wonder.

"What?" everyone seemed to ask in unison.

Heather curved her hand around her tummy. "Oh, God. Is something wrong with the baby?"

"Try," Caleb began, pausing to turn and fire a few cover rounds down the hallway before saying over his shoulder, "talking to him."

She took a deep breath, wondering if she was so far gone crazy that there was never any chance of coming back, then as reasonably as possible, said, "Bean, we need to get out of here, so Daddy and I would really appreciate it if you could—Holy crap!"

She was back in her apartment.

Lark was sprawled on her bed, reading an Italian fashion magazine and popping chilled grapes into her mouth. She glanced up as Heather noisily collapsed into the straight-backed chair at the table.

"You look sweaty. Everything okay?"

Stunned, Heather managed a nod. "Uh. Oh, crap. Damn. I think so." She rubbed her stomach in awe. "I am okay. Apparently my son is already taking care of his mother. He teleported me home." She swallowed, then grinned as she felt the gentle answering flutter in her womb.

Lark crossed her feet, and grinned. "Told you he was going to be powerful."

Heather held onto the chair until the dizziness of reentry faded. "You knew this could happen?"

"I'm an empath, remember?"

Heather frowned as she glanced around, expecting to see Caleb. Wanting to see Caleb, damn it. "Bean only teleported me?"

Lark smiled. "Caleb's a powerful man and a wizard, Heather. Caleb can handle himself."

From your lips, she thought, standing. "Hard to forget," she muttered, going to the kitchen for a glass of water. Wine would have been better, but not when she had a baby onboard. "How come Bean didn't protect me in Matera?" she shouted, filling a glass.

She walked back into the other room, and sat down at the table. Placing her half-empty glass beside her, she started sorting through the small mountain of jewelry still piled there in a jumbled mess. All that was left of her old life. "Well?"

"Timing is everything," Lark said, her expression a mixture of amused and triumphant. "A carrier has to hit the fifteen-week mark before the baby's powers start to develop."

"Carrier?" Heather groaned. "That makes me sound like Typhoid Mary."

"Yeah, sorry, didn't mean for it to come out like that. At any rate, you conceived fifteen weeks ago as of three this afternoon."

"Are you telling me *I* now have wizard powers?" Heather demanded, half horrified, and half intrigued.

And absolutely *not* wondering how Lark knew the exact hour of Bean's conception.

"Not you. Your child. And through Bean, your own natural abilities can come forward."

Say what? "Believe me, I don't have any natural, or *un*natural abilities," Heather assured her.

"Time will tell," Lark said enigmatically.

As much as she wanted to ask Lark what she was talking about, Heather bit her tongue. Lark wouldn't tell her, and frankly she had enough on her plate to think about right now without going down that road.

While Lark reclined on the bed, flipping through her magazine, Heather got up again and paced. "Wherever your father is, I wish he and the others would hurry up and come home," she whispered.

In a matter of seconds, four men crumpled into a heap at her feet. Blood oozed from a cut above Keir's right eye. Dekker had a split lip and what appeared to be the beginnings of a nasty bruise on his cheek. Tony Rook's hand was swelling and black-and-blue already.

Caleb rolled onto his side, wincing as he got to his feet.

"Why do you guys always like to do it the *hard* way?" Lark demanded, shaking her head as she took in their disheveled appearances. "What's the point in being wizards if you don't utilize your powers in these situations?"

Tony Rook grinned. "Perk of the job."

"What the f—What was *that*?" Keir asked, rubbing his lower jaw and looking at the others.

"Warp speed courtesy of Mini Edge," Lark said, barely containing her excitement.

Caleb's blue eyes fixed on Heather. She could tell he was favoring his left side. His ribs? "How'd you make that happen? What did you do?"

Worry about you. Love you. "I just wished you'd hurry up. I guess Bean did the rest."

"Awesome," Rook announced. "We flew through those guys at warp speed. Heather, honey, you can wish me through any op you want. Hey, thanks," he told Caleb as he noticed that his hand was healed. He flexed his fingers and grinned. "That is *so* cool."

Still watching *her,* Caleb fixed his friends' battered bodies. His eyes promised her retribution for showing up at the Aquarium.

Tough.

As usual, his closed expression betrayed nothing more than what she imagined she read in his eyes. And even there she could be way off. Where had he learned to be so damn, *annoyingly* inscrutable?

"Send a detail back to the Aquarium. They've got the place prepped to blow," Caleb told Lark.

"Presidential and environmental group scheduled, ten A.M. tomorrow. I'm on it." She disappeared, taking her grapes and magazine with her.

"Heather, give me whatever it is that has the account numbers, so we can get this tied up."

"Do you have any damn idea how freaking . . . *annoying* that is? 'Get this tied up?' " she repeated through her teeth. "Like you haven't just walked in and disrupted my entire flipping *life*!"

Caleb glanced at the jewelry strewn on the table. "Which piece is it?"

"Bean, Mommy needs to talk to Daddy alone. Could you please send everyone wherever they'd like to go, as long as it isn't here?"

"Hey, w—" The three men disappeared instantly.

Holy crap. Tony was right. This *was* awesome. "Now, please put Daddy's butt in that chair. Gently."

Caleb flew through the air, but landed lightly in the seat.

"Careful," he warned, looking a little shell-shocked. "Power corrupts."

"It's also convenient," she countered, moving closer to him. "I can't have you teleporting off into the sunset when you have so much explaining to do."

"It doesn't matter."

"It does to me," she said, folding her arms over her chest and pinning him in place with a look. "I want to know why you used me. Why you thought it was okay to make me a pawn in the game you were playing with my father."

"It wasn't like that."

"Really. What was it like?"

Caleb rubbed his palms over his face. "It didn't even start out as my assignment, Heather. I agreed to come and talk to you just to get out of the damn hospital. This wasn't even my op. I was supposed to pass you off to another operative."

"To do what?"

"Find your father. Finding him meant finding the money. Finding the money meant chopping the financial legs out from under a dozen terrorist groups."

"Why didn't you just go to Matera and teleport him where you wanted him?"

"Teleportation requires visual contact."

"Oh, for— You could have become invisible, walked into that place any damned time you liked, and *seen* him."

"Tried that. Problem was, the place was a labyrinth. We couldn't *find* him. We knew he was inside. *Then.* But we couldn't be sure he'd stay there while we kept searching. I tried everything before I came to you."

For a moment her eyes were clear and bottomless. "There's one thing you didn't try."

"And that was?"

"You didn't tell me the truth and *ask* for my help."

"Hindsight is twenty-twenty," he said grimly. "But in all honesty, the thought never crossed my mind."

"Too bad. It could have saved a lot of time."

"And a lot of pain."

"Yes. Marrying me was a bit drastic, considering that all you needed from me was a couple of hours at most." She pinned him with her gaze. "I understand that fighting terrorism is more important than, say, trying to find a way to make that Curse null and void." Seeing him wince, she added, "You certainly take that duty thing seriously, don't you?"

"Nairne's Curse has been in force for five hundred years. It is what it is. And completely irrelevant in this case."

"Oh, I think it's very relevant at the moment. I'm your Lifemate."

Caleb's blood ran cold as the word spilled so easily from her lips. "No," he said flatly. "You're not." He'd almost lost her once because he'd refused to acknowledge his feelings. He'd thought that by not acknowledging who and what she was to him, she'd be immune. Wrong. He'd been given a reprieve, that was all. It was as if Nairne had given him a warning.

Do not fall in love.

Duty.

Duty or death.

He shuddered, the pain ripping through his body. He was damned if he'd put her at risk like that again. He'd rather have his beating heart ripped out and fed to dogs than see her hurt again.

She gnawed the corner of her lip and frowned. "Are you saying you don't love me?"

The smell of her skin was making his brain turn to mush. Damn it. He should move away. "I didn't say that."

"So. You do love me."

"Immaterial." His heart was a block of ice beneath her palm, which still rested against his chest. "I have nothing to offer you. Not a damn thing. I can't give you a traditional marriage. I won't live with you. Ever. You and Bean will be well taken care of. Both physically and financially. But I can't, *won't* be a part of your life. Not going to happen."

"Because of the Curse?"

If he told her yes, she'd try to buck it. If he told her no, she'd try to squeeze an admission out of him.

"If nothing else," Caleb said carefully, "Nairne's Curse is as real as death and taxes. Countless ancestors have given breaking it their best shot. It just flat out doesn't work. *Generations* of Edges have tried and failed. Fortunately, that doesn't come into play here." He kept his tone bored and slightly impatient. "To be brutally honest, you were nothing more than a means to an end. That's all."

She blinked at the strike, then lifted her hand off him. Caleb immediately felt the lack of heat.

"That doesn't leave room for interpretation, does it? I—My life has been on hold for long enough," she said with a wobble in her voice. "I want to be settled, *feel* settled before our son is born. I didn't realize until I wasn't living it anymore that my life in Paris didn't quite fit me. But neither does living in a one-room apartment here in San Francisco. I want less of what I had before, but more than this."

She cocked her head to one side, as if she was actually consulting him. He knew better.

"I have to find some sort of middle ground. With or without you. I've been on pause. Now I want to hit 'play' and get my life back on track."

"That's your prerogative." He felt feral. Why wasn't she trying to make him stay? Agreeing to be miserable, just like he would be miserable without her in his life, every single day? It really ticked him off that she was so calm and collected. And that she was making him doubt his decisions. Decisions that he'd made years ago. All three of his brothers had, for Christ's sake! Informed decisions that had always, *always* made perfect sense. Marriage and love equaled death to the Lifemate—therefore, no freaking Lifemate. Simple.

He wasn't exactly taking this lightly. Five hundred years of Edridges and Edges had been foolish enough to think *they* could break the Curse.

Forget himself. His wants.

His son would need his mother.

The decisions he'd had to make were for *her* safety and happiness. He was choking on his martyrdom, God damn it. "I think you should do just that," he said through his teeth.

"Thank you. But I don't need your blessing, Caleb. I'm going to be a mother. That's putting the cart before the horse, but if you don't want me, then it's time I put myself out there to see if there's someone else who *does*."

"What?" He wanted her. He wanted her as badly now as, hell, more so, than he had the second he'd first set eyes on her. But she was already thinking about another man?

He gulped, feeling the sweat on his brow as she waited for him to say something coherent. Why should both of them have to hurt? Heather wasn't Cursed. *He* was Cursed.

His problem. Not hers.

He didn't want her to know just how hard this was for him.

Point was, he reminded himself savagely, she didn't *have* to know.

She'd get over him. Fuck, she practically already had.

Caleb was afraid *he* wasn't going to be so damned lucky.

His life had been exactly the way he liked it. BH—Before Heather. It could be that way again. It would require due diligence. But his life could and would be back to normal. Soon.

Maybe.

"I will of course assume all financial responsibility for both of you."

Her shoulders stiffened, and she went very still. "We don't need your financial *responsibility*. I'm loaded, remember?"

"Nevertheless—"

She lifted her chin and stepped back, her eyes unnaturally bright. Caleb wished he didn't know her well enough to recognize that she was struggling to control her emotions. "I will of course contact an attorney right away."

"You won't need an attorney to enforce my responsibilities, Heather. I've already told you—"

Her eyes met his. "To file for my divorce."

"Div—? Not just no. But *hell* no!" He rubbed the pain piercing his chest near his heart. "No divorce."

"That's extremely disagreeable and unfair of you," she said hotly. "You don't want me, and nobody else can have me either?"

Disagreeable and unfair or not. "Yes." That was exactly it.

"We'll see about that. Bean, let Daddy out of the freaking chair, please." He felt the invisible bonds break.

"You'll be able to see Bean whenever you want." Sorrow and regret surfaced through her annoyance, darkening her eyes to amber.

"Thank you. That's generous of you. I'd still like you to consider moving to Montana and living at Edridge Castle until we're sure we have all the bad guys rounded up. It would mean a lot to me to know you and our child will be safe and well cared for." He sounded as formal as MacBain.

"We'd be safe and well cared for if we were with *you*," she pointed out in an achingly soft voice. Not pleading. Simple, unadorned fact.

She walked toward him, walked into his arms, making every nerve and muscle in his body clench hard and tight. "Hold me one last time, okay?" She slipped her arms tightly around his waist and buried her face against his chest, then just stood there, her body pressed against his, her breath hot through his shirt.

Heather. The aching loss he felt almost knocked him to his knees. He'd hold her this last time. Store up the memory. He pressed his lips to the top of her head. Inhaled the summer fragrance of Heather. His chest hurt so bad he almost cried out.

One more minute. Okay. As long as she'd allow the embrace. Then he'd go . . .

He felt her body shudder in his arms, then she looked up at him, touching his jaw with cool fingers. "Will you look me in the eye and tell me you honestly don't love me? I meant what I said. I can, I will, take care of myself and Bean. If you just say those words, then I'll let you go without a fight."

"I fight for a living."

"I don't have training and I don't have any special skills, but I love you, Caleb."

She wielded the *L* word as expertly as his brother Gabriel wielded his sword. And with as much accuracy. It pierced Caleb deeply, and cut as sharply as that claymore. She had weapons and skills that he envied.

She stood on her toes, cupping his jaw as she brought her mouth up to his. "Kiss me good-bye then."

He slid his hand around her throat to her nape, then up into her hair. "Don't try to beat me at this," he murmured against her damp mouth. "I'll never change my mind."

Never was a long fucking bleak time. He wasn't sure he could survive it.

She slid her hands down his chest, then slipped her arms around to circle his waist. She pressed both palms against the small of his back, urging him closer. "Never is a very long time." She repeated his very thought.

A shiver of raw lust surged through him, pulsing through his veins like a primitive jungle beat. He knew, without a shadow of a doubt, that he would *never* want a woman as he did this one. Knew unequivocally that he would never *love* a woman as much as he loved Heather.

Yeah. All that.

And he was *still* going to let her believe that she'd meant nothing to him. That walking away was one of the easiest things he'd ever done.

His fingers fisted in her hair when she opened her mouth to welcome him, her tongue teasing and taunting his. Damn it. A mere kiss he could have dealt with. Teeth and tongue and lips. But Heather, being Heather, had to play dirty. She tempted him with subliminal promises, tormented him with her beautiful, loving heart. Made him believe, *almost,* in happy endings.

He wrenched his mouth from hers, already feeling bereft and alone. It was going to get a lot worse in the near future. But kissing her, gripping her arms to hold on to her, was not the way he needed to show her that he didn't care.

That would take every scrap of acting ability he could muster.

He knew her. If she realized there was the tiniest chink in his armor, she'd find a way to crawl inside it to reach him. Then he'd never be able to walk away. Gently Caleb put her away from him. He gave her a cool, ironic look. "Thank God we don't have to be in love to be compatible in bed. How about one more for the road?"

Instead of being annoyed, she smiled. "I really would like to make love with you one last time. But unfortunately I don't think you could handle it."

Oh, yeah. She had weapons.

He wanted her with a fierce aching need that threatened to bring him to his knees. Yeah. To the lovemaking. But damn it, he wanted *her*. All of her. He knew that she knew it, too.

"You'd better leave now. I'm going to grab a cab out to the airport and try to get on the next flight to Paris. If I can't, I can always ask Bean to teleport us there." She ran both hands through her hair as she walked to the closet and her suitcase.

"At any rate, I have to settle my parents' estate and decide what I want to do, where I want to live," she told him conversationally, as if he'd responded. "I'd like to establish a home before Bean is born."

She was already separating from him. Caleb couldn't understand why something he needed to have happen, something he wanted to happen—Heather being okay with them going their separate ways—should make him feel as though she'd stuck her hand inside his chest and ripped out his heart.

Be careful what you wish for.

"That's not for more than five months," he pointed out, dying a little inside to realize that she would be making all these choices, all these decisions for herself and Bean, by herself. Without him.

"I've got a lot to do." She gave him a bright, careless smile, but her hazel-green eyes were stark with emotion. "Do you need to call a cab or something?" she asked politely.

"No." He reached out and brushed a strand of hair behind her ear. Her hair felt like silk, her skin was soft and warm. His fingers curved around the shell of her ear, brushed the place on her neck that always made her shiver.

She moved out of reach. "Don't."

Throat impossibly tight, he knew that he hadn't touched her enough. Hadn't stored up sufficient memories to last him the next fifty years.

Damn it. He hadn't left her yet and already he missed her.

How the hell, Caleb thought, bleeding inside, *how the hell had someone he hadn't known existed three months ago become his entire world?*

"I have Gabriel's address and phone number," she said too brightly. "And Duncan's. And Lark's—"

"And mine if you need me."

"I won't. Really. If this is the way you want it, then stop sending me mixed signals. The less contact we have with each other the better." Her voice shook a little. "I love you too much to settle for crumbs when I'm starving for the whole feast," she told him honestly, her heart in her eyes.

"Your job with T-FLAC is important. The world is a safer place because you take your duty so seriously. I'll make sure Bean knows that. And I'll tell him that you loved us. Both of us. I'll try to explain to him why you believed it best to send us away with a lie. Because it's a lie of omission when you refuse to admit how denying what we feel is tearing you apart."

"Jesus, Heather—"

"I'm stuck. What do I *do,* Caleb? I love you. But because of a hundreds-of-years-old curse, you refuse to admit that you love me back." She lifted her eyes to his. "I've spent all my life in a love/hate relationship with my father. I always believed that even when he didn't show it, he genuinely loved me. Yet now I'm not so sure that he gave a damn about me at all. And I'll never know. I'm pretty sure that he killed my mother, the only person who ever loved me for me. And you"—she looked him dead in the eye—"won't allow yourself to love me. So I repeat. What do I do?

"As much as my heart is crying out, insisting that I beg you to give us a chance, I'm not going to do it. You know how I feel, and clearly it's pointless to ask you to admit, even once, how *you* really feel, Curse be damned."

Her eyes, now more green than brown, and as clear as a mountain stream, were focused on him. "I want peace, Caleb. I want love. I want stability. And, damn it, I deserve to have those things. With or without you."

It took everything in him to look at her without flinching. Everything she felt was right there in her beautiful eyes. Love, sadness, hope, and determination.

Caleb was acutely *aware* of her, of the intoxicating fragrance of her skin, of the way her hair brushed her shoulders, and the soft swell of her breasts pushing against her black T-shirt. Every particle of his body knew the sensation of her smooth skin beneath his fingertips, and the feel of her breath against his throat. And every cell in his body mourned the loss.

"Yes," he said, stripped raw emotionally. "You do." He would do anything for her. Anything but admit how he felt.

"How can you do what you do, day in and day out, and still be such a damned . . . *coward*?"

He shrugged. Dealing with tangos was a cakewalk compared to this. *This* was the bravest, most selfless act he'd performed in his life. He deserved an Oscar *and* a fucking Medal of Honor.

She tugged her mother's bracelet off her wrist and held it out to him. "Here. This is yours now. The numbers to the accounts are engraved inside. We'll never know *why* my mother stole the money. I suppose it doesn't matter whether it was greed, or her way of try-ing to even the score for the good guys' side." Her voice trailed off.

"If you like," he said gruffly, "after Bean's born, I'll take you back. You can ask her why she did what she did."

Her smile broke his heart. "I'd like that. Thank you."

He put out his hand to take the bracelet. "Once we se-cure the funds, I'll make sure this gets back to y—" The second his fingers joined Heather's on the cool metal, a blaze of fiery sparks shot out, engulfing them both in a galaxy of brilliant white flame.

"Let. Go." He tried to tell her, attempting to break free of whatever the hell was happening. Magic wasn't always a good thing, although this didn't feel menacing.

He couldn't release the damn thing. His fingers seemed fused to the still-cool metal of the bracelet while blue-centered white flames licked up their arms and en-gulfed their entire bodies. His body hair crackled with static electricity, and he watched Heather's hair dance and halo about her head.

Her eyes were wide, but she didn't look scared. He found his body drawn against hers as if pulled by a mag-net. Between them the bracelet started getting warmer and warmer. Not burning his skin, but heating up to a gleaming molten silver.

In a sudden blinding flare the bracelet disappeared, as if plucked from between their fingers, then quicker than the naked eye, appeared again, this time circling Heather's wrist. It glowed and pulsed against her skin as if lit from within.

"My God." Caleb staggered back, still feeling the sparks and zings of the electricity charging through his body. "Are you all right?"

Looking dazed, Heather nodded. Her long hair was still filled with static electricity.

"Was that Bean?"

"I don't know. I don't think so."

"You're sure Bean didn't—"

"I'm just discovering that the baby *has* powers, but I'm pretty sure *that* wasn't one of them. I think I need to sit down."

"Yeah." He gave her a worried glance as he herded her toward her single bed. "Good plan. Need something to drink?"

She shook her head as she sat on the edge of the mattress.

Caleb sat down beside her, keeping three feet between them. Maybe she needed to lie down. Be held. Comforted. That had been pretty damned scary. And he was familiar with magic.

"I think—No. Never mind. That's crazy."

"You have a theory?" Despite what had just happened, *whatever* the hell that was, he didn't want to talk about magic. Not now. But the alternative was to say good-bye and walk away. "Let's hear it."

"It's way out there," she warned. The glow from the bracelet illuminated her cheek as she scooped her flyaway hair up off her neck and twisted it into a knot. He loved her neck, especially the sensitive spot just below her ear. He wanted to kiss her there. Just lean over and press his mouth against the soft fragrant spot right—there.

She looked so sweet, so damned adorably sweet and sincere, Caleb's heart squeezed. He imagined kissing away the twin lines between her brows. Damn it, he wanted to do a number of things that would start up the entire conversation that had already swirled around the drain. "Try me."

"You told me that Magnus gave Nairne three pieces of jewelry as engagement gifts, right?"

What did the *Curse* have to do with what had just

happened? Other than every Edge wife croaking for five hundred fucking years to prove the Curse was powerful and in effect, there'd been no magical clues to how to break it that he knew of. He doubted the flashy show a minute ago was it.

"Well, yeah, but, sweetheart—*that* had nothing to do with the Curse." *No matter how badly we'd both like to believe it could be.* The thought, however, was intriguing.

Oh, shit, the "sweetheart" had slipped out. She didn't appear to have noticed. She bent her knees up on the bed to fully face him. He could feel the heat of her jean-clad legs almost touching his hip. Cheeks flushed pink, she was practically vibrating with excitement. She touched her fingertips to the gleaming circlet. "I'm positive the baby had nothing to do with what just happened. Aren't you?"

He wasn't positive at all. He had no idea what powers his son had in vitro. "I suppose so."

"I *know* so. Wasn't you, right? Wasn't me. Who else *is* there? The ghost of Flood Street? 'When you've eliminated the impossible, whatever remains, however improbable, must be the truth.' " Her voice gathered speed as she talked, and he couldn't take his attention off her mouth. "I think that bracelet, the bracelet my mother found in the Paris flea market, and had engraved, was one of the three pieces of jewelry that Nairne rec— Caleb?! Are you even listening?"

Not so much. All he had to do was shift slightly and he could take her down. Flat on her back. He'd be right where he longed to be. A little kiss wouldn't hurt . . .

She punched him in the arm. "Talking here."

"I'm hanging on your every word," he assured her. He liked when she said "S" words the best. Loved the way her pink lips puckered . . .

"Your great-great-whatever-grandfather gave her three

pieces of jewelry as an engagement present, right? And when he broke it off with her she threw them back at him and cursed him. I honest to God think that the bracelet was one of those pieces."

Had she moved closer?

He was too stunned to move out of her way. And God only knew, he didn't *want* to. She reached up and traced his cheek with her finger, her beautiful eyes alive with love and anticipation.

She was buying that the Curse had just been broken. " *'Only freely given will this curse be done'*?"

It was practically tattooed on his synapses. His heart started knocking as hope slowly unfurled. "And?"

"The thing that had to be given freely," she said softly, "was that bracelet. The other two pieces she threw back at Magnus must be for Gabriel and Duncan to receive to break the Curse forever."

His heart leapt. Was it possible? After five *freaking* hundred years, was it *remotely* possible she was right? "Why *this* generation? Why us?" As skeptical as he was, Christ, he wanted to believe she was right. That *finally,* at *last* Nairne's Curse was broken . . .

She shrugged. "I don't know."

She was too close. Her nearness muddied his thinking, and made him *want.* He could smell the promise of her skin. Longing welled up inside Caleb in a tidal wave. With a groan he turned to her. Cupping her face, he tunneled his fingers through her hair. "I hope to hell you're right," he whispered against her mouth before he kissed her. And he only did that because not to kiss Heather now would have killed him stone dead.

Touching her tongue to his, she sighed, then tightened her arms around his neck. Caleb couldn't help himself, he put his heart and soul into the kiss. It was like coming home.

But then he'd known it would be.

God help him, she'd better be right, because that one small ray of hope was enough for his brain to hold onto for dear life. Her dear life.

He cupped the back of her head, his thumb stroking the soft, sensitive skin beneath her ear as he broke away from her.

This required a leap of faith.

He held her gaze. "I do love you," he told her thickly, taking a verbal running jump across the dark chasm the Curse had set between them. "Love you with every fiber of my being. More than I ever imagined loving anyone. More than I could have dreamed, if I'd ever allowed myself to dream." He closed the few inches between them and kissed her again, long, slow, and deep.

When Heather opened her eyes again it was to find herself quite naked, and on a bed the size of a small island hung with burgundy velvet drapes. Sunlight streamed through a high, arched window, flooding the opulent room with buttery light and gilding Caleb's bare shoulders to gleaming bronze. He lay, head propped on his hand, watching her. Heather smiled, filled to the brim with happiness. "I'm guessing we're not in Oz anymore?"

"Edridge Castle," he admitted, sliding his hand over the gentle curve of her tummy. "I'd like my brothers to meet you. When we get around to getting out of bed. In about a week or three."

"Hmm." She wound her arms around his neck, pushing him onto his back, and sliding her body over his. "It's not going to be easy, you know."

"Having to deal with two wizards?" he asked sympathetically, running his hands down her back.

Her smile felt as though it started at her toes and worked its way all the way through her body to curve her mouth.

"*Training* two wizards."

He nibbled her throat. "How long do you think that'll take?"

"Bean and I are already negotiating terms. You're a hard case. At *least* fifty years."

He smiled as he kissed his way up her neck to her jaw. "With time added for good behavior?"

"And extra time for very, very bad behavior," she whispered against his mouth. "We'd better get started—Bean? It's time for your nap, sweetheart."

Read on to catch a sneak peek at

EDGE *of* DARKNESS

*the final sizzling adventure in the
Edge Brothers Trilogy
by*

CHERRY ADAIR

CHAPTER ONE

Thud!

A flash of orange lightening lit the room, followed by the sudden materialization of a man, dumped unceremoniously onto the middle of the conference room table. He was soaking wet. Water funneled on the wood surface around him, then started to pour over the sides.

Duncan Edge merely raised a brow as he shifted his chair out of the way. The other five T-FLAC/psi operatives in the meeting jumped to their feet at the unexpected interruption, grabbing up computers, paper, and assorted items before everything was saturated.

"What the hell . . . ?"

"Hey!"

"Holy shit!"

"Who the f—"

Shaking his head, Duncan focused on the rivulets of water, using his power of telekinesis to prevent the stream from reaching his body or cascading to the floor. He knew the who and the why.

Serena Brightman.

One of her strongest powers was her mastery over water. Clearly she hadn't changed. She still had a bad temper, *still* couldn't control it. And still had to have the last damned word.

The woman was a menace.

"This is personal," he told the others. "Take five."

"Hell, take ten. Color me intrigued," Jordan told him affably, closing his computer and setting it on the credenza nearby out of the way. There were general murmurs of agreement from the others.

Great. He'd never allowed his personal life, such as it was, to infiltrate his professional life. But of course he'd never tried to help Serena before. No good deed goes unpunished. Now he had five freaking witnesses to his folly. Crap.

He waited patiently as his man gasped for air like a beached whale trying to regain use of his lungs. Understandable, since the guy had hit the solid wood of the table hard and fast. Duncan retrieved the note pinned to Chang's crumpled shirt while he waited.

"I believe this belongs to you," he read the curlicue handwriting out loud. Oh, yeah. He knew the who. Absently he touched the scar bisecting his left eyebrow. Damn woman had lost her temper that time, too. He'd almost been blinded by a flying pencil. "You gonna make it, buddy?" he asked the young half wizard.

"S-she made me," Chang managed, gray faced and still spread-eagle in the middle of the highly polished Koa wood table. He'd had the air knocked out of him. His pride, too, if Duncan knew Serena.

"Yeah. Figured that one out for myself," he said dryly. "Told you she was sharp." *Too damned sharp,* Duncan thought with a stab of irritation. He'd sent Chang, Jensen, and Prost in to watch her back. Serena Brightman had been a stubborn pain in Duncan's ass since wizard grade school. But for some annoying reason he always needed to know where she was and what the hell she was doing.

Apparently, time and maturity hadn't improved her temper or her stubbornness one iota. He hadn't seen her in what, five? Six years? Not since some Foundation charity fundraiser he'd been dragged to by a date whose name he now couldn't remember. Odd, since he remembered with photographic clarity the backless emerald gown Serena had worn that night.

The glittering material had clung to every curvaceous inch of her body, but had left the upper swell of her creamy breasts and one long, *long* leg exposed. The leg men attending the black tie function that night had salivated when they'd looked at her, the breast men had their tongues hanging out, and every straight man with a pulse had wanted her.

That was Serena.

Help her echoed in his head like a broken record. He recognized Henry Morgan's voice, weak though it was. His old mentor was not only head of the Wizard Council, but he also worked in some scientific capacity for the Campbell Foundation which Serena now ran. He'd been 'calling' Duncan for the past three days.

"Help her."

The only 'her' he and Henry had in common was Serena.

Serena was Henry Morgan's Goddaughter, and the old man loved and treated her as his own. Which had sometimes made his and Duncan's friendship difficult.

"Help her. Stop her."

A running litany with growing telepathic urgency but no clear explanation. Why didn't the guy just pick up the damned phone? Henry was one of the few people who had Duncan's private cell number.

Henry's insistence that he help Serena, and Chang's untimely return, were indicative of something. *What*, he had no idea. Now he realized it was time to pay both Henry and Serena a visit. If nothing else, it would be amusing to see if he could get a civil answer out of her. Probably not.

He'd contact both of them later that evening when

he returned to London, he decided. See what was what. Helping Chang off the table, he noticed that the guy's stick-straight black hair was covered with sand, as if he'd rolled around on a beach. Interesting.

Albert Chang ran a shaky hand over his jaw, his eyes still a little glassy, his breathing ragged. His triangular face flushed with embarrassment as he saw who else was in the room. "I can t-try again."

"Don't sweat it," Duncan crumpled Serena's note and lobbed it into the trash can in the corner. He could almost feel her animosity radiating off the orange colored, flowery scented paper. "The others will keep tabs."

"Man, I'm sorry, Edg—"

Duncan sent the kid home.

The men picked up their scattered papers and reassumed their seats. "That was interesting," Jordan said mildly, reaching for his pen. "Are you using halves as minions these days?"

'Half' was the term for someone with muted wizard powers. Their claim to fame was that they couldn't be detected by full-breed wizards which was why Duncan had sent the three to watch over Serena. They had a few powers of their own, but nothing major. They were neither fish nor fowl. Not fully integrated into the wizard world, but not part of the non-wizard world either.

"Just a little side job," Duncan told them. Prost and Jensen had more experience working side jobs for him than Chang. Serena wasn't going to know *they* were around.

Satisfied that he still had the Serena problem covered, Duncan glanced around. "Now, where were we?"

Zzzft. Orange lightening fizzled and blinked. "Ah, shit," he muttered, shimmering all the miscellaneous papers off the table before they got soaked.

A saturated Prost, swearing a blue streak, crashed into the spot in the middle of the table that Chang had just vacated. The coral Post-it note protruding from the top of his shirt pocket was dry, and read: *"And this!"*

Duncan got rid of the puddles, and crushed the note in his fist. This was just bullshit, not to mention a serious waste of his time. "Get *anything?*"

"Other than, she's drop dead gorgeous with a temper to match that bright red hair?" Gingerly Prost swung himself off the table. "No."

Duncan rubbed a hand over his jaw. "See anything suspicious? Dangerous? Out of place?"

"Not in the forty-eight hours I was tailing her. Just so you know, they're having an unseasonably hot January, and it's one hundred and nine in the Gobi desert right now."

Duncan was feeling a lot hotter. "Miss Brightman returned Chang as well," he said through gritted teeth.

"You mean Mrs. *Campbell?* Yeah," Prost said with a grimace. "She let me know in no uncertain terms that my presence was far from welcome. That woman can yell without raising her voice. Scary, that. Want me to go back in?"

Campbell. Right. As if he could damn well forget. She'd married. And buried Ian Campbell last year. "No. Jensen's still th—"

Zzft

"Goddamn it!"

It was the weakest of lightening flashes. Serena sucked at creating fire. Tom Jensen landed on all fours, just shy of the table, tucked and rolled, then sprayed water in all directions like a dog after a swim. He staggered to his feet and handed Duncan his note. It had been attached to his shirt with what looked like a diaper pin.

"I'm trying to *help* her," Duncan said more to himself than the others. He glanced at the note. *And this one as well!* "What the hell is she doing sending you guys *back?*"

"Says, and I quote: She doesn't need your freaking watchdogs following her around, and not to send any more. She'll send all of us back to you, and she won't be nice about it." Prost caught Jensen's eye before both men turned back to Duncan. "Think she pretty much means it, boss."

"I gotta tell you, Duncan," Jensen grimaced, tucking his shirt into his shorts and looking both embarrassed and annoyed. "That woman scares the crap outta me."

Both men had clearly been out in the desert sun. Even in the few days they'd been wherever Serena was—the *Gobi* for Christ's sake?—their skin was already painfully red and peeling. "Duncan, nobody's gonna hurt that one, *believe* me," Jensen muttered. "She'd flay their skin open with that tongue of hers before anyone could draw a weapon."

Yeah. Duncan knew that only too well. "Thanks for your help, guys. You did good." *All things considered.* These half wizards weren't employed by T-FLAC, they weren't trained in covert ops. They'd done as he'd asked. Kept a low profile, stayed invisible, and watched over Serena. Doing what, he wasn't sure.

"Where can I send you?" Each man told him where they wanted to be teleported, and Duncan sent them on their way. The sizable deposits in their bank accounts would come from his own pocket.

"What'cha do?" Brown asked curiously. "Send those yahoo Halves to observe a female tango?"

Worse than a female tango. "Serena Brightman-Campbell." The name said it all.

"Ah. The bimbo who married that multimillionaire old guy, Ian Campbell?" Chapman asked curiously. "He died last year, didn't he?"

"Yeah." They'd been married all of two years. It had made Duncan's flesh crawl seeing the front page pictures in all the newspapers. Thirty-year-old Serena and that old fart arm in arm at her white—*white* for Christ's sake!—wedding three years ago. There was only one reason a beautiful young woman married a guy like Campbell. Duncan figured not even the combo of Serena and a blue pill could get a rise out of the seventy-nine-year-old groom.

Still, they'd both been grinning like besotted fools in the pictures. Duncan knew that forcing himself to look at every one of the pictures was like holding his tongue to dry ice. Not too bright and a touch on the painful side.

Serena Brightman-Campbell had gotten every last freaking dime when her doddering old husband had reached his expiration date. Word out there was that Campbell's two sons—older than Serena by a good thirty years—were gunning for blood. Their pretty, young stepmother's blood. *All* of it.

By calling out to him telepathically, Henry Morgan had made Serena's problem *Duncan's* problem.

"She's an old friend. Her judgment has pissed off a few members of the Campbell family," Duncan said, figuring discretion was the better part of valor. "I hired a few guys to watch her back."

"You gonna send more Halves to keep an eye on your 'friend,' Edge?" Hart asked curiously. "I've seen pictures. She's *gorgeous*. Shitloads of cash as well. Too plum an assignment for a Half. Beauty, bucks, and she's a full wizard to boot. You've got some downtime coming. Maybe this requires your personal attention."

"Not interested." One freaking Curse on his head was enough. "Let's finish this up so we can get out of here.

NEW YORK CITY

Serena teleported directly from the desert into her New York apartment bathroom. Dirty, tired, and still seriously pissed off, she turned on the shower, then yanked off her boots, and stripped off her sweat-stained, sand-encrusted shorts and tank top, kicking the pile aside. She still wasn't sure if she'd been antsy all week because she'd somehow sensed she was being watched. Or if it was a presentiment of impending—*what*? She had no idea. Things at the Foundation had been copacetic. Much-needed money had poured in from the last fundraiser. Ian's two adult sons had been ominously quiet.

Which was almost more disconcerting than when they were harassing her with their latest attempt to vacate the terms of Ian's will. Maybe someday the greedy bastards will understand that their father had left everything to her for a reason. Ian had known long before he'd married Serena that his sons didn't share his humanitarian leanings. And she would use the very last breath in her body to make sure Ian's wishes were followed to the letter.

Had Duncan Edge somehow gotten involved with Paul and Hugh Campbell? It seemed doubtful. But, hell, anything was possible.

This, however, wasn't the hour to worry about it. Right now she was going to take a lovely hot shower, slather herself in scented lotion, and crawl between her one-thousand-thread-count sheets. After a good night's sleep she'd look into Duncan's intrusion. She shivered just thinking about Duncan joining forces with Ian's greed-driven sons. Hell, she shivered just thinking about Duncan period.

She gave herself a shake, enjoying the glide of her long hair down her bare back. Tonight was for her.

Used to extreme temperatures in the places she visited for the Foundation, weather barely phased Serena. Hot or cold, it was a given that each location she and her team visited would be poor and rural; she was used to sleeping on the ground wrapped in a blanket, used to not looking too closely at what she was eating, used to primitive facilities—assuming there were any facilities at all. Which was why she relished her infrequent visits home. She could hike the jungles with the best of them, but that didn't mean she wasn't a girl who appreciated the indulgence and sanctuary of her perfectly appointed penthouse.

Like the rest of the apartment, her bathroom was spacious, and opulently luxurious. Creamy, peach-veined marble, twenty-four carat gold fixtures, and plush carpeting the color of ripe apricots. They were her favorite colors. But knowing exactly what she loved was just one of the many things her husband, Ian, had been good at. He'd spoiled her, and loved her, and known her, sometimes better than she knew herself.

Her heart squeezed painfully. God she missed him. Missed his dry sense of humor. Missed the love he'd lavished unstintingly on her. Missed his council and his wisdom.

The fact that he'd given her almost everything her heart could desire, and countless things she hadn't even known she'd needed or wanted, was immaterial. Those had only been *things*.

She missed him every day. And at night, when she lay in their vast empty bed, she missed the comfort of his arms around her.

Neither of them had cared what people said. Their world was complete. They'd had each other, and they'd had the Foundation. And knowing intellectually that her husband would die decades before she did, hadn't softened the heart-wrenching emotional blow when he'd closed his eyes that night a year ago and never woken up. How stupid to think that just because she'd anticipated being a widow, Ian's death wouldn't have a devastating emotional impact on her.

Their luxurious home wasn't home anymore. The

apartment, which overlooked Central Park, was much too big for just her. She'd sell it eventually. Find something smaller. But not now. It was too soon. Too complicated. Too painful.

Ian would have known how to deal with Duncan. Henry, too would know what needed to be done. She couldn't even think about Henry lying in a hospital bed, so pale and lifeless. Did everyone she love have to die? "Oh, for goodness' sake. Get a grip. Stop being so damned melodramatic!" she told herself out loud. "*Henry's* not dead." As for Duncan Edge—"Damn that interfering son of a bitch. What is he up to?"

The mirror over the sink bounced against the wall and three bottles of scented lotion on the counter skittered across the marble in response to her inner turmoil. Closing her eyes, she willed herself calm, forcibly reigning in her temper. Only Duncan Edge had this infuriating affect on her telekinetic skills. Another annoying thing she could lay at his door. His *revolving door.*

Playboy jerk.

The last bottle fell to the floor. Damn, damn! *That's* what he did to her. Made her curse *and* lose her temper. She'd always had a problem containing her telekinetic power, Duncan made that control snap like no one else. And even after all these years, all her hard work to channel the power constructively, just the *thought* of him made it go haywire.

It hadn't changed a bit, from fourth grade all the way to twelfth. Serena scratched an insect bite on her arm as the large bathroom started filling with steam. The mirror stopped moving as she regained control of her temper.

Duncan had always mocked her lack of emotional control.

Her temper was *perfectly* controlled, thank you very much. Yanking off the scrunchy holding back her hair too fast, she swore as she pulled long strands of hair out with it. The large antique mirror started dancing against the wall, and her favorite perfume bottle crashed to the floor filling the room with the fragrance of jasmine.

Did Edge have *more* than three of his minions watching her? It was pure fluke that she'd managed to catch the men at all. They'd been Halves. Annoying of Duncan, but clever since she hadn't sensed the presence of the half-breeds. She'd never have known they were there if they hadn't been so careless. The Halves hadn't bothered to check before levitating food and water to their hiding spot behind a sand dune.

She opened the wide, clear glass shower door and stepped inside the enormous steam filled stall. The water was hot and plentiful. Bliss. Lord, she needed this, she thought with a happy sigh. Her parched skin almost sucked up the liquid before she could soap up. It had been an unofficial visit to Mongolia. *Unofficial* meaning she'd telepored in and out instead of using the Foundation's private plane.

Her team there was doing a terrific job as always. The two-room school house/medical center was almost ready for occupancy. The village was already using the basic latrines they'd built for them, and the people had enough food, medicine, and livestock to sustain them until the new cattle bred, and the newly planted crops came in.

She was a little embarrassed and a lot irritated that she'd dispatched Duncan's men back to him with more force than necessary. It wasn't their fault that she had a grudge against their boss. Still, none of Edge's men had cooperated with her when she'd demanded to know what they were doing in a small village on the outskirts of nowhere Mongolia.

Had they even *known* why their hellish boss had sent them to the Gobi to spy on her? Probably not. Duncan liked to play things close to the chest.

She hadn't spoken to him in five years, seven months and three days. Not that she was counting, she thought with irritation as she reached for the soap. It flew off the soap dish, missed her shoulder by an inch and thunked hard into the glass door before shooting upward to hit the ceiling. The scented bar skimmed the marble tile, and crashed down again, hitting the shower head and breaking in half.

"Oh, for—" She made a grab for the long handled back scrubber as it flew around the inside of the stall in counterpoint to the soap.

Deep breath. Hold it. Hold it. Hold it. Breathe out.

She caught the soap and the back scrubber's handle before they hit her. She hadn't lost her temper in years. Five years, seven months and three days to be exact.

What possible reason could he have for sending people to spy on her? *None.* Their paths had no reason to cross. They didn't stay in touch, they rarely saw each other. They'd had an adversarial, highly competitive "relationship" for want of a better word, in wizard school. These days they occasionally bumped into each other at some fundraiser or charity event.

Pouring a generous blob of fragrant shampoo into her palm, Serena started washing her hair. It was long and thick and she rarely wore it down. Wearing her hair pinned up in a classic, if old-fashioned, chignon suited her perfectly.

Duncan preferred cool blondes.

She'd spotted him with a gorgeous Nordic model at the Met a few months ago, but he hadn't seen her, and she hadn't gone over to say hi. She remembered how damned drop-dead gorgeous he'd looked in a stark black tux, his dark hair curling against his collar, that annoying single dimple in his cheek flashing as he spoke intimately to his companion.

It hadn't been her fault that an urn had toppled to the

floor, or that a pile of programs had gone flying like projectiles all over the lobby. Could have been a gust of wind from an open door. Or not. Serena dug her fingers into her scalp and scrubbed her—

She felt a sudden tingle, and blinked. "Holy shit!"

She'd been teleported from her lovely hot shower to a chilly, ultra-modern kitchen. She knew only one man who'd have a stark black and silver kitchen. One man rude enough, and confident enough, to do this without permission.

"Hello, Serena." Duncan's translucent blue eyes scanned her naked, dripping body. "You've lost some weight. Been working out?"

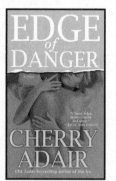 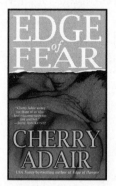 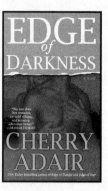